# New Fallen
## The Spiritscape Chronicles
## Book Two

I0533927

By Doug Romig

*If you do see any angels, let me know. I'd like to get some feedback from them.*

# Dedication

To Judy DaMetz
Thanks for getting up early on March 31, Mom.
Sorry about the labor pains and the headaches afterwards.

# About the Author

DOUG ROMIG lives in Knoxville, Tennessee where he enjoys writing, playing his guitar, hiking and spending time with his sons.

His first book, *The Spiritscape Chronicles Book One: Angelcide*, was followed by *Shrink: An Abby Chilton Novel*. His third book, a novella called *The Cryptos Files:* ICE, was about a cyber-thief named Ian Edos. Upcoming titles include *Reunion: An Abby Chilton Novel, Interpol: A Jonas Lange Adventure*, and *The Spiritscape Chronicles Book Three: Demonize*.

Follow Doug's blog at **http://dougromig.blogspot.com**, see what's happening on Twitter **@DougRomigWriter**, follow on his Facebook page at **DougRomigWriter** or just send him an email at **dougromig68@gmail.com**.

### Novels by Doug Romig
*The Spiritscape Chronicles Book One: Angelcide*
*The Spiritscape Chronicles Book One: New Fallen*
*Shrink: An Abby Chilton Novel*

### Novellas by Doug Romig
*The Cryptos Files: ICE*

### Short Stories by Doug Romig
*The Spiritscape Chronicles: Casadore*
*The Spiritscape Chronicles: Praetorac*

# Table of Contents

# An Offbeat Pronunciation Guide

**Acumenite** .... ack – you – men – night (There may be a hidden meaning)

**Adoneal** ........ add – on – eel (Not that you need an eel)

**Adsendelk** ..... add – send – elk (via UPS?)

**Alecto** ........... Think elect with a short A and a long O on the end.

**Arino** ............ Short A – reen – long O (Don't call her a rhino)

**Ba'al** ............. Bail (If you've been arrested, you know the word)

**Chabef** .......... CH – short A – beef (It's the newest kind of steak)

**Crotil** ............ CR – long O – til (like until, but not)

**Dossdril** ........ Doss (like floss with a D) and drill (like teeth)

**Dovhavhads**.. Dove – Have – hads (Just like it's spelled)

**Dracomil** ....... Drac (drat with a c) – long O – mill (think of wind)

**Enna** ............. Like Anna with a long E instead of A.

**Eqemp** .......... Long E – kemp (I know it's missing the U)

**Esiuol** ........... Long E – psi – oo (like food) – all

**Fantazmil** ..... Fan (what I want you to be) – taz (short a) – mill

**Fidrol** ........... Like Fido with the extra letters.

**F'nial** ........... Fin – long E – Al (like my barber)

**Frabby** .......... Like grabby with an F. (I have no clue what it means either.)

**Garrol** ........... Like Carol with a G. (Not named after my aunt)

**Hajile-R** ........ Ha (like the laugh) – ge (like the letter) – lee – ar (like the letter again)

**Halalio** .......... Hal (think 2001) – long A – leo (lion)

**Halidore** ........ Hal (evil computer) – short I – door (think pod bay doors Hal)

**H'tes** ............. The H sound – tess (think Thomas Hardy)

**Ih'duiwqec** ... Short I – dewy – keg but with a C. (Although a keg would be good)

**Iofiup** ............ Long I – long O – fi (like fe fi fo fum) – up

**Irkja** .............. Irk – ja (like someone angry but agreeing in German)

**J'fanasd** ........ Ju (long u) – fan (are you one yet?) – ask with a D

**J'niuav** .......... Ju (ditto) – new – ave (think avenue)

**Jehim** ............. Jay – him (as opposed to Jay – her)

**Je'relir** .......... Jay – ray – leer (It has two heads so it's going to leer)

**Kafplee** ......... Kaf (as in caffeine) plea (as in bargain)

**Kample** ......... Sample with a K. (Not sure what this one means either.)

**Klamoria** ...... Clay – more – long E – short A (think of the mine with an EA)

**Kra'illa** ......... Kra (like gray) – ill (like sick) – short A. (Sound a little like gorilla.)

**Lamptil** ......... Lamp (like you have overhead) – till (until you turn it off)

**L'kanso** ......... La – can – sew (And I am happy La can because I can't)

**Mishava** ........ Miss – have – short A (What she has, I don't know)

**Motmik** ......... Mot (like dot) – mik (like Jagger)

**Nakdol** .......... Nak (think smack) – doll (like Barbie)

**Nandif** ........... Nan (short A) – dif (like difference from a teenager)

**Nasarg** .......... Na (like the one above without the extra N) – sarg (think army)

**Nazilaq** .......... Na (ditto) – zil (like sill) – lack (He has no windows either)

**P'marka** ........ P sound – mark (like the name) – short A

**P'rama** .......... P sound (again) – ram (think curly horned deer) – short A

**Pha'ard** ......... Fa (short A) – ard (like lard)

**Praetorac** ...... Pray – tor (like your) – ac (like act)

**R'Loom** ......... Ra (short A) – loom (think of making cloth)

**Relir** .............. Re (short E) – leer (He has lots of eyes)

**Rheesmil** ....... Re (ditto) – he – smile (Not sure why he's smiling)

**Rialc** ............. Ri (long I) – alc (like talc)

**Samael** .......... Sam (like Sam) – long A – el (think Samuel with an A)

**Shorpy** .......... Shore – pee (Another word for which I don't know the real meaning)

**Spires** ............ Spy – ers (think of the CIA)

**Spiritscape** .... Spirit – scape (scrape without the R)

**Talgram** ........ Tall – gram (think metrics)

**Tam'niq** ........ Tam (gram with a T) – nick (small cut while shaving)

**Tepsam** ......... Tep (like step) – sam (like Uncle)

**Tone** .............. Tone (like the sound) – NOT Tony (He gets upset when you call him that)

~~**Torkel** ........... Think snorkel with a T~~

**Uqump** .......... Long U – kwump (short U)

**Vret** .............. Like Rhett from Gone With the Wind but with a V. (She does give a damn)

**Ximsor** .......... Zim (short I) – soar (like the birds)

**Yeroc** ............. Yeah – rock (think heavy lead guitar rips)

**Zhi Zhao** ....... Zi (long I) – Zow (like Wow)

**Zoobs** ........... Boobs with a Z.

# Prologue

A green glow began to fill the space around Kafplee, causing a rare look of panic on the face of the demon. It was accustomed to causing panic in those encountered. This was an unwelcome role reversal. There had been stories circulating about something new going after demons, but none who had seen anything was around to tell. All that had gotten back was word of a green haze that was left, like an afterglow where many devils had disappeared.

Kafplee was not going down without a fight no matter what this was. The angels claimed to have taken out the beast who had consumed so many, but could they be trusted? *What if they were now using the annihilator as an agent to destroy their enemies? What the heaven was happening?*

"I know you are here. Show yourself, coward!" screeched the twin mouths of the hellion.

A subtle chuckle filled the ether around the demon. "And why would I do that?" came the soft voice that seemed to be everywhere. "I am your judge, jury and will carry out your sentencing. You are guilty." More soft laughter seem to come from everywhere and nowhere as the Spiritscape became greener than its usual amber.

The demon found new fear as the soft sounds created a sense of foreboding that had not been sensed since the defeat of the Demonslayer. *What was this thing that could play hide and seek and still cause fear?* Kafplee did what all but the most powerful demons did when faced with an unknown enemy – run! No matter where the incubus moved, there was a green fog blocking the way. It was like the voice knew where the demon was going. With desperation grasping Kafplee, a mad dash through the mist seemed to be the only option.

Knowing the demon's strategy, the mist enveloped Kafplee before the plan could be implemented. Now Kafplee experienced another new sensation: immobilization. The soft, terrifying laughter seemed to be coming from within as pain permeated the core of the demon causing an anguished cry and a flood of curses. The blue essence of the demon was bleeding through the many gashes appearing on the Hadian.

"Now, now," came the voice. "Watch your language, Kafplee. You never know who may be listening."

A screech came from the mouths of the demon. "Just do your worst and send me to Hell. I will be back and find your ass no matter how long it takes!"

The silence was deafening. For a moment the devil thought that all sound had been stolen and that was its torment. Blue oozing wounds appeared from nowhere but were everywhere on the surface of the devil. Then a sound filled the green haze that stopped Kafplee from even feeling fear. There was nothing to describe the dread of the demon when the voice spoke again.

"What makes you think I will send you to Hell? You are now part of my collection," laughed the voice. The green glow encompassed and filled the demon. Kafplee screamed silently.

# Chapter 1

Ezekiel had been spending the past few months hunting in the entire Western Hemisphere. The pyramids of Mexico's Teotihuacan had been a fascinating experience as the legends of the locals combined with his vision to look into the past. He had found it hard not to laugh when the reality and the legends were so vastly different. Being an angel gave him access to all the facts that even the archeologists had not been able to uncover. He quickly found his prey. It was an imp who was tormenting a scientist by discouraging him when he was on the edge of a great discovery.

Since Zeke was not one for giving a demon a warning, he simply appeared beside the tiny creature whose many eyes widened with terror an instant before it was encompassed in a wave of golden angelic fire. The singed remnants of the scrawny devil were dumped through a rip in the Earthscape that led straight to the hellish prison for the demons. Nothing made Zeke happier than a crispy critter and a job well done. The hunter smiled as he considered leaving the next one medium rare.

Zeke had also gone for a hidden swim in the Panama Canal as he explored the sites of so many deaths of the workers. He was interested in the remains of an Antonio Rubiero, one of the many thousands who had died during the construction. Antonio's death was listed as an accident on one obscure ledger. The truth was far more sinister. One of the crew bosses had been using some substandard materials, and Antonio discovered how the boss had been lining his pockets. After a tense confrontation, the deceitful manager had been influenced by a hazy blue mist that was invisible to human eyes. With the mist guiding him, he had bludgeoned the hapless Antonio and left his body to be carried by the currents, becoming part of the mythology of the Canal. Zeke knew where to look for the last fragments of bones, and laid them to rest in a small cemetery not far from the lock where he had been killed. He had begun to realize that it is the little things that really matter.

The traces of the blue mist were still to be found where the worker had died. With a thought, Zeke slipped through the timescape and arrived mere moments after the death. The blue mist was a succubus named L'kanso. It was notorious for being hard to capture. Zeke was also notorious among demons for capturing them. Before the insubstantial spirit even knew he was there, Zeke had opened a hole into a portion of the Spiritscape that sucked the hellion out of the Earthscape into a realm where Zeke was waiting with a spirit sphere to contain the beast. Once within the sphere that could capture angel and demon alike, Zeke moved to the only transparent part of the glowing device. Waiting to make sure it knew who caught it, the warrior created a rift into Hell and tossed the entire sphere into the darkest recesses of the abyss.

After the hole had closed and he had stepped back into the present, Zeke snapped his fingers and slapped his head mockingly saying, "I forgot to tell L'kanso to go to Hell. Oh well. I'm sure the sentiment was there."

In Columbia, while tracking the demon named Ba'al, he found a beautiful field of flowers that the demon had fertilized. Zeke "accidentally" killed the entire poppy crop with a small campfire. *"How careless of me?"* the hunter thought, smiling at all the drug overdoses he had just prevented. In Argentina, he wandered the Pampas and saved a gaucho from being gored by a Ba'al possessed bull. The beast did make for a decent bar-b-que with the entire group of cowboys. Zeke enjoyed the meal as Ba'al screamed curses beyond the hearing of the humans while locked in the cooking form. After they had eaten the bull, the demon was released and tossed away where he would cause no problems for a few decades in human time.

Peru found the hunter in the Andes sharing stories with a couple from Japan who had always dreamed of climbing the mountains around Machu Picchu. It was here amongst the ruins of the once great city where Michael found him. Ezekiel had been looking through time at the ancient activity and enjoying seeing the past overlay with the present, searching for traces of Faque, his new demon target, when the archangel brought him back with a word.

"Zeke?" called out Michael.

The name caught him off guard. He had been lost in his cross-millennial exploration. Returning his vision to the present ruined Machu Picchu, Zeke greeted his mentor who was sitting on the ruins. "Michael! Good to see you. Why didn't you just call out?" There was something in the aura of his friend that gave Ezekiel pause. Something was wrong.

"I needed to speak to you directly. Something has happened. You know I trust you, don't you?" asked Michael.

Zeke did not like the way this conversation was starting. "Yes," he said cautiously. "Michael, what's wrong?"

"Have you been on Earth since you met up with Tone?" inquired the greatest of the angels.

"After capturing Darius, I was on Earth in the Twenty-first Century. Other than the time I caught L'kanso in the Spiritscape, I have stayed here. You already know that," answer the confused Zeke. "What's wrong, Michael? Is it Tone?"

Michael was looking at his protégée with eyes that saw so much more than human eyes. "Tone is fine. Garrol never leaves his side. But there is a problem. You have not been in the Spiritscape other than that one time? You are certain?"

"Michael, I may have been touched by a human, but I've lost none of my power. Link up with me and you can see for yourself where I have been," said the warrior. "I have been kicking demon asses all over." Michael looked surprised at Zeke's word choice. Zeke explained, "Tone's influence. I did burn down a poppy field in Columbia, but that was not outside my mandate. It helped humans in the long run. See? I'm actually doing my part to make their lives better. Also, Tone's influence."

Zeke could see concern in Michael. "Something has been attacking demons," he said simply. "Do you understand why I am asking you?"

Michael's words sunk in quickly. "You think I'm taking out demons? Well I don't see that as a bad thing since it is my job. But I've been hunting on Earth. I'm hunting here. You have legions cleaning up the Spiritscape. Have you asked F'nial? He's a loose cannon at times."

"I already did. And he was with me when one of the demons was attacked." Michael's gaze would easily intimidate a lesser angel, but not Zeke. Zeke was the second greatest of the warrior angels in a staring contest with the greatest of the warriors. "Let me see all your thoughts." The two angels were instantly connected and Michael could look into every part of Zeke's essence... almost. There was a small part of Ezekiel that was blocked off from even the archangel's power. "Open up to me, Zeke," ordered Michael.

"I am," replied the genuinely confused Zeke. "What can't you see?"

"The Tone touched place is a blind spot." Several months earlier in Earth time, Zeke had worked with an unusual human who could enter the area between Earth, Heaven and Hell called the Spiritscape. Anthony, Tone to his friends, had accidentally damaged Zeke and put him back together while leaving a trace of himself in the angel. That trace made Zeke more powerful in many ways, but also made him more volatile than other angels. Since Tone could not be read by any angel, or even seen unless he wanted to be, this also created a blind spot in Ezekiel where no one else could see in his essence.

Zeke stared at his friend, mentor and leader with what a human would call shock. "Why don't you just go ask the demons who is attacking them? They'll tell you it's not me. I'll go with you to Nasarg and he can take us to see them in Hell." He looked at Michael, who was not moving. "What? Let's go!"

Michael's words hit like a sledge hammer. "There are no demons to question. They are just gone."

It took a few moments for Zeke to speak. This was the last thing he expected to hear. "What do you mean gone? Dead? How can that be? We stopped Bubba!" The name of the beast had been a joke of Tone's based on a childhood bully. Somehow, the name had stuck.

Michael took on a calming glow. "I know. Was there any part of the beast that could have survived? Other than the part in Arino?" The healer, Arino, had been touched by the last traces of humanity in Bubba and, due to that, had been changed for the better. "I have checked, and she was nowhere near any of the attacks to answer your question before you ask."

Zeke laughed. "You know that Tone finds it annoying when you answer questions before they are asked, don't you?"

The archangel smiled. "It is one of my greatest joys."

"There was nothing left. Did you ever find the human side of Bubba?" inquired the angel.

"We suspect we did, but still don't know for sure. If it is who we think it was, she is dead." Michael paused looking at Zeke to gauge his reaction. Stunned was the only word that could describe the look. "The death of her spirit was followed by the death of her body after what the humans are calling a stroke. There was no soul to leave that husk. She was a friend of Tone's; as close as he ever had to a girlfriend."

Ezekiel, the warrior angel, could not find the words. Finally he asked, "Did Tone know?"

"Not as far as we know. On Earth he may have suspected when he got back; but it is hard to tell with Tone." Michael continued, "Back to the missing demons. We are not sure if there is something consuming them, or if it is something else. That is why I'm here speaking to you in person."

Zeke understood. Opening his spirit, leaving himself totally at Michael's mercy, he declared, "I swear to you I'm not the one taking out the devils, but it sounds like you have job for me."

Michael had a twinkle in his glow. "I think we may have need of your partner sooner than we expected. He has only gone for three Spiritscape strolls that we know of. But I need you both to look into this. If it is a demon taking out demons, then Tone can track them and we can take care of this quickly. If it is not, then we may have a bigger problem on our hands."

Zeke grinned with every part of his being. "I guess I need to go to Tennessee. Is he at home?"

Michael paused and said, "Not exactly. He is on a field trip."

# Chapter 2

Ezekiel had changed so much, far more than he had ever envisioned possible. Angels can change, but he never knew this radical growth could occur. Zeke knew there was more to his metamorphosis than just the extra time he was spending hunting on Earth. The source of much of his change was the reason behind the latest leg of his travels. He had left Peru and traveled there with a thought. The sensitivity of the place was legendary. Throughout the last sixty years of the Twentieth Century, there had been major discoveries at this laboratory. During the Second World War, the United States government denied its very existence. That is what gave Oak Ridge, Tennessee the nickname of "The Secret City."

At the Oak Ridge National Laboratory, nuclear secrets were kept safe, as well as other secrets that most of the world would never see. It was strange for Ezekiel to find himself in this mysterious locale. He already knew all the secrets contained within. The hunter knew the secrets of the atom and the subatomic particles. He was even aware of particles that would not be discovered for another fifty years, leading to the reality of sustained clean power. That day, the entire world would celebrate as so many of the problems of the past would fade, only to be quickly replaced by all new problems. *Damn demons.*

The source of his change was standing nearby. There was a diminutive thirty-six year-old black man in a rather unconventional group of people. Of the group of nine there were six women and three men. Each one was dressed eclectically and either seemed to be talking over one another or totally silent. The confusing cacophony of chatter had Tone at its center.

"No. No. No. No. No," repeated Anthony. "Wrong. Wrong. Wrong. Wrong. Wrong." And then he stopped as if that settled the matter. In his mind, the matter was settled. As an autistic, his mind worked very differently than any other human, angel or demon. Anthony had a gift that most humans coveted more than any other. He was one of the rare prodigious savants on the Earth. Angels can usually read information about a human in their spirit; however, a combination of his autism and savantism made that impossible. Tone had kept his identity on Earth a mystery until their previous adventure had ended.

It turned out that Tone had total recall of everything he had ever read. When Zeke finally met him, he discovered that Tone was famous for his ability to recite, word for word, any literary reference he had seen. When an internet search was unfruitful, those in the know would call upon Tone. If it was in literature he had read, it would be instantly shared for a small fee. For fifty dollars, anyone could call upon Tone's mind. That fifty dollars would lead to a five page report on the topic in question. Many students spent that money to have an excellent start to their procrastinated term papers. Tone even had a website.

It also turned out that he could absorb a language in a matter of days when he chose to learn one. Based on the books that Ezekiel had seen in his small house, he could read at least seven. English, Spanish, French, German and Mandarin were the most common and most expected. Even after looking carefully, Zeke was still not certain why Tone knew Xhosa from South Africa or Sengseng from Papua, New Guinea. With Tone, who knew?

Tone was becoming more and more adamant in his argument with a man who seemed to be giving the tour. "No! Wrong! No! Wrong!" He began shaking his head and was on the verge of losing his temper. His caregiver, whom Zeke had met previously, was trying to calm him down. The angel had taken on a different appearance than the last time they had met, so Rachel did not recognize him when he approached.

"May I help?" asked the angel with a thick French accent. Disguised as an office worker, his security badge read "Ezekiel

Ange". Speaking in fluid, fluent French, he addressed Tone, *"It's me. Zeke. I need you in the Spiritscape, my friend."*

"That is so sweet of you to offer but when he gets in these moods no one..." began Rachel.

"Zeke Angel. Yes! Zeke the angel. Need to leave. Need to leave," declared Tone and promptly sat down on the floor, rocking back and forth. That led to an even more impressive ability that no one on Earth could ever even guess. Tone could leave his body behind and travel in the Spiritscape.

"See what I mean," said the caregiver, as Zeke stepped outside of time and to meet Tone in that spiritual world.

Many belief systems understand the concepts of Earth, Heaven and Hell regardless of the words used to describe them. Few living souls know of the space between these places that those inhabiting it call the Spiritscape. It is a place of great beauty beyond human imagination, and some of the most obscene horrors beyond human nightmares. The natural amber glow of the Spiritscape is augmented by colors that defy the human eye's ability to process. There was every conceivable shade of every color known to humanity, plus almost twice that number that were not known.

It was in this Spiritscape where Tone was waiting for the tardy angel. "Zeke! How's it hanging?" asked the effervescent human. Tone was not one for subtlety.

"Hey, Tone! Glad to see you!" said the angel, giving the human a warm hug. Tone's spiritual form was radically different from his body in more than just communication skills. When they had first met, Tone was wraith-like in his appearance. There was nothing substantial to hug! In an accident, while trying to boost his abilities, Tone had been transformed by Ezekiel's power into a solid spirit that even the warrior could not pierce. There was a downside. Only one other angel, Arino, the healer, was able to touch Tone without it causing serious damage to all parties involved. He was also unlike other spirits because his aura was in a constant state of change. His appearance could best be described as psychedelic. The tone of Tone glowed brightly with the warm embrace of his friend.

"So what's up? Where have you been? You didn't call. You didn't write. Your mother and I have been worried sick about you?" joked the human. "Seriously, dude. Would it have killed you to send me a post card?"

The sense of humor of this very unusual human took some getting used to. "I did send you post cards. Didn't you read them?" taunted Zeke.

"Let's see. There was... no. Then I saw... no." Tone looked like he was genuinely thinking. "Nope. Not a damn one! You sure you had the right address?"

Zeke could give as well as he got. "Well since it wasn't more than three hundred pages, it probably didn't look interesting to you."

Tone grinned with his whole being. "Touché!" Then looking around he asked, "Where is my body guard? Garrol!?"

An impressive looking angel appeared beside Tone. It had the look of a linebacker who also happened to be an angel. It was huge. Most angels did not have a gender and this one also seemed to be genderless but for the size. Garrol also had a feature that made it perfect for the job of keeping an eye on Tone: Garrol smiled all the time in stark contrast to the intimidating appearance.

"I'm right here, Tone," squeaked the voice of the guardian. The voice did not match the appearance.

Tone giggled. "I love your voice, Garry. It makes me laugh every time you say, well, anything."

"As does yours for me," retorted the angel, unoffended.

Turning to Zeke, Tone said, "It is impossible to piss him off. Believe me. I've tried!" The smiling Garrol nodded vigorously in agreement.

"I know. That's why I recommended him for the job," replied Ezekiel. "I knew you needed a very patient babysitter."

Tone was known for having many extraordinary abilities. Acting was not one of them. He failed miserably at looking offended, while betraying his amusement. "What do you think I am? A temperamental, tantrum throwing, self-absorbed asshole who needs someone to keep him out of trouble?"

"Pretty much," answered Zeke and Garrol.

"At least we're all on the same page," said the smiling human. "So what's up? I have a funny feeling this isn't a social call? Or are you here to take me to Arino's for that berries and cream oatmeal bath in her hot tub?"

"Anthony Cameron Edmonds, we have a job," declared the warrior.

"Am I in trouble? My mom used to use all my names when I was in trouble. Whatever it is you think I did, there is no proof!" said the half joking human.

Garrol looked at Zeke, asking, "Are you sure you want to do this? I must stay with his body but you have to deal with... this!" The guardian gestured to Tone who was doing the spiritual equivalent of sticking his tongue out.

Ezekiel smiled. "'Want' may be too strong of a word, but we all have our orders."

"You know you missed me! That's why you have concocted a mission." Tone did his version of a belly dance. "I'm irresistible!" Garrol sighed and went back to Earth to stand like the rock of Gibraltar over the body Anthony had left behind.

Zeke became serious. "Tone, something is taking out demons. And it's not an angel."

Tone froze in mid dance and looked at the warrior, finally noticing the concern in his spirit. "I'm guessing that you don't think it is another demon. Enlighten me, oh great halo-less one. Who are they blaming? If they say I did it, they are lying. I've only been in the Spiritscape five times since Bubba."

Zeke began, "The problem is that they... wait. Five times? I heard you had only been over here three."

Tone smiled with his entire spirit. "Garrol's not that smart. It is so easy to sneak away, It's not even a challenge." Tone had obvious pride in his ability to hide his disappearance from the angel. "Now about those demons?"

"That's the problem. We can't ask them what happened. They're just gone," stated the angel. The perpetual smile on Tone's face faded away.

He stared at his friend hoping he had misunderstood. "Are you telling me that something else is eating demons? Didn't we have enough of that last time? I'm still trying to get the taste out of my... everything."

Zeke was always amazed at the way Tone could take a difficult situation and diffuse it with his own brand of off the wall, across the ceiling and around the corner, humor. During the trials and tribulations they had shared fighting Bubba, the angel had gotten accustomed to the rapid-fire verbal shots that Tone would send flying in every direction. This human had even verbally jousted and jested with the beast until the very end. He was unstoppable.

"We really have no clue what's happening. We need my hunting and battle skills, and, unfortunately, we are in need of your unique set of skills." The hunter knew he was giving his friend a straight line that was irresistible and was curious to see what he would do with it.

Mock shock appeared on Tone's essence. "You mean you actually admit that you don't know something? Does Mike know you're giving away such secrets? I bet it makes his halo itch knowing that y'all need little ol' me."

The friendship between Zeke and Tone was a bond that was growing beyond anything the angels had ever seen. The two worked well together, like a comedy team that has enough similarities to find common ground; but substantial differences that make them complement one another.

The relationship Tone had with Michael was very different from his camaraderie with Zeke. They liked and respected one another; but Tone enjoyed trying to play games with the most powerful of the archangels. Michael was not above teasing him back.

This constant teasing was the basis for, what looked like an adversarial relationship on the surface, but was truly a friendship based on respect and the twisted humor of the two.

"Michael is worried. That's why he needs us," said Ezekiel. Then he added, "Besides, he hasn't had anyone to tease since you've been gone."

Tone took the bait. "He is just tired of all those dusty old angels kissing his ass. He likes me cause I don't give a damn what he thinks, and I say whatever the hell I want!" Looking around, he asked, "Where is he? I thought he'd want to brief me himself. Or boxer brief me in my case."

Zeke laughed. "How do you always manage to bring up underwear?" Looking around, he called out to his friend. "Michael!"

The archangel appeared without fanfare or pomp. As he was not preparing for a battle, he looked very similar to Zeke in the Spiritscape. Angels all look the same, yet different. Both Zeke and Michael were warriors, but had the appearance of an anthropomorphic being with human-like limbs on their gold and white spirit. Although Zeke's was slightly lighter, they each had hair of a darkish shade that was somewhere in the brown spectrum, but was difficult to categorize. The essence of an angel shines with pure peace, joy and love. However, there are some things that most humans would never see, nor would they want to. Different angels have different functions. Both of these angels were warriors who would fight battles against any and all demons, or anything else that threatened humans. When in full battle regalia, they were beautiful, terrifying sights, as Tone had learned firsthand. He was grateful that neither of the angels were preparing to fight. *I don't have on the right kind of underwear to deal with that kind of scary.*

"Well, Tone. How are you doing?" asked the too casual Michael. Tone was immediately suspicious.

"I'm good, Mikey," said a cautious Tone. "How are the wings? Have you lost weight? So what's new in your world? Shall we chit-chat some more or is there something else on your mind, like my chili dog recipe? Or how 'bout those disappearing demons? What's up with that? Are they scared? Don't they have any courage? Demons today just are not the same caliber they were in the old days. No character to them."

Laughing, Michael replied. "They can be characters; kind of like some humans I know."

"There's the Mike I know and tolerate!" joked Tone. "Okay. Tell me about the rabbits. Tell me about the rabbits." The two angels looked at one another and then at Tone, unsure how to reply to that. *"Of Mice and Men* is a classic. I like Lennie for some reason."

Zeke looked at him. "You are so strange sometimes."

Michael took over. "The demons' disappearances are troubling. We may have something like the beast on our hands again. But we need your help tracking their last movements. If there is something like Bubba out there, I want it stopped before it gets out of control. We have just barely recovered from our last anomaly."

"Anomaly? You call Bubba an anomaly? You really need to find a better word. Let me show you how it's done. So this thing, if it is another Bandersnatch, we need to get a vorpal blade and stop it. See how easy that was? But that brings up a little matter of armaments." There was a smile on the face and essence of the human that spoke volumes.

"You are mixing your frumious Carroll characters," said Zeke.

"I know. But I like saying Bandersnatch better than Jabberwocky. It sounds dirty," giggled Tone. "Now about my knife?"

A crystal box appeared in Ezekiel's hand. "All I have is this case. Too bad I can't open it," teased the angel.

Grabbing the case from his tormentor, Tone said, "Give me that, asshole!" The crystal case opened at the touch of the human, revealing one of the most dangerous weapons ever created. The blade was called a H'tes, and had been made exclusively for Tone. This was only the third one made during the history of history. Each blade only worked for the one for whom it had been created. All three had some common properties. The crystal blades could cut through the spirit of any demon encountered. If it slashed across the demon, it would cause angel fire to begin burning from within the demon until it was consumed. The damage would cause it to be blasted back to Hell to heal from the wounds. An even more devastating attack occurred when the H'tes was stabbed into the demon. That would immediately send the angel fire throughout it, causing the demon to be consumed. Whatever was left would have to be carried to Hell. These blades were also capable of sending those same flames flying out of the tip of the blade at any target the wielder chose. That distance attack caused fear in the spirits of demons throughout the Spiritscape.

Tone smiled at the rune covered blade. "Hello, old friend. Did you miss me?" He reached out and held the blade, touching a series of symbols. The blade seemed to melt into his spirit, attaching itself to the hand of the human causing a change in his aura. His constantly changing hues glowed brighter with the power of the H'tes adding to his already impressive array of abilities. "Ah. Feels good." The H'tes moved through the ether of the Spiritscape making a sound similar to a throaty hum. Tone moved the blade back and forth as he became reacquainted with this unique tool. Angel fire flew from the tip of the blade that faded away as it spread out into the Spiritscape.

Michael reached out and grasped the crystal blade, imbuing it with some of his power. That was another feature of a H'tes. It could drain power from an angel that touched it. If an angel were cut or stabbed with the knife, it would drain more energy even faster. Few angels could or would touch a H'tes without it causing pain or unconsciousness. Michael was one of the few who could spare the power.

"Thanks, Mike. Now," said Tone, who with a thought caused the blade to swing around and hide itself within his arm, "time to get to work. Whose ass are we going to kick first? And by 'we', I mean you, Zeke."

# Chapter 3

Michael smiled, "Well the first thing we need to do is see if you can track this Bandersnatch."

"I got you to say snatch!" Anthony giggled.

Zeke sighed. "Well played, Tone." There were times when the human could be frustratingly funny. Then there were times when Zeke wished he could focus, but suspected that would take away something of the uniqueness that made him so extraordinary

Tone had an ability that even the angels envied. When he focused, he could see trails left in the Spiritscape by any spiritual being. He had discovered demons leave a trail like oily sludge, while angels left trails resembling marshmallow cream. The truly fascinating part of this unusual talent was something even more spectacular. Tone was learning to tell the angel or demon who made the trail based on the way it looked. He had only been able to discern a few; but in time he would be able to tell as many as his human brain could hold. On Earth, he had an eidetic memory that seemed to be even more powerful in the Spiritscape.

Turning to the archangel, Zeke asked, "Where do you want us to start?"

There was a smile that seemed to flow outward from Michael that captured Ezekiel in its joy. For Tone, it created a nervousness since it meant that Michael knew something that was bound to make his life more interesting. "I think you two need to pay Vret a visit," said the archangel. "She has some information for both of you, and she wants to have a chat with Tone."

Tone smiled cautiously. "That could be fun. Now we can talk a little more freely than last time." He tried to laugh a confident laugh. It sounded fake and forced, revealing his nervousness. The previous time Tone had met Vret and the entire Council of Archangels, he had not revealed his human identity to any of them. Vret, the archangel of wisdom, had been able to deduce the most about him based on what he did and didn't say. This time, Tone had none of the same secrets to keep; however, he wondered if Vret would be trying to find out even more about him.

"I'm actually looking forward to this meeting," said Ezekiel, with an enigmatic smile.

Tone gave him his best pseudo-exasperated look. "Have I ever told you how much I hate that smile?"

"Why do you think I use it on you so much?" replied the warrior, not letting his smile slip in the slightest.

A doorway appeared right beside Michael. Movement through the ethereal essence of the Spiritscape was problematic for Tone. He only had four real options. He could move on his own, which was painfully slow compared to angels and demons. He could be carried by Ezekiel which was better, humiliating but better. There was always a skimmer, a type of ship that was piloted through the Spiritscape by angels. But the most efficient was the doorway in front of him. These portals took him directly from place to place without having to pass through the ether in between. It was like stepping from one room to another.

"We are going to her?" asked Tone.

Chuckling, Michael replied. "Actually you are going to... well... let's call it her office."

Tone looked aghast. "I'm being sent to the office? Not again! Why am I suddenly having a flashback to third grade when I was accused of tying Kerri's pig tails in a square knot?" He looked at the angels. "I was innocent of that crime. It was a bowline in her pony tail."

Michael turned to Zeke, gestured to Tone, and said, "Do you have this?"

"As much as anyone can, I suppose," laughed the angel.

"'This' is right here, guys. I am not an object to be watched like a dog sitting next to a T-bone waiting to get into trouble when you aren't looking." Both angels gave him a look. He replied, "I just described myself perfectly, didn't I?"

Instantly, Michael was gone. "Shall we go meet up with one of your fans?" asked Zeke.

"After you, mighty warrior," replied Tone, opening the door and making a slight, flourishing bow. Zeke pushed him through first anyway.

"Will you stop doing that to..." began Tone, as he emerged on the other side of the portal. His words faded away as he looked at the space around him. This was not like any office he had been sent to as a child. They were in the middle of a decagonal room. Each of the towering ten walls was covered in words and images relating to a wide variety of topics, stretching as high as Tone could see. There were images from movies, words from books, and pictures of a vast array of sources. Tone could somehow see a lecture with the words taking on a visual form as they left the mouth of the speaker. Before his eyes, a picture linked to a book as the lecture was weaving through them, while two movies overlapped to create a multidimensional painting that showed the many levels of meaning behind the one simple book.

In the center of the room was the archangel of wisdom, Vret. She was looking from one wall to another, continuously weaving her tapestries of wisdom, as she saw all knowledge and linked it together. Her dazzling strawberry blond hair was radiating out from her lithe frame, casting an image in the minds of all who saw her of a woman with intellect that was a blazing fury bursting out of her head. The smile on her face at the appearance of the detective duo was genuine and captivating.

"Ezekiel! Tone! It is wonderful to see you both! How have you been?" asked the amicable archangel.

"Why do I get the feeling you already know the answer to that question, hot stuff?" asked Tone.

"Well, I wouldn't be much of an archangel of wisdom if I didn't, now would I?" replied the unoffended angel. "But I'm trying to be sociable. You are quite the enigma, Tone. It is not often I say this, but," she paused for effect, "you fooled me. I really should have known it was you. But even on Earth you are difficult to read."

"You should see his home," said Zeke. "There are books everywhere."

"I see that," said Vret, as a wall cleared and showed the books amassed in the home of Tone. All the books were quickly combined into an eight dimensional sculpture that looked like the Earthbound Tone, and the spiritual form of Tone combined with countless stories, books and websites; intermixing to create a bizarre, unfinished work of art that was constantly changing and morphing into new things as more and more information came into view.

"You are intriguing to portray," declared Vret, with obvious joy in the challenge.

Tone beamed at her. "I'm one of a kind, babe!" he flirted.

"You think so?" asked Vret, throwing Tone off his rhythm. Even Zeke looked at her with shock.

"You mean there are more like him?" asked Ezekiel. "Please tell me you're joking!"

"For once, I agree with the wingless wonder. I want to be unique," whined the human.

A lilting laugh spread through the room, lightening the tension that had invaded. "I never said there was anyone like you. I merely asked a question," said the smiling Vret.

Tone was not willing to let that go. "Well, you implied something, didn't you?" Now he was like the aforementioned dog with the T-bone from the steak he had devoured.

"Did I?" asked the wise one. "We know that there was the beast you called Bubba who was like you. Why couldn't there be another?"

Zeke chimed in. "Is that what we are up against? Another human sneaking into the Spiritscape?"

The smile faded from the archangel. "No, Zeke. This is worse than that."

"Do you know what I really hate about archangels?" asked Tone to no one in particular. Hearing no one asking what he hated, Tone continued unabated, "They are always so cryptic. What kind of person or angel or being is intentionally vague just to get a reaction?" He seemed to be genuinely irritated.

"This, coming from the man who had a secret identity for how long?" asked Vret. It was not a good idea to play games with an angel who had all the wisdom of all time right at her beck and call.

Tone gave her a look that totally failed to convey shock. "I am hurt by that accusation." After pausing to consider the word he added, "Or that implication. Or that unfair comparison. Or that..."

"Bald faced truth?" asked the smiling Vret. Her ever-waving ruby hair seemed to be growing and glowing brighter with the banter. She was truly enjoying the sparring.

Turing to Zeke, Anthony asked, "I'm not going to win this one, am I?"

"No," stated the angel. "You never stood a campfire's chance in Hell." Zeke was enjoying this almost as much as watching a verbal duel between Tone and Michael.

Looking from the warrior to the archangel and back to the warrior, then back to the archangel, Tone finally ended the discussion by saying, "But I did fool you, so there!" He smiled and stage whispered to Zeke, "It's all I've got to work with here."

Shaking his head in wonder, Zeke looked away from his friend to Vret. "So why are you so certain that what is happening is not a human? Have you found a way to keep track of Tone and others who may be like him?" Zeke did not need to see the human to know that he had paled at that thought.

The warmth of Vret was evident as she spoke. "Keeping track may be too strong of a description. But I do keep tabs on Mr. Edmonds here. I saw all five times he left Earth."

Tone was shocked for real this time. "You saw me those two other times and didn't tell Garrol? That was sweet of you; but, if you don't mind me asking, why didn't you tell him? And, more importantly, how the hell did you do that?"

Tone, though he had noticed the green eyes of the archangel, had never taken the time to seriously look at them. This was not the right moment to more than casually glance at them because the normal emerald green of her eyes burned with an intense jade flame that was both terribly beautiful and just terrible. Those eyes could see so much more than any other eyes of any other being. They were looking through Tone to his essence and he was afraid they were seeing so much more than he wanted. The wisdom sculpture that was Anthony Cameron Edmonds morphed into something more through that gaze.

"I know things, Tone. It is what I am – not just what I do." Vret was the first to break the gaze with Tone. Looking at the walls around them, she caused many spiritual sculptures, painting, tapestries and some other things that looked like wads of multicolored string to appear all around them. "Before I met you, I had no concept that a human could do what you do. Now, I have watched you enough to know when you leave your body. My angels are out watching for those same signs in others who may have similar gifts." She met Anthony's gaze once again. "We watch and record. Right now, as far as we know, you are the only human able to access the Spiritscape and still return to Earth."

Zeke was impressed. "That is amazing Vret. How do you track Tone when he is here?" Glancing at Tone, the angel became concerned that his friend was about to become so pale as to be transparent. In many ways, he did seem to be transparent to Vret's impressive array of abilities.

Vret turned her gaze to Ezekiel. It did not have the same effect on an angel. Zeke already shared all that he knew with all the angels. Strangely, she seemed to be trying to look more deeply at him. Finally she said, "Sadly, I still have no way of tracking his spirit once he has crossed over. But I can tell where he enters and where he leaves. There is a slight scar left on the Spiritscape similar to the port marks that Tone is able to see." She broke off her stare and said, "Plus it smells like chili dogs."

Tone began to get some of his usual luster back as he said, "You don't like my Coney Cologne? I wore it just for you, beautiful." Turning to Zeke, he asked, "Do I really smell like chili dogs?"

Smiling, Zeke said, "Yes, you do. It is part of what makes you special."

"I've got to start eating more salads," said Tone to himself. "Before we talk about what the critter really is, I've got to ask you, what is that thing you do with your eyes? I've seen people with metaphorical flames in their eyes, but you have real ones?"

It was Vret's turn to be at a disadvantage. That was not a question she had expected. She quickly regained her composure as she asked, "Really? What are you seeing in my eyes, Tone?"

Taking on his best pseudo-romantic tone of voice, the human said, "Oh my darling, your eyes are like pools of emerald seas that seem to be burning from some horrific chemical spill of toxic waste; burning a bright green that makes me want to kiss you, and then run and hide from your gaze before it melts my brain, three of my ribs, pancreas, the toe nail on my left pinky toe and a few other body parts that I am rather fond of."

Zeke looked at Tone, unable to hide his shock. "You can see the flames? Green flames? In Vret's eyes? Are you serious?"

Tone looked at both angels, bewildered. "Of course I can. What's the big deal? She has lovely eyes that also scare the shit out of me. I had the same thing with this girl I knew in high school, but it wasn't because of her eyes. She wore all these low cut shirts that were very distracting."

Vret's stare was burning brightly as she asked, "You can see my spirit gaze? The flames in my eyes?"

"Okay. For the last time, yes! They are lovely eyes. I like the way you can make them do that flame thing without burning my brain. Very cool trick!" Tone was getting frustrated with the lack of knowledge coming his way from the archangel of wisdom. "What's going on? There's something you're not telling me. If it's because my ass has gotten bigger, I promise to cut back on the chili dogs." Vret's eyes returned to their normal emerald green. "Now, they are not trying to burn a hole in my skull." Looking at the angels, "Do you have skulls?"

The room became instantly empty of all the spiritual artistic expressions of the wisdom, leaving them in a vacuum of information. It was strange for Tone and Zeke to see the room this way. After what seemed like an eternity of looking at the human, Vret finally spoke, "Tone, I need to ask you a question and I need a serious answer. Do you understand?"

Tone looked at Zeke, who was staring at him like he had never seen him before. He then looked back at Vret and answered, "I'll try, but you know how I get."

"Close enough to a yes for me," said the smiling archangel. "In as few words as possible, tell me how you felt when you saw the flames in my eyes? Did you feel good? Bad? Happy? Sad?"

"Yes," said Tone. "All those, and also scared. It's spooky seeing your eyes like that. It made me feel like you were looking through me to see what color underwear I am wearing."

"It is red," said Vret. "But that is all? You didn't feel pain or the need to run?"

"Pain? No. The desire to run? Sure." He thought for a moment and added, "But I also felt like a bug going toward one of those shocker lamps. Even though I knew it was going to fry me, I couldn't help but be drawn to it." The unusual human looked at both the angels near him. Both had the same looks about them. To Tone their spirits were communicating: *Holy shit!*

"Tone," began Vret, "this may be hard for you to totally understand. I was using a spirit gaze on you. That is something I use to gather information, but you should not have seen it. Humans cannot see a spirit gaze without it causing them... problems."

"Problems?" asked Anthony. "Why do I think that needs a little more definition? And why am I afraid to hear about that definition?"

Vret replied, "Let's just say, the only other human to have ever seen a spirit gaze is still being cared for by Raphael's healers. There was not much left of her spirit when she saw my angel using a spirit gaze. It was just bad timing. She was leaving her body and had a fraction of a second of being able to see both worlds just as Nakdol was using a spirit gaze. You looked at my spirit gaze for quite some time without it causing any harmful effects. You should not have been able to see it. And if you saw it, you should have felt pain or gone insane. On top of all that, I still couldn't read anything."

"Don't you know yet? I'm special! And, come on. How sane am I, really?" joked Tone, trying to lighten the mood.

Zeke chimed in. "Buddy, you are impossible to read. You know that and love it." Tone nodded vigorously. "But the soul gaze should have given Vret more information. She could not use it on you last time because you were encased in the spirit sphere. It disrupted everything in both directions. You couldn't hurt anyone, and they couldn't hurt you. Nor could anyone read you. But there is no barrier here, and Vret still can't read anything. Yet, you could see what she was doing."

Tone was still confused. "I still don't see the big deal. I do all kinds of things that surprise you all the time. Why are you two so freaked out?"

Vret smiled. "Only angels can see soul gazes without damage. That means that the portion of Zeke that changed you is still making changes. You are continuing your metamorphosis into something greater than you were before."

The archangel caused a spirit sphere to drop from the ceiling and land on Ezekiel, trapping and protecting him inside. Vret began moving slowly toward the human. Tone began trying to move away from the angel to protect them both. His explosive nature meant that only those angels touched by human spirits could also touch him without both he and the angel being blasted into pieces. Vret continued to move closer until she had Tone trapped in a corner.

"What are you doing? Get back!" shouted a frightened Tone.

"It also means that I can do this." Vret reached out and embraced the human.

# Chapter 4

"What the hell are you doing?" screeched a terrified Tone.

The smiling archangel of wisdom replied, "I learned why you are dangerous. Isn't that nice?" She continued to hug the human. Tone slowly and reluctantly reached out to return the embrace. "As long as I keep all my power in check, it is possible to touch you without any execrable effects."

"True. And nothing bad will happen either!" jested Anthony, as Vret went over to release Ezekiel from the spirit sphere.

The warrior emerged from the sphere looking ready for a battle. His full warrior attributes were shining brightly, with energy that looked like wings stretching from his spirit all around him. He was a bright golden with blazing eyes that showed his righteous indignation at being placed in a spirit sphere, even though he knew it was meant to protect him.

"Vret!" The name of the archangel from the mouth of the warrior sounded ominous. Zeke had not shouted the name, nor had he raised his voice. Quite the contrary. The name was spoken with such a low, smoldering whisper that is was almost inaudible. Yet there was power and anger in the speaking that caused all to pay attention.

Vret was not about to be intimidated by the perceived insult to an angel. "Ezekiel!" said the wise angel with the same quiet intensity. They both stared at one another for what seemed to Tone to be something just short of forever.

After a time, Zeke was the first to speak. "Please do not do that to me again. Tone is my responsibility in the Spiritscape. You know that as well as Michael."

The soothing voice used by Vret made Tone instantly relaxed. "You know I did that to protect you. I was not totally certain that we would not be damaged. But I also knew that you would be the only one who could save Tone should anything bad happen."

"Which would have been difficult to do from inside there," said Zeke, pointing to a fading spirit sphere. He looked at it with new appreciation. Returning his gaze to Vret, he began to smile. "It was a temporally bound sphere?" asked the warrior, quickly understanding. He would have been released by the sphere as it faded allowing him to tend to them if needed. "Brilliant!"

"Thank you," replied Vret, humbly.

"Excuse me. May I ask a couple dozen questions at this point?" asked a slightly relaxed Tone.

Vret's laughter erased all the tension in the room. "Your first question, how did I know that I could touch you? I saw through you and realized that the one part of you that caused so many problems in the past is also the part that made you substantial. Because of the traces of Zeke in you, your spirit will try to draw more power into it. It is like what happened with the beast you called Bubba. There is a part of you that will always try to draw more power. You have felt it. But, you were able to see my spirit gaze which told me you were seeing something deeper inside me. Being able to sense that, was something that only an angel should be able to do. By removing the angelic power from your reach, there would be no issues or danger. I deduced if I pulled all my power into the core of my spirit without any reaching the outer portion, I could touch you without disastrous consequences."

"No. My first question was where the hell is the bathroom because you scared the shit out of me," declared Tone. "But that other stuff was number two on my list. Make that number three because the bathroom was both number one and number two, if you catch my drift."

Zeke sighed. "Maybe you should have blown him up."

"There is always later," joked Vret. "Next, I'm sure you are curious about the disappearing spirit sphere?" asked Vret to a nodding Tone. "There are a few spirit spheres that are basically floating around the Spiritscape. Many are in Heaven for emergencies. Most are in Hell for punishments. Four are on the Earth for when they are needed there. The ones on Earth can be borrowed and placed anywhere for a limited duration. They are bound in time on Earth, so sooner or later they will be pulled back into time, leaving anything in them here. I pulled that one in so that it would stay just long enough to test my theory."

"So that if something went wrong, Zeke would be safe, but would be freed in time to play all the king's horses and all the king's men," added Tone.

"Exactly," stated Vret. "Now, Tone. You can see so much, but now you need to know something you can't see. This may be painful to learn, but you need to know." Tone could read the essence of any angel if they kept things simple. But the angels had learned how to overload his ability to read their thoughts, minds and spirits by sending too much information at him. If an angel chose, they could simplify their spirits and Tone could read everything. Vret did just that.

Tone saw in her essence, a story. A mother was giving birth. It was a glorious day for the family. Months earlier, the doctor had given them the great news that it would be time to buy a stroller for two. Both babies were fine and growing well. The ultrasound showed them seeming to hold one another even though it was not really possible. The son and daughter would be the joy of their parents' lives and the answer to so many prayers. As the day approached, there was something that was wrong.

One of the babies had turned with the head down, ready to enter the world. The other one was ready to start life by hitting the ground feet first. Nakdol was the angel sent to help the family along. The angel began using a spirit gaze on the doctor to try to see if the knowledge, skill and desire was present to save the child. Just as the gaze began, two other things happen at the same time. A demon had been hiding within the room, subtly trying to manipulate the situation so that both children would be lost and the family would be torn apart. The angel had not noticed the demon, who took that moment to attack. That led to the second thing that happened at that moment. The daughter, whose umbilical cord had wrapped around her neck, began to crown which cut off her blood flow. The infant's spirit left the tiny body just as the gaze of the angel was deflected right at her by the demonic attack.

Four screams rang out. The first was the angel's scream of pain and anguish at what had happened. The attack was dealt with by several angels at once. The demon was placed in the lowest depths in a spirit sphere and never left Hell again. The second scream was from the mother who could sense that something was wrong. One of her children had died, she could sense it. The third scream was from the soul of the child who had been torn from her body only to encounter a spirit gaze that ravaged her infant spirit, leaving her with little more than nothing to her spirit.

The fourth scream was heard by no one. Not even the angels realized a scream came from her brother. He had been touching his sister when she was passing from Earth to eternity. He could feel her dying. This newborn also felt his sister being touched by the soul gaze as it touched him as well. No one knew. Even as the emergency C-section removed him from his mother, his cries continued. Eventually, the screams and cries of the baby faded as exhaustion overcame all the humans in the room.

The parents cried over the loss of their little Anna. She would have been their only daughter. As the mother fell asleep with her surviving baby in her arms, she tried to comfort him. "Just rest little one. Mommy has you. I love you, Anthony."

Tone crumpled. He was turning in on himself as if he was diminishing away with the news of his lost sister. He had lost someone he had never known; yet he felt as though she had always been a missing part of him. Now he knew why he was not quite whole.

So many thoughts were going through his spirit. It was impossible to tell where one thought ended and another began.

Tone's emotions were all over the place as well, leaving him unsure how he felt, or even if he felt anything at all. A great emotional tornado had him spinning in ways he could not process.

One second he was thinking of the loss of a sister he had never even met and the sorrow and pain of the loss. The next there was disgust with the angel who had been responsible for harming the helpless soul of Anna as she had tried to free herself from the tiny failing body. Then came the anger at the demon who had caused all the heartache and heartbreak for his family. There was also a perverse joy knowing that the demon would never be allowed out of the confines of the deepest recesses of Hell for eternity. *Payback's a bitch!*

Then the dam truly burst, "HOW LONG?!" demanded Tone of Vret. "How long have you known?!" The usually prismatic colors of his spirit were absent except for the bright green of his anger. Most other spiritual beings showed anger with the blue of the demon.

Leave it to Tone to have green as anger instead of red, thought Zeke.

Tone glared at the warrior. "Shut the hell up, buddy!" The way he said "buddy" left no doubt that word was said with contempt. Zeke felt suitably chastised until he realized what Tone had done. Under normal circumstances, Anthony would not have been able to read the complex patterns of thought that Zeke used to elude his abilities. Right now he was processing at a level that was totally beyond anything he had done before. Anger was a tremendous stimulant for Tone. "And it makes me want to rip things apart so watch your step." The human glared at the archangel still waiting for a reply.

Vret stared at Tone. Trying to ease his fury with her soft voice, she said, "I did not know until I found out who you were on Earth. It took no time to discern what had happened. But only four beings know this truth. You, Ezekiel, Michael and myself. I am trying to protect your privacy, Tone."

"Only my friends call me Tone, archangel," retorted Anthony. Turning to Zeke, he asked, "How could you keep this from me?"

"Zeke found out the same time you did," interrupted Vret. "I made the decision not to tell him until now."

Tone's anger was not to be assuaged. "Why the hell not? He's a big, badass mother. He can take the story of another poor, helpless human getting his life shit on!"

"No, I can't," said Zeke. Tone really looked at him for the first time since hearing the news. The warrior's glow was unlike anything Tone had seen since he had met his friend. He wished Zeke would show some of the righteous anger that he was feeling right now; but that part of Zeke's nature was reserved for demons. Instead of the anger and vengeance that came so quickly and easily to Tone, Zeke felt horror and a soul crushing sadness down to his very core. It was the sadness that shocked Tone out of his retaliation-fueled rage to a sorrow-filled sadness. He collapsed into the arms of his friend as the most unlikely duo shared the loss of the sibling Tone had never known.

There was a sudden warmth as Tone looked up, expecting to see Vret giving comfort to two spirits in distress. Instead of the flaming red of the archangel's hair, he saw a raven-haired angel wrapping them both in a healing mist from her raised hands. The only other angel who had been able to touch Tone and still use her power had arrived to bring healing to the troubled twosome.

"I'm glad to see you, Arino," sobbed Tone. "I need a hug." The angel wrapped them both in her arms that continued to wrap around them multiple times. She looked like a golden amoeba being stretched beyond belief.

Arino had been called from the mind of Zeke when he had discovered what had happened. Previously, Arino had been part of the four who had defeated the beast known as Bubba. Until a small fragment of the last of Bubba's humanity had accidentally attached itself to Arino, she had not been able to help, heal, or even touch Tone without the danger of having her spirit phased apart. After trying to help that piece that Bubba had discarded as trash, it had become part of her in a similar way that Tone had become part of Zeke. The two angels who had traces of human within them also discovered they were quite a formidable weapon. They could cause an angelic blast that made even Michael's battle power seem less impressive. Now was not a time for fighting. It was a time for healing.

"I'm here for you Tone," stated the lovely, calming voice of Arino. "You too, Zeke. Let me ease some of your pain." The healer send wave after wave of calm and love into her arms that sent the same feelings into both of her friends. After more waves of healing than she ever thought Tone would need, she finally spoke. "Do I want to know what happened?" she asked with a lilt to her voice and a smile that would have melted the coldest heart.

Tone turned to Vret and said, "Tell her all of it." Looking long into her flaming eyes, with a great deal of difficulty, he said, "I'm sorry I yelled at you. Please don't stop calling me Tone."

Angels multitask like humans breathe. While bringing Arino up to speed, she smiled at Tone and replied, "It is quite all right, Tone. I was ready for that reaction. If you had responded with one of your jokes, I don't know what I would have done."

"Me neither," said Tone, both serious and trying to get his human humor back.

Arino looked shocked as she learned the origin of Tone. "Anna is your sister. I'm so sorry, Tone. I never knew."

The way the healer said the name caught Tone's attention. "Do you know Anna?"

"Of course I do, Tone. I have spent many quolls with her. She is the sweetest spirit you could ever want to meet," smiled Arino. A quoll was a measure of thought. It was the way the passage of time was measured in a place that was beyond the human concept of time. A quoll for Arino was based on how long it took her to heal an angel who had been phased apart.

"Can I meet her?" begged Tone. There was a desperation in his voice that Arino had never heard.

Vret spoke up. "That could be difficult, Tone. She never leaves Heaven. She has to stay there for her comfort and safety. And you can't go there because you are still living and the power of Heaven or Hell is too much for a living soul."

Defiantly, Tone stared into the eyes of the archangel. "We have fought off demons. Bubba's ass was totally kicked by us! I even know how to do the chicken dance! Difficult is what we do best. Now tell me what you're not telling me." Then he looked around the room, asking, "And where the hell are we right now if we're not in Heaven?"

Vret smiled at the tenacity of Tone. "You are far cleverer than you like to let on," she said, as the sculpture that was Vret's version of Tone appeared and began to morph yet again. "You are in my sanctum. This room can be anywhere I choose. You are actually in the Spiritscape not too far from where you entered." Then she looked at Tone and said, "And before you ask, yes, we just may be able to bring Anna here."

Tone wondered if he would ever stop being surprised by these angels. Zeke wondered if he would ever get tired of seeing Tone speechless. Arino wondered about the human's state of mind and the angel's state of spirit. Vret just wondered about everything, as was her nature.

Vret was the first to break the silence that had ensued after her revelation. "Tone, we must set some rules that cannot be broken, bent or ignored. I know your proclivity for finding ways around the rules and I applaud your tenacity. But this is one time when you cannot cheat and expect there to be no consequences."

"Babe, after what your people did to my twin, you've got to know that I am not willing to lay down and be a nice lap dog on this one. I will be making my own rules for you!" challenged Tone.

Vret actually smiled at the challenge. "I know you will, Tone. Assuming we can come to an arrangement where we both follow the rules set down by the other, then I can arrange this meeting." The way the archangel spoke made Zeke nervous. Vret was not known for her willingness to compromise since she was the most knowledgeable of all the angels. She could be quite adamant about what she knew was right and wrong, and was not open to discussion as a rule.

"Vret, you know that Tone is not on your level," said the hunter." I know you will be fair, but please keep his emotions in mind."

Vret glanced at Zeke, and told him with a thought that she would. But she also conveyed clearly that he would not be part of this discussion. Zeke backed off...for the moment.

Tone had watched the interchange and caught the message that Zeke had intended: *Be careful.* He looked over at his angelic adversary and considered his words far more carefully than usual and decided to hear what she had to say first. "What are you rules, sweetie pie?" He didn't consider them THAT carefully.

Knowing full well what he was trying, Vret began. "First, you cannot upset Anna. If things begin to get out of control, I will end the reunion, and you will not be allowed another. She is a fragile soul who can be easily damaged or damage herself without proper care. In many ways, she is not unlike you on Earth."

"I can live with that. I will be on my best behavior," said Tone. Seeing the curious look on Arino's spirit, he added, "Better than any of you have ever seen."

"Second," continued the wise angel, "you cannot tell her who you really are since she does not have any experience with living human spirits. It may be beyond her ability to understand, and that has been known to cause her to be upset. I cannot allow that to happen."

"Hold on! I can't tell her I'm her long, lost brother? That is not fair!" interjected Tone.

Vret saw that objection coming. "It may not be fair, but I'm not concerned about what you think is fair as much as I am concerned about what is best for Anna. If she is hurt by this encounter, then it is not worth it. Do you not think she has been through enough pain?" The question hung in the ether like a weight on all who heard.

"I agree," said a slightly dejected Tone. "Provisionally..."

Her laughter was musical as she responded, "Your provision is based on what?"

It was Tone's turn to smile. "You don't know me as well as you think. If she recognizes me, then rule dos is null, void and nada. Agreed?"

Vret gave the exception careful consideration before saying, "Agreed." Continuing, she said, "And the final rule, you cannot tell her about your Earthly life. Nothing about your autism, your savantism, not even about your wealth due to your business. She cannot know you are still Earthbound. She has no concept of that."

"Wealth?" asked Arino. "I don't understand."

Tone winked at Arino. "I make good money, babe. Check out my website sometime." Turning to Vret, he said, "No problem."

"Now for my other rule. I get to give her a hug." Tone was being very firm in his demand.

"May I ask why?" inquired Vret, unsure as to the nature of the demand.

Tone looked at her, incredulously. "Don't you ever need a hug? After all she went through, she needs a hug from someone who is blood. No offense, but you angels really have no idea what it's like to be human. I do. What she went through was close to my imagination of what Hell is really like. She needs a hug from her little brother."

Vret knew there was something else going on behind the prismatic glow of the human, but could not tell what it was. She felt that he really had earned the right to meet his long, lost sister; but also knew that she had to put Anna's welfare ahead of Tone's desires. "You are hiding something from me, Tone. What is it?"

Tone's normal flippancy returned. "Whatever do you mean, Vretty-poo? How could I possible sneak something past the wisest of the wise? I'm just a simple, little human." he laughed.

The archangel couldn't help but smile. "Tone, you are many things, but 'simple, little human' is not one of them. Unlike everyone else who has ever met you, I make it a point to never underestimate you. You may be one of the most brilliant minds I have ever met, and I know you are one of the most complex. So, if you don't mind, I'd like to know what is going on in that devious, hidden, Machiavellian, human mind."

Tone was genuinely taken aback. "That was a long winded response. Machiavellian? I'm not sure whether to be flattered or insulted. I think I'll go with flattered."

Vret was not to be distracted. "It was meant to be flattering. But you did not answer my question."

Tone grimaced. "You noticed that, did you?" He paused, considering his options. He opted for the truth. "In my heart and soul I know that she will recognize me if I can touch her just once."

Zeke broke his long silence. "And what happens if she doesn't?" He knew that Tone would be devastated if that occurred. The warrior wanted his friend to be prepared just in case his plan failed.

Tone smiled weakly. He had not even considered that. "Well, a hug is still a hug."

Arino began preparing for the arrival of Anna, and any damage control to either of the human spirits through this encounter. She gave Vret a nod that said she was ready, but also showed that she was concerned with this plan. It was never a good idea to move Anna very far. Vret communicated her understanding.

The archangel looked at the human. "There is one more thing. I would like your permission to bring one more entity into the know about you and Anna. Arino is one of the best of the angel healers and can handle Anna's needs quite well. But if I am going to bring Anna here, then I would like Raphael to know about it, and know why. As you well know, he is the greatest healer and we may need an archangel here to help if there are any issues."

Tone did not even need to think about it. "Absolutely. I like Raph. He's a nice archangel. But he can't talk if he comes. I need to be able to think, and his voice makes me a little too happy."

"You mean loopy," added Zeke, laughing at the memory of Raphael and Tone's first encounter.

"That too!" smiled Tone. "Bring him up to speed."

"Already done," said Vret. "Now as to the rest of the preparations..." With a thought, the room seemed to melt into a new form. Gone were the ten walls which were replaced by a normal-looking, four-walled room with very comfortable accoutrements. The walls appeared to Tone to be a rich mahogany paneling with gaslight sconces; which created a flickering, upward lighting that drew your attention to a low vaulted ceiling. Tone could not tell if the ceiling was painted to look like Van Gough's *Starry Night,* or the actual painting. The movement of the stars made it apparent that it was neither. The large plush chairs placed in a circle in the center of the room were focused on a large crystal bowl filled with pillows and blankets.

"Everyone, please have seat," said Vret. It was clear she was inviting everyone to make themselves comfortable; however, it was also clear that it was not optional. "Raphael will be here shortly."

The angels all sat in the provided chairs and relaxed. Tone was the last to sit, knowing that there was no way to relax with what was coming. As soon as he sat, all his tension seemed to melt into the cushion of the chair. "It's like all my problems were sucked out through my ass and into the chair," sighed Tone. Thinking for a moment and then lifting himself up to check the seat of the chair, he said, "That sounded better in my head. What kind of chairs are these anyway? And can I get one for my living room?"

Arino answered, "They are just chairs, Tone. Granted, they are created by angels, making them more comfortable than anything you have on Earth, but they are just chairs."

"No magic angel mojo? That's disappointing." Bouncing in his chair, he continued, "I'll be taking this with me when I go."

Raphael appeared through a portal along the far wall. The archangel of healing was by far the most beautiful being Tone had ever encountered. Androgynous and beyond the concept of gender, Raphael could have a profound effect on humans. His voice was known to reduce Tone to a babbling, happy idiot. Often his presence would have a similar affect; however, this time he had chosen to reign in his power to allow Tone and Anna to be intelligent in his presence. In his arms was a tiny bundle wrapped in shimmering cloth that seemed to glow with angelic warmth.

A soft voice spoke from the bundle. "Why are you stopping the feel good, Rapel?"

# Chapter 5

Tone wanted to jump from his chair, grab Anna from Raphael, and hold her until everyone just left them alone. There was something that held him back. Passion and logic both screamed at Tone to follow his instincts. Yet, there was something that still kept him in his seat. The chair itself was calming him in ways he never suspected.

Arino rose and took the bundle from Raphael. "It's all right, Anna. Raphael is just trying to help you so you can talk to some friends of mine." She began to unfold the many layers around the tiny spirit, "Are you comfortable, little one?"

A giggle came from the bundle. "I'm feeling shorpy. Thanks."

Arino unblocked Tone from reading her essence. Shorpy is a word she uses meaning, 'good, happy and something like well-fed' but in a spiritual kind of way, thought Arino for the sake of Tone. She has many words like that. Some of the things she says, we are not totally sure what she means since her thoughts are very disjointed.

As Arino removed the last layer of shimmering fabric from her precious package, Tone got his first glimpse of a sister he had never known. The spirit that the healer placed in the crystal container was unlike anything Tone had ever seen. His expectations were totally obliterated. This was not the golden, glowing, angelic baby he had expected. She had an indigo tint to her spirit that reminded Tone entirely too much of many of the demons he had met. She also did not have a form like his or the angels around him. She more closely resembled a tiny, malformed gelatin sculpture that seemed to be constantly falling apart and reforming into something new. Tone could not tell where, or whether there even were anything like eyes, ears, nose or a mouth on his sister. This was not what he had hoped.

"Who is with you, Rino? I can't tell who is here." Anna was inquisitive.

Arino considered her words carefully. "Well, you already know that Raphael is here."

"He is?" asked Anna.

"Yes, Anna. He carried you. Do you remember?" asked Arino patiently.

"I think so," she said unconvincingly. "He did something; but I can't remember what."

Arino beamed at the tiny spirit. "Yes, sweet one. He stopped the 'feel good'. Vret is here. Do you remember her? She is the one who makes you laugh by changing her colors."

"Colors! I love Colors. Where are you, Colors?" asked a joyful Anna.

"I'm right here," said Vret, as she rose from her chair to move to be near the little one. Tone was impressed by this side of the archangel as she took on all the hues of the Spiritscape, making her appear more like Tone than an angel. The tender laughter reminiscent of a wind chime that came from the crystal cradle almost made Tone cry. Her laugh brought out all the emotions that he kept hidden behind his sarcasm and false bravado.

"Who is crying?" asked a concerned Anna. "Someone is sad. Don't be sad. Be happy like me."

Arino intervened to allow Tone to compose himself. "Don't worry, Anna. That is my other friend. His name is Tone. He wanted to meet you."

"A new friend? Yea! I like new friends. They are frabby! What's his name?" asked the forgetful spirit. All Arino could tell Tone was that "frabby" was a good thing.

"My name is Tone," came the shaky voice. He was able to slowly rise to meet his sibling. As she turned to him, he understood why he could not see any kind of facial expression. Her entire being became all senses examining him. She had no need of eyes, ears, nose or mouth. Anna could sense all with her whole spirit. It was unnerving to Tone having someone else reading him the way he read the angels. He was so taken with Anna, he didn't even make a smartass remark.

"Tone? Tone. Tone. Tone. Tone," said the sweet spirit. "I like the tone of Tone." The giggle was back. "Say something else. I like the zoobs you make, Tone." Through Arino, Tone learned that "zoobs" was a combination of seeing, hearing, smelling and a few other things that they weren't totally sure about.

"You have no idea how glad I am to meet you, Anna." He was regaining the normal sound to his voice. Vret had moved to be near him. Tone was not sure who she had moved to protect: him or Anna or both? Raphael was sending some kind of healing energy into Anna. She giggled again. She seemed to do that frequently.

Raphael opened his thoughts to Tone. She needs constant care. Right now she is struggling but I can compensate. I will need to get her back home before much longer. Even his thoughts were soothing.

"Anna, are you happy?" asked Tone with genuine curiosity.

She laughed at his question. "I am shorpiest! Is there any other way to be?"

"You asked if I was sad a little bit ago," replied Tone.

Laughter filled the ether. "Other people get sad. I only get happy and happier and happiest! You should try to be happy all the time like me. Why are you sad, Tone?"

Tone was not sure how to reply. Vret came to his rescue. "He lost his sister a long time ago. It makes him sad."

"Colors! You're here too!" exclaimed Anna, who had forgotten seeing her. "That makes me happier and happiest and happiest-est! Shorped out! Shorped out!" Her joy was contagious.

"I wish I could give you a hug, sweetie," said a very loving Tone.

"Tone. Tone. Tone. You can't hug me. I love too much!" said Anna.

Arino corrected. "You 'move' too much, Anna."

"That too! But I can hug you, Tone. Rapel, can I hug Tone? He needs a hug. He is sad because his sister is gone."

The look on the entire essence of Tone was begging Raphael to say "yes". Raphael, Arino, Vret and Zeke seemed to be having a conference at angel speed. After a long discussion by angel standards, but more like the blink of an eye by humans, Arino moved to lift the tiniest spirit in all the spirit worlds. Anna giggled again as she was lifted by the heavenly healer. Tone could almost feel the angels holding their breath as Arino approached.

"Be gentle with Tone, Anna. I don't want either of you to get hurt when you hug. You know how strong you are!" said Arino, all the while thinking to Tone: *That goes for you too, sweetie.* Tone was so absorbed in meeting his sister, he didn't even make a comment about, or even notice being called, "sweetie."

As Tone held out his arms, Arino shook her head and moved to place Anna on his back. As Anna was lifted onto Tone's back, her gelatinous form began to expand and move to wrap herself around his spirit several times. The feeling went all the way through every part of him. It was like being smothered by love. Every iota of Tone's spirit felt the love of his sister filling him to the point that he felt as though he were about to explode. He wanted to explode. He never wanted this feeling to end. There was nothing that could ever make him want this peace, happiness and love to end. He passed out.

As Arino cared for the overwhelmed Tone, Raphael held out his hand to Anna. She unentwined herself from around Tone and moved once again into Raphael's arms. The archangel of healing restored his normal state of comfort in her presence.

"Feel good!" giggled Anna. "Is Tone hurt? Did I hug too hard? I hope he's kample."

Raphael finally spoke. "He is more than kample, Anna. He is happy."

"I like Tone. He reminds me of my brother. Did I ever tell you I had a brother?" asked Anna, as Raphael walked out through the portal, carrying the tiny bundle.

When Tone came back to his senses, he was looking for Anna. "Where did she go?" demanded the usually casual human. He had a wild look about him that seemed ready to escalate to panic. Arino was quick with the calming power of the healer to bring him back from his manic state.

"Relax, my friend. She had to get back. Anna is fragile. There are limits to how long she can be away from her home," explained Arino. "But that was a very moving moment between the two of you. I wish you could have seen the spirit spectrum from my perspective. It was beautiful."

Tone was calming down even though he was not happy. "What happened to me? It felt like I was smothered by Anna." He considered that for a moment and corrected himself. "Smothered is not the right word. Filled up, maybe? Not quite. Pushed to my limits? I don't know. But it was better than a foot long chili-cheese dog with onions."

Vret, Arino and Zeke looked at each other and, as one, looked at Tone. Vret spoke, "If you say so, Tone. Now that we have explored that and discovered your softer side, I'm afraid that we have a task before us that will take you into some less happy places."

"Bring it on, babe!" The old Tone was back and charged for action now that he knew about Anna. "I'm torn right now. I'm pissed at what happened to Anna. But I also know there was nothing you could have done about it. I owe you for taking care of her all this time and for letting me see her." Tone looked as though he had come to a conclusion. "Anything you want, I can do. But if it is something that requires an elk, a pair of rubber waders, and a unicycle, I will need some time to prepare the mojitos." The glow of Tone showed his joy was reaching new heights.

Zeke looked at Vret and asked, "Do you have any clue what he is talking about when he comes up with these random items? There is a fine line between genius and insanity. I wonder sometimes."

Arino laughed, saying, "There are times when I hope there is some hidden meaning and other days I hope there isn't. I am not sure which is worse."

Vret joked, "Trust me. You do not want to know the answer to either of those questions. It is more than an angel should have to suffer."

Tone had been looking from angel to angel to angel as they discussed his randomness. "You really don't. But if you ever see me running away from something, carrying a pot of armadillo green stew, keep up. It's not good."

The archangel recaptured control of the conversation. "Tone, there is an issue that needs to be fixed regarding your travels in the Spiritscape. With this new problem, we will need you to travel to other levels."

The Spiritscape was a complex area between Heaven and Hell that was also able to touch most places on Earth. Time was not a constant. In fact, the Spiritscape worked outside of time as humans understood it on Earth. Very little, if any, time passed for Tone on Earth when he was in the Spiritscape. The passage of actions was measured by effort of spirit or thought. The unit of measure, a quoll, could be different for each being. Zeke measured one quoll by the effort it took for him to go through every piece of information in his unlimited memory from all time and all places he or any other angels had visited. The time Tone had spent with him, Vret, and Anna had amounted to one quoll this trip.

Since time did not pass in the Spiritscape, even though the space was limitless, there were occasions when the same activities would take place at the same location, but with different individuals. Sometimes the same individuals would be in the same place for different purposes. Instead of angels and demons overlapping and having contact with each other, the same spiritual location in the Spiritscape had layers above and below to allow for simultaneous actions in the same place, but on a slightly different level.

With all of his gifts, Tone was confined to whatever level he was on. Changing levels for a human could cause damage to the link between body and spirit. As the infamous Bubba has shown, skipping randomly from level to level created damage to the link that could not be repaired. Tone had been forced across layers once before with no discernible damage; however, it was not something that the angels wanted to tempt again.

Vret's declaration caught all present off guard. Tone was the first to reply. "Now that you know about my autism on Earth, you see why I was not that worried about damage. I'm already pretty wacky. But let's not try that again. I'd hate to lose any important books from my memory. With my luck, I'd lose something crucial like *The Republic* or *The Iliad* or, even worse, *The Hitchhiker's Guide to the Galaxy*!"

Zeke did not know where Vret was going with this, and hoped she was not suggesting what he feared. "You don't really want Tone level hopping do you?"

Vret smiled a knowing smile. "Yes, I do. But we have found a way so that he will be safe. Adoneal?" She had called out for the archangel of service.

Adoneal appeared without fanfare or flourish. He was a simple looking angel, but quite unique. This archangel had the ability to create anything that was needed in the Spiritscape. He had made everything from spirit spheres to skimmers to the room used by Vret. But Adoneal had been injured and phased apart by an archdemon. An angel damaged in battle could be easily healed, unless the damage was severe enough that parts were severed – phased apart. The archangel had been phased into hundreds of pieces, and taken to the farthest reached of the Spiritscape. When he was eventually able to be healed, part of him had been too damaged to be repaired. A choice had to be made between his personality, and his ability to create. It was Arino who had been forced to make the choice that made him into an even greater inventor; but had sacrificed his personality and his ability to link with other angels. He rarely remembered other beings names. He and Tone had much in common, but Adoneal had not known this the last time they had met.

Vret spoke to the inventor. "Adoneal, Tone, the H'tes Bearer, is here."

Not being one for idle chit chat, he approached the human and began. "H'tes Bearer, we have found a way to augment your blade that will allow you protection while moving from level to level in the Spiritscape. This is something that you will need to activate each time you take up the H'tes. It will be in a passive mode, drawing power from the ether which will allow it to protect you. Level hopping will drain power from the blade; however, it will recharge from the ether without needing any assistance from you. You must remember to make sure it has enough power for the hop or it will not be able to protect you. Do you understand?"

Tone looked at Adoneal with amazement. "I get it. But I think that is the most I have ever heard you talk."

"That is likely," replied Adoneal without elaboration. "May I have your H'tes? It needs to be removed to make this change." Tone caused the blade to swing out of his arm and touched the series of runes that released the bond. The blade floated in the ether between the human and the archangel. Adoneal touched the blade in one of the few spots that was devoid of the tiny runes that covered it. The angel carved a new rune into the blade that was different from the others in design as it lacked the same glow. After carving the new rune in the crystal, the inventor touched the rune to give it power. "You may take your blade back," said the angel, without a trace of pride. Adoneal existed to serve and took no pride in the work that was so extraordinary. He was totally devoid of ego.

Tone grasped his H'tes and reattached it to his hand. "So I touch this rune once, and it protects me when we hop from level to level in the Spiritscape?"

"Yes," said the archangel. Adoneal looked at Tone longer than he normally looked at anything other than a device he was creating. "You can leave Earth and return?"

Shock was on the essence of the other angels in the room. Tone was surprised as well. "Yes, Adoneal. I am special. Why do you ask?"

Ignoring the question, Adoneal continued, "There is something of the astonishing about you. You are different on Earth than here." It was a statement.

Tone was not sure how to respond. "Yes. I am an autistic savant. Everything I have ever read I can remember. Why do you ask?" The same question was on the minds of the angels who had never seen Adoneal take an interest in anything other than his inventions.

"As am I," replied the archangel. "I will talk to you again when I'm not needed elsewhere." With those words, the archangel of service was gone.

All eyes were on Tone. "What can I say? I'm a charmer."

# Chapter 6

Zeke and Tone soon found themselves alone in the beauty of the Spiritscape. Floating amidst towering, misty canyons and majestic reversed mountains was still breathtaking to Tone. *Well, it would be if I had breath here.* The angel knew to give Tone a chance to see what was to be seen. Zeke enjoyed watching the childlike innocence of the human seeing so much for the first time. This place was home away from home for an angel. Zeke spent most of his time on Earth, but was quite comfortable in the spiritual realm. Tone had been coming into the Spiritscape for two decades of his earthly life, but had not been able to see it in all its splendor until he had begun his metamorphosis. Now, all the detail – filled with nuances of color, light and darkness – was fully seen by the human.

Tone broke the silence. "So what do you want to do first? Scene of the crime? Interrogate a demon? Hot tubbing at Arino's?"

"Arino prefers the pool," bantered the hunter, evoking a chuckle from Tone. "Michael suggested we talk to Yeroc. He is a smartass, but he may know something."

Tone gazed at his partner. "Dude, you said 'smartass'! And you used it grammatically correctly. I'm so proud of you!"

Zeke smiled. "Yeah. I've noticed that you are not the only one who has been changing. Just try not to tick me off." He began forming a portal in the ether around them. Since his focus was on hunting and combat, it took him longer to form portals than it did some other angels.

"Like that's gonna happen," laughed the human. "I'll have you saying 'pissed off' before we're done with this little adventure." As his H'tes came out of his arm, he pressed the rune that would keep him safe from level jumping within the Spiritscape. "Just making sure it's on."

"Good plan. This time we're porting farther than you have ever done. Sort of." Zeke left it open just to tease his friend. Tone took the lure, hook, line and sinker.

"Okay. What does that mean? And do I need to get a barf bag for this flight? Did you know they look at you strange when you keep your chili in those?" asked Anthony.

Concentrating on the portal, Ezekiel replied, "I'm sure they do." Finishing the portal, a goldenrod door was floating in the middle of the ether. "This time we are traveling across the space of the Spiritscape, and down and over around thirty-two hundred levels. It'll feel a little funny."

Tone backed away from the door. "Are we talking funny 'ha ha' or funny 'why did my toe end up in my armpit and my ass between my nipples'?" The human continued to back away from the yellow door that looked all too peaceful to him.

Zeke came toward him, smiling in a way that did not calm Tone's nerves. "Tone, would I do anything to mess with you like that? I thought we were buddies?" The closer Zeke came the more Tone moved back.

"Yep, we are buddies. But most buddies like to play pranks on each other. I am far above such juvenile antics since I can't get the 'kick me' sign on your back without you noticing." Zeke continued moving closer as Tone felt himself backed against something.

"Relax, it probably won't hurt a bit," laughed Zeke, as he turned the handle on the real portal he had made behind Tone. The human was through the door before he knew what had happened. "I have missed him," the angel mused to himself, following his friend through the portal.

Tone was not a happy camper when Zeke stepped through behind him. "Ezekiel Angel! If I thought you had a middle name I would use it. That was downright mean, manipulative, deceptive, and just plain ol' sneaky." The human couldn't fake mad very well, breaking into a smile. "I'm so proud of you," he said, giving the angel an unwanted hug.

"Yeah, that's something else I've noticed. I'm not sure you are the best influence on me, but it has been fun watching the demons react to me." Looking around, the hunter smiled. "Speaking of demons, I think I see who we need to harass. I think you'll like this." A rip opened in the ether and Tone could see a beautiful landscape beyond. It looked like an idyllic mountain stream with two men fly-fishing. Ezekiel reached through the tear, grabbing something that Tone couldn't see. A screech pierced the Spiritscape as fish jumped in the stream. Pulling his arm back through the hole, the hunter had one of the oddest looking demons Tone had yet seen.

Yeroc was tinted blue like most of the demons. Many demons had multiple eyes that seemed to look everywhere. This devil had four eyes together making it into a square. The mouth of the devil was twisted into a wicked smile, showing a few pointed teeth. The most distinguishing feature was the rotund body of the evil spirit. It was fat, very fat. Tone was certain it was as big around as it was tall. It looked like a bloated, blue beach ball.

Zeke gave Tone a warning look and the human backed off. He knew better than to mess with demons. A bad experience with a demon shard had enabled a dying demon to temporarily to take him over. It was not an experience he had any desire to repeat. With his H'tes hidden safely away, Tone watched the interaction.

"Yeroc, I think you've lost weight. How are you today?" began the hunter, the tone of his voice contrasted the friendliness of the words.

The demon was terrified of the hunter and pained by Zeke calling him by name. Quaking and stammering, it replied, "E-e-e-zekiel. H-h-how nice to see you. I'm sure y-y-you were wondering what I was doing there. It wasn't what it looked like."

"Really?" inquired the angel. "It looked like you were whispering to the fishermen about the girl they both have been seeing. If I didn't know better, I'd think you were trying to start a fight between them in the middle of nowhere with all kinds of rocks to use as weapons. I'm so glad it wasn't what it looked like."

The blue tinged spirit of the devil lost most of its glow. "I have no idea what you are…" Words were cut off in mid-sentence as Zeke's arms expanded and grabbed it around the midsection. Between screams and curses, the Hadian wheezed, "Can't… we… come… to…" Again, words trailed off as the grip around the demon tightened.

"I'm sorry. I missed that last part. Were you asking if we can come to an understanding?" asked Ezekiel, loosening his stranglehold on the demon. "Come to think of it, there is something you could do to help. I need some information."

The sniveling spirit was all too happy to oblige. "Of course. Anything you want. How can I help?"

Zeke looked at Tone with a sneer on his face. "Do you have any pride at all?" he taunted. The frightened figure remained silent. "Where was the last place a demon disappeared? It seems I have to stop something from making you disappear."

Yeroc looked at Ezekiel in stunned silence. Tone was amused by the whole situation. Zeke had become more aggressive. It was a good thing from Tone's perspective since demons had made his last trip with the hunter very unpleasant. *Revenge is a dish best served with lemon juice poured over the wounds.* Tone chuckled at his own joke.

A quick squeeze of the demon produced a flood of words. "Kafplee disappeared not long ago over at Rheesmil Falls, and that is the only one I know about so please don't squeeze me any harder or my eyes might pop out and roll around, and I won't be able to find them cause I won't be able to see what I'm doing and…" Another squeeze shut the demon up.

"Your cooperation is appreciated, Yeroc. You get a head start. I'll start looking for you as soon as I'm done with this little dilemma. Now, run along." Zeke released the ball-shaped demon who ported away.

"You've gotten more badass-itude going. I like it," admitted Tone. "My influence?" There was hope in his voice.

"Maybe a little. Now, we need another portal to Rheesmil Falls." A door soon appeared that Tone, approached, opened and jumped through, with a wink at Zeke. "That was easier than chasing him," the angel mused, following the human.

Tone was silent when Zeke arrived. At first the warrior thought he was thinking of a smartass comment, but soon saw that the human was just staring at the area where the demon had disappeared. There was a look on his essence that showed him to be awestruck and horrified.

"Tone? Are you all right?"

"Ummm… yeah. Ummm… huh." Tone speechless in a funny situation was a pleasure for Ezekiel. Tone speechless right now sent off warning bells in the angel's spirit.

"Talk to me, Tone. All I can see is a faint green tint to this area. And that will be gone in a few more quolls. What's wrong?"

Tone tore his gaze away from the sight before him. "What a mess? This looks worse than my bathroom after the deer stew diarrhea incident in '04. I can't really find a trail. The green goo is… well… everywhere. It's like whatever did this went all over the place." Moving around, Tone began to trace the outer edge of the solid trail. "I can see an oil trail going in there," he pointed to the spot where Kafplee had been. "But then it does something strange. And I'm not talking about strange like washing your hair with club soda so it fizzes. I mean strange like… well…"

Zeke understood the severity of the situation in the lack of information coming from the normally verbose human. "Tell me as best you can. We'll figure it out."

"It's like the green stopped the black, but the demon didn't port away. It just stayed put like it was a fly stuck in amber or Becky or any of those other girls who sat at the cool table." Tone was uncertain where to look. "I know some demons can stop angels from porting like Je'relir did. Are there any angels who can do that?"

"Sure. Plenty of them. I probably could, given enough time. No port marks for the demon? So it didn't get away. Any puddles like we had with Bubba eating them?" asked the hunter, his instincts on alert for anything approaching. Zeke was getting a bad feeling about this.

Tone continued moving around. "There might be one. If this is a port mark, it's the biggest one I've seen. It looks like a huge port happened all over the place." Moving to another angle, he continued, "And over here there is a green trail that is…" Tone stopped moving, his essence turning pink. "Michael!" he yelled with all his spirit.

Zeke went into battle mode, decked out in full warrior regalia ready for attack. Michael appeared a heartbeat later and transformed into his terrifying form, prepared to devastate anything he found. Tone remained stock still, staring at the trail only he could see. When no attack seemed imminent, Michael, who had been instantly briefed by a thought from Zeke, approached Tone as he returned to his normal form. Zeke remained on guard, ready for battle.

"Tone? What's wrong?" Michael shared Zeke's concern. "You look like you've seen a demon."

Tone continued looking at the invisible trail. "Mike, who knows I'm here?"

The archangel had not expected that question. The absence of a smart remark or insult only increased his concern. "Well, Tone, every angel that is linked knows. It's not a secret."

"And when did this mess happen?" asked the human.

Michael was not sure where this was going. "Best guess is thirteen quolls ago. What are you seeing, Tone?"

"And no demons know about me, right?" asked Anthony, still failing to say anything amusing.

"Right. Talk to me Tone. I can't help if I don't know what's wrong," said Michael, getting more and more worried.

"I think we have a problem. Whatever did this left a note in its trail. It's kind of like sky writing that only I can see. It says, 'Hi Tone. How's life?'" Tone's aura looked washed out with fear.

# Chapter 7

Zeke was immediately by Tone's side asking, "How?" Michael was looking where Tone had been staring, trying to will the invisible trail to appear. Tone looked from one angel to the other, imploring them for an explanation.

"You two are the angels. You tell me," pleaded Tone. He was obviously scared, but Zeke could tell he was also curious. This was not the same frightened rabbit that he had met not so long ago. Tone was becoming something more. "Besides, it's time for a chili dog break and my brain is sweating bacon grease from thinking so hard." Then again, maybe not. The hunter was relieved to hear Tone make a joke.

Michael replied to Tone's request. "Something in the Spiritscape knows about you, Tone. All angels are accounted for… unless…" The ether was thick with the anticipation left by that one word.

Ezekiel, knowing Michael's thoughts, looked hard at his friend. "You can't be serious, Michael. That's not possible." Remembering Tone, Zeke explained. "Michael was wondering if we have a rogue angel when he first sent me on our Bandersnatch quest. Now, he is ready to start an inquisition."

"And that is a bad thing?" Then he added, "Would an angel fit on the rack? That would have to be a really big rack. Or a Judas cradle? That would be a strange pain in the ass for an angel." The angels were looking at him with concern that he knew so much about medieval torture. "I read a lot," Tone said in his defense.

Michael, still looking at Tone, replied, "It's not an inquisition, but I have to investigate all possibilities." Then he turned his gaze to Zeke. "While you were investigating here, I have been double checking your story. You are cleared."

Ezekiel nodded, accepting his acquittal nonchalantly. Tone was less generous. "What the hell, Mike? You didn't really think Zeke would do something like this, did you? Sure, he has been touched by a human spirit after being blown apart, making him undergo some pretty radical changes that are making him say things like 'ass' and giving him even more attitude, but… Oh…" He looked at Zeke. "I just made his point didn't I?"

"Yeah," replied Zeke. "I was the most likely suspect." The angel refrained from telling Tone about the part within him that even Michael couldn't read. He wanted to keep that to himself until he learned more about it.

"So if this is a rogue angel, what are you gonna do about it?" asked Tone. He wanted this to all be over. Something leaving him messages was really creepy.

Michael was multitasking on an archangel level. "I may need both of you to help with my part of the investigation. Let me clear the archangels first then they can check their own angels." Looking at the waiting duo, Michael continued, "For now, keep trying to sort out what you can. F'nial has found two more places where demons have disappeared. Head to Uqump and Ximsor. I need to know if there are any more messages, Tone. This is troubling." The archangel warrior looked worried. "I don't like this," he said as he ported away.

"HE doesn't like this? I'm the one with the stalker," mused Tone. "I hope this one is not like the last one. Bubba really annoyed the shit out of me." He made a show of looking thoughtful. "The real question is not why something chose me to stalk. What I want to know is whether it is my charm, wit, vast knowledge of penguin cosmetology, or uncanny sense of soul style that keeps the creepies coming. I'm pretty sure it's the penguin thing." The old Tone was slowly coming back.

"I'm sure that's what it is." Ezekiel was getting better at sarcasm. "Now we need to meet up with Nazilaq. Portaling to Uqump is totally impossible. We are better off using a skimmer."

"Oh yeah!" Tone began trying to moonwalk while shaking his everything. He couldn't dance if his life depended on it. It looked like he was having a full-spirit spasm.

Nazilaq was the pilot of one of the most unique vessels in all the realms. Naz's skimmer, the *Hajile-R,* was a large crystal ring designed to ride on the surfaces of the energy rivers in the Spiritscape. Since there was no up or down and no gravity, rivers of energy were tubes that flowed from one part of the Spiritscape to another to maintain an energy equilibrium.

These energy rivers were not safe to travel without the protection of a skimmer because of the creatures that could be found within. In his first ride in a skimmer, Tone had discovered that bits and pieces of angels and demons could be found moving in these rivers. These creatures – pha'ards – were pieces that were slowing fading away after they had been lost in battles. Since they came off spiritual beings, the larger ones could retain a fraction of the consciousness of the original angel or demon. Most of them were more like piranhas – pure animal instinct – that wanted to devour anything they could, to hold on to their form in a losing battle to continue to exist.

"Are you done with your gyrations, yet?" asked the amused angel.

"Almost," said Tone, doing a flip, ending right in front of Zeke. "Ta da! You've got to admit, I'm getting better."

Zeke began making a portal. "I may be changing, but I still don't lie to my friends, Tone." The door was opened, and the two friends left to meet up with another old friend.

Arriving in a new place was always an adventure for Tone. He never knew what to expect each time he went through a portal. It could be a river of energy; mountainous, amber-colored crevices; or even a waterfall of gems. Tone was prepared for anything as he exited the doorway, or so he thought. This time he found himself inside a huge cylinder with twenty large, crystal rings lined up – each with angels working on various parts.

"Welcome to the shop," said Zeke. "This is where the…"

"There's more than one?!" interrupted Tone. "I thought there was just our skimmer. How many of those bad boys are out there?" Tone looked like a bouncing puppy, ready to go for a ride in the back of a pickup.

"There are thirty of them. There are always at least ten on patrol at any given time. Usually more, but right now they are doing upgrades." Looking around, he approached an angel. "Torkel, where is Nazilaq? We have a job."

Although more beautiful than any human, this angel was rather plain by angelic standards. He greeted Zeke warmly. "Ezekiel, good to see you. Nazilaq is meeting with Adoneal and Michael. He should be back any quoll now. Are you going to damage my skimmer again?" joked the angel. Then he looked at the human. "Hello, Tone. I'm Torkel. Just think of me as the mechanic for the *Hajile-R*. When it's in the shop, I make sure it's ready to go."

Offering a jaunty salute, Tone replied, "Naz has a pit crew? How cool is that? So tell me, Tork, is the *Hajile-R* the best skimmer or should we be trading it in on a new model with bucket seats, a bitchin' Bose sound system, and steel-belted radials?" Tone was trying for a reaction, but what he got was unexpected.

"Let me tell you a little secret," he stage whispered, "We upgrade them so they all have the same base, but it's the pilot that makes all the difference. Every one of these ships has been upgraded with all the extras that Adoneal added to the *Hajile-R* during your battle with the beast. Plus we have added a few more things that may just come in handy. With Crotil or R'Loom piloting you are in safe hands. But with Nazilaq at the helm, you are with the best. He teaches others how to sail the skimmers."

"I'm almost blushing," came a voice nearby. Nazilaq flew up to greet them. "Zeke, good to see you. Tone! How is my favorite explosive human? I've missed your weirdness." Nazilaq, plain looking like Torkel, was one of friendliest angels Tone had ever met. They had bonded almost instantly on their first adventure.

"Naz, pull your power back and give me a hug!" demanded the human, causing the pilot to move away. Nazilaq was notorious among the angels for not linking up to keep abreast of what was happening. He preferred to hear it from angels rather than having it wash over him in a wave. He dealt with enough of those while skimming.

Looking at Zeke, he reluctantly linked into the angel network. "That is interesting. Leave it to Vret to figure it out." Pulling in his power, he reached out and touched the human cautiously. After verifying that he wasn't about to be phased apart, he gave the human the first hug he had ever given. "Good to see you, friend."

Looking around, Tone said, "So this is where you hang out when you're not surfing the waves? Cool place. Do you get your own room like they do at the firehouse? Oh wait. Is there a pole you get to slide down when there's an emergency call?"

Zeke met Nazilaq's gaze. "Some things never change," sighed the hunter. "How soon can you be ready to go?"

"How soon can you get in?" laughed Naz. "Tone, we added a special thing just for you. It's this new device called a door."

Tone attempted to look confused. "A door? I've heard of those before. What are they used for again? Oh, that's right. They are those things with glass and screens you slide open to let fresh air in. Or is that a window? I get them confused." Laughing alone at his own joke, he added, "You would think a door would be something you would have thought to add earlier."

Torkel defended his ship. "Well, Tone, angels don't really need doors. We pass through or port in."

"So you did that just for lil' ol' me? How thoughtful. I feel bad that I didn't get you anything. Can I send you something later? A subscription to Popular Angel Mechanics? A new set of Craftsangel tools?" The mechanic was not sure if Tone was serious or not.

"Let's go before Tone offers him a Victoria's Secret angel's phone number," laughed Zeke.

"Dude, do you have that?" Looking at Torkel, he said, "Sorry bud, but I'm keeping that for myself. Now, Zeke, about that phone number…"

Shoving Tone through the new door in the skimmer, Zeke entered with Nazilaq close behind. The words of Torkel rang through the vessel as he sealed the door behind them. "Try not to break it this time."

The interior of the skimmer was minimalistic. Only one feature distinguished itself from the smooth walls that curved around. Jutting out of the wall was a raised portion where Nazilaq positioned himself. The crystal wall rose up and surrounded the lower portion of the pilot, partially encompassing him within the wall of the *Hajile-R*. The angel and vessel were now linked – what happened to one, happened to the other. That link allowed Naz to use his angelic power to be sent through the skimmer allowing it to be a travelling vessel or a battleship depending on the situation. It also meant that if the skimmer was damaged, so was Nazilaq.

Angels cleared out of the way as the wall of shop began to move inward, revealing a device that created an enormous portal. The skimmer slowly moved forward, entered the portal and exited as close to Uqump as was safe. Since there were no rivers to cruise, Nazilaq caused a transformation in the crystal ring. The *Hajile-R* elongated into an egg-shaped ship, giving it a more streamlined profile with the pilot in the center of the skimmer.

"This is new," admired Tone. "Resisting the urge to make any yolk references." Looking around, he added, "You would think there would be at least one chick in here."

"I'll call Arino later," sighed Zeke. "Naz, we don't know what to expect here. Be ready for anything."

"Always am," smiled the angel. Nazilaq was happiest when he was gliding through the Spiritscape in the *Hajile-R* at the highest speeds possible. The scenery of the Spiritscape was zipping past faster than Tone could process. He could have sworn he saw four angels sending their fire at a warthog-looking demon. Another place had angels removing the carved face of a particularly ugly, boil-covered devil off a silver and copper-colored bluff. Naz offered commentary. "Demon graffiti."

"Mount Rashmore? He needs some ointment or something?" retorted Tone.

Zeke interjected, "Uqump is coming up." Tone looked to see what was so special about the place where a portal couldn't go. What he saw was unusual in a place of such spectacular splendor. Uqump was an area that looked like nothing. It was a large, dark gray, area floating in the middle of the amber of the ether. Something about it made Tone not want to get any closer to it. It felt wrong, like it was missing something that made it not belong in the Spiritscape.

"Umm, guys, what is that? And why does it make me want to go hide under my bed 'til it goes away? You would think with a sexy name like Uqump, it would have more girls, shrimp cocktails and a spiced rum waterslide."

"That would be nice, but it won't be quite that much fun." Nazilaq had slowed the skimmer as they approached. The *Hajile-R* began press against the flexible gray surface. "I hate this part."

As the ship penetrated the barrier of the area, Tone lost all senses as he felt the gray all the way to his core.

# Chapter 8

Tone was certain this is what madness felt like. There was nothing to touch, nothing to see, nothing to hear. None of his senses registered anything. He couldn't even think straight. There was only gray. It even tasted and smelled gray, even though Tone wasn't sure how gray tasted. It seemed to go on forever.

When there was some movement within the gray nothingness, Tone was momentarily relieved to have some sensory input. That relief gave way to horror as a deformed demonic face loomed out of the gray, ready to devour him. The blue skinned monster had dull, hollow eyes that looked through the human as Tone passed harmlessly through the maw of the frozen spirit. And then everything was back.

When Tone looked up, Zeke looked like he was trying to shake off the cold and Nazilaq appeared to be shivering. The human moved closer to the hunter, concern winning out over confusion. "You okay, amigo? I think you have frostbite on your wings."

Zeke's voice was shaky. "That stuff is a nightmare. How long were we in there, Naz?"

The pilot was looking at something Tone had never seen. It was an actual display in the crystal around him. "Just a little less than a quoll. It would have been faster if we hadn't passed through Ih'duiwqec. I thought she would have drifted out by now."

Tone had questions. "Hey, guys? Human here. Context would be as nice as being the bikini picker for the Sports Illustrated Swimsuit Issue." Getting lost in the image he had just created, he corrected, "Well, not as nice as that. But I would kinda sorta like to know… WHAT THE HELL THAT WAS!"

Zeke tried to calm down his excited friend. "Relax, Tone. It's harmless. There are some parts of the Spiritscape that have to be isolated. This is one of those areas. Energy doesn't flow through the

Gray. It is reflected back into the rest of the Spiritscape. And you have to rely on drifting through it, you can't force your way through. The harder you push, the more it pushes back and the longer it takes. If you try to port or portal in or out... Well, you saw Ih'duiwqec."

It was Tone's turn to shiver. "That was not cool. I thought I was about to be a chili-cheese Toney-dog for... whatever the hell his name was."

"Well, SHE tried to port out of there a couple hundred quolls ago. She has been drifting ever since. Another couple hundred quolls and she will be in or out." Zeke didn't seem concerned that she would ever make it. Tone didn't blame him.

"Well, SHE is one ugly-assed, faced and bodied bitch," acquiesced Tone. "So, what's so special about this place that it gets its own security system with gray fences and guard demons?" Tone looked through the clear walls of the skimmer for the first time since they had passed the barrier. It was very different than the other parts of the Spiritscape he had seen. There was no amber glow casting everything with a golden hue here. A dark savanna stretched out in one direction as far as Tone could see. A mountain jutted out above them with the tip almost reaching to the flat plain beneath it. This was an area where shadows dominated creating an eerie feel to the place. To Tone it felt like...

"It's haunted," said Zeke, letting the words hang in the ether between them. The hunter loved watching Tone reacting to new things that did not make sense to him. This was a perfect example.

"I'm not going to play with you when you act like that," pouted Tone. "Naz, what's the deal with this place?" There was a pleading in Tone's eyes he hoped would cause the pilot to give him a different answer.

Nazilaq, though not touched by a human, still had a great sense of humor. "Well, in your terms, that may be the best description," admitted the angel. "It's... well... let me show you."

The *Hajile-R* cruised along the flatland until Naz spotted what he wanted the human to see. Tone looked at the apparition before him and understood. What was on the savanna was a shadowy leopard. Though larger than anything Tone had ever seen, it did not have a solid substance to its spirit. Another odd thing were the blue vapors that trailed off behind it. The beast went into a crouch as the skimmer approached. The eyes of the phantom cat glowed with blue flames as it sprang at the vessel. The beast bounced harmlessly off the hull of the skimmer.

Tone was confused. "So it's a haunted zoo? I've been to one on Halloween. Why the heavy-duty, scare-the-shit-out-of-you, make-you-want-a-shot-of-rum security system? They are just ghost animals" Looking through the crystal hull, Tone knocked and called, "Here kitty, kitty."

The leopard flew at Tone. Leaving its skin behind, blue and gray goo oozing, skeletal version of itself began clawing futilely at the hardened crystal of the skimmer. Tone stood frozen in place at the display of animal blood-lust and transformation, watching in horrified awe. As the ghoulish version of the animal fell back to the plains beneath it, the flesh crawled back around the bone leaving, it looking as it had before.

"You may not want to knock on the crystal. They hate that," said Naz, making a joke out of the obvious. "The animal spirits in here are protected. All the spirits in here are too dangerous to allow into one of the other realms. They were used by demons on earth, leaving them touched. Some animals we can purify and they have a special place, too. These are all just too far gone for the healers to find enough left to restore. Ripping the demon essence from them would destroy them."

"So you really think it's better to give them a half-existence than none at all? I think I'd prefer none… unless there are unicorns." Pressing his face against the wall, "Are there unicorns?" When neither angel answered, Tone pulled back to look at his friends. "You know I was kidding… Well, mostly." Between the two angels, a look was shared that Tone couldn't read. "There really aren't unicorns, are there?" The human was starting to get excited.

"I know this is useless to say, but just keep them in your imagination." Zeke added, knowing it was hopeless, "Tone, you really don't want to see them."

Tone placed his hands on his friend's shoulders, looked him in the eyes, and said, "I hear you. You're right." Zeke had not expected that. "That was useless to say. Now, where the hell are the unicorns?" Zeke had expected that.

Laughing, the pilot replied, "That is funnier than you know. Zeke, he would probably have seen them anyway." Back to business, Nazilaq continued, "But, first things first. I'm going to run a search route along in the inner walls of Uqump. Tone, I need you to look for trails that are unusual. We need to track where this… I can't believe we let Tone name these things… Bandersnatch came in." Tone giggled.

"It was either that or Bubba Dos or Phil. Bandersnatch sounds funnier because I get angels to say snatch." Tone moved to the forward-most section of the oblong skimmer. "How big is this place? Is this going to take long? I have unicorns to see!"

"Shouldn't take longer than three and a half quolls if we have to cover the whole thing." Nazilaq only took the *Hajile-R* to one-quarter speed so Tone wouldn't miss anything.

"Three quoll? This place is huge!" commented Tone. It was challenging for Tone to maintain his focus with all the bizarre scenery and creatures that appeared. A lake that was made of energy housed scores of fish of every shape and variety. All of them looked like parts had been eaten, leaving organs and gills hanging out at odd and unnatural angles. The sharks were continuously trying to eat the smaller fish, only to have them swim out through voids in the predators.

After searching for two quolls, a cry from Tone stopped the skimmer. "What is that?" asked the human. With a few nudges, he guided Nazilaq to a spot on the wall that had traces of green haze. Examining the trail, Tone declared, "I think we have a trail. It is a smooth kind of green like the message trail. Not really like demon oil trails or angel marshmallow cream trails. This is… well… different." Looking around, Tone noticed something. "I wonder why the animals don't have trails."

"Focus Tone," insisted Zeke. "Where does the green trail go? Can you tell if this is where it entered or left?"

"I can't really tell how old it is. I need to see more of it. Naz, that way," said the human, pointing toward a group of smooth mountains floating in the distance.

As the skimmer glided smoothly, following the trail only Tone could see, a flock of beasts flew into their path. The animals had sickly-yellow bodies of large horses, more massive than the famed draft horses of earth. Their amazing hooves were throwing orange fire as the animals ran on the ether, snake-like tails whipped around behind them. It was the heads that were shocking to Tone. Instead of a horse's head, each looked like a fleshless gorilla's skull had been placed on the body, with thousands of skeletal porcupine quills all over the face. As they saw the skimmer, the group changed course, heading directly toward the *Hajile-R*. Every one of the beasts had covered their faces, quills coming to a central point with eyes being the only things visible.

Tone shuddered. "Those are the ugliest horses I have ever seen. I don't suppose we can get behind them. Their asses have to look better than their heads."

Zeke smirked. "You're the one who wanted to see unicorns. Naz, slow down. I'd better check with Halidore. They may have seen something."

Tone just stared. "You call that a unicorn?" He kept looking. "Why did you make me see these? I told you I didn't want to and now it's ruined for me for life. You can be so cruel to us poor defenseless humans who never do anything to deserve things like this."

Both angels laughed. "Really, Tone?" asked Naz.

"Not buying the bullshit?" Both shook their heads. "Can't blame a guy for trying." Attempting to change the subject, he asked, "So, who is Halidore?"

"That is," said Zeke, pointing at the approaching form of the largest unicorn. Tone looked the beast up and down but couldn't sense anything. It just seemed like the other beastly spirits in Uqump. There was nothing to sense.

Halidore stopped by Zeke, the color of his spirit shifting. Zeke's aura changed as well as a silent greeting took place, leaving Tone still gawking. The human watched the shades of the angel change as did his form. Zeke was communicating with the unicorn without thought or words. Even though the warrior had lowered his spiritual defenses, Tone still had no clue what was being said.

Nazilaq came to his rescue. "Zeke is almost done with the greeting. Basically, he just said, 'Hello. It's good to see you.' You don't ever want to have a long conversation with a unicorn. It takes a while."

"Damn, I'd hate to have one giving a lecture on Spiritscape physics at Angel High. Please tell me their mascot isn't the unicorn. That would suck unless you are playing football against Hell High, and then that mascot would make them afraid to show up."

Nazilaq laughed. "You are more accurate than you know. They are the protectors of Uqump. If anything gets in here, they chase it back out – especially demons. They really hate demons for making them the way they are." Looking at conversation, Naz added, "Zeke just asked about the green cloud."

Tone, bored with unicorn conversation, pursued the origins of the beasts. "How did demons make them? And why aren't they psychotic? They look scary enough to be axe murderers and goat milkers." Naz gave him a questioning look. "I had a bad experience on a field trip to a farm once. A goat ate my underwear."

"You have a long history of bad experiences," observed Naz. "No one knows exactly what happened to create them. All we know is that a group of demons was trying to make them to terrorize humans. It didn't work out well for the demons. The unicorns burst out of Hell with demons stuck to their horns. It was actually funny in a horrible kind of way. Halalio was able to calm them and brought them here. Halidore took his name from Halalio, the only archangel he trusts." Watching the conversation, the pilot added, "And I never said they weren't psychotic; but they do know what we are looking for. Zeke is saying good bye now."

After a long display of colors and shapes, Zeke turned back. "We're on the right track. Halidore said that something happened right ahead of us. They never saw what took out the demon, but it was fast. It was in and out before they even knew it was there. This thing seems like it has the inside track on everything."

Arriving where the unicorn said, Tone confirmed the trail ended there. "It's just like the other place. Naz, can you spin us a little bit? It's like one big trail all over again." As the *Hajile-R* moved all around, Tone spotted what he wanted. "And there are the other trails." He did a double take. "This is bad. There is only one demon trail. We were following the exit trail of the Bandersnatch. Umm... angels? There is no exit trail for the demon. Either Greenie ate it or it tried to port out or it's still here. I don't see a port mark and there is nothing hiding here so... oh shit," mumbled Tone.

The skimmer glowed as Naz prepared for a battle. Zeke was beside Tone, wings of power radiating out from his back. Tone just stared at an empty spot.

"There's another trail note," whispered Tone. "It says, 'Hey Tone. Tell Nazilaq I said hi.'"

# Chapter 9

"What is doing this?" demanded Zeke. "It knows us too well." The hunter hated the feeling of being the hunted. It was beginning to show as his anger welled up.

Usually the calming voice of reason, Nazilaq was uncharacteristically excited. "How could it have known I would be here? I don't like this. We need backup for this one, Zeke. A legion or two of angels should be enough. Warriors, not healers."

Strangely, it was Tone who made the most sense. "Gentle-angels, can we have this discussion somewhere else?" Pointing at things that made him wonder if Picasso had drawn the purple and green offspring of an eagle and a warthog, "I don't know what the hell those are, but I'd prefer to be somewhere else when they get here. They look like they are craving omelets and we're kind of shaped like an egg."

Naz began moving the skimmer back the way it had come, heading to the place where the trail had exited the Uqump. The pilot had shaken off his initial concern. "Sorry, Zeke. I think one legion would be enough for now."

"Have you called Mike, yet? Did he blow his halo when you told him the Bandersnatch knows about me riding with Naz?" inquired the human. "Hey, Mike! What do you think?" There was no answer.

"Tone, he can't hear us when we're in here. Nothing gets through the Gray. I'm sure he will be waiting for us when we get out." Zeke seemed on edge. "We shouldn't be here. It feels like a trap." The warrior had expanded his form, filling much of the open space of the *Hajile-R*. Tone's H'tes flipped into his hand. "Tone, do you see anything I'm missing?"

The eccentric human was spinning around, looking through the crystal walls. "There are no trails other than the green one." It hit

Tone like a blaze of angel fire. "Oh… Okay. This is very not good. There are no trails other than the green one."

Ezekiel and Nazilaq didn't understand. The pilot responded, "We get it Tone. What's the problem?"

"All the critters in here don't leave trails. At least none that I can see. That tells me two things. First, the Bandersnatch isn't one of them. And second, there could be beasties anywhere in here and I won't be able to tell you where they are." The realization of that settled in. "I'm sure that we can handle anything that comes along, but…" Tone's words were lost as the skimmer flew right into the gaping maw of a waiting creature, coming out from behind a peak.

Under Nazilaq's command, the *Hajile-R* transformed once again. No longer a smooth, egg-shaped vessel; it turned into a crystal, spike-covered orb with the pilot encased in his own shell in the center. Naz was taking no chances on Tone accidentally bouncing into him. The spikes all glowed with power as golden fire erupted from each, sending flames in every direction simultaneously. Another surge of power flew out in a solid wave, causing a howl of agony all around them. One last burst of fire in one focused stream created an opening for the skimmer. It soared through totally unscathed by the attack.

Tone was sure that Naz hadn't even changed the speed of the ship as it sailed through whatever had just tried to eat them. Looking back, he wished he hadn't. The green thing that had swallowed them had the trunk of an elephant, the body of a whale, and things that best resembled centipede legs along its underside. Unlike other creatures, this one was as substantial as the unicorns.

"Well, that was fun. How often do you get inhaled through an elephant-whale and shoot your way out through its butt?" Tone was trying to make light of the incident.

Zeke, returning to his normal form, joined in. "Yes, Naz. How often does that happen to you?"

The pilot smiled. "That's all I get? How often do I get swallowed? Nothing about the new spikes or flame throwers?" He chuckled, "There's a first time for everything and a last time. I don't think that dossdril will want to do that again."

"Dossdril? Is that angel for 'piece of shit that just got its ass handed to it'? That sounds more like a new kind of underwear," stated Tone.

"Tone, you have such a way with words," mused Zeke. "The elephant-whale is called a dossdril. I think your Bandersnatch may have had something to do with that. That dossdril was more substantial than any other I've seen. Naz?"

Nazilaq agreed. "The green glow was also a hint. I've never seen one attack anything before. They are usually docile. That one was also about twice the size of any I've ever seen."

Tone summarized the situation. "So what we have is the Bandersnatch pissing off critters around here, making them more like the blob than the fog, and giving them a taste for skimmers even when they don't look like doughnuts. Did I miss anything?"

Zeke added, "You forgot that it sneaks past the unicorns, and that nothing else has ever super-charged any of the Uqumps."

"They have enough problems without being called Uqumps." Tone took the opening, "That is not even close to flattering. Call them beasts or animals or fuzzy wuzzy fizzles. Anything is better than Uqumps."

As they approached the spot where the trail entered the Gray, they were met by a unicorn. "Is that your old buddy, Halo-door?" asked Tone. He couldn't tell one unicorn from another. They all creeped him out.

Naz spoke up. "No. I know this one. He has no name. He's never spoken to me before." The pilot slowed the skimmer, keeping it charged with power. The pilot moved to the side closest to the unicorn and began greeting the guardian. Before Nazilaq could change more than a few colors, the unicorn flashed several of its own.

"Wow!" exclaimed Zeke. "That's never happened. They never interrupt."

Zeke watched as Naz and the unicorn conversed. The unicorn was upset about something. It stopped the pilot three times as he tried to calm it down while gathering information. Tone could not understand any of what was happening. It seemed like the unicorn was throwing a temper tantrum to him. As if reading his thoughts, it flashed crimson five times and then began to leak green mist from every orifice.

"No!" screamed Zeke and Nazilaq, as the guardian threw itself backward into the Gray. The unicorn was stretched beyond breaking, shredding it into infinitesimal pieces that were absorbed into the barrier. All three occupants of the skimmer watched in horror as the unicorn disappeared into nothingness. Even Tone couldn't find humor in the tragedy.

"That was not supposed to happen. Right?" asked the human, showing some respect.

"No," was all he heard as Nazilaq returned to his position at the center of the craft.

Ezekiel explained. "Everything that has been put in here is repelled by the Gray, including the unicorns. If they approach it, the pain is excruciating. Nothing has ever tried to enter the Gray. That unicorn was trying to tell us something about the Bandersnatch. All it said was: 'Green took the blue. Green goes into beasts. Green goes into unicorn.' Then the last thing it said was: 'Die. Die. Die. Die. Die.'"

It all became clear to Tone. The Bandersnatch had taken the demon, influenced the dossdril, and tried to take over the unicorn. It threw itself into the Gray to prevent that. *What is this thing?*

"We need to tell Halidore about this," muttered Nazilaq, turning the skimmer away from the barrier. "I'm not sure he will understand."

"Then don't." The words came from an unexpected source. Zeke continued, "Naz, we can come back later and explain. I respect Halidore, but you know how this will go down. He will attack us when we explain. Right now, we need to find this Bandersnatch before any more damage is done."

The skimmer stopped. It was clear that Nazilaq was torn. There was a silent battle of wills going on between the pilot and the hunter. With a resigned expression on his spirit, Naz turned the *Hajile-R* back toward the Gray, reverting the ship to its egg-shaped form for the transition.

The journey out was better than the trip in. Tone had no idea how long they travelled through the barrier, but this time there were no demons passing through him. Once his head cleared on the other side, he looked for the trail. The skimmer had to maneuver a short distance around the perimeter of the Gray until they found where the green exited. They followed the trail until it ended in a port mark, a safe distance away from the Uqump.

Tone looked carefully at that mark. "Hey angels. I should have noticed this before. The Bandersnatch leaves a bigger port mark than angels or demons. It's not twice as big, but close to it. It almost like it's…" Tone looked at Zeke. "You can't carry me when you port, right? I mean, that's not possible. Right?"

Zeke understood where Tone was going with this. "An angel could port with another spiritual being, but not with you. You have one foot here and another on Earth. You're thinking the Bandersnatch ported with the demon?" He looked at Nazilaq. "How dangerous would that be for you? You ported more extra objects that I ever will." Zeke gestured to the skimmer around them.

"I usually use a portal. It's safer. Porting a skimmer is one thing. If I make a mistake, I can get the skimmer repaired. Making a mistake while porting a demon means part of it might not make the trip." The servant angel looked thoughtful. "As long as you knew exactly where you were porting, it's not too bad. Irkja is the only one who was ever any good at it."

Irkja had been the spotter for the *Hajile-R* during their tracking of Bubba. He had a gift unlike any other angel. He had foresight in the Spiritscape. All angels could travel along time lines on Earth.

Since Irkja could see things coming even in the spirit realm, they were able to avoid disasters. Unfortunately, Irkja was the last angelic casualty of the ravenous Bubba prior to the final battle.

"We really could use his help on this one," admitted Zeke. "Tone, do you remember if the other port mark of your Bandersnatch was as big as this?"

Tone looked thoughtful. "It's hard to say. Probably. This thing is really messing with my head. I mean worse that it's usually messed up. Am I the only one who feels like I'm drinking a boilermaker with a white Russian chaser?"

Naz smiled for the first time since leaving the Uqump. "And how many boilermakers have you tried, Tone?"

"I read a lot," replied Tone, defensively.

# Chapter 10

The *Hajile-R* cruised along at its normal insane speed. After telling him about the new message, Michael sent them on. His information had been solid at Uqump. Ximsor was the new destination. Tone was giddy with anticipation.

"So what is this place like? Do they have a field of food? Are there canyons of cotton candy with hot fudge waterfalls? Dibs on the cream cheese massage beds!" Pressing his nose against the clear wall, he continued, "If you tell me I am going to get to see dragons, I can die a happy man."

Zeke was accustomed to Tone's unusual way of looking at things, but there were times when he just didn't want to know what he was thinking. "If you take everything you just said and imagine the opposite, then you have Ximsor. We could portal, but there's no telling what we would find when we get there, or if the portal would work right. Skimming there is safer."

Tone, H'tes in hand, slashed the ether. "I can take on anything that would be waiting for me as long as it's not a demon, or a unicorn, or a really grouchy hedgehog." Tone had proven himself in battle, but there were times when Zeke was not sure what he would do. If face to face with a demon, he would more than hold his own. The simple truth was, no one wanted the demons to know that Tone was able to defend himself. If it became widely known that Tone was a H'tes bearer, it would make him a target for every demon everywhere. Unknown to Tone, the previous H'tes bearers had died in battles on Earth. He was not able to defend himself away from the Spiritscape. The H'tes needed to be a secret for as long as possible. Zeke dreaded the day when that secret was revealed.

Ximsor was dangerous place for the skimmer. Few pilots would even consider flying through the zone. Nazilaq had transformed it into the smallest version Tone had ever seen. It resembled a stubby, crystal needle that could bend and flow. The *Hajile-R* was a combination of strength and flexibility not found in the rigid crystals of Earth. This one obeyed the commands of Nazilaq. If the crystal needed to be harder than diamonds, it was just that. If it needed to be flexible as rubber, that was what it became. In Ximsor it needed to be both, and that is where the skill of the pilot made all the difference.

The danger of Ximsor was more than just the presence of demons. They were bad enough. Ximsor was the junk yard of the Spiritscape. Any and everything could be found floating around in a random fashion. Letting your guard drop a millionth of a quoll could be disastrous. If there were any demonic problems, Zeke would be dealing with those, while Naz attempted to keep the skimmer in one piece. As they approached, Tone was amazed.

"Just when I thought you couldn't surprise me anymore." Tone tried to take it all in from a distance. This dump was stranger than even Tone's wildest imaginings. It was bordered on five sides by a glittering, inverted mountain of sapphire. The blue bowl went on as far as Tone could see. Seeing to the bottom of this bowl was impossible with the constant movement of the 'trash'. What counted as trash in the Spiritscape, Tone thought, would be a fortune beyond the wildest dreams of Midas. Diamond boulders, slivers of ruby, precious gems of every kind and size floated within Ximsor, crashing together and crumbling, only to reform into new, exotic combinations. Splinters of crystal drifted haphazardly around, piercing anything touched.

"If you need someone to pick up your trash and store it somewhere like my closet, I'll be glad to take some of those disgusting diamonds off your hands." Tone was in awe of the riches just floating in this dump.

"Tone, those are not what you think they are. Keep watching." Naz was more cryptic than usual. The human watched as the huge gems bounced around, gasping when he realized what he was seeing. What he had mistaken for precious stones were flowing like the crystal of the skimmer. Those gems that were moving around almost looked…

"Alive? Those things are alive?! How the hell is that…?" He looked at the smiling pilot. "No. Bullshit! You can't be serious. You don't mean…" It was becoming increasingly difficult for Tone to finish a sentence.

Zeke laughed at his companion as Naz explained. "Those are parts of various devices that were too damaged to remain in service. But they still have power in them, and the imprint of the angel who used them. Look at that golden one." One large, golden, crystal boulder rolled over several others, scattering them like a cue in a game of nine-ball. "That is what is left of Adoneal's skimmer. After his accident, he couldn't fly it safely. So now it is down there, enjoying its retirement."

"So the *Hajile-R* is alive? Good girl," said Tone, petting a wall. "Does she have a belly to scratch?"

"Alive is not the right word," corrected Nazilaq. "Those crystals down there have power, but no will. They are always reforming themselves until the power all drains away. Each time they shatter, a little more drains off and falls down into the basin. Sooner or later, all of these will fade away. There are even a few pieces of spirit spheres floating around in here. The golden crystal will outlast several generations of others because of Adoneal's power within it." He looked at Tone who was still rubbing the wall. "Is any of this making sense?"

"So the *Hajile-R* is alive?" asked Tone.

"Sure," conceded Naz. "She's a good girl, too. But now we have to take her through all that. I'll keep it as smooth as I can, but you may want to sheath for safety." A crystal casing like the one Nazilaq used came out of the wall near Tone. "It will keep you from being thrown around too much." Tone moved inside the sheath, it closed around him.

"Okay, this is freaky feeling. It's like I'm floating in snot. Crystal clear snot." His arms and legs could move, not much, but they could move. He tested it to discover that the outer edge of this crystal would move outward if he pushed, but would not allow him to get out. "Why do I need this again? Not that I'm complaining. Do you think I could get Arino to ride in this with me?"

"I don't see that ever happening," replied Zeke. Tone smiled as he detected a note of jealousy in his friend. Zeke positioned himself in a sheath on the far end of the skimmer, moving his arm through the hull to reach outside, then pulling it back in. "Just making sure I can reach out in case you need my help."

"Thanks. I'm sure I will. Ready? Here we go," said the smiling pilot. The *Hajile-R* began moving through the debris of Ximsor, first making small course adjustments and then bending around larger crystals. A small violet crystal attached itself to the hull near Zeke, smoothly flowing, trying to make it completely around the ship to secure itself. The skimmer began spinning as spikes came out of the skin of the ship to push the violet crystal away.

As two larger crystals crashed into one another, Tone was certain there was not enough space for the skimmer to avoid being absorbed. Naz caused the ship to bend, flex, and dodge through the middle of the merging crystals, emerging on the far side to be met by a swarm of clear, crystal needles. A ball of angel fire flew out of the side of the skimmer, drawing most of them away. Tone looked over to see Zeke pulling his arm back through the wall after sending the fireball. Most of the remaining needles bounced harmlessly off the hull, a handful stuck and attempted to burrow in. A blade morphed out of the aft of the skimmer, moving over the needles, shaving them off.

As they travelled deeper into the sapphire chasm, the ether became a shade of blue-gray that Tone remembered all too well from his previous adventure. "Are we going on another river?" he asked, whining. "I have had enough Spiritscape rivers to last me at least two lifetimes. They are just too tube-ish for me. Rivers are not supposed to look like really mean, stoned snakes with the munchies for Tone-chips."

Zeke reassured his friend. "Tone, that is not from any river. There are no rivers in Ximsor."

"Well, that's one good thing it's got going for it," said Tone winking at Zeke. He looked up in time to see the energy flow of the Ximsor Lake as the ship dove straight in. "I hate you sometimes."

"But Tone, it's not a river. This is much worse," laughed Naz. "The pha'ards in here are a lot bigger." The *Hajile-R* dodged around a large yellow blob with a tooth-filled mouth snapping at them. Tone screamed.

# Chapter 11

"Have I told you lately how much those things scare the shit out of me?" said a breathless Tone. "Why do they always want to eat me?"

The angels laughed at his reaction. "Tone, these are nothing like the pha'ards you have seen." Nazilaq explained while dodging another pha'ard. "They wouldn't know what to do with you if they caught you. These are more interested in the *Hajile-R* than you. You wouldn't taste good."

Tone regained his composure and humor. "Again with the bad taste comments? You wear one lime green pair of chaps over fluorescent orange riding pants with a neon purple pirate shirt to the inauguration party of the president of Uzbekistan and you're branded for life. How many times can I apologize for not wearing the bright pink wizard hat?"

"I'm grateful I don't have a digestive system right about now," laughed Zeke, making a face like he wanted to vomit. "Where do you come up with this stuff? On second thought, I don't want to know." Turning to the pilot, "How long to the bubble?"

"Almost there. Let me get around that." The skimmer tried to avoid a green pha'ard. It immediately expanded in the direction the skimmer had moved. It seemed to be leaking green into the lake of energy. "It's one of the Bandersnatch's drones!" exclaimed Nazilaq. The ship spun around, trying to get out of the way. The pha'ard hit the tail of the skimmer sending the needle-shaped vessel spinning away from its destination.

Tone was grateful to be in the sheath. Even though gravity was not an issue in the Spiritscape, the walls of the *Hajile-R* would have bounced him around the ship. Movement was by will, not by walking. His will would not be tuned to the drastic movements of the ship. He felt helpless as he watched the angels defending the vessel. That was when he spotted the bubble.

"Over there!" shouted Tone, pointing to an area that looked like a place where the lake was kept at bay.

The skimmer ducked and dodged three more attacks of the green monster, moving in ways that Tone couldn't begin to understand. Next, the ship went back to ring-shaped as another pha'ard charged, only to find itself passing harmlessly through the middle of the ring. It then morphed into the egg-shaped ship to cause another to bounce off the smooth sides. Within the blink of an eye, the *Hajile-R* was a figure-eight, spinning around. One pha'ard passed harmlessly through one of the loops, another bounded around the inside of the other ring like a pinball before falling behind them.

Facing the green-oozing pha'ard, angel fire burst from the tip of the now needle-shaped skimmer, boring a hole through the center. As the ship passed through the pha'ard, a blast of power from the ship destroyed the pha'ard from the inside out. The many pha'ards that had been pursuing the skimmer were now devouring the remains of the green-infused crystal pha'ard.

"Umm... Wow," said Tone. "I have no clue what you did, but... Wow."

"That was fun," said Naz. Tone looked to see if he was serious. He was. "We need to come back here sometime and just play."

The human understood the thrill of the chase, but Nazilaq was an angel-fighter pilot. He existed for times like this when he could test his skills against impossible odds. If angels had adrenaline, Naz would have been addicted to the rush. Tone smiled, saying, "You're not right. And trust me, I know what that looks like from my mirror."

The skimmer reached the bottom of the basin, passing through the bubble. "The energy of the lake stays back from here. There was a battle here that left scars on the ether that repel the energy. This is where Adoneal was injured." Nazilaq pointed to the center point of the bubble beneath the lake.

Adoneal, the insanely creative archangel, had taken a blow meant to phase Ezekiel into hundreds of pieces by the archdemon Je'relir. The demon had been defeated during their last adventure, but Zeke still bore the burden of guilt over the losses the archangel suffered saving him.

The space within had a golden hue with traces of blue scattered around. The central point had a glow all its own, casting light everywhere. It was not a huge place by Spiritscape standards, but it was sizable enough to make seeing everything at once impossible. There were small spires from the sapphire walls of Ximsor that gave many places for something to hide.

"Tone? Any trails?" asked Zeke, freeing himself from his sheath.

Joining his friend, Tone moved freely around the skimmer, looking for traces of green. It wasn't hard to find. "Right there, heading to the glowing spot in the middle."

The *Hajile-R,* once more egg-shaped, moved close to the glow. Tone could feel the heat even through the wall of the skimmer. It was not painful in the least, it felt good. It felt too good. Previously, Tone had been touched by Bubba and infected by the same essences that the beast had been absorbing. Bubba had consumed both angel and demon spirits in an attempt to become something greater than those who were just food. The angel essence that Tone experienced was something that could easily become an addiction, leading him to become like Bubba. Tone didn't want to get any closer.

"That's close enough. It is a little too much like the angel essence Bubba gave me." When Tone got serious, everyone listened. It didn't happen often. "Besides, I had two chili dogs for lunch so I'm stuffed." That was more like it.

Zeke knew his friend was trying to make light of a serious situation. Then it occurred to him, "Tone, how close does the trail get to the glow? Does it just approach it and move away? Or does it go in?"

Naz changed the crystal wall Tone was using as window into a magnifier. The human looked at the sheath-incased pilot. "Cool trick. You could have done that sooner, you know." Looking out the magnified crystal, he continued, "It goes up to the edge and moves around. Wait, there it goes inside. Is that important?"

Nazilaq and Zeke shared a look that conveyed concern. "I'll let Michael know about this. That is disturbing. It would seem to confirm his suspicions it's an angel. Something just seems wrong about that to me."

"So only an angel could go into the glow? What does it do for an angel?"

Naz responded, "It really doesn't do much. It is like linking with others, but just gives a power boost. We consider it rude to use that for a power boost though. It would be like walking over a grave. You can do it without anything bad happening…"

"Unless there's a zombie down there that grabs your foot, bites you and turns you so that you end up walking the Earth as one of the living dead, seeking brains to devour," added Tone. Zeke and Naz gave him the look. "Well, it's rude, too."

"That's my point. It is just a scar of where Adoneal was injured, but it is a powerful scar that no angel would use unless there was no other choice," concluded Nazilaq. Those words were not lost on the human or the hunter. *What would have to happen to an angel to make it use this?*

"I found the other end of the trail. It's heading toward the pretty blue rocks on the wall." Looking more, Tone exclaimed, "Okay. That's not good. There are three oil trails going over there too." As the skimmer began slowly moving toward the outcropping, Tone spoke up. "There is something else. There are four trails going in, but nothing coming out. They might still be in there."

The skimmer was battle ready in an instant. Zeke had moved outside the skimmer, looking terrifying and beautiful in his battle form. All Tone could do was watch as he got back into the sheath. Slowly coming around the corner, all the angels saw was a portal door in the side of the sapphire wall. Tone saw trails, two oil slicks, and a green mess as its trail expanded to take up most of the space.

Zeke moved all around the area, looking for anything that could be hiding in the many nooks and crannies. Returning to the ship, he reported. "There's nothing here. The portal is not linked to anywhere. I'm not even sure why it's here. Tone, do you want to look around? There may be another message hidden here."

A door in the wall of the skimmer appeared next to Tone, allowing him to move out into the heat of the ether. It was amazing how good it felt to the human. Remembering the reason for the bubble, he looked back in the direction of the glowing monument to Adoneal's sacrifice. This place was sacred to the angels, like Arlington National Cemetery was to Americans. It just had that feel.

"Why do you have a junk yard over a... what would you call this? A monument?" asked Tone.

"It's more of a shrine," admitted Zeke. "It was the best way to keep this place safe. Demons hate traveling through Ximsor. The crystals remember them and attack. Few make it through them to get here. When they do, it is painful for them to stay too long. Why would three have come here? Could your Bandersnatch have been chasing them?"

"Seems as good as any reason. Unless," began Tone, with a look that told the angels this would be good, "they were going to try to piss you off by roasting brats over that campfire you have for Adoneal. They were interrupted by the Bandersnatch, who ate their marshmallows and then put them in a martini shaker to carry them off to be his personal bartenders."

"Chasing them here seems more likely," said Naz, agreeing with the hunter.

Shrugging, the human examined the trails. Tone was able to discern that two of the three demons had been handily beaten by the Bandersnatch. There were two oil slicks, but not like they had been destroyed. These were like other places where the trails just stopped. The green trail was difficult to find, it was everywhere at once. With some effort, Tone finally found the trail moving off to the side and then toward the portal door in the wall.

As he feared, there was another message in the side trail that he read aloud. "'Having fun with Zeke, Tone? See you soon.'" Tone shivered. "That is just too creepy. I'm really getting tired of this thing playing with..."

The door to the portal burst open. Entering the space with roar, a demon burst onto the scene, slamming the door behind it, leaning on it to keep it closed. The Hadian had once been a multi-limbed, squid-like demon named Motmik. The blue body of the demon had gashes that bled a blue, pus-like ooze. Green haze drifted off the places where it had lost most of its limbs. It didn't notice that it wasn't alone, being focused on keeping the door secure. When it saw them, it struggled to speak through what remained of its face. The words that came out were nothing like any of them expected.

"Angels? Good. I was afraid you were something worse," came the strangled voice like nails on a chalkboard. "Send me to Hell!"

# Chapter 12

Tone moved behind Zeke, ready to use the hidden blade. The skimmer was glowing with angelic power, ready to fulfill the demon's demand. Ezekiel was in complete battle form, preparing to devastate the demon or anything else that came through the door.

The demon raised what was left of its tentacles in surrender. "Hell is better than that thing! Do it!" The screeching was painful to the angels and human. The skimmer moved behind the hunter, opening a door. Zeke, with a subtle burst of power, knocked Tone inside the skimmer while blocking the view of the demon.

"Hey," came the voice of the human, skidding to a stop against the far wall of the ship.

Naz closed the door, sealing the *Hajile-R*. "I think the word you were looking for was 'thanks'." He moved the skimmer so that it was covering both the devil and door. "Or did you want to be out there with an injured, crazed demon?"

"Thanks," said Tone, grudgingly. Moving to his spot at the front of the ship, he watched the battle of wills.

Zeke was in control of the situation. "Nothing would give me more pleasure than opening a rip into Hell for you." He made a movement like he was about to grant the request, then stopped. "Well, almost nothing. So Motmik, what has you spooked?" When an angel used the name of a demon, it would make them uncomfortable in the best of situations. When injured, the power of the words was excruciating. The demon shrieked.

Even inside the *Hajile-R* with Naz muffling the sound, the voice of the demon still gave Tone the willies. The hoarse voice shouted, "Just get me out of here and I'll tell you all about it." The demand was clear, as was the false promise.

"You know, I like it here. It would make a nice place for a summer cottage. You can tell me now, Motmik," he said, sending extra power through the words making the demon writhe, "Or you can lose the rest of your limbs while we wait for whatever is after you." Making his point, a wing of power reached out from the warrior and severed one of the few remaining tentacles of the demon. Zeke handed the severed appendage to the Hadian, a malicious smile on his face.

Tone whispered to Nazilaq, "Is it just me, or is Zeke getting kind of ruthless?"

"Well, doing what he does, he has to be," replied Naz. "But he is pushing the limits more lately." The pilot called out to the one angel who could reign Zeke in.

Zeke continued his interrogation. "Now, Motmik, are you ready to have a reasonable conversation? Or do I need to throw you back through that portal?"

The demon quaked with unbridled terror. "No! It's over there. The green. It's just a green fog. It's…" The demon seemed to be searching for the words. "…collecting us. It laughs at us. Just throw me to Hell. I'm begging you, dammit! I don't know what it's done with J'niuav and Nandif. They just stopped moving." Hysteria was building in the devil, "Now it wants me. It said, there is a spot on the mantle for me! You can't let it take me. Don't you have some dumbass angel code? Do your damned job! Send me to Hell!" The demon was frenzied as it slid down the door, repeating the same thing over and over. "Send me to Hell!"

Zeke reached out, causing a tear in the ether, opening a rip into Hell. A blue mist arose from the gash, making Tone shudder as he tried to see inside. The demon, seeing the tear, leapt toward it, hope shining bright blue to its core. As soon as it moved away, the door opened. A pillar of green fog came through the portal, latched onto the last of the tentacles of the demon, dragging it back through the portal. The door closed softly behind the screaming demon.

The three friends stared at the closed portal, shock saturating their spirits. They had their first glimpse of the Bandersnatch. None of them liked what they saw. It was far too much like a green version of..."

"Bubba?" asked Tone. "That can't be Bubba. She's dead here and on Earth. I killed her, didn't I?" His question revealed what all of them were wondering. *Could Bubba have survived?*

Zeke looked at his friend, replying honestly. "We don't know. As far as any of us can tell, you did. The body of Bobbi died right after you stabbed her spirit here. There is so much we don't know about how you and she operate that we really can't say for sure."

"You know about Bobbi? Of course you do. Dammit Vret!" Tone called to the archangel. "All of that was my fault. I made her when I kissed her on Earth. But I ended her, too. I cleaned up the mess. Well, I thought I did. Did that remind anyone else of what happened to Irkja?"

Nazilaq spoke up. "Yes, Tone. That was just like it." Changing the painful subject, Naz asked Zeke, "Do we go after it? You're in command. Or do you want to wait for reinforcements?"

The hunter looked at his friends. "We have to follow it now. It will take too long for anyone else to get here. Unless..." Zeke looked at the smiling pilot, who was pointing behind him.

A skimmer burst through the bubble, Arino clearly in the front flanked by Michael and Adoneal. Several warrior angels could be seen in sheaths all over the elongated crystal cylinder. The *Rialc* was a sister ship to the *Hajile-R* piloted by Esiuol, Nazilaq's protégé. Angels flew from the skimmer, surrounding the *Hajile-R* and the portal, ready for battle.

Zeke was joined by Tone as they approached the archangels and Arino. The healer moved around, checking all three of the friends. She sent strengthening power into Tone and Naz. To Zeke, she sent wave after wave of calm healing. It was one of the few things she could send to him without risking an overload. That was exactly what he needed. She and Tone could both see the difference in his spirit.

Instantly up to date, Michael took charge. With a thought, ten of the warriors opened the portal, going through in full battle regalia. The door closed behind them. Turning to the trio, he said, "So it is true. There is something that is not a demon collecting them. Now we need to figure out what it is. Thoughts?"

"No, 'hi guys'? No 'glad you're still alive'? How about: 'I'm relieved that you weren't grabbed by the green fog.'" Tone was relieving stress by tormenting the archangel.

Michael smiled. "No 'thank you for coming to the rescue'? I'm glad you and Nazilaq are safe Zeke. Tone, nice glow you have there." Getting serious again, he asked, "Any thoughts? Does it feel like Bubba to you, Tone?"

"Not really. It feels familiar and alien all at the same time. And I'm not talking about friendly *Star Trek* aliens here. Imagine Sigourney Weaver fighting acid-drooling, bat-shit crazy aliens on steroids." He looked around at the angels guarding the portal. "Do any of these guys have red shirts? The red shirt guys always die first."

Ignoring the *Star Trek* reference, Zeke added, "It reminds me of Bubba, but it also seems less evil, less hungry. Motmik said it was collecting demons. Are any angels missing?"

Michael was firm. "All angels are accounted for. Plus, every angel who was alone during the attacks has been checked. Zeke, it can't be one of us." Looking back at the glowing spot where Adoneal had been injured, he asked, "Tone, are you sure it went all the way into the glow?"

"Positive," said the human. "It went in one side and out the other…" He was pointing toward the glow as his words died in the ether. All the angels looked to where he was pointing, in time to see Adoneal entering the glow where he had been injured. "What is Adoneal doing?"

Arino spoke up, "I have no idea." The healer went up to, but not into the glow. It seemed like Adoneal was inside the glowing spot for far too long. The archangel exited on the far side of the glow, in the same spot the Bandersnatch had left. "Adoneal, are you all right?"

"Of course," replied the inventor, nonplussed. "Since all of you fear this point, it made sense that I should go in. The last time I was here I got hurt. Inside the glow, I saw what happened. Very... what's the word? Is it 'sad'?"

"Sad will work. Did you discover anything that explains why it went in there?" asked Michael. "How much power did it take?"

"No. There is no change. The glow was not diminished," replied Adoneal, moving toward the *Hajile-R*, checking it for damage. He was done with the conversation.

"If I walk away from you, Mike, will you leave me alone, too?" asked Tone.

Michael didn't miss a beat. "I should be so lucky. Do any of you have any ideas? I'm even ready to listen to Tone. That's how bad this is."

"Damn, you are worried," joked Anthony. "I have a question. Who really cares? If this thing is collecting demons, doesn't that mean they won't be getting out of Hell and making trouble by causing plagues and famines and diseases and reality TV shows? You have less work, and we don't have any more shows that find the dumbest people on Earth to put on TV, or any of that other stuff that's almost as bad. It seems like a win-win-win-win-win."

Michael took that troubling question. "If it were as simple as that, I'd hire it. What this thing is doing – collecting demons – is not safe for the Bandersnatch, the demons, or anything nearby. Hell is Hell because of the proximity of all the devils in there. They give off demon-power making everything touched in Hell like them. If your Bandersnatch has a collection of demons, they will eventually have an influence over it – corrupting it. Sooner or later, it will become more like them. Anything near this collection could be influenced so slightly that it may not be detectable at first. We are trying to save this collector from its collection."

"So it is making a mini-Hell? That sounds bad," agreed Tone.

The portal door opened again, sending every angel into battle mode until they saw the ten warriors returning. The report was simple enough. The portal led to a part of the Spiritscape with nothing going on. It was quiet. The general opinion was that the Bandersnatch had ported as soon as it was safely away from Ximsor.

"Another dead end?" fumed Nazilaq. "When will we catch a break?"

Zeke shared the frustration. "Not any time soon. Tone and I will take the portal so he can make sure that this thing really did port away. Maybe we'll get lucky and it just ran off carrying three demons on its back."

"Anyone who believes that, I have a bridge in Brooklyn, an opera house in Sidney, and a big-ass clock in London that I will sell you for one low price." Tone had a unique way of summarizing what everyone else was feeling.

"Why is this portal here?" The question came from Adoneal.

Tone replied before anyone else could. "It was here when we got here. I thought it was one of yours."

"It is one of mine. But why is it here?" the archangel asked again.

Nazilaq was confused. "One of yours? You mean a fixed gate? I thought you kept those in your workshop."

"I do. This one is the first one I made. It should be in my workshop on the right corner next to the second one I made. Why is it here?" Adoneal was becoming agitated.

As the archangel reached out to touch the door he had made, it opened. The same green fog moved with lightning speed, grabbing Adoneal and disappearing through the closing door.

# Chapter 13

Angels flew to the portal, flinging the door open, prepared to attack and battle the thing that had taken Adoneal. The only thing beyond the door was the blue wall behind. The portal was gone.

Michael turned to Nazilaq. "Go!" he shouted.

Grabbing Tone, Zeke and Arino ducked into the *Hajile-R* as it went instantly to full speed. Entering the lake, the pilot made no attempts to avoid the crystalline pha'ards that were swarming, waiting for something to exit the bubble. The skimmer was a javelin, hurtling through Ximsor Lake. A golden jet of flame was roaring through the tip of the ship, continuously incinerating anything in its path. Nazilaq had the ship halfway out of the lake by the time the other occupants were in sheaths.

Zeke had wings of power that were going through the hull, sending bursts of angel fire at anything that approached from the sides. Arino was doing her best to calm Nazilaq, who was panic-stricken thinking of the archangel he served in the clutches of whatever had stolen him. Tone was silently wishing there was something he could do.

As the ship exploded out of the lake and back into Ximsor, the skimmer remained steadfastly on a straight course. Crystals were shattered or blasted out of the way. A few bounced off the hull as the ship moved too fast and too hot for the trash to catch. The *Hajile-R* began spinning, faster and faster, causing any crystals that got past the pilot or the hunter to bound off the hull at speeds that sent them crashing into other crystals.

By the time the skimmer was out of Ximsor, Tone began to relax. The ship remained a javelin but it had stopped spinning. When he saw the huge portal in front of them, he was worried what would be on the other side. Nazilaq didn't even slow down as the skimmer shot through. For an instant, Tone was sure they were in the skimmer hanger. Then, they were in the Spiritscape, flying with countless other skimmers.

"Did we just fly through the skimmer fix-it shop?" asked Tone, confused. "I thought I saw it for a second." He looked at Nazilaq for the first time since they left the bubble. The pilot was fused with the skimmer, the lower part of his spirit was stretched out and into the walls. He was not even paying attention to those in the ship.

"Yes, Tone. We did," answered Arino. "Nazilaq had Torkel open a portal for the *Hajile-R* to the shop, then he flew straight through another portal that was already open to go where the portal in the bubble had been. I don't even think the tail of the ship was through the first before the tip was going through the second."

"It wasn't," came the words from a new source. Tone looked up to see Torkel beside him. "I barely made it in as you passed." The jovial mechanic was different than when they had last met. Gone was the light-hearted jokester. The angel looked pissed, and Tone decided not to piss him off more.

"What's happening, Tork?" asked the human. "Has anyone found Adoneal?"

"No," said the angel, without elaboration.

"Let me see what I can see. Naz?" He turned to the pilot. Nazilaq nodded and moved the skimmer past three others to a spot where the ten angels had previously passed through the defunct portal. Tone looked around and saw the trails of the ten angels. "Wow! They went everywhere!" They had scattered in ten directions, covering an enormous swath of the Spiritscape. The human could also see trails left by the skimmers that were scouring the area, looking for their lost mentor. It was what he couldn't see that was troubling.

"There is no trail for the Bandersnatch. Not even a trace of green. It's like…" he was interrupted by Zeke.

"It never came here." The statement caught all by surprise. Realization hit every angel at once. The fixed portals were special. Unlike the portals Zeke and other angels made, those doors never faded. They were used to go anywhere the user wished. But they were bonded to Adoneal. He was the one who could control them. He was the archangel who used them to help create gateways where long term portals were needed. All the angels shared the same thought: *How had that thing used a fixed portal?* That was impossible.

Michael appeared in the center of the action surrounded by archangels. He cleared his spirit so that Tone could understand what was happening as he gave silent orders. All skimmers but the *Hajile-R* were to keep searching this area. The fastest angels, the cherubs, would take the fourteen adjoining areas. Vret was to gather all information and send it to all angels and Tone, as soon as she discovered any kind of clue. Archangel Gabriel's messengers were sent to Earth just in case this creature had taken Adoneal there. A team of Nasarg's angels, led by the archangel, would explore all the depths of Hell. All other angels not otherwise occupied, were to spend every free quoll searching every layer of every part of the Spiritscape.

Turning to the *Hajile-R*, Michael asked, "Do you have any clues where to go from here? This thing has outflanked us at every turn. It knows what we will do before we know."

Tone was mystified. "Mike, I can't track a spirit when it ports. This thing," he refrained from calling it a Bandersnatch, "barely moves anywhere without porting. I'm good, but I'm not that good." The look of frustration going to the core of Michael was screaming out to Tone. "Dammit! I said it for you, Mike."

"Great," he responded without enthusiasm. The archangel was in no mood for Tone's levity.

The *Rialc* arrived carrying cargo that Tone had not expected. The fixed portal that had been in the bubble was secured in a crystal case within the skimmer. Esiuol brought the ship close as the portal was dropped in their midst. Without a word, the skimmer shot off to continue the search for the lost archangel.

"Something is wrong with that," said Torkel. He examined the portal, expanding his spirit to surround the device. All watched as the mechanic's aura glowed more brightly. His voice came from the portal shaped angel. "Something has been changing the graswil of this one. It can't work right like this." The angel slowly melted off the device and returned to a normal form.

"That explains everything," exclaimed Tone. "How could something mess with the graswil? Isn't it supposed to be impossible to change the graswil? I mean, come on! The graswil!!"

"You have no idea what graswil is, do you?" asked Zeke.

"No clue," admitted Tone.

Torkel explained. "Whenever Adoneal creates something that has power independent of an angel, he infuses it with some energy from the ether. It is neither angelic nor demon. It is just neutral power called graswil. The device will draw energy from the ether. This one was drawing energy from Ximsor Lake. That energy is very unstable. That's why you don't port around there unless you have no choice. It makes for a rough landing. Using the lake made this fixed portal have multiple destinations."

Nazilaq understood and explained to Tone. "It means that your Bandersnatch may have never been anywhere around here. It could be anywhere."

Arino was doing her best to keep everyone calm but was having difficulties. She called out and Raphael appeared by her side, sending out waves of peaceful power into all around. "Is there anything I can do?" asked the archangel of the healers. The effect on Tone was instantaneous and humorous.

Tone spoke in a voice that sounded like he had just taken a more than the recommended dosage of muscle relaxers. "Hi, Raph. You are a nice archangel. You need to hang out with us more often. You are my favorite archangel."

Michael interrupted. "Not now, Tone. Raphael, can you and Torkel change the power of the portal back to the way it is supposed to work?"

The healer looked at the portal. "I could, but do you want me to do that?"

"Raph, did you bring any chili dogs? I bet you make great chili dogs. You're such a nice archangel," slurred Tone, becoming even more entranced with the voice of the archangel. Arino and Zeke pulled Tone away from Raphael to allow him to sober up. "But I don't want to go to bed, yet. I want to play *Operation* with Raph. He's such a…" His words trailed off.

"Why not? What is it?" asked Michael, ignoring the stoned human.

Torkel spoke up first. "I agree with Raphael. If we can determine how the power was used, we may be able to find the last few destinations it went to. But that means taking it back to the bubble."

Nazilaq volunteered. "I can take it back. If it helps us find Adoneal, I'll do whatever it takes." The loyalty of those who worked under Adoneal was unassailable. Each one understood the unusual genius of the archangel and took care of him in spite of his injuries. Nazilaq would have gladly allowed himself to be phased apart and scattered to the ends of the Spiritscape to save Adoneal.

"I know you want to do anything to help, but I need you with Tone. He may be the key to tracking this thing down." Michael was adamant.

"I will follow your orders, Michael, but we need Tone, too. If we are going to try to find where this thing went, then we need him to look for trails." Nazilaq made a perfectly logical point. "With Zeke to fight and Arino to keep us all in one piece, it makes sense to send us on this long shot while everyone else is searching."

Raphael looked at Michael. "You know Nazilaq is correct. This long shot is better than no shot at all."

"Chocolate pudding!" shouted Tone, still not far enough away from Raphael.

Glancing at Tone, Michael conceded, "It's a solid plan. But Torkel, if you can't make it work, I want it fixed."

"We will get going as soon as they can get Tone in the skimmer," said Naz, trying not to be amused in this serious situation. The human always managed to make him smile no matter what was happening.

Nazilaq, Arino, Zeke, Torkel and Tone sped back to the scene of the crime, leaving the archangels to coordinate other efforts. Tone was back to his normal, annoying self soon after he was away from Raphael's voice.

"It is so cool feeling like I'm stoned out of my gourd when Raphael's around. I would ask if I made a fool of myself, but that is how I am normally, so I guess it doesn't matter."

Zeke chuckled. "You're even worse when you hear Raphael's voice." He turned to Arino, "Who would have thought that would be possible?"

"Not me," laughed Arino.

"Me neither," agreed Naz.

"Me either," added Tone.

All eyes turned to Torkel who said, "I really don't know him well enough to say." Although he was being serious, it got a laugh.

Nazilaq chose to fly instead of portaling. This gave them more opportunities to look for trails in the Spiritscape. Tone was in the front on the elongated egg-shaped skimmer once again. The sights and spectacle of the Spiritscape was still amazing to the easily distracted human. More than once his enthusiasm caused Nazilaq to stop the skimmer, thinking the human saw a trail. Each time it was only the Spiritscape's splendor showing scenes unimaginable to his human mind.

"Stop," shouted Tone. "Really, this time." The *Hajile-R* came to an abrupt halt, changing shape for battle. "Something is wrong. Do any of you see anything? I feel like something is watching us."

None of the angels could detect anything. Arino asked, "Are you sure, Tone? Maybe you are just jumpy. It's been a trying few quolls."

"You know how you get an itch on the bottom of your foot and want to scratch it; but you can't because you're in public and don't want to set off poisonous gas detectors when you take off your shoe?" The angels all looked at him blankly. "Well, it's like that. Something is making me itchy."

"I understand what you mean, Tone," said Zeke.

"You do?" asked Torkel. "Really? I have no idea what he's talking about."

"You get used to it," admitted Arino. "What are you sensing, Zeke?" Arino knew that the bond between Zeke and Tone was strong. She also knew that she would be the voice of reason to keep the hunter from being blind to the flights of fantasy of the human.

"I'm not totally sure, Arino. Let me try something. Naz, keep moving. I'll catch up," said the warrior, porting away.

The ship moved forward as it had done, with Tone scanning in front of them for a trail. Nothing had changed. Tone still felt itchy. Arino's senses were reaching out to find what was plaguing Tone. Naz and Torkel kept the *Hajile-R* moving forward.

A scream unlike anything Tone had ever imagined pierced the ether. The skimmer spun around, ready for battle and shot along the way it had come. It was not difficult to find the source of the wailing. In the middle of the Spiritscape, they discovered Ezekiel grasping a raven-winged demon, stretching and folding it like a taffy-puller.

# Chapter 14

"Hey, Zeke. What ya doing?" asked Tone. "Can you tie it like a bowtie?" The hunter continued stretching the demon.

"Zeke! Stop! Adsendelk will shatter if you pull much more," pleaded Arino.

Zeke's aura had more shades than usual. "That's the idea," he growled. "It's getting what it deserves." Zeke continued pulling the demon apart. Demon spirits are more rigid than angels'. Part of their corruption made them inflexible in thought, rendering their spirits more likely to break than bend. Adsendelk had already been stretched farther than most demons. "This thing knows something. I think it's about ready to talk." One more pull and the demon shattered into shards. "Oops. Too far," said the hunter, offhandedly.

The occupants of the skimmer watched in shock as Zeke opened a rip to Hell and tossed the pieces of the demon away like garbage. Before any of them could speak, Zeke stretched his spirit out to grab another demon that had been trying to hide. He pulled it close, smiling maliciously.

"Now that you see what happens when you don't answer a question. How are you today, Fidrol?" The tiny imp looked terrified. Its small blue body shook as three of its four eyes looked pleadingly at those in the skimmer. The thick, wrinkled, blue-gray skin quivered in fear and all four of its arms were held up in surrender. With a nose between two of its eyes and three ears between the others, it was prepared to use its senses to do anything it could to survive. Imps were known for information – not courage or battle.

"S-s-scared. Y-y-you can't do that! A-a-angels don't..." Its voice stopped as Zeke wrapped his spirit around it, squeezing. The angel laughed.

Tone looked at Arino. "What the hell is he doing?"

---

"I don't know. He is closed off." The effervescent Arino looked like she was in pain. "Zeke?" Her voice was pleading with the warrior.

Ezekiel ignored her. "Now, Fidrol, I assume I have your attention?" The silenced imp nodded vigorously. "Excellent. So let's talk about this green shit that is taking demons. What do you know? If you lie to me… well… just don't."

As the hunter eased his grip, Fidrol replied, "You said 'shit'? What is wrong…?" The demon gagged as Zeke tightened his grip again. The demon motioned that it wanted to speak, Zeke released it. "We don't really know. It has taken seven demons so far. We aren't finding anything left. It's like the Demonslayer is back. Only worse. At least we found remains before." The imp focused all three of its eyes on Zeke. "Or maybe it's a rogue angel. You are not a normal."

Zeke ignored the jab. "And that is all you know?" The angel expanded to herd the imp, causing it to move backwards until it was pressed against the *Hajile-R*. Two of the eyes of the demon were looking in at the passengers.

"Well, there is something else that may be helpful, but I want them to promise that you won't do to me what you did to Adsendelk." The imp was terrified of the hunter. "You are out of your damned mind!"

"I give you *their* word that I won't shatter you into billions of fragments and toss the trembling pieces into Lake Hades if what you have to tell me is worth it."

The demon looked at Arino. "I-I-I want her to say it." Zeke pressed the imp against the side of the skimmer, causing it to flatten. It reminded Tone of a cartoon. He would have laughed if he weren't worried about Zeke. Arino looked at the imp and then at Zeke. A silent agreement was made between the angels.

"He will not harm you further if you share worthwhile information," said the sad healer. She had no idea what was happening to Zeke, but felt the need to help him.

Zeke allowed Fidrol to move. "Some of the imps saw it at the Dovhavhads Spires before all this began. None of us go anywhere near there now. Too much bad graswil around there. It feels wrong."

Zeke shrank himself, returning to his normal appearance and size. The freed demon looked from the hunter to the skimmer. Glaring at the imp, Zeke whispered, "Go." The sound of the whisper was more menacing than a battle cry. Fidrol shot off, porting as soon as it was far enough away. Zeke began laughing, as he went to the wall of the canyon to open a hidden spot. Within was the intact demon he had shattered.

Adsendelk had been subdued, wrapped in its own wings. As the warrior untangled the demon, he said, "As promised, you can run away now. Next time, I won't be so nice." The demon flew away without making a sound. Zeke smiled at his friends. "Sorry about that."

"Dibs on the first thousand questions!" claimed Tone. "How did you make that winged thing into a puzzle and then put it back together? Superglue? Duct tape? Bailing wire?"

Arino broke in, "Zeke, what was that?" She was angry at the hunter. "You are playing with fire."

Ezekiel looked at Nazilaq, expecting questions. "They asked everything I wanted to know," said the smiling pilot, seeming to suspect the truth. Torkel was still looking at Zeke like he wasn't sure what he was.

"Well, I didn't shatter any demons. When I ported out, I found Adsendelk flying behind us. The ravens are not that smart, so I was sure it wasn't working alone. The imp was trailing too far behind to see everything. Once Adsendelk couldn't be seen by Fidrol, I tucked it in the crevasse and explained that it could be quiet and survive, or make a sound I would toss it into Lake Hades for a few centuries. It was very agreeable for some reason."

"Well played," said Tone. "But what did you turn into Stretch Armstrong?" Naz smiled at the deception as Arino looked a little relieved, but still was concerned. Torkel was still wondering what had happened.

"Relax beautiful," said the warrior to Arino, sounding more like Tone than himself. "It was an illusion. I can't make one that looks believable normally. But if you want one that looks like it has been skewed or skewered, I can do those."

Naz was impressed. "When did you develop that skill? I only know of a handful of angels who can make anything like that here." All the angels make them on Earth. The Spiritscape had too much ethereal energy to maintain illusions for all but the most powerful angels. Half of the archangels couldn't have even done what Zeke had just pulled off.

Tone was grinning. "And can you make an angel for me that looks like Arino, but blonde with really big…"

"No, Tone," interjected Zeke. "It isn't easy to do. As to when, I've always been able to make small illusions to distract demons when I'm hunting them. Ever since Arino and I teamed up, most of my talents have jumped up a notch or two." He turned to Arino, "Sorry for blocking you. I needed Fidrol to believe I was willing to shatter him. Sometimes you can be too sweet." He held out his hand to the healer.

She had been examining him the entire time, trying to determine what was going on. Reluctantly, she placed her hand in his. The two hands merged into one, two angels shared their power. They controlled the angel-embrace, preventing it from raging out of control. The link they shared allowed them to cause a blast of energy greater than any individual angel. If used by Ezekiel, it would devastate the most powerful enemies. If used by Arino, if would send a wave of healing over countless angels. This time, neither was needed. Both angels just shared their power, restoring the bond that had been weakened recently.

Tone felt guilty watching the angels. He tried to talk to Nazilaq and Torkel to distract himself. "So, do you come here often? Do you guys really help out that California baseball team? Who do you think will win the Superbowl? I only watch it for the commercials."

Naz chuckled at the human's discomfort. "Relax Tone. They are not doing what you are thinking. They are just sharing power, sharing thoughts, sharing plans and hopes."

"It sounds like they are doing exactly what I think they're doing." He still refused to look at them. "Do you hook up with anyone like that?"

Nazilaq smiled. "My connection is not to other angels but to the *Hajile-R*. Many angels have a best friend or two. Healers will share with many angels during the healing. They share with each other all the time. I'm more of a loner. It is a price I'm willing to pay to fly. 'Hooking up' with another angel would take the energy I need to be the best with my skimmer."

"So Tork, do you have someone that you share energy with?" asked the human, trying to get a handle on the closest thing he had found to angel sexuality.

Torkel was not sure how to take everything that had just happened. "No, I really don't get out much. I'm just a mechanic."

The connection between Zeke and Arino ended with both of them smiling. Arino was able to understand all that Zeke had experienced and knew his plans. Zeke's power was restored to full, even though it would never be as pure as it once had been. The traces of Tone within him had become so infused that it was impossible to separate the two. Zeke would have never allowed it to be removed anyway. He liked what he was becoming.

"Do you two need a cigarette?" asked Tone.

Taking charge, the warrior changed the topic. "We have two options right now. We can head back to Ximsor and work on the portal. Or we can check out the Spires."

Torkel spoke first. "I think we could do both. Just drop me off and let me work on the portal. It will take a couple of quolls to get it placed and ready to test. I'll wait for you to get back to try anything."

Nazilaq voiced his thoughts. "I'm not sure leaving Torkel by himself is the best idea. There may be some problems if the Bandersnatch tries to open it again."

"Or if demons show up," added Tone. "No offence, Tork, but you don't seem like the most badass of angels."

The mechanic laughed. "You'd be surprised, Tone. I can take care of myself." A crystal shell surrounded Torkel. It looked like a mini-skimmer to Tone. "It's little more than a sheath, but it will protect me from most things. And, it can channel enough power to make a demon think twice before attacking." The shell melted away at a thought.

Zeke was convinced. "I think we should drop off the portal and Torkel, then see what we can see." With that, the skimmer was back on course for Ximsor. With no more demons trailing them, they arrived within a quoll.

As they approached the junk yard, a thought crossed Tone's mind. "After we drop off Torky, we should really cruise around here. I never saw a Bandersnatch trail going in this place. We may be able to follow it a little ways."

Nazilaq transformed the skimmer and sailed harmlessly through Ximsor, no crystals approached the skimmer. Entering the lake, they once again found themselves surrounded by pha'ard of all shapes, sizes and colors. Tone was growing accustomed to seeing the strange creatures. The knowledge that Nazilaq could burn through anything in there made him much more relaxed as well.

Once back in the bubble, Zeke checked the entire space for anything that should not be there. After covering every bit of the space, he declared it safe for Torkel and the portal. In no time, the portal was returned to the same place it had been. The mechanic went around the immediate area, placing crystals at random intervals.

Seeing Tone watching, he explained, "Think of those as demon land mines. If one tries to sneak up behind me…" Torkel tore a sapphire from the wall and threw it near one of the mines. It cocooned the gem in a crystal container, creating a noise that strangely made Tone want to take a shower. "It won't hold them too long, but it will keep them from surprising me."

"I don't suppose you have any more of those handy that you could give to your old buddy Tone, do you?" The human was doing his best to look friendly and helpless at the same time.

"Sorry Tone. These things would suck you in. I don't think you really want that."

"That would suck," agreed Tone.

Nazilaq moaned. "You didn't just say that. That was bad even for you."

"Don't encourage him," giggled Arino.

"I have a whole Hoover routine about sucking if you want to hear it," teased Tone.

"No!" shouted all the angels in perfect harmony.

Leaving Torkel to his work, the skimmer shot out through Ximsor Lake and into Ximsor. To Tone, it looked like most of the larger crystals were giving them a wide berth. *That's putting the fear of Naz in them!* Once outside the basin, the skimmer began a search pattern, looking for the elusive green trail.

After covering the enormous mouth of the basin, Tone spoke. "That is weird. There are no trails going in there. Not green ones, at least. Some oily and several marshmallow, but no green slime. Does that mean this thing had something else take the portal down there? Is that possible?"

"I hope not," said Zeke. "It's bad enough that we have one Bandersnatch to deal with. I don't want to think about two."

# Chapter 15

The *Hajile-R* once again looked like an elongated egg as it cruised toward the Dovhavhads Spires. This part of the Spiritscape was notorious as a demon-infested region. Zeke and Nazilaq had each spent many quolls rounding up the dark spirits from these needle-like peaks. A rumored secret exit from Hell was thought to be here, but the angels could never locate it. There were many nooks and crannies, peaks and crevices, making this area a haven of hiding places.

The last time any of them had been to this place was still a fresh memory – a painful memory. This was where the beast, Bubba, had been defeated by all four of them. It had taken all of them fighting in synchronicity to stop the human spirit that had absorbed demons and angels, making it more powerful than anything in the Spiritscape.

Of the five who had tracked the monster, only four had returned from the battle. Irkja was an angel with a talent for sensing things others did not. Being quiet with little sense of humor, he made up for it with his ability to sense everything else. He had been the last casualty of Bubba.

Irkja had been captured by Zadrol, an imp in league with the beast. The imp and his minions had tortured Irkja to the point he was nearly phased apart. The four who now traveled to the scene of the battle had saved Irkja from the demons, only to have Bubba steal him from their hands right before the final battle. That memory made the approach to the Dovhavhads Spires more bitter than sweet.

Naz was the first to speak. "He died doing what he was meant to do. We can't mourn forever. Let's do this and get out of here." The pilot had been the closest to the lost angel and had no desire to stay in the area any longer than necessary.

"Holy shit! Look at that," declared Tone, examining the spires. No one else saw anything noteworthy.

"Tone, sweetie, we can't see what you are seeing," explained Arino.

"Sorry, babe. It's… I don't know what the hell it is," replied Anthony. "I never even looked at the trails the last time we were here. Most of them have faded so they are really hard to see. But there is one that is… ummm… old and fresh at the same time. It's like a fast food burger that's been sitting out for three years, two months, and eighteen days. You know it's been there a while, but it doesn't look like it."

"Odd," agreed Zeke. "Angel, demon or something else?"

"Well, I'd have to say, yes. It looks angel, demon and something else." Tone looked at the trail from the safety of the skimmer, guiding Naz closer. Under Tone's tutelage, the pilot reverted the skimmer to its normal ring shape with the trail going through the center. This allowed Tone to look at it from every angle. "The trail has traces of oil, marshmallow cream and the gray shit of Bubba. We really did kill her, right?"

Arino was by Tone's side as Zeke continually scanned the spires around them for trouble. She assured Tone, "Her body died. Between the three of us, we damaged Bubba to the point that you were able to release her. Tone, the last vestiges of Bubba faded into…" The glow on Arino's spirit went from calm to horror. "Oh no," she gasped.

All eyes were on her. "What is it?" asked Tone, afraid of the answer. "Leaving people hanging is my thing, babe. Talk to us."

Zeke was by her side, hands joined as he shared his strength and she shared her thoughts. "Why didn't we consider that at the time?" asked the hunter. Turning to Tone and Naz, Ezekiel explained as Arino ported outside the skimmer to test her theory. "Assuming we were successful in destroying Bubba, whatever was blasted away by Arino and me when we merged would have gone in all directions. That includes going down into the crevices where any number of demons could have been hiding. What if one of them was supercharged by what was left of Bubba?"

"That would be worse than a celebrity chicken pot pie eating contest at a vegan dieting convention," agreed Tone. "Something just doesn't seem to fit, though. I don't know what it is, but there is something missing."

Arino had transformed from her normal angelic shape to her healing form that had no discernable contours. She looked like a big amoeba to Tone. With Zeke moving to a defensive position nearby, the healer covered the raised dais that had first held Irkja and then been the place where Tone had used his H'tes to destroy the last bits of Bubba. Arino moved around the platform, expanding and contracting in odd directions. Tone could see that she was following trails of the beast each direction she moved. Arino was making certain that no part of Bubba had survived to reclaim power.

After moving in every other direction, Arino resumed her normal form. "There is only one place I can't be certain about. It feels like there was a trace of a bit of Bubba going down into the shadows, but not exactly. Tone, does your mystery trail come up right here?" She moved to a spot that positioned her directly over it.

"That's right where it comes out, babe. You are good," commented the human. "I didn't know you could sense where Bubba was. That's a cool trick. I wonder if I can do it with Zeke. I really wonder where he is when he's not hanging out with me. I think he's been at the strip clubs in Rio, but I can't prove it."

"I wonder if she can teach me to sense you," added Zeke, causing Tone to pale at the thought.

"Arino, sweetie, we need to talk about things you should and shouldn't teach your badass boyfriend over there. Tracking people named Tone is not nice," said a nervous Anthony.

The lilting laughter of Arino lightened the mood and made this spire seems less like a mausoleum. "I couldn't teach him if I wanted to, Tone. It is more of a feel than anything else." Getting serious, she continued, "Naz, is there any way you can make the skimmer small enough to fit down there?" The narrow opening looked barely large enough for two angels, making the skimmer far too large for the passage.

"I'm good, but I'm not that good. We could send part of the skimmer down there but the hull would take all the space. Sorry," he said as he exited the *Hajile-R*, patting it like a puppy. The skimmer captain knew that his ship would not be taking the trip.

Smiling as the H'tes moved from his arm to his hand, Tone declared, "Field trip! It was getting stuffy in here anyway." Moving to the invisible door, Tone looked to Naz. "Open says a-me." The door opened with Zeke standing right outside, blocking the way. "Excuse me. Trying to go spelunking here."

"Cool your jets, or whatever kind of exhaust you have from your chili dogs. Let me look around first." The warrior was adamant. There was no way he would let Tone put himself in harm's way.

"Dude, you made a fart joke! I'm so proud of you. As to letting you look around first, let me offer a counter proposal." Tone disappeared, moving quickly and quietly around the warrior. "Try to keep up," came the ethereal voice of the human.

Moving quickly after the voice, Zeke muttered. "Anyone have a spirit sphere handy?" Nazilaq and Arino were right behind him.

"It makes me want to have a spirit belt for him," agreed Naz, thinking of a device that was used on a particularly nasty demon on their previous adventure.

"But we are never bored," added Arino, as they angels flew into the dark fissure, never seeing the green form that watched from a distance.

Tone followed the trail until it became too muddled to make out. There was way too much gray snot trail, a remnant of Bubba. That made sense since she had come up from this before challenging them in battle. There was something else mixed in that was far too pure for Bubba. Tone realized that it was the trail of the lost Irkja that he was seeing. He wanted to look away, having no desire to see how the angel's trail would have faded and become part of the gray of the beast.

Before long, Tone was surprised to find the narrow passage opening to a large cavern, filled with the gray trail. This was where Bubba had been lying in wait to take Irkja before rising out of the cracks to surround them. Tone made himself visible to the angels as they joined him in this spacious cavity under the spires.

Nazilaq was impressed. "I had no idea this was here. If there are many of these I can see why we are never able to find all the devils hiding around here."

Zeke, recalling a report from one of the warriors, agreed. "Mishava has located a few of these grottos around here. This one is bigger than any he's found. Arino, are you sensing what I think you're sensing?"

The healer shivered. "This place feels like Bubba. It may be where she stayed when she wasn't out hunting. Not very homey."

"True, but it is the perfect hiding place and a good spot to hunt demons," agreed Ezekiel. "It would explain why we couldn't find her. If she hid here, it's way too close to Hell for any of us to get a good read. To be honest, it's brilliant." The hunter knew when to acknowledge the skill of his prey.

Naz smiled. "My friend, you need to take a vacation once in a while."

Zeke laughed. "You're probably right. It can be brilliant and evil at the same time. Look at Tone. He's a perfect example." Tone didn't respond. Zeke looked over at his friend. "You're going to let me get away with that?" Looking closer, he asked, "Tone, what are you doing? You look lost."

The human was moving all over the cave, looking like a basset trying to catch a scent. "There is something wrong here. It's like that strange trail I saw. It is angel, demon and Bubba, but it starts over here," he was in the far point of the cave, "and then it moves straight to the tunnel that goes out. No port marks or anything else. What the hell could make a trail like that? And, I'm not evil. Well, not usually."

Zeke was confused as well. "The trail begins right there? No entrance. That is very strange."

Arino made the same connection. "It seems like it was created right there. Tone, how old is the trail?" She had a suspicion that she hoped was wrong.

"It's hard to tell. If I had to guess I'd say it was made when the others were. This one may be a little newer. Why? What's going on in that pretty little head of yours?"

Arino looked concerned. "What if Bubba kept demons imprisoned here? It would make sense that she would want to have a food source. When you think about it, there were plenty of imps around here right before she came out to face us. What if one of them was down here when we blew most of Bubba's mist away. If enough came down here, it could have infused the demon with some power, turning it into something that had traces of angel, demon and Bubba."

"There's a problem with that theory," chimed in Nazilaq. "By the time you two hit him, I had pulled all the angel power out of him with a draining pulse from the *Hajile-R*. The combination trail would not have resulted from your blast."

"Oh shit! I am so stupid! I get it now." declared Tone. Moving as fast as he could, the human darted to the passageway leading back to the surface. "Please be wrong. Please be wrong. Please be wrong," he murmured the whole way.

"What is it?" asked Zeke, right behind him.

"All the angel power was gone. There is only one way it could have any angel power," said Tone, shooting out of the rift in the spire. "He had to have it with him."

The angels understood the implication of the power. There was only one possibility. Each one hoped the same thing as Tone. *Please be wrong.*

Leaning against the *Hajile-R*, was something they never expected to see. "It took you long enough," chuckled Irkja, green mist encircling him.

# Chapter 16

It was strange seeing Irkja smiling. It was even stranger seeing him at all. Even Tone was at a loss for words. Irkja watched and waited for someone to say something. At last he decided that he should be the one to break the ice.

"You look surprised to see me. I guess that makes sense since the last time you saw me, you assumed I had been... Tone, is there a way to say 'eaten alive' without it sounding horrific?" The human still had not regained the power of speech. Irkja continued. "There is nothing like being half eaten, then getting spit out when someone hits you with a blast from a skimmer. Thanks so much, Naz." The skimmer pilot was at a loss.

Arino was the first to respond. "Irkja, is that really you? You don't look like yourself." She was trying to move closer, but Irkja was gone from where he had been standing.

"Yes, it really is me, Arino." The voice was behind them. All spun at once to see Irkja casually sitting atop one of the shorter spires. "It is truly amazing having of half your spirit devoured. It can really change you. It also hurts like hell."

Zeke ported to Irkja to find he was no longer there. The hunter looked around to see him lounging in the middle of the skimmer. The hunter flew at the speed of thought to find himself alone in the ring. Ezekiel looked around to see Irkja happily waving at him, from behind Nazilaq.

"Now we can play tag for a few quolls, if you want," joked the green spirit. "Or we can have a nice chat. What's it going to be, Zeke?"

The internal debate within the warrior played out in his spirit for all to see. He considered trying again to catch his quarry, believing that Irkja would make the first mistake. It was Arino who helped him make the decision when she calmly seated herself on the dais, motioning the warrior to join her. She reached out with an overlong arm and pulled Tone down beside her.

Nazilaq faced the angel who had been the spotter in the *Hajile-R* for countless missions. The two looked at one another, staring deep into their spirits. The usual joviality of Nazilaq had fled leaving a hurt, angry angel.

"What happened?" It was all the pilot could ask. He moved away from his former friend, looking at all the damage that had been done. He had been ripped apart right down the middle. Half of Irkja looked almost the same as it had always looked. He still had many spots all over half his spirit that allowed him to sense far more than other angels. Extra eyes and additional places that allowed him to use all ten angelic senses in ways like no other angel. The only difference was his spirit no longer had the golden glow of an angel, it had a green aura that was unlike anything Naz had ever seen.

It was the other half of his spirit that was terrible and terrifying. It lacked the substance of a normal spirit, but it seemed to be trying to duplicate the solid form. It was a liquid flowing in and around Irkja, making that half look more like Arino when she transformed into her amorphous form. Where the flowing green met the solid form of his spirit, it flowed over and under, giving his face a bizarre look that made it hard to look into his one unsteady eye.

"I got eaten," replied Irkja, simply. That was the first time he sounded like the angel they had known. Then he added, "I had to make do with what I had to work with when you left me behind." There was anger in his voice and a green glow to his spirit that scared Tone.

"Didn't it occur to you to make sure I was dead before you sailed away? I was in anguish! Imagine if you could feel the part that thing consumed. That part of me died!" Turning to Arino and Zeke, Irkja went instantly from angry to calm. "How do you like what I was able to do to with the bits and pieces you left me to work with? I know it's not up to your standards, Arino." His temper began to rise. "But if you consider that I was clawing my way out of that pit when

I was flooded by the shit that was blown off Bubba…" He seemed to be looking at something none of them could see. "Zeke, don't bother. I'll port away and then you can't ask any of your questions."

Tone had been staring at Irkja the entire time. It was like a horror movie monster was standing in front of him. A monster he had once known and liked. When Irkja addressed Zeke, Tone snapped out of his stupor. "What do you mean? Um… Zeke is just sitting there. And can you make your face hold still. I'm not sure which eye to look at."

"There's the Tone I remember. This is the best I can do." Looking at the hunter while talking to Tone, Irkja continued. "He was considering ripping a hole to Hell to see if he could shove me in. It won't work."

Arino spoke. "You can still see ahead." Irkja had an eleventh sense that no other angel possessed. On Earth, time was easy for any angel to traverse. They could move to any point in any place at any time. Time in the Spiritscape was different. It was possible to be in the same place over and over, but still not encounter yourself. The Spiritscape had infinite layers of the same place that allowed things to happen at the same time without interfering with one another. Irkja could see the things that were about to happen giving him a type of precognition. It had helped them when dealing with Bubba. Now, it gave the damaged angel an advantage. He saw moves before they were made.

"Damn, that's cool," admired Tone. "What am I going to do now?"

"Make a smartass comment?" asked the green-tinted spirit.

"You are good!" admitted Tone. Looking at closer, he added, "You have some serious demon issues, buddy. There are traces of all kinds of demons in your squishy parts. I think I even see a little bit of Bubba snot in there too. Your after-market parts are invading your factory parts."

Arino agreed. "Irkja, I want to help you. My power can't restore you to what you once were, but I can help you purify what's left of you."

The former angel barked out a vicious chortle. "Arino, what makes you think I want your help? I really don't have time for your nonsense. There are things that must be done and I'm the only one who can do it. Save your power for someone who wants it."

Zeke spoke up. "Why are you taking demons? And what did you do with Adoneal? If you think they can help you, it won't work. The demons will just…"

"Corrupt me further?" interjected Irkja. "You have a very limited vision, Zeke. They are not for me. I have something much more interesting planned for them." Addressing them all, he pontificated, "Here is the deal, boys and girl. I am not your enemy. Adoneal is willingly helping me with a project. I will not harm him or any of you. All I ask is that you stay out of my way until I'm done. I'm doing what you can't do. That part of me that was locked into your narrow view of right and wrong, well… it got eaten. My goals are not evil, even if my methods are outside your box."

Nazilaq joined the debate. "What are you doing, Irkja? Let us help. If your goals are that good, then why not let us join whatever crusade you are on?"

Raising a liquid hand, Irkja shook a finger at his old friend. "Now, now. When the time is right, you will be very helpful. It's not time yet." The green-glowing angel appeared to be looking at something none of them could see. Sounding euphoric, he sighed, "It will be amazing. If you only had the vision…" His voice trailed off. He looked sharply at Ezekiel, smiling half a smile. "You sure you want to try that? I think Tone would say, 'chill out.'"

"More like 'chili dog out', but that was close enough," bantered Tone. Irkja laughed at the levity.

Zeke was not amused and not willing to back down. "And if we don't let you do whatever it is you're doing? To be honest, you're just pissing me off right now."

For the first time, Irkja looked shocked. "Zeke, you just said I'm pissing you off. What happened to you?" The former angel's spirit glowed as all his senses focused on the warrior. "You are not so pure yourself, Zeke." He focused his sense on Tone. "Well, well, well. We have something in common. You have been touched, too. It seems Tone's influence is having some interesting effects on you. Anyone else?" He looked first to Nazilaq and then at Arino. "Arino? What is that? You have a trace of human in there, too? Tone?"

"Bubba," admitted Arino. "Long story. Irkja, you are not yourself. Please, let me help." The healer was begging as she sent out a wave of healing power. Irkja was gone when the power arrived.

In the distance, they could see the green glow of Irkja. "Just stay out of the way. I don't want to fight you, but I will if you force the issue." He disappeared leaving a port mark that only Tone could see.

"He's really gone," said Tone. "I like him a little better like this. He has a better sense of humor."

Zeke rounded on the human. "Better? Were you awake for any of that? He is collecting demons for who knows what?"

Arino touched the hunter. "Exactly. We don't know what Irkja is doing with the demons. He could have attacked if he wanted to harm us. Naz, what is he like in battle?"

Nazilaq looked at them. "Scary. I've only seen him fight eight times. Nothing has ever touched him. He always did what he did to you, Zeke. He isn't where they are going to attack. To be honest, I don't even know how he was captured."

It was Tone's turn to speak. "It had to have been Bubba. I don't think he can sense what I am doing. I almost jumped up and tried to use my H'tes to drain him. If he had tried anything, I would have shish kabobbed him. He looked right past me like I wasn't worth worrying about. I'd guess Bubba snuck up on him and let the imps play."

Nazilaq also joined in. "That's not really Irkja anymore. I don't know what that is, but it's not my friend. He laughed. Well, he had the evil, megalomaniac laugh down."

"Megalomaniac? Dude, I have never heard you use a six-syllable word before," joked Tone, trying to lighten the mood. "What else can you say? Anatidaephobia? Psychopharmaceutical? Antidisestablishmentarianism? Dog?"

Ignoring Tone's inane chatter, Zeke took charge. "We need to meet with Michael. Get us out of here, Naz." Soon, they were all in the skimmer, moving at the usual insane speeds. Once they were a sufficient distance from the Dovhavhads Spires, Zeke turned to Arino. "What did you sense from Irkja? I couldn't read a damn thing."

Ignoring his language, Arino responded, "That really was Irkja. Well, what's left of him. Parts of him are gone. Obviously, his sense of right and wrong has been inhibited…"

Tone chimed in. "Inhibited? Are you sure that's the right word for a former angel who is devil-napping demons, borrowing an archangel for something nasty, and half-way melted into a creepy version of evil pudding? Did I miss anything? Oh yeah, he also has an evil, megalomaniac laugh." He winked at Nazilaq.

"His sense of right and wrong is twisted around. Better?" asked Arino. Tone gave her a courtly bow. "His personality is radically different. He spoke more just then that I have heard him all other times combined. Plus the evil, megalomaniac laugh is the first time any of us heard him laugh at all. There is something else that I couldn't get a handle on. He is struggling with good and evil in a way that I have never seen. I just don't know what he is."

Nazilaq added, "I think you were right about his inhibitions. Irkja, like all of us, had thoughts that were never acted upon. On one mission, he did asked why we don't just lock demons somewhere else. Now he is following through on that thought."

Zeke was worried. "No matter what he's doing, we need to discuss what we are going to do. Or decide if we are going to do anything."

# Chapter 17

"How can we do nothing?" demanded Gabriel. The archangel of the messengers was livid at the suggestion. He was not a fan of Tone or Zeke, and made no secret of his distaste. This was one of those instances where he felt his concerns were more than justified.

Situated in Vret's workspace were four archangels, three angels and one human. In addition to Gabriel were Vret, Raphael and Michael. The other five archangels were listening to the debate, but were not present due to other pressing issues. Three of them were tending to regular duties while the remaining two were assisting with the search for the tenth archangel – Adoneal.

Vret responded to Gabriel's outburst. "It is a logical option, Gabriel. We need to consider all possibilities."

As she spoke, a sculpture of Irkja was forming from the memories and descriptions of those who had met him. To Tone it looked like a damn good example of how scary he looked. All the thoughts of Ezekiel, Arino and Nazilaq had been instantly shared with the angel of wisdom through the angelic link. Tone's observations had been shared through many colorful euphemisms. The phrases "super-villain dipped in battery acid" and "the kind of green that makes you think of pond scum" were included with Arino's more clinical descriptions. Tone described his former friend as "scared the shit out of me so bad I may not poop again for a year," creating an image sufficiently picturesque for Vret to capture the essence of terror instilled.

Michael joined in the debate. "I agree with Gabriel that doing nothing is not an option. The issue is that we do not know what to do. Tone, could you read anything in his spirit that may give us an idea of Irkja's plans?"

Tone looked thoughtful. "Well, it was kind of hard to look at him too long with half of him looking like a stuck special effect. But all I saw was bits and pieces. He was doing the old 'let's block Tone's ability to read us' trick with the solid part of him."

Vret looked at the human. "You're holding back, Tone. What aren't you telling us?" The art behind Vret had frozen as the archangel looked carefully at him. She was waiting.

Tone looked at Zeke, who said, "Just get used to it and stop bitching about it."

"I do not bitch about it. Sometimes it gets on my nerves when angels think they know things that I don't want to tell them. I may whine or pout or complain in a really loud, cranky voice, but I don't bitch about it." Arino smiled shaking her head at him. "Just defined bitching pretty well, didn't I?"

"What do you know?" demanded Gabriel. His lack of patience for Tone's antics was one of the reasons the human acted worse when he was around. It was the little things in life – like pissing off archangels – that made it fun for Tone.

Tone began to speak, but Michael interjected, "About Irkja, that is." He knew how to deal with Anthony's notorious fondness for loopholes.

Glaring at Michael for ruining his fun, Tone admitted, "I caught a glimpse of something, but I don't know what it means. It was in the squishy part." Behind Vret, the sculpture moved so that the flowing half of Irkja was all that showed. "It had spots of gray in it. I'm not talking about the blue-gray snot of a Bubba trail or the fart cloud that was around her. Am I the only one who thinks that was unladylike?" He paused for a reaction. Gabriel's eyes were glowing with angel fire, causing Tone to smile. "It was like gray was on Irk's mind and he couldn't hide it as well in the green, gooey part. Does that make sense?"

"No, but what else is new?" joked Zeke.

Vret turned away, looking at the visual representation of Irkja. The insubstantial half glowed and transformed. What remained did not look as much like the Irkja they had seen, but it felt like him.

"How the hell do you do that?" asked Tone. "Mine doesn't look like me either; but it feels like me, too. That is just too funky."

Vret continued her work on her wisdom montage of Irkja. "Don't look with just your eyes, Tone. Use all your senses." The work on the angel art changed as Tone examined it more carefully.

"Stop moving it. Some of us are trying appreciate it," chuckled Anthony. He leaned over to smell the figure only to have it transform again. He looked at Vret. "You did that one on purpose. You wanted it going up my nose, didn't you?"

All the angels were smiling – even Gabriel. Vret explained. "When I make a collage of wisdom, it changes depending on what sense you use. Imagine what it is like for Zeke when he uses a sense you don't have," laughed the wise one. "The archangels can even see more than that." She looked thoughtful. "Tone, would you be willing to use your tracking sense on it? I wonder..." She gazed at the statue, lost in thought.

"For you, anything, pretty lady...err... pretty angel." Tone opened his mind to see trails. He moved closer looking at the art more intently than he had ever looked. Reaching out to touch it, he began, "That is too cool! It's like I can..."

"Tone! Don't!" yelled Vret, too late.

Tone touched the statue.

The scream from the human was deafening, louder than any of them knew was possible from the psychedelic spirit. Instead of curling up in a ball, it appeared that Tone was rapidly expanding. A spirit sphere appeared around him as Michael attempted to contain what was happening. The glowing ball with golden lines was made transparent with a thought from the chief of the archangels. The golden streaks remained, spinning around the globe with movements that blurred the multitude of runes that made up the power giving lines.

Tone was bouncing around the spirit sphere and the art of Irkja. Each time he touched the statue, a new howl of pain came from the blurred movement that was Tone. Zeke was beside the round prison in an instant. Nodding to Michael, he touched the rounded surface. Zeke was sucked inside the orb to be greeted by another cry from Tone as the human bounded straight at him, plastering him against the interior wall. As soon as Tone had moved again, Zeke flew to the statue and wrapped himself around it. The insulation of his friend allowed Tone to bounce harmlessly off Zeke without contacting the instrument of his torture.

Arino appeared within the sphere, entering the same way as Zeke. When Tone came at her, she transformed into her shapeless healing form, capturing Tone and preventing him from moving further. Her healing powers worked on the human as Zeke moved away from the statue to stop beside his two best friends.

"He has stopped moving, Michael," declared Arino. The spirit sphere dissolved leaving Zeke and Arino hovering over the still form of Tone. More and more healing power poured into the human. Still he remained motionless. Raphael moved closer cautiously. His power was dangerous for both he and Tone, but he had to help. With the power of the archangel of healing going into Zeke, the warrior touched the human, acting as a conduit to help.

The constantly changing colors of Tone's spirit had stopped flowing and changing. They were becoming more monochromatic. He had never looked like a human spirit, nor had he looked angelic. On one other occasion, he had been temporarily possessed by the last vestiges of a demon who had been devoured by Bubba. This time he did not have the cold blue of the demon taking over. Tone was turning the sickly green of Irkja.

Gabriel turned to Vret. "Is there anything we can do?" The concern in the archangel of the messengers was genuine. He did not like Tone; however, he did not want him hurt either. Gabriel knew that they needed Tone and Zeke for the jobs none of the angels could or would do. Right now, Tone was their only hope to find Irkja before something terrible happened.

There was a phrase that Vret uttered that was rarely heard from her. "I don't know. That should not have hurt him. I was trying to stop him from influencing the information."

Raphael spoke. "He absorbed your power from the sculpture. It is tearing him apart. His spirit is trying to expel the power. Arino, continue healing. We have to pull power out before... well, we have to pull it out. Ezekiel, get ready." The archangel changed the direction of the power flow, pulling the power from Tone through Ezekiel. Raphael reached out to Vret and began sending the power that was taken from Tone back to the source.

The green tint of Tone's spirit began flowing toward the hand of Zeke. It became lighter until a clear line could be seen. The healing power of Arino filled the void left by the retreating green, restoring the colorful tones to Tone. As the last traces of green were drawn like a poison from his spirit, the form of the human slowly reverted to its normal human-ish shape.

Surrounded by angels, Tone's spirit began to move, twitching and turning. He motioned for Zeke to come near as he whispered to the hunter. Zeke laughed.

"I'm afraid to ask," said Michael, relieved that Tone had made a joke.

Zeke looked up, "He just said, 'ouch'." Moving his friend around, he asked, "Are you okay, buddy? You scared us."

Looking around, Tone said, "I scared me, too. Gabe, you actually look like you give a damn. Don't worry. I won't tell anyone you really do like me. Do you have Wi-Fi? I need to update my Facebook status to: Fried by an angel statue, but Gabe likes me so it's all worth it."

Gabriel defended himself. "Don't mistake relief that a human is not hurt for liking the human. We need your help."

"'Need my help' is the same as thinking I'm the coolest thing since warm socks after sliding down a waterslide during a blizzard." Tone was not letting him off the hook.

"Isn't that called a bobsled run?" asked Nazilaq.

Tone righted himself to a normal floating position. He was prepared to torment the archangel further when he grabbed his own head. "Whoa. Head rush. Okay, that's just freaky." He turned to look at the statue that had caused all his problems. "Now, that is freaky cool." Tone moved around the angelic art, looking at it from every angle while keeping a safe distance. "It's like I can see every piece of information you poured into that bad boy. And the lines flowing out of it are too cool. Do all your art things look like squids?"

All the angels looked at him, confusion showing clearly on their spirits. "I hate it when you look at me like Gracie Williams did in third grade when I made the underwear out of mashed potatoes and wore them out to the playground after lunch." Stage whispering to Nazilaq, he said, "They are surprisingly comfy, but don't last too long when you slide into second."

Vret asked the question all were wondering. "What lines, Tone? There aren't any lines coming out of the Acumenite."

"The what? Acumenite? Really? A funky name for a funky statue. I guess it works." The human moved closer to the Acumenite than he would have preferred, pointing to trails coming out of the statue. "Right there? They look like tiny versions of his trail. You don't see that?"

None of the angels saw what Tone was seeing. Michael asked Vret, "Any thoughts on this one?"

She had not stopped staring at Tone throughout the whole ordeal. Still not moving her gaze, Vret replied, "Five possibilities." Looking closer at the human, she corrected. "No. Three. It could be Tone is still in shock from the power surge and is seeing things that are not there. Or, he may be seeing something that is beginning to grow out of the Acumenite which would be a type of precognition he has never demonstrated." She looked from Tone to the statue and said, "Most likely, it's Tone's trail vision seeing something in the statue that is not visible to us. Tell me Tone, what do you know about Irkja?"

"Just what I've told you. He is…" Tone paused then looked at Vret. "Wow! That is too cool."

"I thought so," said Vret, smiling.

"The bonding is very sweet, but some of us have no clue what you're talking about," interjected Zeke. The hunter was still leery about Tone's health after the accident.

Tone answered. "I know everything there is to know about Irkja. Well, everything that Vret poured into the Aqua-whatever. I can tell you what color socks he would wear if he ever wore them." He looked at all the angels and added. "Oh yeah, and that gray I was seeing. It's not just gray. It's a Gray barrier like over by the ugly unicorns. Irky-boy is hiding inside the Gray."

# Chapter 18

"Wouldn't you have seen a trail in the Uqump? Granted we didn't cover the whole place, but don't you think some kind of trail may have shown up somewhere? Or are we talking about one of the other Grays?" asked Nazilaq.

Even though he tried to jump in, Vret replied to the question before Tone could answer. "Nazilaq, there is always the possibility that Irkja could be in one of the other Gray areas. Unless he was trying to throw us off, it seems unlikely he would hunt where he is hiding. Michael?"

Tone tried to speak again, but was cut off by the chief archangel. "I will have angels explore all of the Grays. Two of them have already been checked. But if this is Irkja we are talking about, he will know our methods well and could be able to hide."

Again, the human had a question, but was cut off by an angel. "I really think Tone's tracking is our only option at this point," injected Ezekiel. "But as much as Irkja is porting, that may be problematic. Tone, you've been quiet. What are you thinking?"

The human looked around. "Anyone one else want to say something first. Not you Gabe. You still need to sit in the corner and think about what you've done." The messenger glared at him. "Now first, how many Gray areas are there? I thought there was just the one around the creepy critters."

Vret replied. "There are ten presently, but Adoneal can make others. At one point we had seventeen and at another point there were only five." Vret looked at the other angels as they shared thoughts. "That may be why he needed Adoneal; to make a Gray for him."

"Here's the sixty-four thousand dollar question, why does that question cost so much?" Tone looked around at the befuddled angels. "Just curious. Anyway, the real question is about shortcuts. I don't enjoy the sensory deprivation experience of floating through those, but it seems to frost your halos with real ice. Now, if it was that really good cream cheese icing, no problem. Is there any way to take a short cut through a Gray? Would a couple of static portals be a good way to do that? If Irky has Donny making Gray shit, why not have him make a couple fixed portals to sneak in and out?"

"Torkel!" shouted Naz. "Porting as close to Ximsor as I can take the *Hajile-R*." The pilot and ship were gone in less than the blink of an eye.

Michael opened a portal beside them. The door opened and, with Zeke's help, Tone was once again shoved somewhere without a word. The startled human looked around to see Zeke, Michael, Arino, and Nazilaq in the skimmer. The skimmer took off toward Ximsor at top speed.

"Excuse me. That was really rude. I thought angels were supposed to be nice," whined Anthony. Tone was doing what he could to ease the high level of tension in the ship.

"Yeah, I'm not that nice," Zeke replied. All of them were focused on Torkel and the fixed portal. If Irkja had decided to use it, the mechanic would be no match for him.

"Porting in there for you would be bad because…?" asked the human.

Zeke replied, "It can be done, but it leaves an angel too drained to defend or fight. If we were just going to the monument, it's not an issue. Heading in there to deal with a potential problem, not a good idea."

Nazilaq spoke, "The *Rialc* and *Enna* will get there first. We won't be far behind them. I had already sent Esiuol there to check on Torkel. He was almost there when Tone figured it out."

"I'm glad I was able to do my small part in making the Spiritscape a safer place. It was really some of my best work and I couldn't be prouder of my contribution to this heroic endeavor," beamed Tone.

Michael actually laughed. "You have no clue what you did, do you?"

"Not a damn clue. Care to share?" laughed Tone. He was pretty sure it had something to do with the fixed portals. Beyond that, no idea. "It's my job to throw out random shit all the time, and then I get to see what makes one of you have a brilliant idea."

Arino explained. "It is the fixed portals. Having one at the base of Ximsor would be one of the few places Irkja could create a strong enough portal to cut through a Gray. Drawing power from the lake could give it the boost it needs."

"And once it has a link to the portal inside a Gray, that side would only need a fraction of the power," added Zeke.

"Entering Ximsor," announced the ever-efficient Nazilaq. "Cutting a direct route. Can anyone hear Torkel, Esiuol, or Kra'illa?"

"You have an angel named Crayola?" asked Tone, giggling. "I will trade my signed copy of *Shrink* if this character wears a pointy hat."

"He's a skimmer pilot," replied Michael, exasperated. With a thoughtful look, he added, "He has made the *Enna* look rocket-shaped before. I never made the connection. I can't hear any of them. The link is cut off."

"No way!" shouted Tone, getting into his sheath for the trip through Ximsor. "Is he messing with me?" He looked from Zeke to Arino, each smiling and shaking their heads negative. "I really need to meet more angels. You people are weird. Coming from me that's a..."

"Compliment?" asked Zeke.

"Insult?" added Michael.

"Fairytale?" asked Arino.

"Impressive feat," concluded Tone. "Not to be confused with impressive feet. That is the aroma of my tootsies after a long day of jogging, pumping iron and teaching refried bean wrestling to all my many female admirers."

Naz looked up from blasting his way through a large chartreuse crystal. "And he says we are the weird ones. Entering Ximsor Lake."

Tone watched the outlandish lake life and added, "Well, not as weird as that," he pointed to a pha'ard that was blasted into tiny pieces by Michael's power. "But pretty close."

There were a large group of multicolored pha'ards near the under-surface of the lake. One large blast from the *Hajile-R* and the mindless crystal fragments scattered. The skimmer burst into the cavern, making a quick turn and sudden stop to prevent the ship from crashing into the devastation in their midst.

One flattened-disc-shaped skimmer was trying to burn its way out of a crystal trap that had been set for demons. Tone was astonished that one trap could encompass an entire skimmer until he realized there were at least four of them covering the ship. The pilot, Kra'illa, was trying everything in his arsenal of tricks to free his vessel, but nothing seemed to work. Michael went to assist the freeing of the *Enna*.

There was another skimmer that was floating as a crystal ring above them, adrift in the ether. Further investigation showed that Esiuol was directly in front of them in a crystal just for him. The prison was filled with angel fire that merely made it look pretty to Tone, without doing any damage to the crystal. Arino moved by his side looking for ways to unlock the device that held him.

"Where is the portal?" asked Zeke, noticing the absence of the device they had left Torkel to repair.

"More importantly, where's Torkel?" asked Naz. "Tone, seeing anything?"

The human was looking all around. "There is so much to see. Ice cream stands and lollypops are conspicuous by their absence. But there are some wacked-out trails. Looks like Irk did come back through where the portal used to be. I think that Torkel was ushered through the portal. Could they have pulled the portal through itself to their side?"

Nazilaq thought for a moment. "I don't think so. Fixed portals need to be moved, not ported. Most of the time we have cherubs do it."

"Zeke, can we go for a walk? I can't see everything I need to see, and it's way too crowded to have Naz shoving everybody all over the place in this puppy." Holding up three fingers, he added, "I'll behave. Scout's honor."

The hunter sighed. "You were never a scout." Opening the door, he gave Tone a stern look. "Try not to get hurt."

"Zeke, Zeke, Zeke. You act like I do stupid things on purpose. It's just a gift for natural stupidity."

"That's what worries me," admitted the angel. Calling to the others, he asked, "Any luck?"

Arino replied, "I've almost got Esiuol out. This stuff blocks me from most communications."

Michael had expanded his spirit, muscling his way through the crystal. "I've almost made enough of a hole to be able to link with Kra'illa. The ship seems agitated. Be careful. Nazilaq, do whatever you need to do if something happens to Zeke and Tone."

"Understood," replied Naz. The *Hajile-R* transformed into a needle-shaped vessel, ready to snake its way around the angels and skimmers in the way.

Tone approached the wall where the portal had been. He followed the fluffy trail of Torkel, noticing where the mechanic had worked on the device. The angel had been floating some distance from the portal when the trail moved in a straight line through the aperture with a green hazy trail moving with it. The green trail moved further into the space. This time there was no large mark from Irkja's expansion or porting. It was a long trail that moved all along the edge of the immediate area before returning to the original spot.

"It looked like Irk grabbed Torkel and then went for a stroll all around here. First he moved up here," Tone moved up to a spot near the feverishly working Michael. "Then he went over there." He pointed to the spot where Arino was trying to free Esiuol. "Then he went over here." Tone moved very cautiously toward another area, not following in the exact tracks of Irkja after seeing what had happened to the angels. It was then that Tone noticed that the trail was almost in the shape of a word. He just needed to move a little higher and to the right.

The words rang out as Michael was able to shatter the deepest layer of crystal surrounding the *Enna*. Kra'illa sounded panicked, "It's a trap!" The words were too late as Tone moved to the see the words left by Irkja.

"Oh shit," muttered the human as he read the message in the trail, dread filling his spirit.

"Got you" were the words that caused Tone to turn around to see one of Torkel's mines racing toward him. Tone held out his H'tes to defend himself as Zeke flew to him. Neither the blade nor the warrior could do anything. Zeke arrived after the crystal avoided the blade and hit Tone in the chest. The shell flowed around Tone, immobilizing him instantly.

Zeke reached out to tear the cocoon to pieces only to have it slip through his fingers. The crystal shell was different than the ones around the skimmer or Esiuol. This one formed into the shape of an elongated jewel with tips that came to points. At Zeke's touch it shot up and out into the Ximsor Lake, carrying Tone away.

Without a thought Zeke was right behind him, going into the lake without anything to protect him from the pha'ards waiting at the edge. The warrior form of Ezekiel was devastating to most demons, the smaller pha'ards never stood a chance. Encompassing himself in angelic fire, he burst through the group of pha'ards sending them all spinning out of control. The hunter could see the distant form of Tone's escaping crystal pod getting farther away.

Tone was trying to use angel fire to break out. He quickly found two problems with that idea. The first problem being the material he was trying to burn was essentially the same basic substance of his H'tes without the added power. Flames would only bounce around and then land back in the blade. The second problem that hit him was obvious: *What am I going to do if I get out right here? Be pha'ard chow? I don't think so.* He could not see anyone behind him, but he hoped they were close.

Zeke poured on the speed to catch up to Tone and almost ran into the maw of a huge pha'ard that had more parts fused into it than he had time to admire. He briefly considered flying through it, but had no idea if he would be able to blast his way out. He dodged around it, skittering around the back of the monstrosity. An unseen second mouth caught the angel around the middle, holding Zeke in place. The hunter could see the escaping pod almost at the surface of the lake. Zeke expanded further, trying to pry the vice-like jaws open while trying to watch where Tone broke the surface of the lake. The angel had just started to move the jaws when the entire pha'ard exploded in a blast of skimmer fire.

Nazilaq flew through the remains of the pha'ard and scooped up Zeke without slowing, bringing him inside the *Hajile-R.* "You're welcome," said the pilot, breaking the surface and changing course to follow Tone.

"Thanks. Good catch." Changing his focus to his friend, Zeke asked, "Where is he?"

"Up there. That thing is dodging crystals better than a skimmer. I think that's Torkel's pod. It's not any use in battle, but it can move. I move faster," declared the pilot, dodging and blasting away as the skimmer got closer to the pod.

The pod left Ximsor and changed course again. Tone had no idea what was happening. He thought he could see a skimmer beneath him, but he wasn't sure. He thought of all the abilities at his disposal, and then it occurred to him. He decided to return to Earth, away from this trap. With a thought, he tried to return to his body. Nothing happened. He tried again. Nothing happened, again.

"Okay, this is very not good," Tone said to himself. "You have a gift for understatement. Now you're talking to yourself, too. That may be worse. Not as bad a vegan chili dogs, but almost." He looked ahead and exclaimed, "Oh shit! I think that tops them all." He had looked to see a doorway in the middle of the ether, opening like a ravenous mouth. It looked just the right size for a pod.

# Chapter 19

The *Hajile-R* flew around a floating orange mountain to see Tone heading toward the unknown. No words were needed between pilot and passenger. The skimmer would not reach the portal in time. Zeke ported.

Tone looked up to see Zeke appear in full power between the speeding pod and the dark opening. A blast of angel fire and the wings of Ezekiel's spirit stretched out toward Tone with the goal of slowing or changing the course of the speeding pod. Neither worked. The pod hit Zeke without losing any speed, taking both the pod-encased Tone and the blazing Zeke through the portal into the unknown. The door closed and disappeared behind them leaving Nazilaq and the skimmer soaring through the empty ether.

The unknown was darker than Tone had expected. The only light was from the warrior's angel fire flying in all directions. If he could have moved, Tone would have knocked on the crystal or at least waved at his best friend. All he could do is mouth the words, "Thank you." It was bad enough to be kidnapped. Being here alone would have been worse. Much worse.

"You're welcome," replied Zeke. "Now if I can just figure out where we are and what is going on."

A chuckle filled the air. "I should have known you'd tag along, Zeke. I really didn't need you just yet. Oh well. I'll make lemonade." The voice did not have a form to accompany it, but there was no doubt as to the owner.

"You may be the first being to ever call me a lemon. To what do we owe the kidnapping, Irkja?" asked Zeke with far more cordiality than he felt.

"Relax Zeke. We don't have to be enemies. Our goals are not that dissimilar," replied the still disembodied Irkja. "As a gesture of good faith, allow me to do this." The pod around Tone dissolved, leaving the human free.

Pretending to take a breath, Tone quipped, "Thank you. I farted in there and it didn't have anywhere to go. I've really got to cut back on the red beans and rice with boiled cabbage."

Zeke looked him over. "Are you okay?"

After pretending to feel all over his spirit, Tone responded, "Well, I did get swallowed up by a gummy crystal and shot who knows where. And I think that pod thing stole my wallet. All in all, a normal day at the office. How about you? Did I miss anything cool?"

Zeke was determined to irritate Irkja by ignoring him. "I went swimming in Ximsor Lake without a skimmer. That was fun."

"Really? You clever bastard. I never knew you could swim. Breaststroke? Crawl? Doggy-paddle?"

The voice of Irkja interjected, "Are you two done?" There was a trace of irritation in the question.

"Not quite," replied Zeke. Turning to Tone he said, "Angelstroke. It's a lot like butterfly with the wings."

Tone nodded sagely. "I can see how that would work. So, shall we keep on stalling to piss him off, or shall we chat and see what he wants?"

"I guess we better talk to him." Making a show of shrugging, the hunter asked, "So Irkja, what's with stealing my friend? If you wanted to talk, we could have met someplace fun. I know where to find these really nice spirit spheres."

There was a prolonged silence that caused the comedy duo to glance at one another. A faint green glow appeared distantly in front of them. It began to grow in size and clarity until they saw what it was. There were lines appearing in the green. Both of them understood. They didn't need to put Irkja in a spirit sphere. He had already dropped them in one. It was a big one too!

As the green grew in brightness, Zeke and Tone moved toward the wall where the glow was brightest. By the time they made the trip across the sphere, the wall had become transparent showing a floating Irkja smiling at them.

"I find this much more relaxing than our last encounter. So Tone, how are you doing? I understand you are autistic on Earth. That explains a great deal. I'm curious, how much of each place do you remember? I'm sure you can't possibly recall all the events that happen here? Or is it that you can remember, but can't articulate it?" Irkja was full of questions.

"Well, Irky, it's like this. I remember most of my Earthly life here and almost none of my fun in the Spiritscape there. I think I did have a dream about the party we had after we kicked Bubba's ass. That whole naked olive oil slide thing with Arino was really hard to forget," taunted Tone. "So sorry you missed it. It was a mind scrambler. And I did not know Michael could sing Cole Porter with the karaoke machine. That was a mind scrambler, too, but not in a good way."

Zeke looked at his friend. "There are times when we need to be serious, Tone. I do agree this is not one of them." He turned toward their captor. "Unless you are going to answer as many questions as you ask."

Irkja looked from one to the other. He asked them both a pointed question. "Why is it that demons are tortured in there when they lie in a spirit sphere, but Tone can say anything he wishes without any consequences?"

That was something neither of them had ever considered. One of the purposes of a spirit sphere is to keep the one inside honest. It was one of the few times when a demon's words could be verified as true. Any lies resulted in the lines running along the outside of the sphere sending pure sheets of power cutting into anything inside like an appalling magic trick gone wrong. Tone had jested and joked inside of these devices and never been hurt.

"Secret power?" asked Zeke, only halfway joking.

"I'm just an honest soul. Deceit is not in my nature. Being so pure can be a hell of a burden," replied Tone. His answer was a message to Zeke that he hoped would not be received by the green ghoul outside. Tone had no idea.

"No. That can't be it," said Irkja, also only halfway joking. "I think you, Tone, are going to be a crucial part of my plan. There is something about you that is unique. It's a shame I can't examine your body on Earth without that lout Garrol causing me problems."

Zeke glowed with righteous indignation. "I'll let you in on a little secret. Garrol is not alone. Since we discovered you were alive, I made extra sure Tone would be safe."

"You did that for me?" asked Tone, pretending to be flattered. "I didn't know you cared. That really moves me and not in the bowel kind of way. You know I hate it when you make me get emotional in front of the bad guy. It's so embarrassing."

"Sorry about that, buddy." Deciding on a new tactic, Ezekiel asked his former teammate, "Irkja, what are you trying to do? Maybe we can help. You know Tone and I don't play by the rules all the time. What do you want with all the spirits you have taken? Are they at least still alive?"

Shaking his head, Irkja looked solemn. "Ezekiel, I know I have changed, but I am not Bubba. None of the spirits that are in my care have been harmed much. I promise you that the angels that are with me will never be harmed by my hand. What I am doing will help all of them."

"And the demons?" asked Zeke. "What about them? Don't get me wrong, I have no problem with knocking them around a little…"

"Or a lot," added Tone.

"Or a lot," agreed Zeke. "But what are you planning on doing with them? Even I draw the line at destroying them." He was trying to keep their jailer talking to discover more of this mysterious plan.

Irkja laughed cruelly. "Destroy them? Zeke, you are an amazing hunter and warrior, but you have no vision. Have none of you found the connection, yet? Not even Vret?" Looking at them, he could see she had not detected his plan. "That is priceless. I would explain it to you, but I don't want to interfere in your quest for knowledge. Besides, only an idiot explains his plan to someone who can stop him."

"Not even if we say pretty please?" asked Tone.

"Well since you asked so nicely," Irkja pretended to consider the request. "No."

The human stage whispered to Zeke, "It was worth a shot."

Zeke whispered back, "No it wasn't." To Irkja he continued, "You still haven't given me a straight answer about Tone. Why did you try to kidnap him? There is something going on that you're not saying."

"I promised to not hurt any angels, Zeke. Isn't that enough?" asked the green spirit.

"Not hurt angels? You will hurt demons." The glow of Zeke's spirit became pale as he made the connection. "You will not!"

"Zeke, sometimes sacrifices need to be made for the greater good. I promise he will not be killed, but I need some of that unusual power. Please know that I take no pleasure in this. You will understand when all this is done. I know you won't thank me, but you will understand." Irkja turned to Tone. "I'm sorry, Tone."

"Hold your horses, Irky. What do you mean some of my unusual power? I am kind of attached to my power." Tone was getting scared. "You do remember I'm armed, dangerous and flatulent, right?"

"I will only take what I need, Tone. Relax, I'll make it as painless as possible. I'll be back once everything is ready." Irkja looked at the two within the sphere with genuine sadness.

"If you touch him, I'll…" began Zeke, only to be left in the dark as the window Irkja was using disappeared.

Tone lit up the area with his glowing dagger. "That could have gone better."

Zeke began flying around the perimeter of the sphere. "We need to get an idea of how big this thing is. It's the same size as the sphere at J'fanasd. If that is where we are, I can get us away from here once we can find a way out." The warrior glided up to Tone, smiling, "Fortunately, Irkja doesn't know I am in here with the only spirit to ever escape from a spirit sphere."

Tone had managed to cut his way out of a spirit sphere when Bubba had dropped one on him prior to their last battle. There were many things that the human could do that were beyond angels, demons and whatever Irkja had become. Fortunately, Michael had decided the information about Tone's escapology was to be kept among a select few. As long as Irkja was not getting information from an archangel or one of the three who had witnessed his escape, their absence should be a surprise to him when he returned.

Tone considered the idea. "Listen, I'm all for getting away from here and spending time on a Caribbean beach with babes who like autistic guys putting suntan oil all over them, but you may be overestimating me. That sphere was only half there. The other half was on a different level or in Cleveland or something like that. This one looks pretty damn solid."

"Then you better get busy cutting while I prepare a portal. All I need is for you to break the surface and that will be enough to use to get out." Zeke began making a portal.

"Start cutting? Sure. Why not? Nothing better to do." The H'tes had never left his hand. Tone moved to the far side of the sphere and began slashing and stabbing. "Cut, Tone. Sure, I'll cut," muttered the hacking human. "Why do they always come after me? It's not like I'm that irresistible. Well, I am, but still..." His blade stuck and he tried to work it deeper into the wall. "Can't just one of these things just ask for a damn..." he grunted, "...autograph?"

Zeke moved the useless portal so that Tone was between it and the wall, shielding him from most views. "You may want to work a little faster, Tone." There was urgency in the angel's voice.

"I'm going as fast as I can. Do you want to do this?" asked an irritated Tone. "It's not like this is like slicing butter."

"Okay, but I can see a green glow from the far side of the sphere. Irky is coming back."

There was urgency in Tone's voice. "Shut up. I'm trying to work on this butter."

Zeke moved to the wall where the green glow had grown into the form of Irkja. The powerless portal was placed to perfectly hide Tone's activities. The angel only hoped that Irkja couldn't foresee things through the sphere.

"Did you really think I wouldn't see you making a portal? Zeke, it won't work. You wasted energy that you are going to need. I brought you some playmates." Behind his former friend, Zeke could see another spirit sphere with several demons raging at the windows.

"Any time now, Tone," called Zeke. "We are about to have company of the blue biting variety."

"The butter is almost ready," came the voice from behind the portal. "Serve them the stuffed mushrooms first. I made them with psychedelic shrooms. It should make them see the walls melt. Watch out," he grunted, "that they don't try to eat your face. That whole," grunting again, "incident where Claudia Green thought my face was a cheeseburger still gives me nightmares."

Irkja was suspicious. "Where is Tone? What is he doing?" He pulled the demon-filled sphere up to the window by Zeke. "I'll know soon enough. Have some toys, boys." The walls began to merge into one another.

"Now!" yelled Tone. The portal glowed as Zeke flew toward it. The door was thrown open as Tone ducked through with Zeke turning to wave to a screaming Irkja and a five raging demons. He closed the door and dissolved the portal on the other side.

"Hey, Zeke? We need to talk about your sense of direction and the phrase: out of the frying pan…" Tone said as he looked at the drooling demons around them.

# Chapter 20

"…and into the fire!" yelled Zeke, sending angelic flames every direction as Tone disappeared from view. "Stay close, bud." A score of demons scattered at the surprise attack by the warrior known as Demonbane. These demons were no more hideous than the others that Tone had seen; however, there were a hell of a lot of them. The majority of these looked like the results of a bad marriage between a warthog and a ballerina. Ugly, piggish faces and portly bodies on tiny pointed legs were everywhere with an imp and a misty blue spirit mixed in. There was also an eel-like demon with a humanoid head that was melting in on itself.

As soon as Zeke sent out a silent call, Michael appeared at the hunter's side. "Tone, Michael needs to be able to see you," shouted the hunter as he dispatched another demon into the rip he had created to Hell. Tone appeared on the far side of Zeke, safely out of Michael's way. Zeke turned, totally covering Tone with his own spirit. With Tone safely out of the way, Michael created an explosion of colorful power, sending the demons scampering and skittering away. Some fled right into a rip that opened like a toothy maw, flinging themselves into Hell. Michael completed the cleanup process as more warriors appeared to chase down the fleeing demons.

"I'm glad you are both all right. Where have you been? We were afraid Irkja had done something terrible to you." Michael looked strangely worried considering they had not been gone that long.

"It was so cool, Mike," said Tone. "You should have seen it. There was this thing that looked like some really bad modern art of a horseshoe embedded in haggis surrounded by garden gnomes peeing. Irky was going to make us write positive reviews for the Psychotic Fall Angel Review. You would have been proud of Zeke.

He wouldn't give it above a three-star rating no matter how much cooked cauliflower Irk made him eat." Tone looked at his friend with insincere admiration. "It was inspiring," he sighed.

The archangel shook his and looked at the hunter. "What really happened?"

Zeke had a question before he answered. "I know that look. How long were we gone, Michael? It was less than a quarter of a quoll for us."

Michael looked incredulous. "A quarter quoll? Zeke, no one has seen either of you for one hundred and three quolls!" Zeke's expression mirrored Michael's. "The only way we knew Tone was still alive is his body has rocked a few times while you were gone. I hoped you were still with us. Zeke, we looked everywhere for you."

Arino appeared beside Zeke. She wrapped herself around him. "I thought Irkja had destroyed you," she whispered, barely able to communicate. As their bodies merged, Arino's eyes opened wide. "That's not possible," she gasped.

"I'm afraid it is," replied Zeke, sharing the experience with Michael as well.

"As usual, the human is lost," complained Tone. "We were gone a hundred quolls? That is longer than it takes for Mike to make a funny joke. Is this one of those thing-a-ma-jigs where the doohickey and the what-ya-ma-call-it get mixed up and the gizmo…?"

Zeke interrupted. "We were in a different thought stream. Apparently Irkja can slow us down now."

Tone pouted. "My description was funnier."

The *Hajile-R* came roaring to a stop. "You two had me worried," said Naz as he ported from the control seat to his friends. He gave Tone a careful hug. Looking at Zeke, he linked with the hunter and instantly went pale. "How can Irkja do that?"

Creating a portal for Tone, Michael ended the debate. "We need to move this conversation someplace more secure. Several things happened while you were gone, but this is not the place.

Nazilaq, please take the *Hajile-R* to Stikes. Tone and Zeke will meet you there." The archangel opened the portal and led the way.

Tone entered a room that he had seen once before. It was a large golden globe. He and his friends were right in the middle. It was his second trip to the Council of the Archangels. Unlike the previous visit, he was not contained in a spirit sphere and he could see all nine of the present archangels. Around the room each angel had a position equidistant from each other. Tone hated to admit it, but he was impressed at the splendor.

Michael moved to his place directly in front of them and called the Council to order. "We all know what has happened, but it is necessary to bring Tone up to date. In the one hundred and three quolls you were missing, Irkja has been busy. An inventory was taken of Adoneal's workshop. Three fixed portals are missing. Additionally, enough skimmer parts are unaccounted for to produce an entire skimmer, provided one knows how to fuse them the correct ways. In addition to Torkel, eleven other angels who worked under Adoneal have gone missing."

Tone raised his hand and then spoke without waiting for the teacher to call on him. "That seems like a lot of stuff. Does anyone know how he got all that shit? And how is he angelnapping your people? Don't you have some kind of security system? Guards? Hell, even a yapping Pekinese is better than nothing. Well, not much better; but at least Irkja might trip over it if it was dark."

It was uncomfortably quiet in the spherical room. Tone looked at his friends, picking up on the problem, asked, "You don't know if your missing angels were taken or went willingly, right? Going on their own is more badder than being grabbed in a drive-by. Yeah. That would be worse than my underwear after fighting Bubba."

Tone spun to face an angel that had no clear form. Halalio was the archangel of miracles. "Your analogy, though crude, is apt. We have no way of knowing if there is a fifth column of angels who are planning a rebellion with Irkja as leader. It is also not apparent what role Adoneal is playing." The misty form of the angel glowed with a shade that was able to convey both concern and fear. Tone was impressed it could do that with so little substance.

"Don't you guys all have that psychic link thing? Can't you just scan everyone's mind and find out?" asked Tone.

A battle scarred angel spoke, causing the human to spin to face him. Nasarg answered, "It is not quite that simple, Anthony. Any angel can hold things back from the others if they so choose. We do it all the time if there is something that needs to be kept confidential. For example, if there was a human who could cut his way out of a spirit sphere, that is not something that all angels need to know. That confidentiality saved you from a rather unpleasant fate."

Uriel explained. "It is against the nature of angels to hide information from one another – unlike thy kind, who continually uses deception and subterfuge to accomplish goals."

"Point taken," agreed Tone, who had been flipped upside down with Uriel's words. "A little insulting, but I'm not going to take that personally." He winked at Uriel. "Archies, since I'm not on trial here, can we stop with the spinning? I just saw some very ugly demons and feel a little pukey already. It would be a shame to hurl all over your pretty gold room here."

The voice of Raphael floated around Tone. "Our apologies, Tone. I hope you feel better now."

Tone went limp. "Thanks Raphael. Have I ever told you that you're my favorite archangel?" he asked dreamily. "We need to hang out more often. When can you come over and see my books. I have lots of books. You're such a nice archangel." The glazed gaze of Tone stared at the archangel of healing.

Gabriel joined the conversation. "Did you really have to do that, Raphael? He's bad enough with what few inhibitions he has normally." Several angels chuckled at the comment.

"Marshmallows!" shouted Tone.

Michael sighed. "We need to figure out what to…"

"More marshmallows!" bellowed Tone. He began spinning in every direction, looking at all the archangels. "I love the paths they leave. Nice creamy marshmallows."

Michael continued, "… do about this situation. Is there a way…"

Tone approached Iofiup – the tiny archangel of the cherubs – saying, "Did you know that different marshmallows have different trails? I like them."

Zeke and Arino grabbed their friend and began pulling him away from Iofiup. "It is the effect of Raphael," explained the healer.

"No," stated the cherub. "Something else. Speak, Anthony."

Every angel in the room was shocked. Cherubs hate noise. Voices are uncomfortable for them to hear. It was rare they placed themselves in situations where they could be in contact with vocalizations of any being. For Iofiup to listen to Tone was unusual. Iofiup speaking and encouraging Tone to speak more was unprecedented.

Giggling, Tone continued. "You look like a marshmallow with itty bitty wings. You have… can I have a chili dog? I promise not to spill it and I'll try not to fart." The human began looking toward Samael, the archangel of death. "He looks so nice."

Iofiup moved quickly into Tone's field of vision. "Focus Tone. Marshmallow trails?" Cherubs were well known for their formal speech patterns. For Iofiup to speak to a human in such a common way spoke to the severity of situation.

"Hmm? Oh, your marshmallow looks different than his." Tone was looking past the cherub to the angel of death. "His has more lumps. You have the cutest little trail. It has wing prints." Tone was batting the air at the trail only he could see. He broke down giggling as Iofiup looked to Vret.

"Brilliant!" declared the archangel of wisdom. They had all deciphered Tone's ramblings in the same instant. Tone might be able to track at least some of the missing angels. If they went willingly, the trails may give some indication. "Now if we can just keep

Raphael from saying anything for a while, we may be able to get some work out of Tone." All of the angels in the room snickered. There was a forced quality to it that was not lost on Zeke.

As the discussion took place, Michael made preparations for the next step of the investigation. A portal appeared next to Zeke, Arino and Tone. "Zeke, I want you three to go to the workshop and see what Tone can detect in the area where the fixed portals disappeared, then try the places where we lost angels. I really need to know if they went willingly."

"Is there anything else?" asked Zeke, suspecting there was another issue on the agenda of the Council. The hunter looked from Michael to each of the other eight in turn. None of them looked away, but none of them offered any information.

"Not at this time," said Michael. The lingering sense that something would soon happen weighed heavily between mentor and student. The portal opened as Arino and Zeke escorted the still high Tone out of the Council.

As the portal faded, Vret asked Michael, "Do you think Zeke knows?"

There was a sagely sadness in the essence of the head of the archangels. "He knows something is happening to him. He would have said something if he knew what."

"Are you certain?" asked the beautiful Samael. The angel of death was not certain at all.

Michael was resolute. "I know Zeke. He will do the right thing."

Gabriel added, "I hope you are right, Michael. You are placing more on him than any other angel."

"He will not let me down," said Michael.

# Chapter 21

"Something is wrong here," said Tone. "There are way too many trails to tell one from the other. Was there an angel rave here that I missed?" He continued looking around but raised his hands in frustration, the hue of his spirit glowing crimson. "Next time you have a party, do it somewhere else."

Arino comforted her friend. "Easy there, Tone. What do you need to sort this out?" It was unusual for the human to get frustrated so quickly.

"Are you all right, buddy?" asked Zeke. He noticed the unusual reaction, too.

"Yeah. Just feeling the pressure. Plus, the pudding content in my blood is getting low and that makes me cranky." Anthony continued to move around the room. He examined the unorthodox workstation of the eccentric archangel. There was a notable absence of tools of any kind. The center of the oblong room was totally barren of anything. Tone had an image of Adoneal using that space to create items he would use out of nothingness.

All along the edges were parts and pieces of various devices. Along one wall were sheets of a blue substance that Tone could imagine being fashioned into the base of a spirit sphere. Beside the sheet were hundreds of thousands of runes floating in the ether. These golden symbols would be placed on the blue material to make the spirit sphere work.

There was a space along the far side of the room that had parts that could be used on a skimmer. Several places had spots that looked bare next to the places that had countless odds and ends. Tone looked around the area, but gave up quickly once he discovered that too many trails had already been all over, looking for the missing parts.

Another wall contained crystals of all shapes, sizes and colors. Some looked to be half finished projects that may now never be completed. Tone approached one that looked like a blue crystal bust of a demon. It was hollow on the inside with enough room for an angel to place a head within.

Tone motioned to the disfigured mask. "Do you have Mardi Gras parties? I bed Arino gets the most beads, right?"

Zeke took the mask from its resting place. "I have no idea what this is." He placed it on his head, causing both Arino and Tone to back away.

"Zeke?" squeaked Tone. "Are you in there, amigo?"

"Of course I am," growled the hunter. "Was that my voice?" The thing that was Zeke appeared grotesque. A blue demon disguise had covered Zeke's body as soon as he placed the mask on his head. It had the blue fur of so many of the demons, but the body of three snakes. The serpent bodies joined together at a head with the mouth of a wolf, the snout of bulldog, and eight ears at odd angles that looked human. It was the eyes that truly terrified. The blood red eyes had black iris slits that went horizontal from the top by the nose to the bottom corners.

Arino linked in with Zeke so he could see how he appeared. "Okay, that is disgusting," said the angel, removing the mask and returning to his normal form. He checked in with the other angels. "No one in the link knows what that was for."

"Can I try it on now?" asked Tone, bouncing up and down like a puppy. "I'll be good. I promise not to stay up past my bedtime for a month. Pretty please?" He gave them both his best sad-eyed expression.

Arino was cautious. "Tone, it may not be made for you. It might not work. Or it may work too well."

Tone stopped bouncing. "Too well? Like my face would stay like that? I thought Mom was lying when she said that could happen."

"I think we should wait until Adoneal is back." Zeke returned the mask back to its place. He tried to decipher what Tone was thinking. He had a bad feeling the human would try to get at the mask regardless of the risks.

"Can we let Arino try it on? Will you use it babe?" asked Tone, regaining some of his enthusiasm.

Arino was less excited. "I don't know, Tone. It seems dangerous to me. There is something strange about that mask…" She looked it over carefully before placing it on her head. "Well, how do I look?"

"Um…" began Tone. "Well, I don't know how to tell you this. You look like yourself with a crystal demon mask on your head. It didn't work on you. But you still look great."

Zeke was confused. "Why did it work on me and not on you? That's very strange. It must be made for warriors. Maybe it is used for infiltration. The imps sneak around us enough that Adoneal must have made this so we could walk freely around them." Zeke sounded like he was trying to convince himself of that.

"It kind of makes you want to see what it would look like on…" Tone paused, pretending to think. "Oh, I don't know… maybe one of the cherubs or a messenger or... it's too bad we don't have any humans to try it on." He moved toward Arino, arms held out to take the mask.

"No," said both angels together. Tone looked genuinely surprised. He backed off, examining his companions carefully.

"What is it? You two know something. Spill it. If it will make me look like a demon, that's okay. It'd be cool to see if I look like the demon version of Zeke, but with more boogers. You're worried I will be one of the blue mists, aren't you. I might just be an imp with a third leg, if you get my meaning." He glowed salaciously.

Arino spoke. "It affected us differently, Tone. There is no telling what it will do to you. I'm sorry but I am exercising my prerogative as a level two healer. There is something dangerous about this." Arino created a large crystal box from nothing and placed the mask within. Sealing it, she said, "Off limits to both of you. End of discussion unless you want to appeal to Raphael." She was adamant. Tone had never seen Arino like this.

"Zeke, do you find her as hot as I do when she gets all authoritative-like? Sweetie, that was sexy!" Tone knew the debate was over so he tried to change the discussion.

"Yes, she is attractive when she does that," agreed Zeke. Arino looked at Zeke, amazed that he would say something like that. "Well, it's true," defended the hunter.

If Arino could have blushed she would have. "You have never communicated that kind of sentiment, Zeke. It felt good. Out of character, but good." She reached out to touch her friend. Their hands merged as they shared the essence that allowed them to connect more intensely than a simple link. Tone felt like a voyeur whenever they did that.

"Excuse me. Human here. We need to figure out what's happening with the trails."

"Sorry Tone. We got caught up in the instance. Can you tell the trails apart?" asked Zeke. Tone sensed that he had formulated a plan.

"For the most part. Adoneal's is easy. I see his all over the place. All the others are similar, but not totally identical," explained Tone. "What are you thinking? I can't tell you who belongs to which one. Just that different ones are doing different things. And they do get mixed, mingled and mangled."

Arino caught on. "But if we can take Tone where we know one of the missing angels has been, then he can see their trails."

Tone moved over to a rack along the wall where seven of the fixed portals were hanging. "Hey, there are several trails here, but the same trail is in all three empty places. It looks familiar. Have I met any of the missing angels?"

"I don't think so. You could have seen their trails in the hanger, though. They all worked in or around there." Zeke was confused. "Were you tracking in the hanger?"

"Not on purpose. Sometimes I see the trails without trying. I just ignore them and turn it off. The hanger might be it…" Tone didn't seem convinced. He kept looking at the trail like he should know it. "I have it memorized. I'll know it again if I see it."

"Let's go check the last places any of our missing comrades were seen," said Arino. She went to a wall and took Tone's arm as they passed through it and into another space adjacent to the workshop. "Six of the nine missing angels worked in here."

The area was huge, Angels were working all around. Tone placed himself between his friends to protect himself and the angels around him from the dangers of being near an exploding human. All the angels were always linked together allowing them to work as one. Zeke joined their link to warn them of Tone's presence and to gain information on the missing angels.

One of the workers stopped what it was doing and approached the threesome. "Good quoll to you. Anthony, I am Tepsam. It will be my pleasure to show you to the workstations of our missing friends."

"Nice to meet you Tipsy." Tone turned to Arino and stage whispered, "I love the names of these guys. It's not even a challenge to make a joke."

Their guide laughed. "I have heard about Tone's tone of voice. This will be fun."

"Another angel who recognizes quality entertainment! Who says angels have no sense of humor?" asked Tone. Three angels nearby raised their hands in response. The human shook his head. "No. Too easy." Calling out to the hand raisers, "It was rhetorical."

Tepsam led the trio to a work station. "This is where Tam'niq worked."

Tone gave the trail careful consideration. Looking all over the table with crystals that were in different stages of completion, he came to a conclusion. "This trail was in the workshop, but it isn't the one that was by all three of the fixed portals. Next."

Tepsam led them to the other five workstations with the same results. All of them had been in the workshop, but none of them were by all three of the portals recently. Their guide bid them goodbye and went back to work.

"Am I the only one who wants to sing a work song for these guys?" asked Tone. "Ninety-nine bottles of beer on the wall. Ninety-nine bottles of beer. Take one down. Pass it around. Ninety-eight bottle of beer. Everybody!" Tone motioned for the angels to join him. "Ninety-eight bottle of beer on the wall…" No one joined in. Several looked at him, chuckling. A few gave him exasperated, but amused, looks. Most just ignored him entirely. "Okay. See if I help you again."

"That had to sting," joked Zeke. "I'm sure they don't know how they will get along without you."

Arino laughed. "The other three worked in the skimmer hanger." Taking Tone's hand again, she moved through several walls as they passed through other shops to get to the hanger. All the skimmers were still out looking for the missing angels, leaving only a skeleton crew behind. They easily found the spots where the three worked.

After each trail was examined and each trail was dismissed. Zeke and Tone were frustrated with the lack of progress. Arino, always finding the bright side, pointed out the positive. "We have eliminated nine possibilities. We are making progress. At least we can tell Michael that none of the missing workers were responsible for the theft of the fixed gates."

"You're right, as always," agreed Zeke. "We should go and meet up with Naz. Michael wants us to check out Stikes and see if we can find anything there."

"Can we use the big-ass skimmer portals?" begged Tone. "They look so cool and I want to show up so I can see Naz's face when we stroll in, arm in arm, singing 'Follow the Amber Brick Road'." Laughing, Zeke started the portals sequence. The walls opened to show the portal glowing.

"Stop!" shouted Tone, flying through the inactive portal. He moved as fast as he could through the ether, coming to a sudden stop with both his friends right beside him. "This is the trail I saw!" The bloodhound-human followed the trail all over the hanger making turns and stops all over. He finally stopped at a work station not far from where he had first spotted the trail. "The trail is all over this place. Who is the asshole who worked here? This is the bastard who stole the portals!" Tone looked triumphantly at the angels.

The angels looked anything but triumphant. "Are you sure, Tone?" asked Arino, with a tremor in her voice. "You need to be positive."

"On a scale of one to ten, it's a fourteen and three-eighths," declared Tone. "What's wrong?"

Arino said, "Tone, that's Nazilaq's work station. This is where the *Hajile-R* docks." She looked shocked by the implication.

"I know Naz's trail. This isn't it. But I'm sure this is the trail."

"No doubt at all?" asked Zeke, sadly.

"None whatsoever." Tone was getting frustrated. "Who is it?"

"We helped him get the fixed portal back to Irkja," murmured Zeke. "This is the station for one other angel that works on the *Hajile-R*. It was Torkel."

# Chapter 22


Tone, Zeke and Arino had been joined by Michael, Vret and Gabriel in the vast empty hanger. As the human looked around, it felt bare, naked without all the activity he had seen previously. Tone wondered why there was no echo in there. Then he wondered if there was any real sound anywhere in the Spiritscape. Before he could ask, a portal opened and the *Hajile-R* came to rest at its dock. A dozen angels swarmed around it to verify it had not been sabotaged. Nazilaq was nowhere to be seen. As soon as the skimmer had arrived, he had been taken away by two archangels.

"Why would Torkel be helping Irkja? We are missing a piece to this puzzle. Ideas?" Michael looked around at the group assembled.

"I have no idea, but the one who would know the most is in a windowless room surrounded by bright lights with his feet in Thousand Island dressing and his arms tied up with red licorice ropes. Isn't that against the Geneva Convention?" Tone was not happy that his friend was being interrogated. "We need Naz in here to help us brainstorm."

Vret interceded. "Tone, he's not being interrogated. He went willingly with Samael and Nasarg so we can make sure he has not been influenced by Irkja. At this point, we don't really know who to trust."

Tone knew he was fighting a losing battle. "This is Nazilaq we're talking about. Think about it."

Michael's patience was reaching its limit. "Yes, Tone. Think about it. Naz rarely links with the other angels. He was Irkja's closest friend. Being a skimmer pilot puts him out in the Spiritscape alone most of the time. Are you telling me that doesn't make him susceptible to Irkja's influence?"

Tone stood his ground, trying to stare down all three archangels at once. "Well, sure. If you want to be logical. But since when do we work in logic around here?"

Zeke joined Tone's side. "If Naz was working with Irkja, don't you think we would have noticed? Tone can be annoying, but he can read us better than we can read each other. Add Arino and me to the mix and you have a team that knows one another."

Vret joined the debate. "Tone, he is not being punished. Nazilaq will be back with you as soon as possible. We also need to make sure that the *Hajile-R* is still safe. Torkel was very instrumental in the upgrades. If he had done something, then Irkja might be able to gain access to you. We don't want him to take you apart like he suggested. All of this is for your safety." She ignored Zeke's objections.

Arino watched her two friends closely as the archangels gave them time to absorb all that had been said. Tone moved in circles thinking, trying to come up with an effective argument. Zeke was frustrated as well, but kept his composure by brooding. Lately, it had been the angel who had been getting angry and the human had kept his cool. Arino wondered if there was a correlation. She sent a message to Raphael.

At last Tone asked, "Can I see Naz so I know he's ok? I promise not to sneak him a file hidden between the chocolate bars and the Uzi in his care package."

Before the question was complete, a trapezoid appeared beside Tone. The silver edged shape went from transparent to filled. Within was a view of Nazilaq, Samael, and Nasarg. Tone reached out and found there was a transparent barrier between the angels and him. He knocked and waved at Naz who smiled and waved back.

His voice came through crystal clear. "Hey Tone. I'm fine. Don't worry about me. I just have to go over a few things with the bosses." He winked at Tone. "I'll be back out there saving you in no time." With that, Tone saw him turn back to his interrogators as the picture and frame faded away.

"Satisfied?" asked Michael, knowing he was giving Tone a straight line he couldn't resist.

Tone folded his hands and placed his pointing index fingers on his chin, trying to look thoughtful. "That show needs more drama. No plot twists. Nothing to get you excited. They didn't even have a rubber hose to beat him with. Now if you want to go with intimidating, try that whole feet in Thousand Island dressing thing I mentioned. Very scary."

Gabriel chimed in. "He's satisfied." Suddenly the hanger was gone and they were all in a room that looked like a smaller version of the room for the Council of Archangels. "This part of our conversation needs some privacy."

"Dude, did you just port me? That was way too cool. I may start liking you if do cool shit like this all the time." Tone was impressed.

The archangel of the messengers smiled at Tone for the first time. "We are in the same spot. I just ported the sphere in. I have an issue with letting the service angels hear what I'm about to say."

"Agreed," said Vret. "Tone, as much as you can, please keep this between us."

"I'll try, but you know how I get after I have a few shots of Jennifer's Orgasms." Tone grinned. "I can be more chatty than usual."

Zeke looked at his friend. "First, chattier than usual is scary. Second, how often do you drink spiced rum and butterscotch schnapps in the Spiritscape?"

The human was impressed until he remembered who he was talking to. "Of course you know the drink. You know EVERYTHING." The sarcasm in his voice was not subtle in the least.

"Back to the topic," interrupted Michael.

Gabriel began. "All of the angels who are missing worked under Adoneal. They may or may not have gone willingly. It seems likely that Torkel is working with Irkja. It could be willingly or under some kind of duress."

"If you consider the loyalty the servants feel toward their archangel, then it wouldn't take much of a threat against Adoneal to get them to do virtually anything," agreed Zeke.

"Irkja wanted to toss me into the Fanjil River when I made some rude comments. And I was just joking," added Tone.

Vret was contemplating something. "I hate to even suggest this. What if Irkja is working under someone else's orders? When he was injured, who would he have tried to reach? A healer? Not Irkja. Not first anyway. Nazilaq? He had left and Irkja could have seen that as a betrayal. Would he not have reached out to the angel who could help him? Does anyone know where Adoneal was right after the Battle of the Beast?"

Gabriel was horrorstruck. "You cannot be serious. Adoneal is an archangel. He does not have the capacity to be deceitful. With Adoneal, what you see is what you get."

Michael spoke up. "As far as we know, what you see is what you get. None of us can link with him since the accident. Even I don't know what is happening inside of him. Gabriel, I don't want it to be true either, but I think we have to give this fair consideration."

"Wow!" said Tone. "Just, wow. Are you three always this paranoid? Or is this something new?" Then he added, "If we are going to talk about conspiracy theories, can we discuss who killed JFK?"

Zeke replied, "It was Oswald. The other five in the area were just backup in case he missed." Returning to the topic, he continued, "IF – and this is a very big if – Adoneal is a willing party to all of this, what do we do? Can we trust any angel who worked under him? Should we be having them crawling all over the *Hajile-R*? What if they are doing more harm than good?"

Michael replied, "The skimmer is being checked by ten service angels and then double checked by two warriors. I trust my warriors.

We cannot start pointing fingers at angels who have done nothing wrong. Well, nothing yet."

Gabriel stepped back into the conversation, "We need to check up on all of the service angels. Michael, I'll help with that if I can get Vret, Samael and Nasarg to help, we can check them all in two quolls."

"Do it." As the orb disappeared from around them, they were greeted by a familiar face. "Nazilaq, I'm glad that you are cleared."

The ever-jovial angel was nonplused by the situation. "If I had been you, I'd have wondered about me, too. I understand. But now, I'd like to find Adoneal if that's…" He stopped as Michael silently brought him up to speed. "You can't be serious. Adoneal was taken. We all saw it. I refuse to believe he is a part of all this." The pilot was more upset about the accusation against his archangel than being accused himself.

"We must consider everything," reassured Vret. "I feel certain you are right, but all options must be considered."

Naz was not to be dissuaded. "You can consider them. I'm ready to go out there and prove you wrong."

Michael was pleased. "That's the way I need you four to be. Get out there and find out what's going on." With a thought, orders were given to Zeke. The hunter and archangel seemed to stare at each other, silently communicating, for longer than necessary to just receive orders. When they finally broke contact, Michael was gone.

"Care to share with the class?" asked Tone. "That looked as intense as I do when I'm making my world famous cherry chocolate chipotle chimichangas. It also looked as scary as I do in the bathroom after eating my world famous cherry chocolate chipotle chimichangas."

"Once again I'm glad I don't have a digestive system," chucked Ezekiel. "I'll tell you about the debate later. Right now we need to head to Eqemp. Ready for more Gray?"

Nazilaq ported to his command sheath in the skimmer while the other three moved to their sheaths for Tone's sake. Once inside, the skimmer portal activated as the *Hajile-R* moved slowly through, coming out in another area that Tone had never seen. This part of the Spiritscape was devoid of the usual mountains and valley going at odd angles. This was somewhat round, but far from smooth. It more closely resemble a purple asteroid than anything Tone could think of to describe it. The closer he looked the more he saw a symmetry to the bumpy planet. It was made up of more than two dozen diamond shaped sections.

"Are we ever going to go someplace I recognize?" asked Tone, pseudo-frustration in his voice.

"We went back to the Spires," replied Arino, smiling.

"Let me rephrase the question," retorted Tone. "Are we ever going to go someplace I recognize that doesn't scare the hell out of me?"

"I doubt it," replied Zeke. "You scare pretty easily."

The Eqemp was huge. Tone had not realized how far they had been when he first saw it. Even flying at the speeds of the skimmer, the Eqemp grew slowly until they were skimming along its surface. Each of the elongated diamond-shaped sections would be big enough to hold a hundred skimmers and still have room left.

"This thing is big. I mean really big. I'm talking really big-ass big!" said Tone, trying to convey his astonishment.

Naz joked. "I think Tone thinks this thing is big."

"I'm not sure," teased Zeke.

"Tone, dear," began Arino. "The Eqemp has 59 of these flat places surrounding it. It is the biggest structure that has been made by the angels in the Spiritscape. It is the most," she paused as if choosing her words carefully, "secure location we have."

Tone did not like the sound of that. "By secure, you mean…?" he let the question float in the ether.

"It is where we take anything dangerous," said Zeke bluntly. "Think of it as a high security lab."

"More dangerous than the things that are out here?" asked an incredulous Anthony. "Let me get this straight. You have rivers of energy with bits and pieces of spirits floating around. You have a junk yard full of living crystals beating the hell out of each other. You have lakes with both of those things floating in them. Plus, you have demons and unicorns running around. And THIS is where you put the really dangerous things? Did I miss anything?"

Arino laughed. "That about sums it up. You did forget the spiritual animals in the Uqump though."

Naz came to his rescue. "Our definition of dangerous is a little different than yours, Tone." The human could see an opening appearing in the Eqemp coming up over the horizon. "There are a few things in there than can harm a spirit, but most things in here can warp your mind."

"As if he needed to be any more warped," joked Zeke. "Relax, Tone, the place is perfectly safe."

At those words, a flock of angels came flying out of the opening, pursued by an enormous charcoal black beast with wings that pushed the ether. A group of angels turned to fight, only to be captured in an indigo mist than came from the mouth of the dragon.

# Chapter 23

"How did the dragon get out?" screamed Nazilaq, transforming the skimmer into battle mode.

"Holy shit!" yelled Tone. "A dragon? A real dragon?" His excitement was mirrored by the angels within the vessel. He looked at Zeke and Arino who had both transformed, ready to fight or heal.

They ported together to a spot near the angels who had been caught in the blast. The dragon turned its massive, horned head toward Zeke as Arino moved to care for the injured. The warrior sent out a wave of energy that hit the breast of the beast, causing it to roar in agony. A sweep of an icy wing was dodged as the angel flew back, flipping in the ether while sending a rain of angel fire down in the back of the blue skinned behemoth. Fire flew from the *Hajile-R,* enveloping the dragon in flames.

"What is everyone doing?" asked the human, looking around.

A confused Nazilaq replied, "Fighting the dragon. What do you think we are doing?"

"Playing charades? Working on a really lame mime act? Shooting at nothing? Putting on the worst revival of *Singing the Rain* I've ever seen?" Tone was equally confused.

The angel was shocked. "Wait. You can't see Dracomil? It's right in front of us."

"I see Zeke acting like he's in *Lord of the Rings* before they do the special effects. You are sending blasts of some kind of fire at the same imaginary critter. Arino is trying to help several angels who are shaking like they are coming down off a bad acid trip." Tone considered that for a moment. "Maybe you are all on the same acid trip. I wish I could see what you are seeing. Does it have tambourines and elephants?"

Naz brought the skimmer to a dead stop, still keeping the spikes and weapons powered. "Do you see a small demon around here anywhere? It would look like a blue ball with a face."

The human laughed. "You said 'blue ball'. I'll never get tired of angels saying silly shit. Wait 'til I get Gabe to say 'douche'."

"Hilarious," droned Naz. Tone's timing left much to be desired. "Now about the demon?"

Tone looked around. "That's weird. There is a tiny trail by the entrance moving away from the action. Nothing seems to be making it. That may be Blue Balls."

In front of his sheath, two crystal levers appeared as a set of crosshairs split the wall of the skimmer. Naz smiled. "Tone, if you would be so kind as to aim the weapons at that trail. Just get close and I'll make sure there is a wide enough attack to get it."

"I get to shoot the guns? Too cool!" Tone began moving the levers at random, causing the *Hajile-R* to bounce like a bull being ridden by a mountain lion. "This thing is hard to steer, amigo."

"Gentle movements, Tone. It takes a light touch."

Slowing down, the jerking movements of the skimmer seemed more like a vessel-wide seizure. After several tries, Tone said, "I led the trail a little. It should be right there."

No sooner had the words left his mouth than six fireballs leapt from the spikes of the skimmer and blazed toward the target, erupting all around the area. A screech of agony was felt more than heard by the angels. The dragon disappeared as a seared demon faded into view. Zeke stopped his attack on the illusory dragon, flying at top speed to capture the blue-ball of a demon.

Looking at the skimmer, the hunter saluted, declaring, "I hate it when this thing gets loose. Hello, Fantazmil. You look a little worse for the wear."

The demon squeaked, "I've been better, hunter. Tell the skimmer I owe him for this. How did that bastard find me?"

Zeke blasted the demon with angel fire, causing it to screech again. Tone saw the skimmer glow brightly with the same kind of fire, ready to send more fireballs at the demon.

"I'm guessing that questioning your parentage tends to piss you off? Mental note: don't tell angels they don't have a daddy." Tone's efforts to lighten the mood failed.

Naz explained. "The little blue beach ball of a demon is one of the three most dangerous demons in all the realms. He has phased more angels than any other single demon." It looked to Tone like the glare of Nazilaq was shooting daggers, swords and chainsaws, too.

Tone looked at the demon and back at Naz. It was rare to see the pilot angry, Tone surmised there was a story behind the venom. "So Naz, what did he do to make you look like a recently circumcised Brahma bull at a Hasidic rabbi convention?"

"He destroyed the *Hajile-J*," replied Naz flatly. "Well, he tricked me into destroying it by flying it into a crystalline volcano. Long story. Let's just say, we have issues."

Tone stared at his friend. "There is so much you just said that sends up the 'what the hell?' flags."

Naz finally smiled. "Another time."

Zeke was holding the squirming demon by the ears as other angels came shooting out of the opening of the Eqemp with a small spirit sphere. The lead angel spotted the hunter right away and changed his flight to stop beside him.

"Thank you, Ezekiel. I was afraid it got away. After the last time…" the angel began.

Zeke cut him off. "Don't worry about it, P'talgid. I'm just glad we were passing by. You really should be thanking Nazilaq. He's the one who fireballed the blue ball." The skimmer came to a stop beside the angels.

"Thank Tone. He's the one who spotted the trail," said Naz. "Plus, he didn't even see the illusion."

P'talgid ported inside the skimmer next to Tone, startling him. "Hello Anthony. I'm P'talgid, one of Vret's researchers and chief of security in Eqemp. I have to say it is an unexpected pleasure to make your acquaintance." He held out his hand to shake Tone's.

The human looked out at Zeke. "Does he know about the boom issue?" Zeke smiled and nodded. Cautiously taking the offered hand, Tone replied, "Hey Spit-Tal. Nice to meet you. You are more forward than most angels. Kind of in an invading my space way. I like it. By the way, it won't work."

P'talgid smiled at Anthony. "What won't work?" he asked knowingly.

"You're trying to read me with the handshake thing. You'll get more from me with a chocolate milkshake. No one reads me. Sorry, dude. Nice try."

"You can't blame me for trying." Turning to Nazilaq, the angel asked, "Are you bringing the *Hajile-R* inside?" A nod from Naz and the opening of the door was all the invitation the angels guarding the sphere needed. The tiny spirit sphere containing the oddest looking demon Tone had yet seen was moved to a position far from the human. The last thing Tone saw before the walls of the spirit sphere went opaque was the blue face of Fantazmil peering straight at him. It made Tone shudder.

Naz spoke, "Stand by for a trip through the Gray." The skimmer was positioned over the opening which led to a wall of Gray.

"Again?" asked an exasperated Tone. "I hate this stuff."

Arino had brought the injured angels into the skimmer for the trip. "Trust me, Tone. It's even worse for us. It saps our warmth." She had just placed the last injured angel in a sheath. To Tone, it looked like she was doing more than protecting them. Those sheaths seemed like they were more cocoons than just places to ride through the Gray. Arino saw his curiosity and explained. "Fantazmil can get inside the minds of angels and make them see things that aren't there."

"Like the dragon?" asked Tone, proud that he had made the connection.

"Good example. But that was just a superficial illusion. When it really gets into an angel, they are convinced that Fantazmil is anything but a demon. An angel got too close and let the demon out. I just want to keep these five safe from any more illusions, hence the cocoons."

Tone looked them over. "It's that one," he said, pointing to a slender angel in the middle. "I can see it in her essence. She thinks the blue ball is a trapped human baby."

P'talgid joined the conversation. "That explains a great deal. Thank you, Anthony. We will get her fixed up in no time. Arino, can you help once we get back inside?"

The smiling healer beamed. "Of course, P'talgid. You know I'm here to help."

"Entering the Gray," declared Nazilaq. The skimmer had slowed for the transition. At that instant the skimmer entered the Gray, the cocoon containing the tainted angel exploded out, as the angel made a dash for the spirit sphere.

Shards of crystal cocoon floated around the *Hajile-R* while Tone watched in horror as everything was enveloped in the Gray. His H'tes swinging into his hand, Tone moved to block all the pieces of crystal that came his way. It was not difficult to block the slow moving shards, but that was not his real concern. Once in the Gray, the angel trying to get to Fantazmil would be slowed substantially; but it would still be ahead of any other angel when they made it through.

The last trips through the Gray had been so strange, Tone had been too frightened to move. This time, he knew he had to try something. His arms moved to free himself from his sheath, feeling like they were moving through a non-Newtonian substance. Tone had read about the corn starch and water combination that created a material that increased the viscosity with increased pressure or stress. He had even watched several internet videos as people ran or sank into the semi-solid material. The Gray seemed to work in the same way for the Spiritscape. He tried moving with less force and found it made no difference. *So much for that idea.*

Looking through the Gray haze around him, something caught his eye. It was a sparkling crystal blade right beside him that had golden flames with traces of black. His own H'tes caused him to wonder if it held the key. Without really thinking, he found a rune he had used in the past and pressed it. Everything within the skimmer froze. Even though he couldn't see through the Gray, he knew that everything had ceased moving within the stillness field. This feature of the H'tes had come in handy while fighting an archdemon in the past. Now, Tone wondered if it would be able to help him in this predicament.

As he moved his arm, the gray parted, moved and piled up around him. He pushed with both hands and discovered that he could easily move this strange substance while it was stilled by the blade. The human freed his body from the sheath and began making his way toward the spirit sphere containing the blue ball of a demon. He knew better than to try and move an angel. Even in the still state, there was no telling what would happen to both of them at his dangerous touch. Plus, this angel was not in her right mind thanks to the demon's manipulation. Better to get the sphere out of the way and let the angels deal with the psyched-out spirit.

Once he was beside the spirit sphere, he used his blade to move the device rather than risk touching it. A touch could either set the demon free or cause Tone to get sucked in himself. Either option sounded hazardous to his health. Tone was surprised to find the spirit sphere cruised through the Gray, pushing the substance out of the way as he guided the sphere to a position right behind Zeke. He was certain he heard movement within the orb while it travelled. Not surprisingly, the demon was not affected by the stillness field. Tone had learned that the hard way when he had been stuck within a spirit sphere before battling the beastly Bubba.

Staying beside Zeke, Tone once again touched the rune that deactivated the stillness field. The places that had been cleared of the

Gray were filled back in with a rush. Tone could feel Zeke trying to move through the Gray to spot where the spirit sphere had been.

"Zeke? Can you hear me?" asked the human.

Zeke's labored movements ceased as his head slowly turned to face his friend. "Tone? How did you get over here?"

Tone laughed. "Dude, you sound like you are talking through a blender full of cottage cheese, ball bearings and really cheap light beer."

"So do you," yelled Zeke through the mist. "We have to stop P'marka from reaching the spirit sphere. If Fantazmil gets out again…"

"Buddy, look behind you," slurred Tone through the Gray. Zeke, with much effort, slowly turned to see the hazy form of a spirit sphere behind him. "Am I good or am I great?" His chuckle sounded evil in the Gray. "This stuff is way cooler than a sound distorter run through a bowl of applesauce and played on an old eight-track player. And yes, I have tried it."

Zeke remained looking at the sphere since it was so difficult to turn his head. "How did you manage that? Can you move better than we can in here?" Even through the distortion, Tone could hear the confusion in his friend's voice.

"Stillness field. It worked pretty well, don't you think?" Tone was proud of himself.

Zeke turned his head to stare at his friend. "You did what?! Tone, that could have been disastrous. That shouldn't have worked. No one has ever used a stillness field in a Gray. They are too similar. It should have made the Gray solid and bound us all for a very long time."

Tone was not to be dissuaded from his sense of accomplishment. "But it worked," chuckled the human. "And that would have been good to know earlier."

"You have a talent for breaking the rules and come out smelling like a rose," sighed the Gray-gnarled voice of the hunter.

"Unless I've had pork and beans," added Tone.

# Chapter 24

As the skimmer emerged from the Gray, three angels ported to the spot where the spirit sphere had been. Arino and P'talgid were trying to prevent P'marka from starting the disaster all over again. P'marka, wanting to free the hurting human, was convinced she was doing the right thing. All three were shocked to discover there was nothing but ether where they appeared. Arino sent a wave of calming power into the tortured angel, placating her for the moment. P'talgid blazed with angelic fire, prepared for an attack by the demon.

"Cool your jets, Talgiddy. It's all under control. Mr. Blue Balls is safe and sound over here," declared Tone, proudly. "I knew you had your wings full with that whole freezing in the Gray thing, so I helped out. No, no! Don't applaud. Your stunned silence is all the thanks I need. But if you have a spare subscription to Pudding of the Month, I wouldn't say 'no' to it."

Arino looked up from her work on P'marka to smile. "I would tell you that you get used to him, but that hasn't happened for me, yet." Turning back to her work, the tortured angel struggled under her ministrations, but slowly acquiesced to her care.

With a thought, Zeke brought all the angels up to date on what Tone had been able to do. P'talgid was impressed. "Nicely done, Tone. You are quite the handy human to have around. I would love the opportunity to work with you. I wonder how it is that you are not affected by Fantazmil when every angel is. If we could find out what…"

"If this involves jumper cables attached to certain body parts," interjected Tone, "I'm really not into that. Now, if you want to put tickling sensors on my knees and butt cheeks we can talk about that! Just know that can make me kick or fart. Does the testing involve riding a greased pig through a mud bog made from modeling clay and grape soda?"

P'talgid looked at Tone as if he were insane. "Umm... no jumper cables..." He looked at Zeke, still wondering about the sanity of the human.

"That's good news. He hates that," verified Zeke. P'talgid looked from hunter to human several times, assessing if they were serious or joking, crazy or kidding. "Don't try. You will never understand."

Tone looked out the side of the *Hajile-R* for the first time since they had exited the Gray. Once again, he was amazed at the new vision stretching out in the distance. Spirit spheres of all sizes were scattered and placed at odd intervals. Angels with strange looking devices were poking and prodding the globe-shaped prisons. In the distance, Tone could see the largest spirit sphere he had ever seen, having more lines than any other. Within the crisscrossed pattern of moving runes, Tone caught his first glimpse of what the angels thought they had been fighting.

The demon-dragon had the same blue tint and glow that most other demons shared. Though most of the demon had the leathery skin Tone expected of a dragon, there were still tuffs of softly flowing feathers sprouting from numerous locations that seemed out of place on such a powerful looking monster. The massive, undulating body of the demon constantly stretched and compressed making it impossible for even Tone to fully comprehend. The wings grew and shrank based on the actions of the dragon. First they seemed to fill the sphere, then they disappeared behind it. Its head had strange angles that would have been impossibly painful to move had the being been physical instead of spiritual. Eyes bulged from sockets on stalks that allowed it to look in any direction it chose. The mouth of the dragon was something out of Tone's worst nightmares. It opened with six hinges as it roared and blew icy, blue breath against the walls of the sphere, clouding the view.

"Okay, that thing is too scary to joke about. Well, almost." Tone glanced around, asking, "Did you loan him out for *The Hobbit*?"

P'talgid explained. "That is Dracomil. That demon is far too dangerous to ever leave here. It has no intelligence left. The only thing it feels is rage. It would destroy anything – angel, demon, human, or…" the angels stopped before saying more, "or anything else that it contacted. There were many shattered demons and phased angels before it was captured and placed in here. That is one of the few times angels and demons worked together."

"No wonder you were all shitting cupcakes when that came out of here. It doesn't look like it is happy." Tone looked around at the spheres. Naz guided the skimmer near one of the sphere-incased demons. That one contained a baby faced demon. "Is that part of Je'relir?"

Zeke smiled. "I think Relir looks good in there. They keep Jehim as far away as possible. They both have an uncontrollable urge to merge. It is really sick to be honest."

Arino shuddered. "Make sure they stay apart. I still feel chilled when I think of what they did." All who had been at that battle agreed.

Tone had to add, "Besides, I can only save your asses so many times before I start charging for it. Next time, I expect a dozen roses, a box of chocolates, and new purple lederhosen with lime green suspenders." All the angels gave him the same look. "I just read *Springtime for Germany*. Now, I want to be a little black man in purple lederhosen. Is that a bad thing?"

"Yes!" said four angels in unison.

The group of angels and Tone took the small spirit sphere to its resting place. It was in a section all by itself. No other demons were even remotely close. It was as near as the angels came to solitary confinement.

"Fantazmil is too dangerous to keep near other spiritual beings. Well, except for you, Tone. That is really fascinating," declared P'talgid. The angel was looking at Tone in a way that made him feel like he was a disease under a microscope. Tone was beginning to wonder about P'talgid.

Zeke could sense the tension between the two. He got them moving. "P'talgid, we need to speak with Darius. It's about the Grays." The two angels linked, bringing the studious spirit into the loop.

"A new Gray? That seems unlikely. Don't you think one of the patrols would have found it by now?" asked P'talgid. There was almost a hint of condescension in his spirit. The skimmer flew toward a distant section of the Eqemp, passing demon after demon, encased in orb-shaped prisons until they came up to an opaque spirit sphere. "You sure you want to do this, Zeke? Remember last time?"

"Want to? No. Need to? Yes. Let's get this over with," said Zeke, resignation to the situation he dreaded rang in his voice. He moved quickly toward the sphere and touched it to allow it to become transparent. Tone watched his friend, certain he was moving quickly so he would do this before changing his mind. The sphere went from gray to clear, slowly revealing one of the strangest spirit spheres Tone had seen.

The interior of the cell was truly gilded. It closely resembled a Victorian sitting room with a roaring fire within an ornately decorated fireplace. There were piles of books all around the orb which seemed to be stacked in haphazard piles, ready to topple over at the slightest breath. A large armchair surrounded by books was facing away from Zeke and the rest of the party. A large leather-bound copy of *War and Peace* flew over the high backed chair, hitting the wall of the sphere near Tone, as an orange tinted hand reached from the chair to snatch a book from the nearest stack.

"What do you want?" came a strangely gentle voice from the chair. "Can't you see I'm otherwise occupied?" Another book flew at the wall, its cover shredded by claws.

The orange hand froze in mid reach as Zeke captured its attention with just one word. "Darius," said the hunter, with more than a little menace in the tenor of voice.

"Ezekiel," replied the voice with a level of threat that mirrored Zeke's. "How nice of you to stop by. It hasn't been long enough since we last met." Darius did not rise or turn to face the angel as another book struck the wall of the sphere squarely by Zeke's face.

"It's not my choice to be here," bantered the angel. Ezekiel paused, gathering the nerve to say what needed to be said. "I need to ask you about the Grays." Tone was certain he saw pain in the aura of his friend as he uttered those words. There was a story here that he really wanted to hear.

A book floated in the ether, paused in mid-flight. Pages turned on their own, revealing words that floated off the page:

"The words so pleas'd me, that desire to know

"The spirit, from whose lip they seem'd to come,

"Did draw me onward."

Tone was impressed. "Dante's *Purgatorio*, canto twenty. Nice quote."

The first sound he had heard from the chair was a shuffle of movement. "A new voice? I don't know you. Interesting." Still not facing the group, Darius asked, "Why do you want to know about the Grays? Are you having trouble getting through them again? How long were you stuck in there this time?"

Zeke seethed. "Not stuck this time. But we think someone has created a new Gray that we can't find." The anger behind his words was not well hidden. The hunter looked at Tone and silently communicated, "I'll tell you later."

Another book plastered itself to the side of the sphere. The words of "The Tell-Tale Heart" jumping off the page: "You fancy me mad. Madmen know nothing." The message was clear. Darius was going to make this long and difficult.

Nazilaq piped in. "I knew this was a waste of our time. Let's go talk to Vret. She knows more than Darius does." The temptation the pilot tossed out was meant to goad the being in the chair to action. It failed.

"Nazilaq, thank you for stopping by. How is the *Hajile-J* doing? Wait. I am so sorry. I forgot that it was destroyed. Is the new one the *Hajile-R* or *Hajile-L*?" Buttons pushed, Darius continued,

"So Ezekiel, who do you think has the power, intellect and courage to create a new Gray area? It can't be a demon. Do you have another rouge angel on your hands?"

Arino opened up, allowing Tone to read her essence. *"Darius is one of the Praetorac. They are neither angel nor demon. He was once human. They are somewhere between angel and demon, but Darius is far too powerful and unpredictable to be let loose. The last time he was free, he caused problems during World War II."*

Tone looked at the hand that reached for another book. It looked like a muscular, orange arm with large warts all over it. The long fingers were tipped with razor-sharp claws. Now that he knew this was once a human, curiosity about the appearance of the remainder of this Praetorac became all consuming.

"So why don't you come over here and chat with us? I think we should be buddies," said Tone. "Do you like strawberry-rhubarb pie with cream cheese topping? Personally, I find it as repulsive as reality TV; but it seems like something an orange guy like you would like."

A silence emanated from the chair. The hand waved dismissively. "I think not. So Ezekiel, what is in this deal for me? I do not see you letting me out for a few quolls to explore the Spiritscape. I already have all the books I can digest."

"Can we offer him Fleetwood Mac's greatest hits on an mp3 player?" asked Tone. "How about some Weird Al? Wait, I know! Let's give him the Wiggles live album. He'd love them."

More rustling came from the chair as the Praetorac moved around. "I do not recognize any of the words that creature spews forth. Please muzzle it."

"I will arrange for you to receive books from the 1950's so you can see the results of your work. Now, about the Gray?" Zeke was using more patience than he had shown recently. Arino looked him over carefully, trying to decipher his Machiavellian scheme.

A sound like a sigh issued from Darius. "You know I had nothing to do with any new Gray. Ask my captors. They do not like letting me out of my cage."

"Yes," began Zeke, "but you may know of someone who might have something to do with making one. I know how you work, Darius."

"Yeah. What he said! And I'd like to see you try to put a muzz…" Arino sent a massive wave of calming power into Tone. The effect was instantaneous. "Can we stop for ice cream?" asked Tone dreamily. Nazilaq chuckled at the change.

The voice from the chair sighed. "None of my brothers bother with the Spiritscape. They have more Earthly interests. It is much more fun."

"You're very pretty, Arino," sighed Tone, still feeling the effects of her power.

"Not even Zhi Zhao?" asked P'talgid. A book flew over the back of the chair, striking the side of spirit sphere where the angel floated.

The voice of the being in the chair was openly hostile. "Never mention that traitor's name in my presence." Then, after a pause for reflection. "Zhi Zhao could make one if she chose. But there would have to be something in it for her clan. Now, may I please get back to the task at hand? There is so much to read."

"Zee Zo. That's a funny name," rambled Tone. "It sounds like a cool aminal in the Zee Zo zoo." He laughed at his own joke, as Naz began ushering him toward the skimmer. "I said aminal." His giggles made it hard for the pilot to remain serious.

Zeke turned to leave with Naz and Tone, but the healer stayed at the sphere. Arino addressed Darius, "My offer stands. I will always be here to help you when you are ready to cross over."

The hand that had been reaching for the book again waved dismissively. It grabbed a copy of *A Tale of Two Cities*. Arino helped Nazilaq get a wandering Tone back into the skimmer, reducing the power she was sending so that he could think straight.

"I thought Raph was the only one who could do that to me," whined Tone once they were safely inside. "Now there are two of you who make me sound like a babbling idiot."

"Well…" began Nazilaq.

"Don't go there," laughed Tone. Getting serious, he asked, "So who is going to explain what the hell Dar-race is? I thought I was the only human who could come over here. You have been holding out on me."

Arino explained. "The Praetorac are human spirits that get stuck on Earth. For some reason they do not cross over, and neither angel nor demon notices them until it's too late. They are what most humans call ghosts. A select few learn how to manipulate things on earth. Most of the stories of the supernatural on Earth are nothing more than one of the Praetorac being mischievous or, worst case, malicious."

"Hold on there, hot stuff. Are you telling me that all those ghost stories are really ghosts?" Tone was excited at the prospect. "Since I've been coming here, I always thought they were demons causing problems."

"Maybe a few of them are demons," explained P'talgid. "Not nearly as many as you would think. Demons don't like to draw that much attention to themselves. It doesn't suit their purposes. With only a dozen exceptions, the Praetorac are all the ghosts, ghouls, goblins and gremlins."

"What about vampires?" asked Tone, more enthusiastically than any of the angels found comfortable.

Zeke sounded somber, "Especially vampires."

# Chapter 25

Flying in the *Hajile-R* toward the exit of the Eqemp, Tone asked the question that was gnawing at him. "Let me try to wrap my brain around this," he began. "These Pray-Terry-Acks are humans who just hang out on Earth?" He was looking at each of the angels in turn. None of them seemed interested in explaining. Finally, he looked right at Zeke. "Right?"

Zeke sighed. "It's not that simple. You are one of the Exceptionals – a human with some skills that are beyond normal human abilities. When the archangels gave you the H'tes, do your remember hearing how we didn't discover all of the Exceptionals? A few of them died before they were discovered?"

"Yeah. I'm only the third one to get a H'tes." The human grinned. "That makes me exceptionally exceptional, not to mention a dynamite dancer."

"Well…" began Nazilaq, smiling with his whole being, pausing long enough for Tone to interject.

"Again, don't go there," laughed the human.

Zeke continued, "There have been five Exceptionals that have slipped through the cracks. Two simply died and are doing some amazing things in the spirit realms." Tone missed the look shared between Zeke and Arino. It hinted at a much larger story that neither wanted to tell Tone. "Three of them died, but didn't cross over. They had the power to remain on Earth. One of them, Joachim, actually works with me from time to time hunting demons. The other two are…" The hunter's voice trailed off.

"'Less than helpful' would be a kind way to describe them," filled in Arino. "They prefer to stay on Earth out of fear of the Spiritscape and the other realms."

"Plus they like being ghosts on earth," added P'talgid. "Darius lived in Persia. We had to look through 3000 years of Earth before we tracked him down. It is strange that no angel was there for his death since…"

Zeke interrupted. "What we need to do is check and see if Zhi Zhao has made any trips into the Spiritscape lately." Another silent expression was shared, but this one was between Zeke and P'talgid. Tone didn't miss that look.

"You do know I will be asking about all this later, right?" Tone asked, grinning mischievously. "I don't forget things like that unless there is something a lot cooler to… Is that a llama?" He pointed to a spirit sphere with an odd looking demon.

P'talgid shook his head, wondering about the strange human. "I have work to do. Sorry I can't play along with your snipe hunt." The angel gave them all a salute. "Tone, I look forward to spending some quality time getting to know you better."

"I'll bring the cream soda, you bring the tickle sensors and the butterscotch schnapps," said Tone, trying to imitate the angelic salute. He didn't even get close.

After leaving the angels in the Eqemp behind, the foursome within the skimmer emerged from the Gray surrounding the prison. Tone posed the question that all were wondering.

"So this Zi Zoo. Where can we find him?" asked Tone, stating a question they all were wondering. "Is he more talkative than Delirious back there?"

Zeke began, "Well, buddy, SHE is not as helpful as Darius. We need to check in with Vret."

At the mention of the name, the archangel of wisdom ported into the skimmer. Tone spun around, surprised. "I hate it when you do that!" screeched the startled Tone.

"I have never done that to you," said Vret, laughing as her flaming red hair spread out in a panorama of crimson colors. That only made her look more powerful than ever in Tone's eyes. The hair looked like scarlet tendrils reaching out and pulling ideas from the ether.

"There's a first time for everything," retorted Tone. Without even thinking he asked, "Do you suck up ideas through your hair?"

The look on Vret's face showed even more surprised than Tone's at her sudden appearance. She looked at him, spirit gaze blazing like a green inferno in her eyes. The archangel couldn't see past his psychedelic spirit. After what felt like an extremely uncomfortable silence, she replied, "Yes, Tone. I do. How did you discern that?"

Zeke looked at his friend and the archangel. "You do? Why didn't we know that?"

"It was not important to share. My hair always reaches out for knowledge. It is just how I developed my abilities." Turning to Tone, she asked again, "How did you know that?" The verdant conflagration in her eyes never dimmed.

"They just looked like that. I can't read your spirit very well. You are too good at keeping me out. But your hair looks kind of... I guess the right word is hungry?" Tone was enjoying playing with Vret. He knew it would not be often that he would have the upper hand. "Plus, when your hair spelled out the words 'Eat at Joe's', I thought it might mean something."

Vret continued her scrutiny of the human while enlightening the group. "I got your message about Zhi Zhao. P'rama has been tracking her for quite some time. There was a point in 1898 when she was missing from Ontario. It is possible that she was in the Spiritscape. If it was Irkja who pulled her over, he would have had to do it from one of eight spots." To Tone she explained, "Praetorac are notoriously difficult to get into the Spiritscape. It's even harder to get them back to Earth. They are not easy to find there, either. I actually entertained the idea that you were one, before you showed Zeke who you were."

The archangel shared with the angels the possible locations for Zhi Zhao's crossover. Nazilaq had a startled look about him. He looked closely at Vret before asking, "Are you sure about the fourth one? That seems like an unlikely spot for an Earth-touch."

"As unlikely as it is, that is one of them. Without Irkja to help you, that could be a challenging place to fly."

Tone spoke up. "Human here. It's not nice to talk about stuff and not share. Seriously, is there no such thing as angel kindergarten to teach these things? I bet you still eat paste, too."

Vret, who had never stopped looking at him, explained. "There are eight possible places that Ontario in 1898 touches the Spiritscape. Six of them are simple spots like you use all the time without realizing it. There is another that is not useable due to its proximity to Iqimp – that's another place surrounded by one of the known Grays. But the fourth one on the list is even worse than that. It is a spot that is at a nexus point of three rivers. It tends to be overrun with pha'ards on the layer of the Spiritscape where you would have to look. That is the one where the *Hajile-R* must go. Other skimmers are checking the other seven."

Tone looked depressed at the news. "What is it with you angels and those damned pha'ards? I think you need to get pha'ard shredders on all the rivers. It would be a nice touch for those of us who so closely resemble pha'ard chow."

Vret looked somber. "If you save Adoneal, I'm sure he can make one." With those words killing the cheery mood Tone had created, the archangel of wisdom ported away.

"Well that was fun," said Arino, trying to restore the spirits of the others. Sending out a wave of energy meant to raise their spirits, she added, "We are the best chance Adoneal has. If the four of us can't find him, no one can."

Zeke looked scary as he muttered, "That's what I'm afraid of." Then, like flipping a switch, he was upbeat. "Let's get going. The place we need is over a thousand layers below us. Tone, you good on your H'tes charge?"

The blade flipped out of Tone's arm. He could feel the power blazing within the crystal dagger. "Pretty much a full charge, amigo. Let's jump some layers."

"Hopping layers in five, four, three, two, one," announced Naz.

Tone had only gone through layers twice before. This was the first time he had travelled through them instead of porting at Bubba's whim, or portaling by Michael's power. Each part of the Spiritscape had more than one layer. The same thing could be happening in the same spot thousands of times over. Since time was not a factor in the Spiritscape, it had layers that allowed an angel or demon to be in the same spot, but on different layers. Each layer could flow naturally into the one above it or below it, but those spots were difficult to find. With an infinite number of layers, flowing from one into the next was nearly impossible. Angels and demons could simply jump down layer after layer.

Tone watched as layers faded into one another. Most of the time, the only differences were subtle changes in the Spiritscape. A mountain could be a different shade of amber as the layers were traversed. He saw that one layer had a sickly-green valley carved out of the mountain. He tried to mention it, but it was gone to be replaced with a valley that glowed with the blue of demons. He could see Zeke tense at the sight, wishing he could go and kick some ass. That layer faded as another came into view that showed all was restored to its original appearance. Tone had to laugh as the *Hajile-R* slipped through a layer and surprised a raven-winged demon. One blast of angel fire from the skimmer and the demon was flying back to Hell to heal.

Finally reaching the correct level, Tone commented, "That was fun. How many layers was that?"

"1,294 layers," explained Nazilaq. "We didn't move at all during the hopping. Now we can head to the right spot." Looking at Tone, he said, "Whatever happens, don't try to leave the Spiritscape on this level. It would be… messy."

"Define messy, please," said Tone. "Messy like mud wrestling with a bikini clad babe? Or messy like my body would explode into tiny pieces of Tone? If it's the bikini thing, I'm out of here right now."

Zeke explained. "Messy like your spirit would be scattered all over Earth since your body has no connection to this layer. Your timeline doesn't have any touch-points to here. To be blunt, you have no body to go back to from this layer."

"Okay, so what you're saying is, it would be messy. Got it," replied Tone.

The skimmer flew along at blinding speeds, allowing Tone to only glimpse trails every so often. There was an urgency that Tone did not understand. Nazilaq wasn't even taking time to blast the handful of demons Tone saw, not to mention the many more that he had missed. As the skimmer zipped through the center of a doughnut-shaped diamond, Tone saw something that made him yell.

"Stop, Naz. I see a trail of some kind. That is weird."

The vessel went from breakneck speed to still. Tone was glad that inertia didn't apply in the Spiritscape. That would have been messy, too. With some guidance, the *Hajile-R* moved to be near the trail.

"What are you seeing, Tone?" asked Arino. "It is Irkja's trail?"

"No. But it is something else. It's not like any trail I have ever seen. This one looks misty and colorful. It's like something I would make, but I don't leave a trail anymore," replied Tone, "and I've never been here. Or have I?"

Zeke looked tense. "I'm sorry, Tone. I'm sure it's interesting, but we need to keep moving. You see, Adoneal can't last much longer without...." Turning to Nazilaq, "Get going. No more stops."

The skimmer was back to full speed. Tone was still wondering about the trail when Zeke's words hit him. "What do you mean that Adoneal can't last much longer? He's an angel. Hell, he's an archangel. Time is nothing to him."

Arino spoke up. "We have to tell him, Zeke. Adoneal can only function for one thousand quolls before he starts to deteriorate again. He has to receive a special kind of healing. In another twenty-one quolls, Adoneal will begin to lose his cohesion. In twenty-four quolls, he will be phased. In twenty-five quolls, no one will be able to restore his connection to a functional level. We have to find him."

Tone had no smart-ass remark. No snappy comeback. He looked hard at the healer and saw something. She was holding back. As great as she was at keeping him out, he could see it. "What aren't you telling me? Does it have something to do with me?"

Zeke tried to reassure the human. "It is not you. Don't worry about it. We will find him before it's too late."

Tone knew Zeke even better than Arino. Something was happening that they didn't want him to know. "What is it? I know you two. There is something going on that you're not saying. I can feel it."

"Please, Tone," begged Arino. "Just trust us. You don't want to know this" There was sincere pleading in the healer's essence. Tone liked and trusted her, but he knew there was something happening and he could not let it go.

"My friend, I'll tell you; but you will be happier not knowing," said a somber Zeke. Tone had never seen the hunter with a pleading look until now. Everything in Zeke and Arino was sending out the signal that he should let this go. The knowledge they were withholding was not out of spite or evil intent. They really wanted to protect him from something that would be painful to discover. He had almost decided to drop the quest for this hidden knowledge when he looked at Nazilaq. His aura was the opposite of the other two angels. Even though his was focused on piloting the skimmer, he spirit was begging Tone to ask. The angelic sailor wanted Tone to know for the sake of Adoneal. But there was something else in the pilot's aura. There was a piece of the puzzle even Naz didn't want Tone to know.

Turning to Zeke, he flatly said, "Tell me."

A resigned look resided on the spirit of the warrior. "Tone, Adoneal can't function like he does without being healed regularly. Arino and Raphael can help him hold it together for hundreds of quolls. But every thousand quolls, he has to visit a special healer. He helps her stay together by draining off the power that keeps him together. Adoneal is the only one who can handle that power. It would destroy any other angel. It's a very symbiotic relationship. She has to get rid of power that would tear her up from the inside out, while Adoneal needs that power to keep from phasing."

Tone was confused. "So is it some kind of demon that has the opposite power? I'm missing something here."

Arino explained. "Tone, it's not a demon with that power. Anna is the only one who can help him. If he doesn't drain that power in the next twenty quolls, Anna will begin to implode and he will fall apart."

# Chapter 26

Part of what made Tone an invaluable member of that foursome was his unpredictability. When faced with an archdemon, he would make a joke and find a way out of the situation that no angel would even consider. Dealing with angels always made those who didn't know Tone well fly away, shaking their heads as they tried to understand what was wrong with him. It was difficult times like this when the unexpected was a downside. Zeke, Arino and Naz all wished he was more predictable. They had no clue how he would react to this kind of news.

Arino was pleasantly surprised when Tone did not lose what little composure he possessed. He did not turn inward, curl up in a ball, and suck his thumb like Naz halfway expected. Zeke was prepared to restrain an angry Tone, ready to take on the entire Spiritscape to save his sister. None of them expected the words that came out of Tone's mouth.

"That explains a lot. I wondered what no one was telling me about Anna." Tone had a rare, genuine thoughtful look sneaking across his spirit. Turning to Arino and Nazilaq, he said, "Just so you know, I will do whatever it takes to save Anna and Adoneal. Zeke is an angel on the edge of losing it, but he will help me do what it takes. Are you two on board? There are two spirits that we will lose without our brilliant teamwork. This may get messy."

Shocked glows came from all three angels. None of them had ever seen Tone look so serious or driven. They all just stared at the human, not knowing what to do.

"Hello?" asked Tone, showing his lack of patience with the situation. "Do I need to say something silly about pudding and rainbows to snap you out of it?"

Zeke looked at Arino and Naz. "He's right. I can do whatever it takes. You two do not have to come any farther." Looking right at

Arino, he added, "This could get very dark if we have to take on some of our old friends. I don't want you to do something that will hurt your spirit – or see things that hurt." Leaving the unsaid hanging in the ether, they all knew that he was referring to the things he might have to do to save Adoneal.

Naz spoke first. "That was the sanest thing I've ever heard you say, Tone. Please don't ever do that again. It is just spooky." The pilot looked at the other two angels and then back at Tone. "I will do anything it takes to save them, Tone. I'm in."

All eyes were on Arino. She was by far the most caring and compassionate of the four. Neither Tone nor Zeke were certain what she would do. After a long look at all three of them, she said, "There needs to be a voice of reason in the midst of all this. Besides, you can't get through this without me. I'm a big angel, Zeke. I can live with whatever you have to do. Besides, who is going to pick up the pieces when you're done?" Tone and Zeke weren't sure if she was referring to the pieces of Zeke's spirit or the pieces of anyone who got in the way. They looked at one another and silently agreed she probably meant both.

Tone smiled with his whole spirit. "Now that we got that out of the way, I think we need to find Irkja's hidey hole right now. So where can we find Zhi Zhao? And can we do the short version of an interview? I don't even give a damn about her resume."

Zeke looked dangerous as he said, "I think I can arrange that." With a look he shared his plan with Nazilaq, who chuckled. Zeke smiled a frightening smile, saying, "I'll crossover, find her, and meet you at Chabef. See you in a bit." With those words, the warrior was gone.

Naz explained for Tone. "He just crossed over onto Earth. He'll track down Zhi Zhao and meet us at Chabef. That's a place where Earth touches the Spiritscape in that timescape."

"Cool. What else did he say? If he is bringing me a pony, I'm going to be so excited!" spouted Tone, sounding more like the quirky human they knew and loved. "Wait. Where would I keep it? Arino, baby, can I keep my pony at your place? I promise I'll feed him, clean up after him and give him all the Twinkies he can eat."

"Okay, serious wasn't that bad after all," laughed Naz, piloting the skimmer around an auburn field of trees that were floating in the ether.

Forcing a laugh, Arino said, "Sure, Tone. If Zeke brings you a pony, I'll make space for him." Tone could see she was tense. Naz had Adoneal's wellbeing as his driving motivation. Tone knew that he would do what it took to save Anna. Zeke had been holding back his new power, but would now be turning it loose. That gave Arino something to worry about. She was wondering who – or what – Zeke would be after all this was done.

Tone put his hand on her shoulder. "He's going to be all right. We won't let him fall too far. Besides, if he goes all demon-side, who will I get to torment me? Naz is good, but he's not on Zeke's level of picking on me."

Arino looked at the human and smiled. "I don't know if there is anything any of us can do when he finally turns loose. But, I will do whatever it takes to save Zeke, even if it's from himself." The look on her face told Tone that Zeke was more important to her than Adoneal or even Anna. She was staying to save Zeke and would take on anyone who got in her way – even him.

"We are going to have so much fun being the heroes!" said Tone, trying to lighten the moment. The eyes of the healer were not smiling as she laughed in agreement with his joke. "Besides, we're the good guys. The good guys always win. Right?"

From the pilot's sheath, Nazilaq muttered, "Don't tell Irkja that." Bringing the *Hajile-R* to an abrupt halt beside the convergence of three energy rivers, Nazilaq announced, "Now we just have to wait for…"

A hole opened in ether of the Spiritscape, the Earth city behind glowed with gaslight street lamps unlike any Tone had seen. A horse drawn carriage passed the opening, without anyone noticing the hole into the Spiritscape right next to them. The view was like looking through a window. The skimmer went right up to the opening as Nazilaq created a cavity through the middle of the vessel.

A spectral being flew right through the hole from Earth and into the waiting compartment. Zeke was right behind it in his full, terrifying angelic glory. Upon reaching the far end of the cell, the being turned and tried to expand through the crystalline walls to face Zeke. It found itself being compressed as the walls did not yield. The open end of the tube closed as the orifice that had led the creature to its capture faded away.

Zeke ported out of the cell and appeared beside Tone and Arino. With a smile, he said, "That was funny. You'd think she thought I was going to drag her ass off to Hell or something."

"Dude, how would you find her ass?" said Tone, looking at the creature. Knocking on the crystal, he shouted, "Hey there! Zhi Zhao, I presume? Do you even have an ass for Zekey to haul off to Hell? We are having a debate out here."

The voice one would expect from a ghost floated through the walls. "Who is the human?" It gave Tone a chill as the voice sounded like several voices speaking in soft harmony, creating a spectral quality.

Arino was not amused. "Drop the special effects, Zhi Zhao. If you help us, we are willing to send you back. Try anything funny, and we will find someplace very unpleasant for you. Any questions?"

Tone raised his hand. "When did you become a scary badass, Arino? Aren't you supposed to be the sweet angel who tries to see the good in everyone?" Turning to Zeke, he said, "You aren't going to start healing the ghost are you? If you do that, then I have to start flying the skimmer and Naz has to be funny, and you know how hard that is for him."

The sound that came out of the crystal container in their midst was radically different. It sounded like a normal human voice. "Arino and I have history. She tends to not put up with any of my shit. You have me at a disadvantage. I've never seen a Praetorac like you. Why are you working with the angels? What do they have on you?"

Tone looked from Zeke to Arino to Naz. They all gave him the same "tell her whatever you want" look. Tone smiled. "They want me to take them through the new Gray I made. I told them we don't know each other, but they suspect we are buddies and threatening you will make me tell them what I did for the green ghoul."

Laughter burst from the clear cage. "You think he made the Gray?! Please tell me you are not that stupid. You can tell just by looking at him that he doesn't even have a hint of that power." A gray mist began to flow from the trapped spirit. "Ditch the pretender and I'll take the deal. But I want to be put right back where you found me, hunter." The Gray faded away as the Praetorac gave Tone an evil look. "Sorry, but you know how it is. Every spirit for themselves."

Arino asked, "So, it was you who made the new Gray?"

"Of course it was me. You really thought he could do it? He won't be able to make anything like that for a few more centuries. He looks like he hasn't..." Zhi Zhao looked at Tone who waved back. "He hasn't died? How the hell can he be here? What are you?"

Tone grinned. "I'm one of a kind, babe. So tell us, where is this Gray that you made for Irkja?" He really enjoyed messing with other spirits, but his crest fell at her words.

"What do you mean Irkja? I didn't make anything for an angel. This was a demon deal. A couple of demons caught me and gave me the choice of making them a hideout far from anyone else, or they were going to drain me dry. It wasn't that hard to choose." The spirit looked around and took a more substantial form. She looked like a translucent human with Asian features. Her face glowed with a crimson shine.

Zeke asked the question that all of them were wondering. "Who was the demon?" Tone looked at his friends, afraid of the answer.

The spirit hesitated, knowing the angels were not going to like the answer. "It was Je'relir. They needed somewhere to hide after really messing up an archangel. Don't you understand? I had to do it or that baby face was going to drain every bit of life force out of me." There was a pleading in Zhi Zhao's voice that almost made Tone feel sorry for her. "They made me make a gray cloud around the outside of a whole new area. It is not thick enough for anything to get lost. It's barely thick enough to get stuck in. All it does is keep spirits from getting in and out easily. No porting. Just travel."

Arino was ready to be done with this. "Just tell us where it is. We have some unfinished business."

"They hid right in plain sight," said the Praetorac. Wanting to make sure the deal was solid, she asked. "You give me your word you will return me to Earth?" Impatient heads nodded all around. "They wanted a place where none of the angels would ever go."

They were all confused. "We go everywhere. We go anywhere," stated Nazilaq. "There is no place we don't go in the Spiritscape."

A light bulb looked like it had gone off over Tone's head. "There is a spot you don't go unless you absolutely have to. It is too sacred to disturb."

Arino gasped. Zeke glowed. Nazilaq growled. Zhi Zhao genuinely loved the power position as she asked, "You didn't know there was a small realm within that glowing place at the bottom of Ximsor? That is hilarious!"

# Chapter 27

Zeke grudgingly returned Zhi Zhao to her place in time, making a promise to pay her a visit the next time he was on Earth. The Praetorac tried to laugh off the not-so-veiled threat while moving faster than he had ever seen. He waved goodbye to the fleeing spirit, making sure to laugh loud enough for her to hear.

"I like her. She could really be handy to know around Halloween. Does she do parties?" asked Tone. "She doesn't even need a costume. She can come as a ghost, a ghoul, a goblin, or a politician. They all look pretty much the same."

Arino wore a sad smile. "You wouldn't want her around your guests, Tone. She tends to… drain people."

Before Zeke had even made it back to the Spiritscape, the *Hajile-R* was soaring toward a portal that Nazilaq had conjured to get them close to Ximsor. He had sent a message to Michael explaining the situation. The archangel was sending angels to meet them under Ximsor Lake. All the angels that could be spared were all on their way to meet skimmers at the rim of Ximsor.

"You need to get into sheaths," said Nazilaq once Zeke had ported back to them. "This will get bumpy. Michael wants us to head straight there. The others will join us as soon as they can. He wants me to…" He trailed off. "We will be going fast and plowing through anything in the way." The skimmer had taken on a needle-like appearance as it cut through mountains and valleys, heading to the portal.

Climbing into his sheath, Tone had to ask. "What did you mean by draining people? I'm a little freaked out by that."

Zeke looked at his friend. "You should be. As far as we know, there are only three genuine Praetorac. You have met two of them. While on Earth, they take living energy from people around them.

Most times it appears as some kind of sickness. Other times it is just weakness and fatigue. But they must drain power to stay strong."

Tone caught something that Zeke hoped he would have missed. "I'm guessing there are ingenuous Praetorac? Are they innocent or just trust too much?"

Arino answered that one. "If a Praetorac drains too much living energy, they can kill a normal person and make them a pseudo-Praetorac. Think of it like…"

"So they are vampires!" interrupted Tone. "That is cool in a mind-blowingly scary kind of way. Do they drink blood or just get transfusions?"

Arino sighed. "That is where your legends of vampires and zombies come from. Zhi Zhao is smart enough to not make too many converts. She has about ten spirits in her coven. They are really hard for angels and demons to find. They like to slip inside people when we are near. And before you ask, they don't possess anyone. They aren't that powerful. But they can hide inside someone long enough for us to move on."

"Approaching the portal. As soon as we are through, I'm taking us the fast way through the levels up to near where we began. Tone, your timeline touches the level where we are going, but it links to several points along your timeline. Be careful if you have to jump back to your body."

"Check. Don't jump back into my body as an old man. I'm gassy enough at thirty-four," joked Tone. No one laughed. "Tough room."

The skimmer morphed into a small sphere as it flew through the open portal. Arriving on the other side, it continued to fly as it went through levels of the Spiritscape. The *Hajile-R* began to shake as Nazilaq pushed it beyond its normal limits, adding more of his power to keep it from losing cohesion. Scenes flashed past Tone far too quickly to comprehend what he was seeing. It was a blur of images and colors that spanned all spectrums making it a beautiful kaleidoscope of the Spiritscape. Tone was positive they had travelled straight through some of the most beautiful locales that he would never be able to process.

The *Hajile-R* approached the right level just as they were reaching top of the bowl that was Ximsor. Nazilaq neither slowed nor hesitated as the skimmer shook violently while passing into the crystal refuse field. The ball shaped skimmer began rolling as it rocked and rocketed through the variety of colored crystals. All of Nazilaq's energy was being used to pilot the ship, Zeke and Arino were sending out wave after wave of angelic fire to do their best to keep the living crystals from approaching the skimmer. As one moved directly into their path, Naz plowed straight through it, shattering it into an infinite number of pieces and creating a crack in the outer shell of the skimmer.

"I can't take much more," grunted Naz. Tone forced his eyes away from the scattering shards to look at his friend. The sheath containing Nazilaq had become so merged with the angel it was impossible to tell where one ended and the other began. The pilot was in incredible pain maintaining the pace, and the beating of the *Hajile-R*. If it had not been for his power and skill, Tone was certain the skimmer would have come apart long before they had reached Ximsor.

As they transitioned from the land of crystals to the lake of pha'ards, Zeke sent a massive series of fireballs ahead of the skimmer to clear the way. Pha'ards scattered and scrambled away from the attack as the skimmer screamed through the flames, passing through the lake untouched. The skimmer burst through the bottom of the lake, slamming into the far wall. It came to rest among a blue outcropping of the walls of Ximsor, near the monument to Adoneal's sacrifice.

Arino was beside Nazilaq the instant they stopped. She began sending healing power into the angel who was nearly unconscious. She stabilized her friend who then pulled away from her healing.

"I'll make it. Save your power. I have a feeling you're going to need it in there." Naz gave them all a look they instantly understood.

"My job was to get you here. I used everything I have to do that. There is no way the *Hajile-R* can get through there. I can't make it small enough to fit through whatever that is. And without my skimmer, I'm not much use in a fight. Others will be here soon to help me, but we can't risk waiting."

Zeke offered his hand to the pilot. "I've seen you fight without a skimmer. You are better than you know."

"Injured like this I'm not," smiled Naz. "Do what it takes, Zeke. Do what none of us can do." An unspoken promise was made between the two angels. As the skimmer morphed into its nature ring shape, Nazilaq opened a door for Tone. "Go! Save Adoneal!"

Arino wanted to argue, but knew that Nazilaq was right. She sent one last wave of healing power into the pilot and followed Zeke to the monument.

"That was an awesome ride. If you ever decide to do that again, make sure you call me so I can sit up front again," said Tone. "See you in a little bit, buddy."

He joined the two angels at the threshold of the glowing monument. Tone could feel the heat and the power of the archangel trying to reach into him, making him want to consume as much angelic power as he could. Using all his willpower, he resisted the urge to draw power off the glowing orb. Tone had no idea how bad it would be for him once they entered the glow. Grabbing the hands of his two friends, they crossed the threshold.

Inside was all light and heat, golden power inundated Tone with angelic power. He pressed back with all his might, but it was impossible to resist all the might that was trying to invade every corner of his essence. A golden hum flooded all his senses leaving him deaf, dumb and blind to anything but the power. Tone could feel it seeping into his spirit as he pulled back all his natural power to avoid explosive reactions. Every point that became devoid of his power was soon filled by the golden glow of the remnants of Adoneal. Each nook and cranny that was touched was far more powerful than anything he had ever imagined.

He began to wonder if it would be so bad to give in to the desire and allow all the power fill him, making him into something greater than a human. He was not like Bubba. Just this one time wouldn't hurt anything. This wasn't even taking the power from an angel. Taking all the power into himself would be doing the angels a favor by exposing the entrance to Irkja's lair. Or better yet, that might just trap Irkja and his followers on the other side.

Tone's mind was beginning to play tricks on him as he forgot about Adoneal and Anna, until he felt healing power washing through his arm. Arino had sensed the confusion building in Tone and sent some calming power into her friend. She silently communicated to Zeke, *"We need to find the Gray. Tone can't take much more of this place."*

Zeke was also struggling to move through the power of Adoneal's memorial. It felt amazing to have that kind of might filling him to his limits. When they found their way through, he felt sorry for the first spirit that got in his way.

Even with Arino helping him, Tone knew that resisting the heat any longer would be impossible. Just as he decided to give in and let the power flood him, Zeke found the Gray and pulled them in.

The chilling, calm of nothingness soothed the human. It was like the cool of fresh summer sheets floating down upon him. The Gray was pulling the golden power out of him like heat from a steaming body on a cold day. Tone was just starting to think all would be hunky-dory when they stopped. The Gray was not wide at all, but it was blocked on the far end. Hitting a wall caused them to begin to float back toward the golden glow. Panic spread through Tone. He knew that another trip through that kind of power would be impossible to resist. His mind raced for a solution, but was paralyzed by fear. An angelic hand slowly touched his wrist, causing his H'tes to swing out of his arm. It touched the rune that activated the stillness field.

Everything stopped for Tone. He brushed aside the thick Gray to reveal Arino's finger touching the blade. He could see her power being slowly sapped into the H'tes. Quickly moving it away, he realized that she knew what was happening and acted, risking herself to save them all. If he hadn't removed her touch from the crystal dagger, it would have drained her power to a dangerous point. Tone was impressed by the healer. She never ceased to amaze him.

The human brushed aside the Gray from the barrier to discover a portal. It was really brilliant of Irkja. If someone was following him through the Gray, he could either close the portal or activate it once he was through, sending them bouncing back, or to another place entirely. Tone could not tell if the portal was active, but he knew that anywhere would be better than being back in the golden glow. Using the point of his dagger, he tried to pry open the door of the portal. It proved to be more resistant than he had expected. No matter where he tried, the doorway refused to yield. That left him one option.

Tone sent a small blast of angelic fire from his H'tes into the center of the portal. The flames licked at the substance of the gateway, causing a slight deterioration of the door. A smile crept across Tone's face as he sent a blast of fire into the opening, causing it to slowly melt. More and more power was drawn from the H'tes to burn through the doorway. Between the stillness field, the angel fire, and using it to keep him safe while jumping countless levels in the Spiritscape, Tone knew he was taxing the power reserves of his blade. Looking at the door, he hoped the one last blast left in the blade would be enough. If this didn't do it, he knew the stillness field would collapse shortly after the flames died away.

He positioned Zeke and Arino between the portal and himself. Holding the H'tes between his friends he pushed them toward the door as he sent one last stream of angelic fire at the weakened gateway. The door flew off the portal, leaving nothing but an opening as they floated through.

The stillness field failed as the H'tes' power died. They found themselves in the strangest realm any of them had ever seen.

# Chapter 28

"Am I the only one who feels like he should be looking for a caterpillar taking hits off a hookah?" asked Tone, looking at the scene all around them.

"I-I think we did go through the looking glass," stammered Arino, at a loss for words. "This is nothing like anything I have ever experienced."

"Yeah," agreed Zeke, looking around in amazement, trying to wrap his mind around this place.

The colors in the Spiritscape were always mind boggling to Tone. Every shade his imagination could conjure was present with many more beyond that. Even with the variety of colors, it all seemed like the design was tastefully done, colors working or contrasting with one another to create a hyper-real display of beauty. This new place looked like an artist's color palette had been spun, flinging colors all around with no rhyme or reason to the color choices or the way the hues would blend together.

Lacking the substance of the Spiritscape, there were no grand and glorious mountains and valleys. The terrain seemed to be fluidic as globs of colors merged and bounced off one another without any sense of purpose to what would merge and what would not. To Tone, it looked like a temperamental toddler was playing with blocks and clay, trying to make something from its ever-changing mind.

"You know it's bad when even I think something is too funky for words," declared Tone. "But I do have to admit I like the color scheme," he added as he looked at his colorful arm in comparison. It was startlingly similar. Looking at his two friends, he asked, "I'm not doing this, am I?"

Zeke laughed. "You know, I thought we might be in one of your nightmares when we arrived."

Not one to let a straight-line pass, Tone replied, "Nah, I'm not wearing my underwear over my head and there are no sumo wrestlers trying to feed me Brussels sprouts dipped in WD-40." Stage whispering, he added, "It makes them go down smoother."

Arino giggled. "Tone, you are the only one who can be in a strange place and say something that is even stranger than the melting colors."

"It's a gift," said the proud human.

"Well," began Zeke, "I wonder how we can find what we need in here. I guess we just have to start moving things out of the way." He reached out to brush aside a blue and crimson bubble, but it made a strange noise and fled from his touch. "Arino, is this what I think it is?"

Arino, startled by the action of the glob of colors, moved close to another that was a fusion of sickly green and a neon blue. Transforming into her amorphous form, she more closely resembled the terrain around them than an angel. Multiple amoeba-like forms drew near to Arino. She sent out tendrils of her spirit to try to touch the bubbles, causing most to flee from her touch. After several failed attempts, one gray-brown globule was finally touched.

"Amazing!" came the voice of Arino from her formless spirit. The gray-brown glob began to take on traces of the golden power of the healer and then broke contact, drifting away. It bumped into two other balls of color, adding traces of gold to each of them. Then the gray-brown blob separated into a brown ball and a gray flattened form – both with traces of gold. Tone and Zeke watched as the gold Arino had shared with the first was shared with more and more of these strange things until it faded into the mixture.

Returning to her normal form, Arino explained. "I have never encountered spirits like these. They are alive, but pure instinct – no intellect. I could sense their natures when I touched that one. No individual thoughts, more of a group-think. It's not quite a hive mentality. They communicate experience – not thought – through touch."

"That is too cool," declared Tone, reaching for the nearest floating ball. Energy flew from Tone's outstretched arm into the cream-colored ball, causing it to explode into thousands of smaller versions of itself that fled into the distance. Looking around like a kid caught frying ants with a magnifying glass, Tone spluttered, "Okay, that was an accident. I think I'll let Arino be the toucher, unless there is one with a badass attitude that we need to blow up." He tried to make light of the incident even though Zeke and Arino knew he felt bad.

"Just relax for a second, Tone. I want to try something." Zeke reached out, expanding his spirit toward a group of colorful globs that were bouncing off one another. As that portion of his spirit approached the meandering blobs, they sensed his proximity. The brown orb that had been part of the entity that first touched Arino, moved closer to Zeke's extended portion, but stopped before it touched him. The appendage Zeke was offering began to take on the multi-colored aspect of Tone. The blobs scattered. "They learn fast."

Arino tore her gaze from the floating forms around her and looked hard at Zeke. "How long have you been able to emulate Tone's appearance? I've never seen you do that." Her concern for her closest friend was plainly visible on her spirit.

"Yeah. You looked pretty good, but that's my shtick, dude," added Tone, more amused than concerned at the imitation.

Zeke smiled with a trace of mischief in his eyes. "I am learning how to focus the parts of Tone in me. It's everywhere all the time, but I can move large parts to places within my spirit." His eyes took on the psychedelic look of Tone. "I'm trying to be able to see things like Tone does. Quite literally." His eyes returned to their normal hazel.

Arino was not angry, but Tone and Zeke could tell she wasn't happy. "I need you to keep me informed about all the changes that are happening within you, Ezekiel. I'm your friend and more. But, I can't help you if you shut me out."

"Dude, she called you Ezekiel. You're in so much trouble," laughed Tone, only to be silenced by a glare from Arino. "Please don't call me Anthony," he begged. "I will have flashbacks to kindergarten and the whole disaster with the glue, the hamster and the funnel."

Ignoring Tone, she stared down the warrior. "Do we understand one another? I'm the one who is keeping the archangels off your back. You have to work with me."

Zeke smiled guiltily. "I guess I should mention the whole reading demons thing then."

Arino approached. "Let me in! All the way in." She merged with the hunter, leaving Tone trying to look anywhere but at the angels.

"So, bubbles, how are you today? Anyone want to be popped? I can do that really well. I love what you've done with the place. Who is your decorator? I'm thinking a wacky Salvador Dali drinking jet fuel."

After what seemed like far too long to Tone, the two angels separated. Arino had a look Tone couldn't discern. She was either shocked, amazed, impressed or all of those feelings at the same time. He figured it was all.

Raising his hand like a schoolboy, Tone asked, "Do I get to know what Zeke can do? Please don't do the whole merge with me thing, buddy. That would be an overshare."

Zeke smiled at his friend. "I can sense what demons are doing. Not quite like you can read us when we let you, but it is like a precognition of what they are likely to do. It's not like Irkja's ability, but along the same spirit lines. It just started when I was pretending to torture Adsendelk. I knew exactly what Fidrol was going to do, and how it would react. I don't know how I knew, but I did."

"Dude, that is going to make you even more of a badass when you are hunting them. Way to go!" Tone tried to offer a high five to his friend. His enthusiasm wasn't matched by either of the angels. "I'm missing something again, aren't I?"

Arino spoke with a solemn voice. "It means he is becoming tuned into the demons' thoughts. It may be a good thing, or it could be the beginning of his falling."

Zeke made light of the issue. "We can worry about that later. Right now, we need to get past all these balloons and find Adoneal."

Behind the trio, the fixed portal that stood at the entry to this strange place made a noise as it activated. As if connected, all three turned in unison to see an angel come through the portal. Seeing them, it turned back to the portal, touched it, and ported away on its own power. The glow of the portal changed.

"I'm no expert, but I don't think that was a good thing," commented Tone.

"No," said Zeke. "That was not a good thing. That was Talgram, one of the angels who disappeared from the hanger. So much for the element of surprise."

Arino looked at the fixed portal. "This is a strange portal. It is still active, but I can't tell where it leads. Talgram changed its destination before he ported."

"Well, I'm not going through it," stated Tone, emphatically. "I am convinced that I will end up someplace nasty every time I use the damned things. And I usually do!"

Zeke examined the portal carefully, using senses that Tone did not possess. "No, Tone. You would not like this one. Not one damn bit. I can tell this one is linked to a place I have sent demons many times. It is a bit chilly there."

"Oh, hell no!" exclaimed Tone.

Zeke had a sad smile. "Hell yeah, would be more accurate." He shared a look with Arino who nodded back to him. "Tone, neither Arino nor I can destroy this portal. We can't even change it. We have to find another way out of here or get someone to change it for us. There is no way you would make it once we were passed the gray on the other side. You wouldn't last a millionth of a quoll getting out of Hell."

Tone seemed nonplussed at the news. "Oh well. We have to find Adoneal anyway. He can fix anything. So enough waiting around. Where are we going, angels?"

Arino smiled her first smile since Zeke's revelation about reading the demons. "I will never understand the way you think, Tone. You are such a mass of incongruities. First, you are the most sarcastic being I have ever encountered. Next, you have the most beautiful, blind optimism of any spirit in any of the realms."

Winking at the healer, Tone replied, "I am a confusing conundrum of contradictions. It's part of my charm."

"I keep telling you to look up that word. I don't think you understand what is meant by 'charm'," jested Zeke. "Tone, can you see any trails?"

Tone focused. "Let's see what I can see." A faint green and several fading angel trails went off in one direction. Tone watched as one of the colorful balls passed through a trail causing it to fade further. "The great balls of color are slowly erasing the trails, but I can tell some went that way." The human pointed the direction the trails travelled. "If these critters are everywhere, this will be the hardest place to follow trails."

Arino shook her head. "I wonder if Irkja knew that. If he did, it's brilliant. I don't think we can count on the trails heading straight to his lair. That would be too easy."

Zeke chuckled. "When do we ever do things the easy way?"

"Bah," said Tone, waving dismissively. "We don't need no stinking easy." Then he looked around at the area they would have to cover. "But, once in a while, it wouldn't break my heart."

"I agree," said Zeke and Arino together.

Zeke carried Tone as they flew along at top angelic speed. It was not as fast as a skimmer, but it was still impressive. With Arino leading the way, sending out waves of power to clear the colorful blobs out of their way, they flew along, stopping periodically so Tone could look for trails. After several backtracks and turns, they entered an area devoid of the bountiful, bouncing balls.

Tone was puzzled. "There are no blobs here, but there are no trails either. Did we take a wrong turn?" Looking back he spied three of the trails they had been following. "No. They just end right there. Why does that fill me with a sense of foreboding just like when I eat five-bean salad with a prune juice chaser?"

Arino looked at Zeke. "I'm fine with not meeting Tone on Earth."

Zeke smiled. "Tell me about it." He looked at the healer. "Arino, are you trembling?"

Arino looked at Tone and Zeke. "I think we all are. What is that?"

"Oh shit!" shouted Tone, pointing.

A gargantuan ball of mixed colors was rolling toward them, absorbing any stray blobs that wandered out onto this strange plain in this strange place, causing the entire region to shake as it thundered along. Zeke grabbed Tone and began flying at an angle away from the oncoming ball with Arino right by his side. The faster they flew, the faster the ball went, slowly gaining ground. The angels took a radical change of direction, only to have the course matched by the rolling ball of color. It was chasing them.

Arino shouted, "Keep going!" She stopped to face the ball, expanding her blob-like form to its maximum potential. Arino send a massive wave of angel-fire at the rolling orb. The fire went right into the gargantuan glob, but had no effect on the speed of the monstrosity dwarfing Arino as it threatened to roll over her.

"We've gotta help her," shouted Tone. "Drop me and save her. I'll blast it apart if it gets to me." Then he wiggled out of Zeke's arms, short-circuiting any debate from the warrior. Hitting him with all his might, he barely nudged his friend toward Arino.

Zeke ported right beside the healer just as the ball was on them. Before they could touch to create their dual-angelic blast, the ball rolled over them both, leaving nothing in its wake. It rolled and raged toward Tone before he even had time to process what had just happened to his partners.

"Okay, this is gonna hurt one of us," muttered Tone, holding up his arms as the colorful ball rolled onto him.

# Chapter 29

Tone felt like a tidal wave of color was washing through him. Bright pinks and sky blues rushed by as they permeated his spirit. He was certain he could feel the ruby reds and fiery oranges burning him from the inside out. A cool, blue wave comforted and cooled him to the point he felt frozen. And then it was all gone.

"Okay, I think I'm half well-done and half icicle," muttered Tone, afraid to open his eyes. A wave of power that cooled his warm parts and warmed his cool parts washed over him. He opened his eyes to see the smiling face of Arino. "Did I die?" asked the human, not sure if he meant that as a joke or not.

"You are very alive. Now get up and help me," snarled Zeke. Tone looked at his friend who was only halfway through the wall of whatever they were in.

Tone gaped at the hunter who was only half-way through the wall. "What happened to you? I bet you look really silly with your ass hanging out this ball thing." He reached and began pulling on Zeke with no discernable effect. Arino was conspicuously not helping. "Hey sweetie, a little help would be appreciated. I'm not sure I can get him out without you doing your healer thing."

She shook her head. "There is something wrong, Tone. I tried to help him out and we almost went supernova with power. One of us is overloaded." She made a nodding gesture to Zeke. "Some angels just can't seem to contain their power around me." Zeke shook his head.

Tone responded, "Well, I hate to break it to you, but some of us humans know how he feels." He made a show of looking her up and down.

"As funny as this is for the two of you," interrupted Zeke, "I am useless right now. Did I mention the pain? A lot of pain! It's not my fault my power is out of control. For some reason this part of me is just angel, but the part that is stuck in the wall is my angel-human mix. I can feel my spirit, but I can't seem to get out of the wall."

H'tes swinging into his hand, Tone stabbed it deep into the surface beside Zeke. The wall yielded to his blade easily. Too easily. It seemed like it was fleeing from the power. Tone used his dagger to make the wall melt away from his friend. With Zeke freed, they took their first look around this unusual space within the unusual place.

"How big was that ball?" asked an astonished Tone. He looked around the large room and discovered that there were countless passages going off in several directions. Each one had a greenish glow just like the room they were in.

Arino explained. "This place is made up of those living blobs, their life energy is being used to make this bigger than it seems when seen from the outside. This is where Irkja is hiding. I can sense him in the green haze."

Zeke looked at her askance. "How do you know about this place?" It was obvious that he was as much in the dark as Tone.

Arino smiled with her whole spirit. "You are not the only one who has power, Ezekiel." The smile faded as she explained, "As a healer, I can sense when other beings are in pain, and this group of beings is suffering by being forced together. I can feel their screams, their suffering, their cries. If I thought it would help, I'd send some healing into them, but I know it won't. We have got to stop Irkja. He is out of control with whatever mission he is on."

The hunter looked at the multicolored walls around them. "It's like looking at Tone all the time."

"But not near as handsome," added Tone.

"Well…" teased Zeke. Before Tone could riposte the jab, Zeke asked, "Can you see any trails in here, Tone? We've got to find Adoneal and stop whatever Irkja is doing. We're running out of quolls."

Tone looked around. "It's useless. There are trails going all over the place. It's like a parade of spirits came through with clowns and acrobats bouncing all over the place. And the spiritual elephants were fed way too much fiber, if you get my meaning."

Arino sighed, "Fecal comments aside, I think I know where to go. I can feel pain coming from the middle corridor. That seems to be a good place to start." She began heading toward the one in pain.

Zeke spoke up. "Wait. Do you really think we should go toward the ones in pain?" He was not comfortable with his loss of control of the situation."

Arino turned to face Zeke and Tone, eyes blazing. "I am going down this corridor. Are you coming?" She resumed her path, continuing toward the ones who were hurting.

Tone patted his friend on the back. "Women. Can't live with 'em. Can't let them go down spooky corridors of rolling hideouts in strange realms." He followed the healer.

Zeke just shook his head. "I have a bad feeling about this." He caught up with his friends before they had made it to the end of the hallway. As they entered the room, Arino and Tone stood still, gaping at the scene before them. "I hate it when I'm right," was all Zeke could say.

The room was a place to torture demons. There were twelve transparent compartments containing twelve different kinds of demons. There was everything from a tiny, lethargic imp to a misty blue haze that looked more sedentary than flowing. One of the cells contained a furious blue-winged, raven-like demon that fluttered and clawed at the clear walls, leaving a blue essence oozing along the barrier. Both a blue, leathery tiger with the face of a child and a gorgonesque demon looked like they were frozen in place. The most terrifying demon was so still Tone wondered if it was dead. It was eel-like in its body with the face of a featherless vulture, frozen in mid scream.

Three of them – the raven-like demon, something that looked like a hellhound with blue frost snorting from its nostrils, and a hog-face demon – raged at the angels as they entered the room, screaming curses that couldn't be heard through the walls of their prisons. Two others – the blue haze and a demon that looked like a gigantic man with putrefying organs on the outside of his body – stared blankly at the trio who had entered the room, no recognition shown in the faded blue eyes. The other seven floated in their cells, completely oblivious to anything happening around them. Each demon was connected to a central basin by green, pulsating tubules that seemed more fluid than solid.

One of the active demons – a hog-faced creature with the body of an enormous, hairless ferret – pounded on the transparent shell of its prison. Amid the spray of spittle, they could see its rage was directed more at the basin in the center of the room, than the angels and Tone. Carefully approaching the basin, Arino looked within and gasped. At the bottom of the caldron was the last thing she had expected to see in this place. It was a small glowing golden piece of an angel.

Zeke growled, "Arino, don't move." The hunter had seen something she had missed. One of the twelve green tubules going from the demons to the basin was growing a tendril, which was snaking toward Arino. Zeke, in his full warrior glory, sent a wing of his spirit out, slashing the green shoot before it reached the healer. Arino turned in time to see the green tendril sliced, saving her from a frightening fate. Zeke wasn't as fortunate as he screamed in agony causing Tone to turn crimson with fear and anger.

The green tubule that Zeke had severed had attached itself to the part of his spirit that had touched it. The area of Zeke that was connected to the tubule began to lose its golden angelic glow.

"It… is…. stealing…. my…. power!" grunted Zeke, futilely trying to pull away from the siphon. Behind Arino, the glow from the basin transformed into a blazing golden light. Tone moved up to Zeke, unsure of what to do. He reached for the tubule, hoping it wouldn't drain him as well.

An angel came flying into the room, sizing up the situation instantly. "Do not touch him," shouted Torkel. "It will sap your power, too. I can get it off him, but it will take me…" Tone's H'tes sliced neatly and quickly through the green tubule, freeing Zeke from the suffering. Torkel looked at Tone, "Or you could do that."

Tone pressed the stillness rune on his blade, freezing everything in place. He checked the barely conscious Zeke, moving him further away from the spirit suckers to be right next to Arino. He turned the healer so she would see the hunter the moment she could move again. Causally moving up to Torkel, he pressed his blade against the angel's throat and hit the rune to remove the stillness field. Terror filled Torkel's eyes as Tone appeared in front of him. The touch of the blade was enough to drain some of the mechanic's power, leaving him at Tone's mercy.

"Do I have your complete and undivided attention, Torky?" asked Tone, the venom in his voice terrifying all three angels in the room. A petrified Torkel managed a bob of his head in acknowledgement. "Excellent. Arino, make sure Zeke is okay while I have a chat with our old friend here." Arino was already sending healing power into the hunter, restoring his essence while keeping an eye on the human.

"Now, Torkel, if I don't like your answers, I may just have to see how much angel power my H'tes can absorb. Don't bother trying to port. While my H'tes is touching you, all the porting power will just go right in here." Tone wasn't even sure that was true, but he pressed the flat of the blade harder onto the angel's spirit to make it seem more believable. "So, think before you answer, because your little mad science experiment here almost killed my best friend. Explain what this place is, Dr. Franken-angel."

"It is for Adoneal," said Torkel, as if that explained everything. Tone twisted the blade so that the edge was against the angel's spirit.

"I need you to explain that a little better. Remember, I'm a special needs kind of guy," whispered Tone, the threat in his voice not matching the humor. The angel was beginning to lose much of his glow as the H'tes drained his power. "You may want to hurry. I really don't know what will happen if I keep doing this, but since it's you, I'm willing to find out."

Torkel looked at the human, trying to decide if he was bluffing. "You are not that vicious. Zeke might push it, but you don't have what it takes to hurt me. It is your conscience that will betray you every…" Torkel screamed louder than Zeke had screamed, as Tone allowed the blade to cut into his spirit, draining exponentially more power.

"Oops. Slipped. How careless of me," said Tone, not even trying to sound sincere. "I hate to bring up someone else's flaws, but I think you need a reminder. You betrayed us. You helped angel-nap Adoneal. You are part of this whole crazy-ass shit that almost killed Zeke. And you almost made Arino cry. That irks me. When I get irked, I get cranky. When I get cranky, the archangels really regret giving me my H'tes." Waving the blade in the face of the angel, "So let's try this again. What the hell are you doing here?"

"We are refining the spiritual essence of these demons to heal Adoneal. Look in the basin, Arino." The healer looked from Tone to the cauldron, and then moved to look inside it again.

Arino examined the glowing fragment at the bottom of the bowl. "It looks like part of an angel." She expanded all of her senses to examine it. "It is not quite right. There is something missing. Even with the extra power it stole from Zeke, it still needs something more. It has the essence, but not the power." She glared up at Torkel. "You have been stealing power from these demons for nothing! Half of them are so weakened they may not ever recover. How can you rationalize this?"

Torkel regained some of his confidence. "I don't have to explain my actions to you." The defiance in his voice was clear. The next sound he made was another scream thanks to the tip of Tone's H'tes making the human's point for him.

"Damn these shaky hands of mine," said a sarcastic Tone. "They tend to slip when someone is rude to my friends. Now, be nice, Torky, and answer the lovely lady's question."

The former service angel glared at Tone, but made no move against him. "We are trying to take from the essences of the demons to make a new piece for Adoneal. We used twelve different ones so we wouldn't kill any of them. We are still angels, Arino. Plus, using twelve different kinds of demons allowed Irkja to create the essence we need to help Adoneal. If it was Raphael, wouldn't you do anything you could to help him?" Gazing at Zeke, who had been listening as Arino continued healing him. "What would you do for Michael?" Turning his attention back to Tone, he asked, "You are showing your true colors, Tone. See what you are doing for your friends? We are willing to do the same thing for Adoneal. It's not that different."

Zeke looked at the mechanic, not sure what to say. He knew that there was nothing he wouldn't do for Michael or Arino or even Tone. "There are limits, Torkel. Part of me can understand using the demons. But, what about Adoneal? How does he feel about all this? Does he want this?"

Torkel just looked at Zeke without answering. Arino read him perfectly. "He doesn't know, does he? You didn't tell him. This is not what he would want, you know that!" Arino was outraged at the hypocrisy. "You are trying to help the greatest inventor in the realms by doing something that would appall him. Do you even know Adoneal? I mean, really know him? I have been deep in his spirit when D'vrash and I healed his phasing. He exists to serve others." She was nearly screaming as she said, "He made the spirit spheres so we could contain demons without causing unnecessary injury. If this works, do you think he will be happy that you caused all this pain for him?"

Torkel remained silent, not having a good answer for the angel. Zeke, finally back to normal, asked, "If the healers couldn't make something like this work, why do you think you can restore Adoneal? Where did you get this stupid-ass idea?"

Tone spoke up. "You know, I was kind of wondering that myself. And I agree, it is a stupid-ass idea."

A chill filled the room as a soft voice responded to Tone's demand. "If you must know, Tone. I got the idea from what happened with you and Zeke," said Irkja from the doorway. "It's about time you three got here."

# Chapter 30

The green glow tinted the entire room with a sickly haze. The demons who had been catatonic or lethargic were instantly resuscitated by the presence of Irkja. The reaction was one unique in Zeke and Arino's vast experience dealing with the satanic spirits. All twelve cringed away from Irkja, as they all moved as far away as their prisons allowed. An enormous, blue-furred demon that was only a snaggletoothed face tried to chew its way through the wall farthest from the green haze of the former angel. Irkja chuckled at the reaction of his prisoners.

"Tone, would you mind removing your dagger from Torkel's neck?" asked Irkja, trying to sound amicable. "He's been drained enough. I believe he's about to pass out," Each of the green tubules going from the demons to the basin sprouted new tendrils. Four surrounded Zeke, four surrounded Arino, and four found their way to Tone. "Or we can always see who can drain more power," added Irkja, the not-so-veiled threat loomed around the trio.

Tone looked over at his friends and knew there was no way he could win. The tendrils around him were positioned at key spots that meant moving would mean touching one. Pulling back from the mechanic, Tone smiled his friendliest smile, saying, "Of course, old buddy. Anything for a friend who has soul-sucking snakes hovering around my real friends." Tone began slowly moving his hand toward the rune for the stillness field.

"Before you freeze us all, Tone, may I ask what you plan to do once you waste all the energy in your H'tes?" asked Irkja, the knowing smile on half of his face was really irritating Tone.

"Well, I was thinking of recharging it by stabbing you. You know, just to see what happens." Tone kept his finger hovering over the rune, still maintaining his friendliest smile.

Zeke, watching the green tendrils carefully, spoke up. "Irkja, you know this won't work. That piece in the bowl won't restore Adoneal. It's just not the right piece. Don't you think the healers tried everything they could?" He was moving around, trying to get in a position where he was not hounded by the green snakes all around him.

"They tried everything they would – not could. There's a difference," retorted Irkja. "That fragment is almost ready. It just needs something special, something unique to make it perfect." He looked at Tone with something akin to desire in his spirit. "I'm sorry Tone, but I need some of your power to make this work. We have done all the calculations and I'm certain we can do this."

Arino joined the conversation. "Why are you doing this, Irkja? Think back to what you once were. Can't you remember what you used to be? The Irkja I knew may have been willing to inflict some pain on a demon or two, but this is horrific! You are killing these demons and…"

The explosion of anger caused Tone and Arino to flinch. "AND THEY DESERVE WORSE!" screamed Irkja. Regaining some his composure, his rant took on a less volatile volume. "I would gladly sacrifice every damned demon in Hell if I thought it would make a difference for Adoneal!"

Zeke had been watching his former friend carefully. His new talent for reading demons had translated to the angel who was infused with some demonic power. This changed things, somewhat balancing the power between the two rivals. Zeke was seeing the truth behind Irkja's madness. He was quite sane. His madness was pure and simple anger, mixed with hatred of the demons who had caused Adoneal so much pain. The hunter understood and could sympathize to a point.

"These are some of the demons who stole parts of Adoneal when he was phased, aren't they?" asked the warrior. He looked at each one, finding a demon he knew. "I personally kicked Alecto's ass back to Hell for her part in it."

Irkja smiled in a way that showed neither happiness nor joy. It was a smile of the vigilante. "Exactly. These demons are not at all innocent, Arino. Their crimes over the eons alone make them deserving of this, but their role in Adoneal's downfall make them even more culpable."

"But what about Tone?" pleaded Arino. "How can you possibly think stealing some of his power is right?" The concern in the healer was genuine. She was beginning to see Irkja for what he was: unredeemable. He had no desire to be salvaged, and she could do nothing without his consent.

Irkja turned to the human. "I promise, you will not die. Pain seems likely, but you will be making a sacrifice that will be remembered by every angel for all eternity." The tendrils around Tone began encircling him, preparing to totally cover every part of the human. "I'll try not to cause any permanent damage, but there are no guarantees here. I'm not even sure what's going to happen when they touch you. It could be catastrophic for all of us, but it's a risk I'm willing to take for Adoneal."

Zeke opened his spirit to allow Tone to read him if he would look over. As it was, Tone was fixated on Irkja, with a look of panic infusing his spirit with shades of orange and yellow. "Tone, tell him what you saw in the basin."

Tone spun to look at the hunter, knowing he hadn't looked at the angelic piece being created. Instantly he saw all that was happening within the hunter. A plan that was so crazy it could just work. "Are you sure you want me to do that?" asked the human, with an evil smile on his face.

"Give him what he needs," said the hunter, glowing as if he prepared to attack.

Irkja laughed. "Do you really think you can attack me, Zeke? I know what you are going to do before you do it, old friend." He began expanding his presence into the room, causing the demons to literally bounce off the cell walls in fear.

"Irkja, I'm not going to touch you," replied the hunter. "Tone?"

"You know, Irky, it's like this," said Tone as he stilled the area by just thinking of the stillness rune on his H'tes. Everything had stopped as he had hoped. With all the strangeness in this area, he wasn't totally certain it would work. Looking at their frozen tormentor, he chuckled, "I don't think you can tell what I'm going to do. Now that I think about it, I really don't know what I'm going to do most of the time either."

Zeke, when he lowered his defenses, had told him exactly what to do. The first order of business was dealing with the tendrils. A few quick cuts and all twelve were safely moved away from the trio of heroes. All of them would be safe for a millionth of a quoll when Tone removed the stillness field. He hoped it would be enough.

The next item on Zeke's checklist was the biggest gamble of the plan. Tone moved up to the nearest demon container and examined it. A thrust of the H'tes revealed that the barrier was made from the same material as the wall. It melted away from his attack. Tone made a hole big enough for the demon to escape. The human went in and cut the green tubules from the demon, allowing it the freedom to cause havoc and confusion. He really hated being that close to demons, but it was safe as long as the stillness field held. Repeating that same tactic on each of the cells, he made it so that all the demons could charge out of their prison. Tone wondered what would happen when all hell broke loose in the room.

"I'm damn sure not going to be visible for this. Too many things in the room want to eat me." Carefully examining his blade, the power was beginning to fade. Tone had not absorbed very much power from Torkel, in spite of the way the wimpy angel acted. There was only a limited amount of power remaining due to the drain of the stillness field. "Let the games begin," he said as moved behind Irkja, while fading from view. The stillness field went away with a thought from the human.

Most of the demons took advantage of the instant holes that appeared in their transparent prisons. Nine of the twelve flew out and around the room, looking for a means of escape. Irkja immediately realized what Tone had done, silently calling for backup as the raven-like demon dove toward its tormentor. Irkja swatted it away and back into a cell, sealing the hole with a wave of power, melting it back to its original state.

Zeke wasted none of the distraction. He hoped that Tone had listened and hid behind Irkja as he sent a blast of angelic power at his former friend. Knowing what would happen, Irkja was able to dodge the blast that continued to the space behind him, disappearing into Tone's drained H'tes.

Arino had been let in on the plan through her link with Zeke and pounced once the stillness field had died. She sent her power that would heal an angel into the three demons that had not found the courage to leave their cells. That shock of pain spurred them into action with two escaping to charge the reinforcements that Irkja had summoned. The third demon moved too slowly as Irkja sent a green spray into the demon, blasting it back into the far wall of its cage. Irkja sealed the demon within its prison as Arino sent a wave of power toward him. He dodged it, allowing Tone to absorb more power into his blade. An attack from Zeke hit Irkja hard, surprising the former angel. A shared look between the two combatants conveyed the balancing of power. Irkja could see what was about to happen, but Zeke could read what Irkja was about to do.

The dozen angels Irkja had summoned, most of whom had never fought another spirit, focused on the escaping demons. If the demons had not been weakened, the angel technicians would have been far out of their league. As it was, they had their hands full trying to reign in the terrified Hadians. One angel entered the room and froze in place. Arino looked at the stunned angel, wondering why it had paused. It then collapsed and Arino caught a flash of a crystal blade receiving power before it disappeared again.

Tendrils of green power shot out of Irkja toward all the demons, connecting to them and causing an immediate end to their resistance. Angels were scrambling to shove the captured demons back into cells, as Irkja sent out misty green globs of power at Zeke and Arino. Arino dodged the one aimed at her which landed in the basin, filling it and protecting the contents. Zeke sent a blast of power directly at the cloud soaring toward him, bisecting it twice, leaving four smaller clouds coming at him, allowing him room to maneuver around them as they crashed harmlessly into the cells behind him. The power Zeke used on the clouds collided with Irkja, spinning him out of control and breaking the links he had with the demons. The four remaining demons attacked the angels trying to corral them. Two of them were able to overpower their captors, as each went flying down a separate corridor, away from the combat.

Irkja hit hard against the clear wall of a caged demon, causing it to scream and claw futilely at the back of the former angel. The fluidic part of Irkja lashed out, shooting through the wall and connected to the demon. The demon stopped its raging as it went from indigo to sky blue. Irkja turned a deeper shade of green, absorbing the demonic energy. He shot a blast of icy demonic power at Zeke who was able to evade most of the attack. Enough of the demon power hit the angel hard enough to send him flipping back into the open door of an empty cell. A wave of green energy followed behind the demon blast, sealing the hole in the wall, buying Irkja time to assess the situation.

Arino sprang into action to free the hunter, mirroring Zeke's efforts with angel fire cutting into the clear wall. Another cloud of green mist shot from Irkja, heading toward the back of the healer. A warning from Zeke and Arino flipped out of the way, sending a blast of healing power at her attacker. Irkja dodge most of the attack, but it still caught him on the side that still had substance. The healing power momentarily stunning Irkja, gave her a moment to check on the situation. She knew Zeke would have to free himself as Arino felt the heat of an attack from one of the Irkja's minions. Normally, angel fire would have no effect on other angels. This fire definitely did not feel good, even though it didn't cause immense pain. Their spirits had been corrupted to the point their fire was dangerous. But that also meant that her power would have an effect on them.

Arino sent a blast of angelic power toward her latest attacker, only to see the angel collapsing and her power absorbed into a H'tes that faded from view after attacking her opponent. Looking around the room, of the dozen angels Irkja had summoned, only three were still in the battle – all three of them were trying to deal with demons, ignoring her. Two others looked like they had not won their battles, being impaired from their wounds. The other seven were laying around in a coma identical to the one who just passed out. Arino smiled in approval at the non-lethal immobilization of the others. Tone had been busy. He should have quite a good charge on his H'tes by now.

As the wall of the Zeke's cage exploded out, it shocked Irkja to his senses. Roaring out of the cell, Zeke send an anticipated blast of power at his nemesis. Irkja didn't dodge, but prepared to receive the blast. The whole essence of the fallen angel glowed with pleasure-filled anticipation as the ball of angelic fire loomed. Zeke and Arino, realizing he was about to absorb the power, watched in horror as the blast hit him full in the chest. Flames encompassed Irkja as they began to be taken in. The flames died away before they could be consumed by the seer. The look of pleasure turned to pain as Irkja screamed, the liquid half of him boiling and with green geysers erupting from the surface. Sending out green tendrils in every direction, Irkja hit his invisible attacker, rendering Tone visible as he was sent flying out of the room. Irkja collapsed, not comatose like his minions, but severely weakened by the unexpected attack.

"Tone!" yelled Zeke and Arino. Arino flew at lightning speed after the human, with Zeke following to watch her back. The warrior looked at the rising Irkja and collapsed the wall above the fallen angel, burying him and buying them time to check on Tone.

The blast from Irkja had sent Tone flying all the way down in the corridor and into the next room. The stunned human had no sense of his surroundings as he looked around trying to sort things out, while his spirit pulsated through every color imaginable.

A calm voice surprised Tone. "Hello," said Adoneal, rising from his workbench. The archangel was totally free to move about as he approached Tone. "What are you doing here?"

# Chapter 31

"You know, the usual. There's a pie eating contest down the hall, and I haven't had any really good boysenberries in so long that I can feel it in my toenails," replied Tone, flipping his H'tes back into his arm to appear less threatening. "There is also the whole turning the Spiritscape upside down trying to find you, but that's just a side project around here."

The archangel stared at the human, trying to decipher what he was saying as Arino and Zeke stormed into the room. Both angels came to a dead stop as they saw Tone and Adoneal right beside one another.

"Hi guys. Donny and I were chatting about pie eating contests and the pros and cons of boysenberries. I was just about to ask him what the hell is going on here." Turning to the archangel, he continued. "So, Adoneal, what the hell is going on here?!"

Zeke flew through the room, searching for any other spirits. Finding nothing, he came to a halt beside his two friends and Adoneal. "Are you all right, Adoneal? We have been worried that Irkja had done something to you?"

The archangel of service gave him a confused look. "Why would you think that? Irkja would never do anything to me against my will. He serves me." Tone looked from Zeke to Arino several times. None of them understood what was happening.

Arino spoke. "Are you in control of this place? Are Irkja and the other angels here working under your orders?"

Adoneal stared blankly at her, trying to process the question. "Why would I not be in charge? I am the archangel of service. All the serving angels work at my command."

Zeke intervened. "Do you know where you are? This looks similar to your workshop, but you know it's not your real workshop, don't you?" The room had the same appearance as Adoneal's workshop in the Spiritscape, but it was not quite a perfect replica. The layout was identical down to the placement of supplies and the position of the workbench. If it were not for the greenish haze that infested everything, it would have been a perfect duplicate.

The archangel examined the room carefully. He moved around, looking at the odds and ends, repositioning a few pieces miniscule amounts so they were right where he wanted them. He regarded Zeke. "This is my workshop, warrior. This is where I do my work." He held up a crystal that morphed into an egg-shaped container, glowing with a golden fire within.

Ezekiel tried a different tactic. "Look around carefully, Adoneal. Don't look at the individual items. Look at this whole place with all your senses. Reach out with your creative flow and tell me if this still feels like your workspace." Tone could see in Zeke's open spirit that Adoneal, unsurprisingly, had senses beyond humans and other angels. One of them was the ability to sense the creative flow – the potential for change and reforming – within a given object. It was part of what made him an extraordinary inventor.

Adoneal froze in place, a look of amazement and awe spreading out from his core of his spirit. "This is not my workspace. It has much more creative flow than anything in my workspace." He continued examining the room, his spirit growing larger as he took in more and more information. "Is this workspace a living spirit?" He looked like he was laying down on the floor of the room, carefully examining the tiniest parts. "I do believe this is a living spirit. Where are we?"

"We are where I can help you," came a voice from behind Tone. The human froze, wishing he still had his H'tes out. He turned to face the flowing form of Irkja. Arino and Zeke joined hands, prepared to use their angel blast to stun the rebel angel.

"Hey, Irkja. We were just about to tell Adoneal that you have been a bad boy. Do you want to tell him about the whole kidnapping him and torturing demons thing?" Tone stage whispered. "I won't say a word about that room with pink hippos doing Russian dance moves in spandex bodysuits. We'll keep that tidbit between us."

Adoneal glowed golden. "What are they talking about Irkja? I thought we were trying to find a way to restore you." The archangel was beginning to expand.

Tone looked closely at Adoneal and began to get nervous. His glow was getting brighter and Tone was beginning to see something he had never seen in the spirit of that archangel: anger! The human could see that the power of Adoneal would become a problem if it reached him. Taking advantage of Irkja's distraction, he moved from between the two to a safe place behind Zeke.

"I never said we were trying to restore me. I said we were going to restore an angel who was grievously injured. Failing to correct you when you thought I was referring to me was my greatest sin, Adoneal." Tone was pretty sure that Irkja was turning a new shade of green as his mentor glowed brighter.

"You are so busted, dude," giggled Tone, as the trio backed away, keeping the angels between the action and the human.

"You would dare to deceive me?!" rumbled Adoneal. "YOU?! Of all my angels, you were one of the few I could recall, one of the few I felt would do anything I needed." His growth in size was only rivaled by the growth of his golden glow. Irkja was trying to face him, but the power coming from the archangel was beginning to reach him.

The fallen angel momentarily regained his confidence. "Yes, Adoneal. I will do anything you need. Even if you don't know you need it. Especially, then." Those words stopped the growth of power that seemed ready to explode in the archangel. He looked at Irkja, waiting for more explanation. "I am going to restore you to what you once were." His voice began to rise. "Don't you miss the way you used to be? Do you remember how you would link with all of us who were serving with you? The addition of your mind to ours was something that made us all better. You shared that massive creativity with those of us who were lowly angels, lifting us higher than we ever dared dream! After Je'relir phased you, things haven't been the same. We want you back. We NEED you back. Can't you understand what we lost when we lost you?"

The golden glow relented as Adoneal began to understand. Soft words came from the archangel, saying, "You have always said you did not care how I was. As long as I was still here. Now, you seem to think differently. Am I not enough of a leader? Of an archangel for you?" Turning to Tone, he asked, "Human…" He seemed to be straining, as he asked, "Anthony?"

He peeked from behind Zeke, "That's me. But Donny, I really don't want to get in the middle of this. It seems like a family feud and, living in Tennessee, I know all about the Hatfields and McCoys. I don't think it worked out too well for the lawmen who tried to referee that little spat. Plus, you two could both slip and blow the shit out of me and I haven't seen a bathroom in the place."

Ignoring his babble, Adoneal asked, "Can you see truth from lies in Irkja?" The question was a simple one, but not something Tone wanted to answer. Adoneal stared at the human until Tone felt like the angel was seeing him naked. He moved so that only the top of his head was visible behind Zeke.

"Sort of. He doesn't really lie as much as he withholds truth and manipulates meanings."

"If he says anything that is deceptive, will you please tell me? I cannot tell truth from lies." A nervous nod from Tone was enough for Adoneal. Looking back at Irkja, he asked again, "Am I not sufficient as the archangel of service for you to follow?"

Irkja glowed brightly, anger spilling out in waves of green on the half of his body that flowed. "No, you are not. But I can restore you. We have a plan. It is almost ready. All we need is some of Tone's power and you can be restored to your former glory."

Adoneal looked at his protégé, the golden glow of his anger replaced by an anemic yellow of sadness. "How long have you thought of me as less than enough?" Arino looked at him, seeing his heartbreak, she sent a wave of healing power to help strengthen him.

The inventor looked at her, gratitude shining bleakly in his sorrow-filled spirit.

"I formulated this plan after my injuries at the Dovhavhads Spires," replied the green glowing spirit.

Adoneal looked at Tone who responded. "True enough, but he didn't answer your question."

A green blob shot out from an angry Irkja that was upon Zeke, Arino and Tone before they could even react. Zeke turned, wrapping himself around Tone to protect him as Arino placed a barrier of angel fire around them. The blob hovered right in front of them, not reaching the wall of fire. An instant later, the green goo shot back across the room, striking Irkja and sending him flying into a shelf full of crystals that were scattered in all directions. A golden glow of energy went back into Adoneal.

"I believe by your reaction that Anthony was accurate. The next time you attack the healer, the warrior, or Anthony, I will not be as gentle." Adoneal turned to the trio. "I apologize for his actions. It will not happen again."

Tone's mouth was hanging open. "If that was gentle, remind me not to piss him off. I would look lousy as a Rorschach Tone-blot."

Zeke joined in the conversation. "Thank you for defending us Adoneal. I'm afraid I have to be the one to inform you that he attacked us in the room with demons being drained."

Adoneal glowed golden with anger again. "What room is that?"

Irkja led the way down the hall toward the scene of the battle. Tone spoke up, "This hallway looks totally different when you're not flying down it, spinning like a turbo-charged tilt-a-whirl. I love what you've done with these walls," said Tone, tapping the sickly gray-green surface of the hallway.

Entering the room, they could see the few angels who were still conscious had managed to cage all but one of the demons. A nod from Irkja sent them searching for the remaining demon elsewhere in the rolling hideout. The nine that Tone had managed to disable had all been moved to one spot where they were stacked together like a pile of broken dolls until their power was restored. Arino wanted to go to them and help, but resisted her natural desire to heal until Adoneal understood the entire situation.

Adoneal looked around the room, trying his best to understand what was being done. He looked carefully at the demons, examining the green tubules going from each one to the basin in the center of the room.

"Those are something I made based on your plan for a device that healers could use to heal one hundred angels at once," explained Irkja, trying to regain some semblance of pride. The archangel grabbed one of the siphons, pulled it out of the demon and the basin and shredded it, examining every detail with a detached objectivity. When he was done, he tossed it away like something unworthy of his attention.

Looking into another cell, the caged demon began to rush the clear wall. It stopped, frozen in mid-roar as Adoneal passed through the wall of the prison, spinning the demon to examine the attachment of the green tube. He pulled it out, examining the spot where it had been connected. Once he was satisfied, he tossed the demon away like he had with the uninteresting siphon and moved out of the cell. A very confused demon sat in the far side of cell, too perplexed to move.

"I have no clue what he just did, but I'd like to see him do it to another one," commented Tone.

"I have a funny feeling, if you wait around a while, you just might," said Zeke. "Adoneal, all the demons are attached to that device in the middle of the room. They are being drained of their power…"

A wave of the archangel's hand and all the green tubules popped out of the demons and the basin, tied themselves together and shot toward Irkja, surrounding him and eventually being absorbed into the rebel angel.

"Or he could do something like that," said Zeke, obviously impressed.

From the hall, a rumbling sound caused everyone – even Irkja – to look and see what was happening. One of the fixed portals from Adoneal's workshop flew into the room, stopping by the archangel.

"Warrior, please send all these demons through the portal," said Adoneal. It was clear this was not a suggestion.

Zeke approached the portal, looking at it carefully and smiling. With Adoneal watching and Irkja scowling, Zeke went to the first cell and tore open a hole in the transparent wall. The imp within cowered away from the hunter. He grabbed the demon, took it to the portal and casually tossed it through. All the demons were watching with unusual interest for Hadians. Zeke approached the second cell, as soon as there was a way out, the raven-like demon freely flew to the portal and left the hellacious prison for the real Hell. Each of the next nine demons willingly flew out through the portal, grateful for their freedom from Irkja's experiments. With one remaining in a cell, the angels who had been searching for the missing demon arrived, a demon struggling against them. Zeke approached, grabbed the hag of a demon, and casually tossed it through the portal.

The last demon would be the most dangerous. As a blue mist, it was the least predictable and hardest to touch. Tone hid behind Arino as Zeke sauntered up to the cell. "Are you going to be a problem?" asked the warrior. "You can leave nice and easy, or you can make this hard. Personally, I'd prefer the hard way." The smile Zeke gave the demonic mist lacked humor or happiness. He was challenging it to try something.

The blue mist glowed as a soft voice drifted from it. "I have no desire to remain here." Zeke tore open the cell, allowing the demon haze to float toward the portal. As it neared the entrance, Irkja moved aside when it tried to send a blast of demonic mist at him.

Zeke moved faster than the demon, placing himself between the mist and the portal. There was a malevolent golden glow in the hunter's eyes. "You really shouldn't have done that." Ezekiel expanded, as the wings of his spirit surrounded the mist. He winked at Tone, "Watch this." Part of his spirit became translucent, allowing a gold-tinted view of a demon struggling to get out of the prison that was Zeke. Angelic fire filled the area, scorching the demon as Zeke smiled at his own ingenuity.

"That is sufficient," stated Adoneal. "Please complete the task, warrior." The archangel was looking closely at Ezekiel, his gaze was inscrutable, but Arino suspected he was curious about the warrior's methods. Zeke turned to face the portal, releasing the seared and singed demon to drift away and back to Hell.

"You have to admit, you deserved that," Zeke said to Irkja, chuckling at the demon's parting shot. Irkja growled at the closing portal. One look from Adoneal and the portal was sent flying back down the hall.

Tone peeked from behind Arino. "Adoneal is scary powerful, isn't he?" There was a little fear and a great deal of awe in his voice.

"Yes, he is," admitted Arino. "More than you know." Tone looked at Arino and could tell she was thinking more than she was communicating. She turned and noticed his gaze. "Later, sweetie."

He smiled at the term of endearment. "You know that won't work every time, right?"

The healer returned the smile. "Yes, it will," she said with a giggle.

"Yes, it will," sighed Tone. "But, we will get back to this."

"Of course we will, sweetie," laughed Arino, looking back to Adoneal, who was watching them like a scientist watching an experiment he couldn't understand.

Irkja spoke his first words since being snubbed by his archangel. "Please just look at what I've been able to create for you. It's in the basin. I know if you let me remove the covering from…" His words were cut off as Adoneal neared the basin, the green goo that Irkja had used to cover it during the battle was sent flying at the fallen angel. Irkja caught the gob of green, but the impact sent him staggering back into the remainder of a cell wall causing it to shatter.

Irkja gazed up, covered with shards of wall, a look of sadness showing in his spirit.

"Yeah, Adoneal has a temper. Noted," came the voice of Tone from behind Arino.

Adoneal looked at the healer. "Anthony, I would never use my power against a human or an angel. Only demons or," he glared at Irkja and his partners in crime, "against these New Fallen." He peered into the basin, looking at the contents for an unusually long amount of time. Reaching in, he removed a few fragments of spirit. "Is this what you created?" asked the archangel, obviously neither pleased nor impressed.

Irkja was by his side in an instant. "No!" he screamed. Looking in the basin, he removed a few more tiny fragments of spirit. "What happened to it?" Turning on Zeke, he raged, "You did this! This is your fault. I could have done it! I could have restored him to his greatness! He would have been the Adoneal of old! How did you destroy it? I covered it before… before…" He looked around the room for Tone. "Where is he?!" Green mist shot out of Irkja in every direction, a wail of loathing screeched, "TONE!!!"

Arino had moved to cover Anthony from the assault, but it was unnecessary. Zeke moved between Irkja and Arino, sending out a counter blast to his fury. All the green mist was sent in other directions. A sound from the workshop caught Zeke's attention. A spirit sphere bounded into the room and came to rest beside the warrior. One nod from Adoneal and Zeke knew what to do. He touched the sphere, causing the lines of runes to spin so quickly they turned into blue lines crisscrossing the golden sphere at odd angels. Once the lines were solid, Zeke touched the wall of the sphere nearest the out-of-control Irkja. With one fast move, a wave of energy swept out from Adoneal, sending Irkja somersaulting back and into the sphere, trapping him within. Zeke went to the pile of semi-conscious New Fallen and threw them into the spirit sphere to join their leader.

Adoneal turned to the remaining New Fallen. He merely looked at them and gestured toward the spirit sphere. Two of them flew straight in without hesitation. The last one approached Adoneal, preparing to make a case. Before the fallen angel could say a word, Adoneal reached out and grabbed it by the neck. "If you try to rationalize torture and kidnapping as something you did to help me, I will not be pleased." He released the New Fallen. It wisely flew straight into the spirit sphere.

The human peeked out from behind Arino. "Are they gone?" He looked over and saw the spirit sphere slowly becoming transparent. The half fluidic face of Irkja leered out at him. "I didn't touch the doohickey to fix Adoneal. Scout's honor," said Tone.

Zeke laughed. "You were never a Boy Scout."

Making a show of holding his finger to his mouth, Tone replied, "Shhhhh. He doesn't know that."

# Chapter 32

Travelling back down the hall to Adoneal's workshop, Arino looked back into the torture room at the crowded spirit sphere and wondered aloud, "What will happen to Irkja and the other angels?" Her loving, healing nature never ceased to look for a means of redemption.

Adoneal spoke without looking back. "I do not know. There are some who are not beyond redemption." The unspoken implication that others were beyond redeemable made hope for Irkja seem slim. "I need to return to the archangels. I am certain that my absence has been the source of some confusion."

Tone looked at the artistic angel. "You could say that. You could also say that penguins are cute when they are the most adorable of all tuxedo wearing animals."

"I do not understand you much of the time," stated Adoneal, without meaning it to sound funny.

Arino responded, "Don't worry, Adoneal. We don't either." She looked closely at the archangel. "Are you feeling odd?" She was sensing growing fissures in his spirit that were along the lines where he had been phased apart. His exertions had increased the speed of his collapse.

"I am," stated the angel. "It has been far too long since I have seen the tiny spirit. I'm certain she is getting overpowered by now. Your assistance is needed." He turned to her and waited for her to react.

The healer sent a massive wave of healing power into Adoneal causing the cracks to shrink a miniscule amount. "Adoneal, we need to get you back to the Spiritscape. Can you use one of your fixed portals to link with another on the outside?"

"We are not in the Spiritscape?" asked the confused archangel. Zeke explained where they were and how they had gotten there.

Adoneal smiled. "That is why I saw gray within the monument to my injury. I assumed it and the other angel were not really there."

Zeke perked up. "What other angel? There was someone in there with you?" The warrior's instincts told him there was something he was missing.

Adoneal appeared distracted by a crystal that was out of place. "Oh. Yes. It was one of my angels, but he did not speak when I spoke to him. Any time I speak and something does not reply, I presume it is something that is not there or it cannot speak. This time it was one of the angels who service the skimmers. I do not recall his name, but he works on the one you used when fighting the beast."

Zeke moved into his way so Adoneal had to look at him. "Torkel. It was Torkel. He must have seen you and gone back to tell Irkja. That made it so much easier to capture you and bring you back here." Zeke shook his head in disgust.

Tone began counting on his fingers, turning to Zeke. "How many New Fallen did you cram into that spirit sphere? I'm counting thirteen, including Irky."

"That sounds about right."

The human continued counting. "Okay. I drained nine of them and they were stacked like a funny looking woodpile in the corner." He closed his eyes, trying to remember. "I drained Torkel, but I didn't drain him as bad as the others. I don't remember him being on the angel-pile. I don't know who the others were helping Irky. Do you remember tossing Torkel in the spirit sphere?"

"Why do you…" Zeke stopped in mid-sentence. "Oh shit," he whispered. Realization dawned on all but Adoneal.

The hunter flew at lightning speed out of the room and down the hall. Tone, Arino and Adoneal followed close behind. Before they entered the room, a shout of frustration could be heard from Zeke. "Stupid! Stupid! Stupid!" screamed the angel, beating the side of the empty spirit sphere. The indestructible device was being put to the test as flames of rage flew from clinched fists with each impact. With one last two fisted slam, Zeke looked up into the fear-filled eyes of Tone and Arino. A glance at Adoneal told him the archangel was looking at him like he was a device gone wrong.

Arino approached him. "Relax, Zeke. We can find them again." She was sending all the calming energy she could into the warrior.

"How could I have missed that? I'm better than this." There was no calming or consoling Zeke. His anger was growing brighter with each word he spoke.

"Dude, we all missed it," said Tone, afraid to reach out to his furious friend. "It's not like they are going to get very far. I'll bet you that Mikey has a butt-load of angels waiting on the other side of the Gray. And if a bunch can dance on the head of pin, you can only imagine how many a butt-load is." Tone's humor failed to get a reaction out of the enraged warrior. Tone made mental note to discuss anger management classes with Zeke when he was less likely to smack him. "Zeke, I'm saying this as a friend – switch to decaf. It is just as tasty as real coffee once you get used to it." Still getting no smile, Tone turned to Arino. "I'm getting nothing here. Give it a try. Show him your boobs or something."

"Ezekiel, our priority is getting Adoneal to open a portal out of…" Arino was interrupted by Zeke.

"The portals!" he shouted, flying back down the hallway. He arrived just in time to see Irkja waving good-bye, as he stepped through an open portal, closing the door behind him. Zeke's rage erupted as an enormous ball of angelic fire hit the fixed portal sending fire in all directions on impact. Tone moved into the room, H'tes in hand and absorbed all the angelic energy.

"Thanks, amigo. I needed a little more power to top off the tank." Tone was trying to distract from the angry angel in the room. Looking at his friend, he could see everything in his spirit. The frustration with the whole situation, and the fear that all this would start over again with Irkja and his minions on the run. As a hunter, he had a near perfect record of tracking and locking away those he hunted. This was a rare case of something he had in his sights slipping away.

Their eyes locked and Tone could see the angel was terrified that something would happen to the human if Irkja had the opportunity to capture him. "Zeke, chill out. I'm okay."

"If that damned piece hadn't been shattered in the battle, we would at least have something to work with. Without it, Irkja will be more dangerous than ever. Who knows how many demons he'll capture next time? For all we know, he may start using angels." Zeke paused for a moment as he considered a new option. "Maybe he can use my power instead of yours. I wonder if I have enough of your power in me to give a fragment the last bit it needs."

Arino neared, sending calming power into Zeke. "That is so sweet of you. But I don't think Irkja would stop at draining Tone's power out of you. He was pretty angry at both of you. Fortunately, I don't think that will be necessary." Arino opened her hand to reveal the fragment that had been in the basin.

Adoneal was by her side instantly. "That is a curious spirit fragment. It is what Irkja wanted to show me." He reached out to touch it but Arino pulled it away.

"Look, but don't touch, Adoneal. I don't know what it will do if you touch it. It will likely try to bond to you. It was made to do that. It's taking a little bit of my power to keep it from trying to absorb into me."

Tone was impressed. "That is too cool. Do you do any other sleight of hand tricks? I have always wanted someone to pull a tuba out of my ass like they do with coins and ears."

Arino made a face at that image. "I am not going anywhere near your tuba. I was able to grab this right before Irkja hit the cauldron with his green goo. I'm guessing those fragments he saw were just new pieces from the demon draining."

Adoneal examined it carefully. "There is some promise to that fragment, but it will not work as it is. With some work, it may restore me." He seemed to be lost in thought. "Do I want this?" He looked at the fragment again. "That thing has been the cause of much suffering. It could be tainted by the cruelty that created it."

"We can debate this later," said Arino, taking charge. "Right now we need to get you someplace safe."

Zeke was still furious that the New Fallen had escaped. "I forgot that Torkel was still free. How could I forget that?"

Adoneal placed a hand on the warrior. "You did all you could. It is better this way. The disruption the New Fallen would have caused…" The archangel's mind drifted as he held up a hand, looking at it as fingers began to spread apart on their own. "I need to leave." The portal that was used by the New Fallen flew across the room and opened beside the foursome.

"Will we be able to get back here?" asked Tone. "I think the portal by the entrance is sending angels someplace unpleasant."

Arino turned to Adoneal. "Can you deactivate the all other portals in the place before we leave?"

"Of course," said the angel, as every portal in the room dimmed and went out. "There is one some distance away that cannot be reactivated either. They will not function until I repair them."

Tone looked at him. "You could have just turned them off, you know. Or do they not have an off switch? That is something that you really need to add on the fixed portals 2.0."

Adoneal walked to the portal, patted the side and said, "These are already fixed portals 536.0."

"Was that a joke?" asked Tone, trying to decide if the archangel had grown a sense of humor.

"No," said Arino with a grin. "He tinkers all the time." Turning again to Zeke, she sent all the calming power she still possessed into her best friend. "Zeke, we need to get you some help, too." The hunter began to object, but she cut him off. "I'm not asking. I'm invoking my authority as your healer to remove you from active status until we determine how to help you control the passions within you."

Zeke looked defiant. "You wouldn't dare," he stated, knowing that he had made a mistake the moment he spoke the words. "Wait," he said, backing away at the look on her spirit.

Arino changed to her amorphous form. Growing larger than Tone had ever seen. A soft, yet frighteningly strong voice came from her spirit. "That was a mistake, Ezekiel. You are removed from active status," she said as her spirit wrapped around him. His eyes glowed brightly while his mouth moved noiselessly. Finally, his glow faded as he passed out.

Tone back away, holding his hands up in surrender. "I'm not saying a word. Please don't put me in a coma. They feed you through tubes and I hate chili dogs in the blender. That one episode with the chipotle chili cheese chewy chocolate malt was a disaster."

Arino laughed as she returned to her normal form. "Relax, Tone. Zeke's just inactive. He's fine."

"I would prefer to remain on active status as well," added Adoneal. Arino looked at the archangel, wondering if he was joking. When he didn't smile or break eye contract, she decided he was serious.

"You two are something else," said Arino. "I'm not going to do anything to either of you. Tone, help me with Zeke."

Grabbing one of Zeke's arms while Arino grabbed the other, they carried him to the portal. "I didn't know you could do that," said Tone.

"Neither did he," said Arino, as all four went through the portal.

# Chapter 33

"Here's what I'm wondering," said Tone, when they emerged from a fixed portal in Adoneal's real workshop. "Can't you use your super-technotronic-megablast healing thing-a-ma-jig to fix up Adoneal? Was that too technical? I think he could use it. Maybe Anna, too."

"No, Tone. That power is the polar opposite of Zeke's blast that devastates demons. I can use it to heal injuries from battles, not something that is related to the essence of the individual." Arino sighed. She smiled at the human, admitting, "I already tried it on Adoneal right after we discovered what I could do."

The archangel look up from organizing the few items that were out of place from the snatch and grab by the New Fallen. "I appreciate your efforts. Hello, Michael." The chief of the archangels had appeared in the room in full battle-form, ready to face any situation.

Instantly aware of all that happened through Arino's angel link, Michael resumed his normal form and asked, "Which is the priority? Ezekiel or Adoneal?"

Arino replied. "I can bring Zeke back right now so you can talk to him, but we need to get Adoneal to the healing house. Raphael will be meeting us there."

"The healing house is being moved near as we speak. Anna is already there, waiting for Adoneal." He looked at Arino, eyes glowing brightly as he read the plan in her essence. "Are you sure you want to do that?" She allowed Tone to see what she was planning.

Arino had studied the fragment that Irkja had created and discovered the flaw. It did need some of the power from Tone, but Arino had discovered that it would only take a minute amount that would leave no lasting damage. In fact, Tone would not even notice the loss. There was a complication. It had to flow through Zeke, transforming the power and also taking a substantial amount of the built-up power of Tone's touch from the warrior. As Arino linked to Raphael across the Spiritscape, Tone could see he agreed the plan was sound; but the archangel also pointed out that it would take his healing power plus the supercharged Arino and Zeke power to make it work properly. Even then, there was a chance there would be unanticipated issues.

"Yes, Michael. I am." Explaining her thoughts, "Tone, you are basically the catalyst to charge the fragment and make it receptive to your unique power. Then, Zeke can infuse it with even more with a mixture of his and your power. That may be enough to restore Adoneal's connection to the angels and return his memories and personality. It is not a total cure because that is not possible. He and Anna will still need one another, but this is Adoneal's best chance at some semblance of normalcy." Looking at the archangel who was still tidying up his workspace, she stated, "Assuming Adoneal is willing to risk this. It could have some unforeseen downsides."

Without looking up, Adoneal added, "Such as causing me to link to demons or the New Fallen." He said it without fear or feeling. It was just a statement of fact. "I believe the risk is worth the potential gain. If I can create better devices, I am willing."

All looked to Michael, knowing he was the only one who could stop the plan. "I agree the risk is worth the potential gains. I miss your humor, Adoneal." The creative archangel looked up, nodded and went back to his cleaning. The head of the warriors, addressed Arino, "I need you to wake Zeke, please." There was something going on within the spirit of Michael, but Tone could only read his spirit when he allowed it.

With a touch from Arino, Zeke sprang back to life, morphing into his full warrior form. He looked around the room and, seeing Michael, returned to his regular appearance. The two locked eyes and had an intense, but silent, conversation. Zeke left his defenses down so that Tone could read the entire conversation.

Michael: *"Zeke, your behavior has become erratic and you have been losing control. It was my choice to let this run its course, but I gave Arino the authority to override my decision. She has done that."*

Zeke: *"And what is your decision about my erratic behavior?"*

Michael: *"We will help you with control. Arino thinks your new power is more of an asset than a liability. We are going to have to drain some of Tone's power from you periodically. It can be placed back into Tone, or may be used for something else as Arino sees fit. Basically, you have your own personal healer from this point on."*

Zeke: *"You mean babysitter, don't you?"*

Michael: *"That, too. She is the only one who can handle both you and Tone. Ezekiel, this is not a request. You are free to refuse, but I cannot allow you to remain in my service if you cannot control the fusion within yourself.*

Zeke: *"You can't be serious! I am the best you have and Tone's influence has made me better. Much better. More powerful. And I am growing, something most angels hardly ever do."*

Michael: *"I agree. You are more powerful and, in many ways, better. But you are also losing control. You have been hiding your new powers from us. I cannot help but wonder why?"*

Zeke: *"You know why. I didn't want you or anyone else getting in the way of me becoming something more. Much more. The power is..."*

Michael: *"Addictive. I can see that in your essence. The spot I could not read is still not open. But I know you well enough to tell when you are keeping something from me. This is your chance to come clean."*

Zeke: *"The new things I can do help me do my job. I never lied to you or any other angel."*

Michael: *"You did not share the truth which is just as bad. The end may occasionally justify the means, but I can see in your spirit that the means are becoming an end in itself. That is a dangerous path."*

Zeke: *"But it is one I can walk without falling..."*

Michael: *"I'm sure Irkja has reasoning just like that."*

Zeke: *"We are nothing alike!"*

Michael: *"You cannot see it because you are too close. Irkja was willing to sacrifice whatever it took to accomplish his purposes. He was willing to drain all of Tone's power to restore Adoneal. I can see that you would do anything it takes to recapture the New Fallen. The greater good is not worth the sacrifice Irkja is willing to make. I want you to stay with us more than anything else, but it has to be under my conditions."*

Zeke: *"And if I cannot abide by your conditions?"*

Michael: *"You have to decide where you choose to go. You are my brother, Zeke. But I love you enough to let you go your own way. I'm certain the New Fallen would welcome you to their ranks. But know this, they cannot come back because they chose a course that is counter to everything the Angel Legions believe. They may someday be our allies, but they will never again be angels. Is that what you want?"*

The hunter looked at Arino and Tone, knowing that he could never leave them.

Zeke: *"I'll never abandon them or the Angel Legions. Why do you ask questions when you already know the answer?"*

Michael: *"Because sometimes I need to hear the answer for myself."*

Tone stared at the two warriors. "Do you two always talk that fast in your heads? That was like the time I took a drink of diet soda with a mouth full of Mentos." Looking at Adoneal, he asked, "Did you know I can shoot Mentos-infused soda twenty-seven feet through my nose? It is a great way to clean out the sinuses even though all you can smell for a week is Mentos and soda."

A perplexed Adoneal turned to Arino. "After you place that fragment within me, will I understand what Anthony is saying?"

Arino's lilting laugh rang out, "If you can, I may get one for myself." Addressing Zeke, she continued, "I am sorry I had to do that. Please know it was for your well-being that I acted as I did. You were on the verge of crossing a line that you would never been able to undo."

Zeke looked at the healer. "I know, Arino. I can't thank you for that, yet. But, we are good. How long have you been able to turn me off?"

Tone stepped in. "And how long have you been able to turn me on? Oh yeah. Ever since I looked into your lovely face and amazing eyes when I thought I had died. Good times." Zeke gave him a good natured smack that sent him flying across the room. "I can fly!" shouted Tone, spinning and bounding off a shelf that sent segments of skimmers flying in strange directions. Adoneal moved at blinding speeds, catching the parts and placing them back where they belonged. Tone apologized, "Sorry. Didn't meet to mess up your O.C.D. mojo."

Arino giggled. "You are not the only one who is growing, Zeke. Some of us can control the strange feelings from our human influences." Zeke was startled at her confession. "Yes, I have issues with the humanity that touched me, too. But it has the opposite effect on me. I wanted to heal every single one of the New Fallen after Tone drained them. You seem to have more new powers than I do. But I'll take mine over all of yours."

"Yeah. About that. Please don't do that again." The hunter was concerned that his friend had that much power over him.

Arino enjoyed his discomfort. "Then you had better behave yourself."

Michael approached Tone who was enjoying spinning through the ether. "Zeke's love tap aside, are you all right, Tone? We were all worried that you wouldn't make it back in one piece. Or the piece that made it back wouldn't be the annoying Tone we know and love."

"All of you were? Even Gabriel?" asked an incredulous Tone.

Michael smiled. "He went through the passage to the new area more times than any other angel. Gabriel hoped he could overwhelm the portal placed on the far side of the Gray with a blast of power and speed. I believe there are a few demons who hope they never see him again. He got a little frustrated by the portal that sent him to random spots in Hell, and may have caught a couple demons escaping when he was trying to get back to us. It wasn't pretty."

"He does love me!" declared Tone, with pseudo-enthusiasm. "I knew it was all just an act to make me think he wanted to beat me across the Gobi desert with really long pieces of spaghetti dipped in cocktail sauce and gummy bears."

"Yes, I'm sure that's it. But are you all right?"

"Dude, I'm the same irritating, awesome asshole with frosting and jelly beans that I have always been. Only now I have a craving for pistachio ice cream. I blame that on Irkja." Tone gave the most powerful archangel a wink.

"That works for me," smiled Michael. Looking at the far wall as if he were seeing through it, the warrior added, "The healing house is nearly here. Is there anything we need to prepare for Adoneal's merging?"

"Well, yes." Turning to Tone, Arino inquired, "Is there any way you can resist the effects of Raphael on you? He will need to be able to speak throughout this, but I could really use your help."

"Sweetie, I have done my best, but Raph gets me all loopy." He thought for a moment. "You know, this is the first time I have ever wanted to resist his stoner effect."

Adoneal looked at Tone, confusion on his face. "Is there a problem with your blade?"

Michael interjected. "Adoneal, we discussed this. Tone needs to discover H'tes features on his own. Especially that one."

"What one?" asked Tone, bouncing up and down like a toddler on a sugar high. "This must be something really, really cool to make Mikey nervous? If you are about to tell me it has a chocolate malt dispenser, I can die a happy man."

"Why would you want to die?" asked Adoneal, genuinely concerned. "I think you have much to offer and dying would…"

"It's a figure of speech, Donny," sighed Tone. "We really need to get that thing-a-ma-bob put in you. Will it restore his ability to tell when people are joking?"

"Most people, yes," said Michael. "You? Well…"

Adoneal addressed the chief archangel. "If Anthony needs the power of the H'tes, it is worthwhile to give him this knowledge. Do you not agree?"

Michael studied both Adoneal and Tone before replying. "That particular aspect of the H'tes makes me very uncomfortable. But, I don't see that we have a choice." Giving Tone a stern look, he added, "The key rune can be removed if this power is abused."

"Okay. Okay. I get it. I'll be good." All the angels gave him the same disbelieving look, even Adoneal. "I'll be the best I can?" asked Tone, trying – and failing – to looking innocent.

Adoneal explained. "There are a series of runes that must be pressed that will allow you to resist the power of Raphael or virtually any specialized power of an angel. With every use of the power it drains the blade, but it can last some time if it is used sparingly."

"Hold on. I can be around Raph without being stoned out of my gourd?" Tone pondered that possibility. "You know, I kind of like it most of the time. But for this, I'll make an exception.

Adoneal showed Tone the complicated sequence that would allow him to resist Raphael's influence. "This rune and this rune," he pointed to two in the series, "allows you to resist healers plus archangels. This will only work on Raphael. Others require different runes."

"My friend," began Tone, "we need to sit down and have a few fuzzy navels and discuss other options that will work on warriors and archangels." The human smiled evilly at Michael.

Adoneal looked at Tone's mid-section. "Does your spirit have a navel? Mine does not. Nor do I have any fuzzy."

Arino announced, "The healing house is here."

Zeke smiled. "Just in time. I didn't want to hear Tone explain that."

# Chapter 34

Opening the wall of the workshop with a thought, Adoneal led the way out and into the healing house. Tone thought he was prepared, having seen the moving angel hospital once before. He was wrong. The over-sized room was not like he expected. Previously, it had looked like a comfortable recovery room, filled with angels going around either healing or receiving the healing. This time it was a stark, golden room that reminded Tone more of his inquisition in the presence of the Council of Archangels than a place of recuperation. In the center of the room was the crystal cradle containing Anna, with Raphael singing softly to her. Even with his H'tes offering protection from the healer's euphoric influence, the voice was still very calming and comforting.

Along the edges of the room were several angels, some of whom Tone recognized. It took no time for the human to realize that all the angels in the room were open books. No one was trying to block him reading their spirits. He spotted Gabriel looking at him with less vehemence than usual, so he gave him a casual salute. He also saw Vret floating near the messenger, red hair blazing all around her as she consumed all the information in the room. The beautiful archangel of death, Samael, was floating off to the side, watching the activities with a vigilance that made Tone very uncomfortable. There was one other angel who was unknown to Tone. This one looked feminine, but also looked like she could hold her own against Zeke. Her medium brown hair was much shorter than most angels, creating a look that was tough, yet inexplicably beautiful.

Tone bowed deeply to the new angel. "Hello, gorgeous! Allow me to introduce myself. The name's Tone, human extraordinaire, chili dog connoisseur, and all around lover of beautiful angels and pudding. May I be so bold as to ask your name?"

The angel smirked. "Zeke warned me about you, Tone. I am Klamoria, warrior angel. Michael has assigned me as Adoneal's personal guard. It is interesting to meet you." Since she was an open book, not even trying to hide her spirit behind a confusing array of thoughts, Tone saw Klamoria had no agendas, and no real interest in Tone's antics. Her function was to protect an archangel who really didn't need that much protection. As he looked closer, he saw that her role was to provide security as long as Irkja's New Fallen were perceived to be a threat. Her eyes blazed a violent violet when she gazed at Tone, highlighting her battle prowess for him. Tone shuddered in fear and respect.

"I'll take interesting. But be warned," jested the human. "I grow on you."

Zeke approached and greeted Klamoria, clasping her in a warm embrace. "He does. He's a lot like a fungus." Both warriors laughed at the image of Tone as a mushroom.

"Well, I am a fun guy," proclaimed Tone. "Get it? Fungi and fun guy?" He looked around hoping for a response.

Klamoria stared at him, mouth agape. "I really thought you were exaggerating about him."

"I'm not that creative," replied Zeke.

Before Tone could strike back, Raphael intervened. "Tone, it's good to see you. I understand we can actually have a conversation without discussing pie this time."

"Well, sort of. I really like listening to you. It is the cheapest buzz around. Besides, I'm into scones right now."

Laughing, the archangel of the healers pointed him toward Anna. "She wants to see you." Raphael smiled at the human, as Tone made a mad dash for the crystal container.

"Hey, Anna. How are you doing today?" he asked, nearing the form draped in shimmering shawls. He froze, any other words became lost at the sight of his sister. Her spirit did not have much substance when he had first seen her, but now she had lost most of her translucence. Her size hadn't changed and she was still flowing constantly, but it was very difficult to see where she ended and the covers around her began.

A whisper of a voice echoed through the room. "Hi, Tone. Do you feel better? Are you shorpy today?"

Tone had to try three times before the words would cooperate and come out of his mouth. "I'm good, Anna. I'm a little worried about you, though." He wanted to pick her up and run over to Adoneal so that the energy that was destroying her could help him. Looking at Raphael, he could see in the angel's spirit that there was still enough time to talk.

"Why are you worried? I am a little lamptil, but Don-el is here to help me. I will be the shorpiest you have ever seen." Giggles floated through the ether. Tone looked around at the angels mouthing the word "lamptil" while raising an eyebrow. No one had a clue what it really meant. It was just another Anna-ism.

"Hey, Tone. I know a secret. Do you want to hear a secret?" asked Anna. "You can't tell Rapel I told you though." Another giggle, this one mischievous came from the tiny spirit.

"Sure, sweetie. Tell me a secret." He looked at Raphael who just smiled and nodded.

Anna's giggles increased. "Don't tell anybody. I know who you are." More giggles stopped her from speaking.

Tone's spirit went a shade of pink Arino and Zeke had never seen. Arino placed a hand on Tone's shoulder and spoke for him. "Who do you think Tone is, sweet one?"

"Rino! Rino! Rino! You're here, too! This is a shorpy day!" The insubstantial spirit jiggled and wiggled with excitement. "What were we talking about?"

Arino spoke sweetly to Anna. "We were talking about Tone." She sent a wave of comforting power into Anna who stopped moving to bask in the healing.

"Ah. Feel good! I like the feel good," sighed Anna.

A shriek shocked everyone in the healing house as all eyes turned to Adoneal. The infinitesimal fissures were now growing rapidly, becoming anything but tiny. A series of cracks split his face down the middle, bringing images of Irkja to Tone's mind. Arino and Raphael were by his side, sending massive amounts of healing power into him. The fissures ceased growing but failed to close back up.

Raphael took charge. "Arino, prepare the fragment. I will maintain Adoneal's integrity. We cannot wait any longer."

The fragment appeared in her hand as she approached Tone. "Take my hand, Tone. This won't hurt you at all." She closed her hand around the fragment and then held it out to the human. Tone, hand shaking, stretched out his hand and wrapped it around the healer's. He glowed brightly, power flowing through his arm and into the fragment concealed in Arino's hand. Tone looked into the eyes of the healer who smiled reassuringly. The hand of the healer glowed with the many colors of the human and then returned to normal as the flow of power ceased. Arino pulled away saying, "See, that wasn't so bad was it?"

"No, but was it good for you?" asked Tone, trying to add some levity.

She opened her hand to reveal a prismatic fragment rapidly flashing a variety of colors in her hand. "Well, it was good for this." She turned to Zeke. "Your turn." Transforming into her formless mode protecting the fragile fragment deep within herself, she reached out to the warrior.

"This is going to hurt," muttered Zeke, as his hand merged with Arino's.

"Yes, it is," said Michael, moving to Tone. "I'm sorry, Tone, but you need to be in a spirit sphere. Do you understand why?" The sphere dropped onto the human before he could object. "This is one made especially for you. It will take you a lot more effort to cut your way out of this one." The archangel was proud of the improvements.

Tone grimaced and then stuck out his tongue, unintentionally licking the side of the wall. "I hate it when you do that. I get it. Too much random angel power floating around in here. No need to make things worse with me blowing someone up. Hey, Gabe, want to hang out with me in here? We can play whack-a-mole with demon heads."

Gabriel wasn't listening to Tone. All eyes in the room were focused on the warrior and the healer. The glow around them began to brighten and expand as they ceased holding back, allowing their powers to merge – the sum of power being substantially greater than the individual's. As the two angels' essences became completely entwined, Ezekiel disappeared within Arino. Tone suspected that Michael was doing something with the sphere to allow him to look past the glaring power so that he could see the healer discharge all of that power into the fragment that made its way to the surface. The constantly changing hues of Tone were gone when the fragment fell into the hands of Raphael as Zeke and Arino collapsed, falling apart. Zeke was out for the count, and Arino could barely move.

Raphael examined the hunter. Turning to Michael and Tone, he explained. "Zeke is fine. Just a little drained. At this point, it seems that the excess power has successfully been removed."

Michael smiled at Arino, "Good work on both parts."

The healer sounded winded. "The fragment is as good as I can make it. As for Zeke," she looked at her unconscious friend. "He sent every bit of power he could give to our blast. That was more healing than I have ever used. I think we may have even rivaled Raphael." The healer looked at her archangel.

"By an order of magnitude," agreed the egoless healer. He held up the fragment for all to see. "Vret, your opinion?"

"The presence of the fragment feels bigger," began the angel of wisdom, "Even though its size has not changed, something is different about it. Tone, do you have an irresistible urge to hold it, touch it, take it?"

"As a matter of fact, I do. I want to eat it and let it flow around inside of me like a Japanese fighting fish in a really big-ass tank," admitted the human. "Why do I feel like it would eat everything else inside of me?"

"Because it would," said Vret. "Everyone else feeling it drawing them in?" The other angels in the healing house could feel the pull of the fragment. "It worked far better than any of us expected."

Raphael smiled as he turned to face the pained Adoneal. "This is going to be rough. Are you prepared," asked the healer, already knowing the answer.

"Yes," gasped Adoneal, trying to control the pain of the barely contained fractures all over his spirit. A look of pleading was shining brightly in his spirit.

Without hesitation, Raphael transformed into pure light, passing into the core of Adoneal. The creative archangel ceased all movement, freezing in place. The two archangels merged as Raphael moved the fragment into an empty place near the center of the archangel of service. The power of the healer moved the fragment, reshaping it within the gap until it was a perfect fit. An energizing shock of healing power fused the fragment to the spirit of Adoneal as Raphael flowed out of his friend, resuming his normal form.

Reaching into the crystal container, he lifted Anna saying, "All right, little one. It's your turn to help Adoneal."

"Rapel! You are here. Can I have more feel good? I'm not shorpy right now." Anna squirmed with delight.

"Oh course, Anna." Raphael sent healing power coursing through her insubstantial spirit. "Now, I am going to need to use some of your power to help Adoneal. Do you remember when I told you about it?"

"Is Don-el hurt again? He needs to be more carefuler," snickered Anna. "Let's make him all better."

Raphael carried her to the motionless form of Adoneal. Holding her tiny spirit up to the archangel, a wave of energy leapt from Anna into Adoneal, causing him to convulse like he was having a seizure. Tone, who was watching the spirit of Raphael for any sign of trouble, noticed almost as quickly as the angels who were linked with the healer. Raphael tried to pull Anna back from transfer only to discover that was a mistake. Anna's spirit folded in on itself, compressing into a pinpoint of glowing power flowing into Adoneal, linking them together. It looked for a moment like Anna was about to shrink into nothing. Tone screamed, pounding on the wall of the spirit sphere. His H'tes sprang into his hand as the blade was buried deep into the side of his safety cell. Tone could only watch helplessly as the archangels and Klamoria flew to help. As they surrounded the speck, a blast of power exploded out from Adoneal and Anna, stunning all the angels as they crashed into the walls of the healing house. None of the angels seemed to be alert as the power flowed from the merged forms in the center of the room. Even the unconscious form of Zeke was plastered next to the spot where Tone was carving his way clear of the sphere, and Arino was on the opposite side of the room, out cold next to a stunned Samael.

From the epicenter of the explosion, a voice rang out. "Tone? Where are you?" A madly slashing Tone was making little progress on the side of the spirit sphere, desperately trying to get free to help his sister. "Tone, I need to tell you who you are, but I don't know where you are?"

"I'm here," grunted Tone, thrusting again as he made another scratch on the surface of the sphere. "I'll be right... unghh... there."

A form grew out from the explosion. It was a larger version of Anna, Tone could see she was different. He froze in mid slash, transfixed by her beauty. She had the same undefinable form, but her spirit was a brighter and more colorful version of Tone.

"I see you, Tone." A hand formed from the flowing spirit of Anna, waving at him.

Tone was panicking. "Anna, move away from Adoneal. Come to me. Please," he begged, "come to me." He looked deep within her spirit and his heart sank.

"I can't move away, silly Tone," giggled Anna. "Don-el needs me. He has a really bad hurt part. I like to help Don-el. He's my friend." She turned to look at the archangel. "He won't be here if I go there." She sounded so sweet, yet determined. "I think I want to stay with Don-el."

Her spirit was easily read. Knowing what she was planning, Tone sent every modicum of power in his H'tes into the scratched surface of the spirit sphere as angelic fire flooded it, causing it to creak and groan. The spiritual protection device held fast at the outburst. He pressed against the wall, willing himself to be closer to Anna.

"Anna! Don't do it! Please!" begged the weeping Tone. His mind raced, trying to come up with something that would convince Anna to stop. "I need to tell you something. It's important. Look at me." As he saw there was no hope of changing her mind, he sobbed, "Please."

The sweetest spirit in all the realms looked back at Tone, smiling with her entire spirit. "I love you, little brother," said Anna, as she flowed into the spirit of Adoneal, creating an explosion of power that destroyed the healing house.

# Chapter 35

Tone bounced around the interior of the spirit sphere as it rocketed away from the epicenter of the explosion. The last thing he saw before the walls turned opaque was the unconscious form of Zeke flying off the exterior of the sphere as it spun out of control from the power of the blast. Once movement stabilized within the sphere, it was impossible for Tone to tell if he was still moving or had come to a stop. He huddled in a ball, floating in the ether of the spirit sphere, crying for his sister. Pulling himself together, he wasn't sure what had happened to Anna, but he knew he needed to get out so he could discover what had happened.

Looking around his prison, he sent a wave of angelic fire from his blade at the far wall. It bounced around until it hit him in the back, sending him tumbling forward unharmed. "I think that could have gone better." Using his H'tes, he tried once again to cut through the wall. The blade stuck in the wall, carving a narrow groove in the surface. The moment he removed the dagger, the sliced section closed up as the sphere repaired itself. "This may be a problem."

The sphere began to shake and groan as a jagged rip began to appear in the center. He had no idea what was out there ripping a spirit sphere apart, but he had no intention of making it easy to find him. Disappearing from view, Tone held his H'tes in front of him, flames oozing from the tip. *I'm ready for anything that comes at me,* thought the human. He was wrong.

The rip down the middle of the sphere widened and opened as the two halves were thrown in opposite directions. The being tossing the pieces away was beyond any of Tone's worst nightmares. That was saying quite a bit since his nightmares had been incredibly vivid since meeting the angels. This thing was huge! There was no definable body to this spiritual being that looked like a vast sheet with countless scowling faces peering out. Tone hoped it was an angel based on the golden color with streaks of black shooting around the spirit; but, at this point, he wasn't taking any chances. As he looked around, he saw there was no real place to go to escape this being.

A thousand voices shrieked in disharmony, "Tone, are you in there? I can sense you but cannot see you. The sphere was damaged so I had to destroy it to get you out."

The voices made his spirit run cold with unbridled terror. Those few words were some of the most awe inspiring, yet horrific, sounds he had ever heard. Speech eluded him as he held a trembling blade in front of him.

The voices spoke again making Tone cringe, "I do not want to risk touching you so I will lessen." The sheet of spirit shrank rapidly back on itself until it slowly morphed into a form that Tone knew, yet still feared. Samael, the beautiful archangel of death, was floating in the Spiritscape, looking in his general direction. His soft, soothing voice rang out, "Come out. Come out. Wherever you are."

Tone's shaky voice came from nowhere, yet the angel looked right at him as soon as he spoke. "Please don't kill m-m-me. I've been relatively good lately."

Samael smiled a gorgeous smile that somehow made Tone even more terrified. "If I was here to bring about your death, you would never have seen me coming," the angel said matter-of-factly. "I was the only one who was not injured by the blast. Raphael is trying to heal the others and he asked me to locate you and bring you to him."

"S-s-so you're not piss... I mean mad at me?" asked Tone, still not appearing.

The smile on the archangel's face never wavered. "If I was angry, you would not have to ask. Now, can we please go? I am not known for having as much patience as Gabriel."

Slowly fading into view, Tone queried, "Gabriel? He has never seemed that patient to me." The human tried to smile, but this was the first time he had ever been alone with this angel who scared him too much to even make a joke. Tone always got the impression the Samael didn't have much of a sense of humor and could kill him without thinking twice about it.

"He isn't," said the angel. Tone could swear the archangel of death had just winked at him. Samael opened a portal and motioned for Tone to lead the way. Afraid to turn his back on the archangel, he backed into the portal and found himself in the remnants of the skimmer hanger.

Raphael was everywhere. The archangel of healers had divided into five versions that were working on injured angels as other healing angels appeared throughout the vast room. All the versions spoke at once, "Tone, make certain your angel filter is on and then please check on Ezekiel when the *Hajile-R* arrives." The sound sent a rush of euphoria into the core of Tone's being, almost sending him into the normal delirium he felt in Raphael's presence. The multiple voices taxed the power of the H'tes. The figure of Samael moving past him snapped him out of the brief haze.

"Will do. Please only use one voice, bro. It is a little much to take all at once," replied Tone, still aghast at everything that had happened.

The nearest version of Raphael spoke without looking up from the injured Arino. "My apologies. Zeke will be here momentarily. I do not want any healer other than Arino helping him. I do not know what state he will be in when he awakens. Can you do anything to help him until I have Arino available?"

Tone nodded, "I'll do what I can." He had been able to put Zeke back together when he had been phased apart shortly after they had met. That phasing and Tone's efforts to put him back together were the reason behind so many of his issues, but was also the reason he was developing new powers. Glancing at Raphael's work, he asked, "How is Arino? Is this from the first blast or the biggie?" His friend still had a golden hue to her spirit, but her glow was the lowest he had ever seen.

Raphael looked up from his work, but his spirit never slowed. "She will be fine. I know her better than she knows herself. We could really use her power combined with Zeke's right now, but everyone should be able to fully recover."

The arrival of the skimmer ended their conversation as Tone met the Zeke-carrying Nazilaq. "How are you feeling, buddy?" asked Tone. "You looked about half dead when we left you by the monument.

"I'm good, Tone. I was on my way back here when I felt the explosion. I doubt there is anywhere in the Spiritscape that didn't feel it. Raphael sent me to look for anyone who was thrown clear of the blast." He let the passenger float beside Tone. "He was flying into a group of demons when I caught up to him. They got a couple of shots in on him before I fried them."

Tone could see his friend had been better. One eye had been knocked to the other side of his spiritual head. The one that was still where it belonged opened. "Hey," muttered Zeke. "I need a healer. Arino?"

"She is going to be okay, but you are stuck with me right now," said Tone, touching the injured eye that began moving back into place.

A pained chuckle came from Zeke. "Try not to leave too much of yourself in me this time."

"You should..." Tone and Zeke both grunted as the human forced the eye back into place, "be so lucky." Moving part of his arm from his leg up to the place where arms belong, he added, "I can give you a facelift while I'm working on you. We all know you need something to make you look less hideous."

Zeke laughed and grimaced. "Just shut up and work."

Tone called out, "Raph, I've done all I can. Everything is more or less where it's supposed to be. I need someone with the right kind of healing energy to boost my bud here."

"Almost ready, Tone." He looked back down, "That… should… do… it!" Arino glowed brightly as her eyes fluttered and then opened.

"That was a new experience," she said, as she moved around, testing her spirit. "You missed a spot," she said to Raphael, holding up her hand. The archangel send a wave of healing power into it. "Thank you," said Arino, and began looking around. "All the angels near the explosion were injured?"

"You caught some of the worst of it. Fortunately, you shielded Samael allowing him to bring everyone here. Then he went and found Tone." Raphael motioned to the human who waved and then motioned to Zeke.

"Oh no," whispered Arino, flying to be by the warrior. "Who did this to you? You look terrible. Your arms are in the wrong place."

Tone looked down at Zeke. "Oops. I thought something didn't look right."

The healer went to work while Tone looked around. Michael was looking back to normal, as was Klamoria who flew out through the gaping hole in the hanger as soon as she was cleared for action. Gabriel was still looking pretty bad and Vret was still out cold. He looked closely as the part of Raphael that had been healing Arino merged with the one working on Vret. The healer had a strange spot on his back that looked like an ugly shark bite.

Tone approached Arino. "Hey, babe. Look at Raph's ass. Has he been in trouble? It looks like someone been chewing it."

Arino glanced up and shuddered. "That has to hurt." Turning to one of her healer colleagues, she communicated without words. That healer went and began healing each of the four versions of Raphael. All four looked up and then looked over at Arino. "No arguments, Raphael. It's your rule. ANY healer who is injured cannot heal others unless a healer is helping them at the same time."

"Thank you," said the archangel, turning back to his work.

Michael approached. "How are you feeling, Zeke? Before you answer, you have looked better." The fact that Michael was teasing him did more to lift his spirit than the healing of Arino.

"Look who's talking. You won't be at full strength for at least a quoll. Maybe two or three," bantered Zeke, smiling as his face seemed to melt and then reform into his normal handsome self. "How is Adoneal? Is Anna okay?"

Michael looked at Arino, a question in his spirit. "He can't link just yet. I wanted to make sure everything was back the way it's supposed to be before I restore it."

Zeke looked at each of them. "What happened?" The look on his face showed his concern for both Adoneal and Anna.

Tone's voice shook. "Anna merged with Adoneal. She was trying to help him. That's what caused the explosion. I don't know the rest."

Zeke looked at Michael. "Is she gone?"

"Yes," said Michael, sadly as he placed a fatherly hand on Tone. "As to Adoneal, we really don't know yet. He is still in the same spot. As soon as you are well enough, we can go see him."

Zeke tried to move. "I'm well enough to…" He froze in place as the amorphous from of Arino grabbed him and gently, but firmly, restrained him. "To stay here and behave like a good little angel." He glanced sheepishly at the healer. Arino was not amused.

"Good answer," she said, without mirth. "I will let you know when you're good enough to do anything. Understood?" The way she asked made it sound like more of demand than question.

"Yes, ma'am," said Zeke.

"You forgot to salute," said Tone. "I prefer the two handed, Australian salute with flair!" Tone's arms moved in strange patterns that the angels followed, but didn't remotely understand. Arino stifled a smile, but not before Tone saw it. "Got ya!"

Within a quarter of a quoll, all angels were restored to a working level. It would take a while for them to fully recover. That blast of power was something none of them had expected nor ever experienced. Even Vret proclaimed it as something new to the astonishment of all, but Tone.

"This is Anna we're talking about. You never know what will happen with either of us."

"We know," said all of the angels in unison, much to the delight of the human.

Moving through the ripped wall of the skimmer hanger, they surveyed the damaged workshop of Adoneal. There was very little left of it. Pieces of portals floated among shards of crystals. Shattered, mysterious devices were intermixed with broken shelves and tables, making it difficult for Tone to tell what was a gizmo, and what was a piece of wall. *I wonder if any of these things will get merged together to make something cool?* thought Tone.

The area where the healing house had been was stark by the absence of anything, except Adoneal and a squad of sixty angels. Klamoria was in the center of the guard, directing the warriors. Half of them were facing out to deal with anything attacking from the Spiritscape. The other half were facing in, ready to deal with whatever Adoneal may do. The creative archangel floated in the ether, completely unconscious.

"So, paranoid much?" asked Tone, looking at Michael.

The voice that answered surprised Tone. "That was my idea," said Samael. "We have had some interesting experience with angels and humans sharing essences lately. It's like the whole Nephilim situation, but worse."

Tone shivered when the death angel spoke. "I want to ask about the Nephilim," began Tone, but was silenced by a look from Samael. "It'll wait."

Michael and Zeke shared a smile at the interaction between the two. Zeke said, "Samael, I may need your help from time to time when Tone gets out of hand."

"Really?" asked the archangel, glancing at Tone.

Tone answered for the hunter. "That won't be necessary. But thank you for your willingness to assist." All eyes looked at the human as most of them chuckled. "It's not funny."

Gabriel spoke for the first time since he was healed. "Yes, it was."

To Tone relief, Raphael changed the subject. "We need to wake Adoneal, but I'm not the one to do it. I feel Arino is better suited for this. She is less likely to create reactions."

All eyes watched Arino as she carefully approached the still form of Adoneal. She sent out a tiny wave of healing power that was quickly absorbed. A touch revealed that Adoneal was not toxic to her. Changing into her healing form, she slowly added more and more healing energy to the unconscious archangel.

"I can sense the fragment has been fused into the spirit of Adoneal. There is no going back now. His entire spirit is changing, adapting to this new state. I think he is almost…"

Hysterical laughter rang out, echoing through the Spiritscape, causing all present to jump and prepare for battle. The laughter came from the spirit of Adoneal, eyes still closed as laughter continued bursting forth. Tone looked around and wished he hadn't, as he saw Samael looking terrifying, Zeke and Michael appeared battle ready, and Gabriel was preparing something that Tone couldn't quite place. It felt like he was going to start moving something around. Then, Tone realized that Gabe was ready to move him to a safe place if the situation dictated.

The laughter stopped after far too long, as Adoneal's eyes opened. "Okay. Shorpy. I get it now."

# Chapter 36

The thirty warriors surrounding Adoneal blazed with power, ready for anything. Adoneal looked around and laughed. "Am I that dangerous?" He looked from one angel to the next, a smile still filling his face. "I guess I am. Arino, would you do the honors? If I am not me, I feel fairly certain they can defend you." The archangel of service winked at the healer.

Tone whispered to Zeke, "I think he's flirting with your girlfriend, dude. I'm the only one allowed to do that."

Zeke remained transfixed on everything happening in front of him. He was shaking with excitement in every part of his spirit. "He sounds just like the old Adoneal."

"Really?" inquired Tone. "He was an archangel and a hound? Cool. I hope I get to know him." Tone turned his attention back to the scene playing out before this unique audience.

Arino reached out with a steady hand, touching Adoneal's chest. Her spirit displayed an unusual array of colors as each one rapidly flashed, only to be replaced by the next shade. After a seemingly endless examination, Arino removed her hand sending a blast of healing power in every direction, creating a display to rival any fireworks Tone could ever hope to see.

"It worked!" shouted Arino, turning to hug the glowing Adoneal. "You had us so scared! Don't ever do that again!" teased the healer. The cadre of warriors dispersed by flying or porting away, leaving the group alone with Adoneal. Each of the archangels flew to their friend, greeting and congratulating him.

Raphael paused, looking at Adoneal carefully, and then looked to Vret. The two archangels expanded, linking while examining Adoneal. Vret spoke first. "You are significantly different Adoneal. I can see traces of Anna in you." Looking at Arino and Zeke, she turned back to Adoneal. "You are more like Arino than Zeke. I believe it is based on the individuals who have joined with you. You both have traces throughout your body; whereas, Zeke has certain parts that have more of Tone than others."

Tone spoke up. "I think I'm offended by that, but not totally sure. Are you saying I'm like an infection of sickly purple parakeets on the back of a red rhino? You are not the first to make the comparison, but it still hurts after the eighty-third time."

Vret sighed. "No, Tone. Adoneal and Arino each absorbed more human essence than you shared with Ezekiel. And, before you ask, Anna is part of Adoneal, through and through."

Tone approached the service archangel, looking him up and down. "Do you have any of her memories? Or is it just a feeling?"

Adoneal smiled. "Anything Anna was or thought, I have within me. She knew who you were and loved you very much. She knew that she was fading, wasn't she Raphael?"

Tone spun on the healer, shock showing in his spirit. Raphael nodded. "I'm sorry, Tone. It's true. She may have lasted two or three more times of draining the energy into Adoneal. But after that, her weakening spirit wouldn't have been able to take the strain. That's why I told her who you are. She needed to know. She wanted to tell you good-bye."

Tone was at a loss. Adoneal placed a hand on his shoulder. "She will always be with me. Anna is a part of me, making me better – more caring, more loving, more creative. In fact, I am changing my name to honor her. As of now, I am Andoneal."

The human broke down, crying in the arms of the newly re-christened archangel. "It's okay, Tone. Let it out," said Andoneal. When Tone finally looked up, Zeke, Arino and Nazilaq were the only other ones with them.

"As soon as Tone is ready, we have some work to do," said Andoneal. "The New Fallen have used the fixed portal I left in their lair." A portal appeared next to the archangel. A wave of his arm and the *Hajile-R* shrank to a fraction of its former size. "If you don't mind, Nazilaq, the *Hajile-R* will now fit into any situation needed.

With a thought, you can expand it to eight times its original size. But for now, I'd say it makes a rather stylish backpack."

The three angels and Tone were stunned into silence. The archangel laughed. "If you are amazed by my ability to make something that has eluded me for eighty-seven trillion quolls, wait until you see what I will be doing in my new workshop." Looking at Tone and winking, he said, "That H'tes needs some upgrades. But for now, we have some unfinished business. Are you coming?" Andoneal stepped through the portal without waiting for an answer.

Tone bounced after him. "I can't believe we have a cool archangel to play with. Andy, wait up. We need to discuss the chili dog cooker on this knife." He disappeared through the portal after Andoneal.

Zeke looked at this two companions. "Andoneal likes Tone. I have a feeling we are going to have our hands full now. We are so screwed, aren't we?"

Nazilaq was excited, too. "What do you mean 'we'? I'm with them!" He laughed disappearing after Tone.

Arino held out her hand to the hunter. "It'll be fun. If you can't beat them, join them," she said, leading him to the portal.

"Are you sure I can't beat Tone? He really needs a spanking sometimes," joked Zeke, as the two entered the portal.

Once they emerged back in Irkja's hideout, Andoneal touched the fixed portal and it dimmed, deactivated. "No need to give them a short cut out. Be right back." The archangel ported away and was back almost immediately, chuckling. "This should be fun."

"What should be fun?" asked Tone, hopping around Andoneal like a puppy with a new master.

Zeke smiled, looking at the archangel. "That is classic Adoneal. I really have missed you."

The archangel winked at the warrior. "Would you do the honors? They are in the siphon room."

"It would be my pleasure," said Zeke with a grin that spoke volumes of mischief. "Tone, you are going to love this." The hunter ported away.

"Human here," said Tone, raising his hand. "Kind of in the dark. Please tell me this plan involves a cream corn trap and duct tape."

Laughing, Andoneal moved at an impossible speed around the room, gathering supplies and creating the pieces that were missing. A large box, similar to the prisons that had held the demons in the siphon room was quickly assembled.

"I believe they are coming," chuckled Andoneal, disappearing to be replaced by twenty warriors. Tone looked carefully, but couldn't sense anything from the new angels. They were an illusion to scare the New Fallen. As soon as the first of the New Fallen flew into the room, it shrieked and ported away. Every one of the New Fallen repeated the process until Irkja ported into the room, saw the numbers, growled in frustration and ported out.

The illusion faded and Andoneal reappeared. "Five, four, three, two, one." He pointed to the cage he had created as a portal opened dumping all fourteen of the New Fallen in the prison. "Welcome. It is so nice you could all drop in. Please don't insult me by trying to escape. Porting won't work." One of the New Fallen turned and flew into the portal, only to bounce off the wall of the cage. "See, I told you."

Irkja moved to the forefront of the group. "Adoneal? Did it work?" asked the leader of the New Fallen, excitement showing in his solid half and causing waves in his liquid parts. He pressed his face against the clear walls followed by every one of his cohorts. They were looking in astounded pleasure, patting one another on their backs in pride. "I think this means that we have earned a little bit of leniency. Am I right?" His pride glowed arrogantly on his face, convinced he had been right and would now be forgiven for all his misdeeds.

Andoneal came as near to Irkja as he could. "No, you were wrong. The fragment didn't work the way it was supposed to. Even with Tone, Zeke and Arino helping Raphael, it almost destroyed me." Looking hard into his eyes, Andoneal repeated, "You were wrong."

"No!" screamed Irkja. "I can see you. I can feel you. You are back, stronger and better than ever. I DID THAT! How can you deny me this victory?" Rage burst out in green steam from Irkja causing his followers to press themselves against the far sections of their shared prison to escape. With a thought from Andoneal, Irkja found himself in a sectioned off portion of the cell that protected his followers from his rage. Pounding on the walls, he screamed over and over, "I DID THAT!" Andoneal let him pound and scream, standing beside the prison, waiting for his rage to abate, pretending to buff his non-existent fingernails.

Tone looked at Andoneal and asked, "What a tantrum. Do you think he needs a timeout? A spanking? No dessert for a millennium?"

"Not bad ideas," admitted the archangel, pretending to examine the buff on his nails. "But I have something else in mind." The smile on the face of the angel made Tone excited and afraid at the same time. There was something incredibly powerful about Andoneal, yet there was an extraordinary sense of compassion.

As Irkja began to quiet down, Andoneal turned his attention back to the prisoner. "Are you done yet? We can come back if you want to throw some toys or hold your breath." Irkja just stared at him, barely controlled fury boiling the liquid portion of his body. "I'll take that as a 'Yes, I'm done.' Now, let me tell you where you failed with the fragment." Andoneal explained all the flaws that had been repaired by Tone, Zeke, Arino and Raphael. "The worst part was the connection. It required something you could never take. My body would never take the fragment. The rejection was catastrophic. The only thing that would have worked was human spiritual power given freely, lovingly, and unconditionally. My name is now

Andoneal in honor of Anna's sacrifice to restore me to something greater than I have ever been."

Andoneal stood before all the New Fallen, staring each one of them down until he reach Irkja. "You were wrong, Irkja. Even though your thoughts and plans were for my well-being, what you wanted was for yourself. You never did accept me as I was: broken, but still the archangel of service. I wish you could have just loved me the way I was. Then Anna could have spent her final quolls with her brother. By saving me, she had to give up getting to know the most extraordinary human I have ever met." He looked at Tone, "Irkja, you stole from demons, your stole from me, and, worst of all, you stole from Tone."

Facing the New Fallen, he proclaimed, "You are all aware of the punishment. Rejection of the laws of the Legions of Angels means you give up the rights to be angels. I am sorry. So, so sorry. But I have interceded on your behalf. You will be allowed to stay here within this new realm. I will send you what you need to build and strive to be better. But your banishment is out of my hands."

Every one of the New Fallen nodded in sad acquiescence except Irkja. He stared at Andoneal, anger and hatred oozing from his body. "I was not wrong. You would not be restored without me."

"Yes, you were wrong. I'm sorry you can't admit that." Andoneal waved his hand around the room as everything shattered into component parts. "But you will have plenty of time to think about it while you decide what you want to build here." Another wave of his arm and the entire place fell apart as colorful blobs bounced away, freed from their imprisonment. "I'm sealing the doorway by the Gray. I'll leave one fixed portal behind, but to activate it you will have to contact me through the silver crystal I'm leaving you." He held up a perfect triangular silver crystal.

Nodding to the portal, it activated. "After you," he said to his four companions. "Turning back to the New Fallen, he smiled. "I wish it could be different. Good luck. I'll check on you in a few hundred quolls. Right now, I have to repair some damage to my workshop."

As they disappeared through the portal, it deactivated as the cell that had held the New Fallen collapsed into its parts. Irkja stared at the triangle of silver. Picking it up, he angrily threw it at the portal causing it to be buried deep within the closed door.

# Chapter 37

Tone looked around. "Anything else you need help with? Demon hoard? Mysterious blob of hot fudge? Angel bikini contest judge?"

Andoneal laughed. "I think Zeke is already in line for the bikini contest judge. We will call you if he is unable to fulfill his duties." The archangel winked at Tone.

The human nudged the hunter. "Zeke, what would it cost me to get you to come down with a sprained halo or something? I really don't want to go back yet. There is so much to see and do. Tell me you don't want to go snowboarding down the Dove-whatever-they-are-called Spires."

Arino giggled. "As tempting as snowboarding down demon-infested spires sounds, I think I'll pass on that one."

Andoneal paused as if listening to something, "Zeke, you and Arino need to take Tone home. Michael is calling for an archangel council. Even in the Spiritscape, we still have meetings. Tone, I look forward to seeing you soon. We have so much to talk about." Pausing again, he looked up, startled. "Get him home, now. We have a problem that you can't help with this time, Tone." Andoneal was gone as he ported away.

"Bye?" said Tone to the empty ether where the angel had been. "Wow! He gets all better and then he's off running around taking care of problems I can't help with. He should have more faith in me."

Zeke smiled. "I think he has more faith in you than you know. Between Andoneal, Michael, Raphael and Vret, you are slowly winning over the Council of Archangels."

"You know Gabe loves me, too. He is just afraid of letting his feelings show. It's got to be a messenger kind of thing," giggled Tone. "Or maybe it's one of those I annoy him kind of things."

Arino chuckled. "You may be on to something with the annoying thing."

Garrol appeared beside Tone. "Hey there," squeaked the huge angel. "I hear it is time for Tone to go home. There have been a few strange spirits coming around Anthony's body, but they seemed to be intimidated by me."

That statement got Zeke's attention. "What kind of spirits? Demons?" Tone and Arino were understandably curious as well.

Garrol shook his enormous head. "Nothing that bad. Just two different pseudo-Praetorac. They looked like some of Darius' minions sniffing around for a new boss. I'm certain it was nothing."

Zeke eyed Tone. "I'm not so sure. I think we need to do some Earth-bound hunting Arino. Anything sniffing around Tone could be a problem." Turning to the human, "That settles that. You can't come along when we hunt on Earth. Sorry, buddy. I guess you have to go back to reading a dozen books a day."

The human had a look of false exasperation on his spirit. "I've told you a million times not to exaggerate. I only read five books a day. Get it right, dude." All four angels laughed. Turning to Nazilaq, Tone held out his hand. "At least we can shake hands this time."

The effervescent angel laughed. "Yes we can, Tone. Once again, it has been a pleasure. See you the next time things go sideways around here."

Tone winked. "Trust me, I make things go diagonal. It's what I do."

"You know, I believe you on that one," laughed the pilot. Removing the crystal backpack, he tossed it away as it grew into the ring of the *Hajile-R*. Porting inside, Naz waved and was gone, leaving a wake in the ether.

Arino watched the skimmer fly away. "He is going to be unstoppable now. Did you see how much faster it is?" Nodding heads from Zeke and Garrol agreed with her. Looking at Tone, he just shrugged.

"It always looks fast to me. Human eyes. Go figure."

Zeke linked to Garrol and discovered how much time had passed on Earth. "How did that happen?" asked the warrior. Realizing Tone was out of the loop. "Your body is in a van travelling back to Knoxville."

Tone smiled guiltily. "Did they give up on trying to get me to move?" Garrol smiled, nodding. "Not the first time that has happened, and won't be the last. I'm sure you will find this hard to believe, but I can be perceived as ever so slightly stubborn on Earth. I know. Hard to fathom, isn't it?"

Garrol squeaked, "He is joking, right?"

"I hope so," said Zeke. "Tone, it is time to give me the H'tes." A crystal case appeared in his hands.

"Do I have to go?" pleaded Anthony. "It is so much fun here. I get to stay up late, eat junk food, kick demon ass, and stab bad angels. I'm living the dream!" He knew it was pointless, but he had to try.

Arino smiled. "Don't worry. I'm sure we will need your unique services soon. Plus, I can only go so long before I start missing random bouts of your one-of-a-kind strangeness."

Tone beamed at the healer, whispering. "I knew you loved me more than Zeke. Don't tell him. It would crush him to think you liked me best." Turning to Zeke, he flipped out his H'tes, touching the series of runes that released it. Placing the blade in the crystal case, he winked at his friend. "Now, take good care of my baby."

Zeke sighed. "I won't let anyone play with your H'tes."

Tone tried to look confused, but cracked a smile as he put an arm around the healer. "I was talking about Arino," giggled the human. "But please take care of my fancy-schmancy pocket knife, too." Arino kissed Tone on the forehead, causing him to glow brighter than ever in a display of colors that would have been blinding on Earth. "Thanks, babe. Don't get jealous, Zeke. I'm sure she likes you, too. Just not as much as me."

Zeke hugged his human friend. "Try to stay out of trouble. Garrol can only do so much."

Tone had his most mischievous look as he said, "I don't try to find trouble. It just likes to follow me around. It would be rude to ignore it. Did you know trouble knows all the best places to get dollar shots and cheese fries?"

Zeke laughed. "Be rude. Garrol, he's all yours. Good luck."

The gentle giant of an angel smiled. "Thanks, I'll need it."

"Yes, you will," said Tone, leaping back into his body with Garrol right behind.

Arino and Zeke sat on top of the van that contained Tone and his friends. Looking at the Cumberland Mountains in the distance, Zeke asked, "Do you think we should pay those pseudo-Praetorac a visit? I don't like them hanging around Tone and we may be able to help them move on if they are part of Darius' coven."

Arino let her legs dangle off the back of the speeding van. "That sounds like a fun outing. You know, I really haven't spent much time on Earth in the Twenty-First century. Will you show me around?"

Zeke grinned. "Having a babysitter may not be so bad after all."

Arino's hand found his and merged with the hunter. "Trust me. This is going to be fun."


Andoneal arrived at the Council of the Archangels to find the place in an uproar. Michael called the meeting to order as each one took their seat. The room was a smaller version of the golden room that Tone had encountered when he received his H'tes. Each archangel had a chair even though none of them needed it. The entire discussion took place as the archangels linked with one another.

*Michael: Welcome back to the Link, Andoneal. You were missed.*

*All: Welcome. Welcome.*

*Andoneal: Thank you. Glad to be back. I need to restore much that was damaged during my healing. My team has been dispatched and are already working on it.*

*Michael: Excellent. We need your assistance in dealing with an issue with the Eqemp.*

*Andoneal: Fantazmil's escape?*

*Vret: Yes. We need to insure that cannot happen again. If Tone had not been there, projections show that we would have a crimson level crisis right now. Fantazmil cannot ever be allowed to escape.*

*Andoneal: I have some new ideas about security around him. It would require a new prison just for him in the Uqump with the unicorns guarding it. That is assuming they are unaffected by his illusions.*

*Halalio: They should be immune. I will ask Halidore to visit and we can see what happens.*

*Michael: That will ease my spirit. Is there any other business that needs our immediate attention?*

*Gabriel: The New Fallen. Are they secure enough? What will they do if they escape?*

*Andoneal: I have sealed the passage from the Spiritscape to their home. They have a silver crystal to contact us should they need anything. Also, the fixed portal I left behind is locked onto one other portal and cannot be energized from that side. As clever as Irkja is, he doesn't have the resources to get out without help.*

*Vret: It is unclear what they would do if they escaped. It depends entirely on Irkja. His instability is troubling. I wish the healers could help him.*

*Raphael: That is not possible. He is unwilling to let us help. Arino offered and he rejected it. There is nothing we can do.*

*Samael: That is tragic. He was such an asset before his fall.*

*Nasarg: I can always make room for him in Hell. I fear he might take over and then what would happen?*

*Iofiup: My cherubs shall be prepared periodically check on the New Fallen. They are the ones most fleet of foot, while able to avoid being seen by those who need not notice their presence.*

*Andoneal: I really missed the way you think things, Iofiup. You have such a way with words.*

*Iofiup: Whilst your troublesome humor has remained unchanged and unimproved, your presence was equally notable by its absence.*

*Michael: Now that we have taken care of that, it there any other business? No? Then, Andoneal, let us know when Fantazmil is secure in a new cell. Council adjourned.*

# Epilogue

Anthony sat back in his favorite chair, reading his newest book about transhumanism. The pages flew past as he took in the contents of each one with a glance. Within twenty minutes, the book was laid on top of a pile of other books to be filed away. A knock on his door revealed a tall blond man, with eyes that glowed golden.

"Anthony, this is Donald. He wanted to talk to you," said Rachel from behind the handsome man. Ignoring the words, Tone grabbed another book and began flying through the pages. She whispered, "He may not listen to you. He is in his reading mode."

"That is quite all right," said Donald. "I'm fine just sitting in here and watching my old friend read. Do you mind if I sit down, Tone?" Tone ignored the visitor who seated himself in a folding chair.

Rachel reached out to place her hand on Donald's shoulder, and then pulled it back when she received a shock. "I'm so sorry," she stammered. "I didn't mean to shock you."

Donald replied, "It's quite all right. Anthony and I will be fine if you have some other work to do." The suggestion ended the conversation as the woman left the room in a trance, closing the door behind her.

Donald reached into his pocket and held out a tiny golden ring with a gem that glowed with a display of colors that was identical to the appearance of Tone's spirit. "I have a gift for you, Tone. You can't keep it, but you can borrow it any time you want."

The word "gift" caused the tiny black man to look up from his book. "Ring! Ring! Ring! My ring?" He snatched it out of Donald's hand and held it to the light. "Shiny. Shiny. Shiny."

"Try it on," suggested Donald. "I bet it will look good on you."

Tone looked at it carefully and looked back at Donald, trying to recall something locked away in his memory. Giving up remembering, he placed the ring on his finger. The demeanor of Anthony changed entirely as his eyes glowed with the prismatic display of his spirit form.

"Okay, this is just too cool." he said, looking at the angel across from him. "So, Andoneal. Do you come here often? More importantly, do I get to keep this mega-cool ring?"

Andoneal laughed. "Sorry, Tone. It is just for special occasions. So, let me tell you all about Anna."

# Demonize

coming in Fall of 2014

## Prologue

The ring-shaped skimmer came to an abrupt halt at the edge of the Gray. The Eqemp was the enormous prison and laboratory of the angels. Kra'illa had his skimmer, the *Enna*, ready for the dangerous journey ahead of them. Andoneal, the archangel of service, had just completed upgrades on the *Enna*, making it the most advanced skimmer in the Spiritscape. It had a special crystalline skin over its normal crystal structure that would make it indistinguishable from the amber-hued Spiritscape. It was essentially a stealth skimmer. The angelic pilot was pleased with the new handling and speed. With this mission, both attributes would be handy in the event something went wrong.

A group of angels emerged from the Gray that surrounded the interior of the Eqemp, towing a spirit sphere on strange looking lines. The sphere contained one of the most dangerous demons in all of the realms. The *Enna* had been specially augmented to carry this particular sphere within the center ring of the skimmer. A special crystal netting was in place to keep the prison cell outside, and keep the angel safe inside.

P'talgid approached the skimmer. "Kra'illa, good to see you. Are you ready for this?"

The smiling angel moved through the wall of the skimmer, stopping next to his friend. "Ready as I'll ever be. How long has it been sealed up?"

The head of the Eqemp angels replied, "It has been safe and sound since Zeke captured it. But I wouldn't want to take any chances. You know how it can be."

The captain of the *Enna* nodded. "I lost the *Onna* thanks to that atrocity. Let's just get it locked up so I can get this over with."

The angels pulled the spirit sphere into position. With a thought, Kra'illa sent tendrils of crystal to surround the sphere, securing it in the open space in the middle of the skimmer. Next, the *Enna* morphed as it became egg-shaped, netting attaching to the sphere as the walls closed. As the last trace of wall encircled the open area, the skimmer became invisible to all but Kra'illa.

"Nice trick," admitted P'talgid. "Andoneal has really taken his game up several notches. You should see the new equipment he made for us."

Kra'illa smiled at his friend. "Next time I bring you some supplies, I expect the complete tour." A group of angels appeared in the distance, porting as close to Eqemp as was safe. "There is my escort." He sensed all the angels around them perfectly. Surprised, he commented, "Michael? Why is he doing escort duty?"

P'talgid shrugged, "He must want to make sure everything goes smoothly." As the chief of the archangels approached, the angelic scientist greeted him. "Hello, Michael. We're surprised to see you."

Michael chuckled, "I get tired of sending everyone else out to have all the fun."

Laughing, Kra'illa commented, "I think you have been around Tone too much if you define this as fun."

"Could be." Turning serious, Michael gave out the orders, "We all know how dangerous this is. The warriors will be your vanguard all the way to Uqump. Five in front. Five in back. Ten circling the perimeter."

"Aye, aye," said the angelic sailor. "Let's get going." Moving through the invisible wall, he said, "Linking with the vanguard so they know where I am."

"Confirmed," acknowledged Michael. "Prepare to…"
The explosion could be felt all the way to Earth.

www.ingramcontent.com/pod-product-compliance
Lightning Source LLC
Chambersburg PA
CBHW031256170626
46807CB00001B/176